THE WAY OF ALL FLESH

The Way of All Flesh

Copyright © 2014 by Corey Furman

Cover Design © 2014 by Michael Moss

Book Website: http://coreyfurman.net

Email: feedback@coreyfurman.net

This is a work of fiction. Names, characters, businesses, organizations, places, events and incidents either are the product of the author's imagination or are used fictitiously. Any resemblance to actual persons, living or dead, events, or locales is entirely coincidental. Only Zarmina's World itself may possibly exist, but it is greatly in question, and if it does, it is certainly not habitable. So, don't go there.

Print ISBN-13: 978-0-9907415-3-4

eBook ISBN-13: 978-0-9907415-2-7

Print ISBN-10: 0990741532

eBook ISBN-10: 0990741524

Library of Congress Control Number: 2014956134

Dedication

John

Thank you for your brutal and much needed honesty, for your technical assistance and tutelage, for your esprit de corps. You always were the smartest one of us.

Any errors in this book are mine, not yours.

—∧=∨—

Mike

Thank you, brother. You possess deft skill, a keen mind, and a warm spirit. Your friendship and your family mean more to me than I can articulate.

—∧=∨—

Nigia

One of my oldest and dearest friends,

My muse, you were there when the going got tough and found ways to inspire me. If it weren't for you, this would have been a bleak and desolate story indeed.

—∧=∨—

Without these my friends, this book would never have seen the light of day, and rightfully so.

Table of Contents

CODA	1
THEME	3
PART 1 – COUNTERPOINT	17
One	19
Two	33
Three	45
Four	57
Five	67
Six	71
Seven	83
Eight	97
Nine	109
Ten	121
Eleven	127
Twelve	149
Thirteen	163
Fourteen	171
Fifteen	191
PART 2 – CRESCENDO	201
Sixteen	203
Seventeen	215
Eighteen	225
Nineteen	231
Twenty	247
Twenty One	261
Twenty Two	277
Twenty Three	293
Twenty Four	307
Twenty Five	323
Twenty Six	339
ELEGY	357
GLOSSARY	*377*

THE WAY OF ALL FLESH

ILLUSIONS CAN BE REAL

—∧ = ∨—

By Corey Furman

Coda

Luna adjusted the translucent container on the coffee table to better see the roses inside, then sat back down and snuggled her head into Maré's lap. "Read it again, Chroma…"

She stroked Luna's hair softly. "Again?" she asked playfully, knowing full well that she would give in. "I just read it last night…"

"Please? It reminds me of when we were children…"

Maré smiled. She loved the feeling of having her twin so close. Her physical presence somehow had an effect on her. With her this close, she could smell the soap she'd used earlier. Leaning forward, she brushed her ear with her lips. "If you like," she whispered. "But then *I* want a story from our childhood."

"It's a deal."

Sitting up, she reached for the small book on the end table next to the sofa. She paused to run her fingers over the knotted whorls and vines of its embossed cover reverently. It was quite beautiful and it occupied an important place in their family history, but it had been hard won, and it still filled her with mixed emotions. Sighing, she flipped it open to the first page, written in her great grandmother's handwriting:

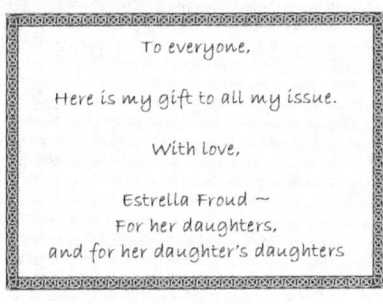

To everyone,

Here is my gift to all my issue.

With love,

Estrella Froud ~
For her daughters,
and for her daughter's daughters

As she cafunéd Luna's hair, she could feel her emotions brew. "You're brooding; what is it?" she said, laying the book aside.

Luna sighed. "It's hard to describe..."

Maré waited for her to find the words.

"We... What we have been through." She looked about the quiet comfort of their modest home almost dazed. "What it took to get here. I'm finding that saying I forgive and actually forgiving are two different things."

"Mmm," Maré grunted, and her own cocktail of feelings threatened to bring tears to her eyes. She would have to help Luna whenever it swept over her like this. "Look, we're together and we'll work through it. It's only been a couple of weeks." She kissed the top of her twin's head. "I have a feeling that if we stick with it, it'll make sense looking back. Enough sense for some peace, anyway."

"I'd like to forget about it for a while. Read to me please. Reading helps."

She laughed, but she hummed a little as she continued to comb Luna's hair, until she felt some of the unease leave her. Again, she picked up the book and flipped it open.

"There was once a beautiful queen who ruled from a grand castle. Near a fountain in the castle's courtyard was a bright garden, and at the center stood two huge rose bushes, one of which bore white and the other red blossoms. She had two daughters who were like the two rose bushes, one named Snow White and the other Rose Red..."

Theme

The vibralarm in Joss Breylin's watch agitated harshly against the skin of his right arm, snatching him halfway out of the grip of a fitful nightmare and startling him enough to thrash against the sweat-soaked sheet. The inky, greasy smell of burned plastic and flesh filled his senses. A half a second later, he recovered enough of his wits to realize where he was, and he began to uncoil. *It was just a memory...*

Normally the band exuded a cocktail onto the skin above the arterial bundle in his wrist in shots timed with the vibrations, and when it worked, it would bring his mind and cardiovascular system alive in a brilliant flash. That it didn't happen this time could only mean one thing, and the thought of having to claw his way to consciousness without it made him anxious. He let the alarm continue to pulse, hoping it would help to jumpstart the various regions of his brain, though it would be so much easier just to roll back over and give in to the comforting abyss that wanted to devour him.

He was too far away from the edge of oblivion though, and thought relentlessly intruded.

Shit, the damn stimpack finally ran out, he thought blearily. *I think there's only one or two left, and the supply drop isn't due for nine months. If the damn storms don't delay it.* He could already tell it was going to be yet another long day.

It seems like forever since I've gotten a decent night of sleep...

The vibrations continued to agitate a lonely warning against his wrist.

Almost nothing could be seen through the darkness of the bedroom. At times, the view from the enormous window beyond the foot of the bed showed a serene, unobstructed view of the edge of the perpetual sunset. It was so perfect that he supposed the house had been precisely situated where it was near the rim of Amity Canyon to present that exact view, likely for some long dead and forgotten mining exec. At the moment though, the view wasn't available; Joss had drawn the opaque protective screens over the gigantic window at the start of the storm cycle, almost nine months ago, securing it against the often fierce gales that were generated. It was now just past the height of the cycle, and last night it had seemed as if the entire world tremored as the house had cleaved the irregular gusts that were even now seeming to be alive and howling under the roofline.

The hell with it for a few more minutes, he thought, and he reached over and touched the screen of his wristband, temporarily hushing it. As he lay in the empty gloom, he pushed his sweaty hair out of his eyes and futilely tried to resist the thoughts that kept trying to steal his attention. Time was an impatient taskmaster though, and the precious seconds ticked away as sleep continued to elude his grasp. Though his mind was still stuffed with lethargy, the meaningless activities of the coming day fought for more consideration, and won with short, quick thrusts.

I hope I didn't misjudge the fuel in the lift... I don't think I did. I better get a couple of cylinders from work just to be safe. They're bigger, but I should be able to adapt the connectors. He knew the ride to work wasn't short. If he ran out of hydrogen, it would be hours before the collectors grabbed enough to get back up. *It would be just my luck to end up sitting in the middle of nowhere,* he thought dourly.

Running out of fuel wasn't the only issue on his mind. Knowing that today he'd be headed out to the subsolar region, he'd have to spend time around the simulant work crew that did most of the heavy labor. He wouldn't really have to interact with them – his boss, Harry, would do most of that, if he came out to the site – but he hated being around them regardless. Trusting them to do even simple tasks could prove to be foolish.

Harry was usually an even tempered guy, but he could be a real pain in the ass when he wanted to get things done. Joss was thinking about the kinds of samples they would need to take, and whether the lousy gas taps would need to be moved, when his alarm buzzed again. Life wasn't going to go away this time, the smug bitch.

Vaguely angry at being defeated yet again by even something so small, he reached over and smacked the band, killing its tiny victory dance. He threw back the coverlet, sat up, and put his feet on the cool, textured floor.

—∧=∨—

In another part of the room, Maré was lying on her thin pallet in the corner. She had just been lost in a dream of Luna, of the comforting smell of her twin's hair and the happy way it would tickle her nose when she used to bury her face in it in their clam-shell bed at night, when she sensed the vibrations emanating from *his* wristband. She came awake instantly, adrenal glands just starting to pump and filling her with the urge to do something. Despite that pressure, she didn't move, because she was here with *him*, and she knew better than to make any noise while the lights were off. Disturbing the peace of the house was very impolite. Worse, it was *unacceptable*.

He stirred, and the vibralarm ceased. *He must have muted it,* she thought fearfully. *Strange... Normally, he likes to get up right away.* Maré silently begged the deaf stars above that it wasn't a sign that when he got up he would be sullen and brooding.

Her bladder was an insistent need, but it wasn't yet an emergency. *When he finally rises, I will hurry to the kitchen and get his breakfast around. After that, I should be allowed to use the facilities.* It might only be a miniscule measure of control, but planning her steps gave her something to do, and maybe increased the chances that she would avoid a painful confrontation. *So many things could go wrong though...*

The winds moaned their annoyance outside, causing the old shutters to pop and tick in their frames, and she shivered. Idly, she wondered if the fittings holding them in place would eventually give way. Slowly easing her blanket tighter around herself against the cool air that crept along the floor looking for the gaps in her protective shell, she was again glad for it, and her pallet. She had been doing well, and as a reward, *he* had given her a few of her possessions back. The floor wasn't *very* cold, but the hard, textured plastic was particularly uncomfortable without them, making it difficult to get any rest, especially when the winds called to each other in their oblivious voices.

If I can just stay focused on doing my chores well, maybe he will let me have my pillow back. Maybe I can even have some of my clothes, if I am extra good.

She knew that line of thinking was futile, though; one way or another, somehow, she would do something stupid, and *he* would be forced to teach her a lesson. She would try to focus, but she knew the trouble would come regardless.

The thought of screwing up turned over and over in her mind, and the fear wormed its way into her gut. *I'm always making mistakes, dammit. It's no wonder I have to be corrected so often.*

But then she started second guessing the inadequacies *he* was quick to point out. *Relax, Maré,* she thought. *Get a hold of yourself. You haven't done anything wrong yet! And Luna would tell you that you can do this!* As the image of Luna's fine hair and smooth, ruddy features came to her, her pulse began to slowly regulate. The grief of their time apart had been so very hard, but she would try to take strength from her missing Chroma; she would have wanted it that way.

Fear, guilt, loneliness and a desperate twist of optimism were still working together to make her sweat when she sensed the alarm again. Maré held her breath for a time measured in a stream of seemingly endless heartbeats. Then she heard *him* quash the alarm and rise.

As he sat on the edge, Breylin turned on the light on the low table next to the bed, creating a small pool of light around his feet and dimly illuminating the rest of the room. She scrambled to a respectful position on her knees with her hands clasped on her thighs. Her quick movement seemed like it must have startled him, as if he had forgotten her existence. He recovered quickly though, oriented himself towards her and continued to sit on the brink of the mattress looking at her with eyes made of shiny fragments of graphite. If felt as if he were studying an insect that had crawled onto his arm – right before he crushed it.

Carefully she said, "Good morning, Mr. Breylin."

"Good morning, Maré," he replied quietly, and stood up. "Let's have a good day, shall we?" he called over his shoulder as he walked into the bathroom with his loose lounge pants swishing with each step.

Maré rose. She folded her blanket, rolled up her pallet, and put her things in her cabinet, hoping that the activity would take the chill off of her nakedness. "Did you sleep well, Sir?"

"No... I dunno. Well enough, I suppose."

"What are your wishes regarding breakfast, Sir? Should Maré make you something?" she called out in what she hoped was a compliant voice. His demand for strict obedience was complete, but sometimes he appeared to take an approving note if she put her heart into it.

"I will take two meal supplements with me." he replied over the sounds of water sloshing around in the sink.

—∧=∨—

After opening the shutter on the bathroom window, he leaned on the counter and let the water run to get hot enough to make an angry, moist cloud of steam shoot upward, hazing the mirror above the sink. His morning ritual of obscuring his own face wouldn't be complete without it.

Today wasn't a regular day, though; today was one of those rare days where he felt like punishing himself. He reached over and used the edge of his hand to expose the mirror, leaving be-hind water beads in narrow, even streaks. He studied his own echo wreathed by the remaining haze. Collar length sandy curls, now darkened with sweat. Even so, it looked a little lighter in spots than normal, and that might be a trick of the sunlight flowing through the bathroom window, but he wondered if maybe a few were more grey than blonde.

He stared deeper. *Crow's feet at the corners of my eyes. Did they always look so pronounced? Or are they heavier? You're not eighteen anymore, Joss... Bags under the eyes, but that's not sur-prising given the lack of decent sleep since the fire...*

Spotting the shadow of stubble on his cheeks and jawline, he resolved to use the razors he hated. Thick neck, strong shoulders. Square chest and large arms, a little more fat than they once were, but still heavy with musculature.

All in all, a decent looking guy, though not so good looking as Riss had once thought. He took in the entire reflection... and he hated what he saw.

—∧=∨—

She padded out to the kitchen and packed the food he wanted into the small, green satchel he carried with him every day. As she was folding its top closed, she regretfully realized that she had forgotten to ask him about coffee. Pestering him was a gamble that gave her pause, but if she did well then maybe he'd reward her. Moving back to stand just outside his bedroom, she could just make out the patter of sprayed water hitting the glass shower door. "What about coffee?" she called out. "You usually want that, Sir."

"Do you think you should try?" he replied. "I will show you one last time if you need it. I don't think either one of us wants a repeat incident from the other day – the coffee is too precious."

Wanting to avoid unpleasant subjects, she considered quickly and made her reply. "Maré will be very careful, Mr. Breylin! She remembers how you showed her you wanted it made!"

She returned to the kitchen and began to get things around. First, she got the kitchen scale out, then the ration canister of coarse, brown powder. Being very careful, she measured out precisely 9.60 grams of the stuff with a tiny spoon. She started to put the container away, but then she began to doubt herself. Had she gotten the weight right? What about the tiny amount of residue that would never make it into the cup? She realized her error, and reopened the canister. *But how much would be left in the basket?* she wondered. She waffled back and forth for a minute, but she finally ended up settling on 9.62g. She hoped it would be right.

—∧=∨—

As the water ran down over his hair, Breylin's thoughts drifted back to his beloved wife, obliterating the trivial ideas of what the day would hold that had been nagging at him. A wave of loneliness washed over him. In a gesture of abject weariness, he rested the back of his head on the white, plastic wall, and the tepid water washed over him. Without realizing it, he slowly beat his fists against the wall behind him. *I miss you Larissa, my beloved. Without you I merely exist here...*

As he returned to washing himself, he noticed a few strands of his long, blonde hair slip towards the drain and circled around its soap-slick edge. They lost their purchase and plunged in, never to be seen again. He knew it was irrational, but he was envious at their escape.

He shut off the water, stepped out onto the small mat and reached for the large, threadbare towel. Feeling tired and fed up with the daily drudgery, Breylin briefly considered returning to bed as he dried off. *The hell with the damn gas taps, Harry, and everything else.* Instead, he forced himself to move, completed his ablutions and slowly got dressed in work fatigues. *The sooner I get out of this house and away from her, the better.*

—∧=∨—

Ignoring the growing urge to pee, Maré put the reclaimed water into the kettle and set it over the fire on the gas stove. Knowing not to waste the gas, she set the fire to a medium flame.

He came into the kitchen, dragged the chair reserved for him out and sat down. Maré was still fussing with the kettle, but she could sense his mood right away. She fidgeted as she waited, the asymmetrical stone pattern of the floor irritating the bare soles of her feet. Outside of herself, the only sensations in the room were tension and the steady hiss of escaping gas.

Breylin began to tap his index finger on the top of the kitchen table using deliberate, measured strokes. *Snick. Snick. Snick.* It produced a deafening punctuation in the cramped space, and managed to ratchet the tension a few notches higher. The message was clear to Maré: *don't make me wait.* Nervously, she set an empty mug in front of him; it was better than doing nothing.

Finally, the water began to boil. She turned off the gas and took the kettle to the table. Carefully, she poured the water into the mug against the inside, making sure not to splash any. After setting the kettle back on the stove, she waited with hands folded in front of her, covering some of her nakedness.

Breylin stopped tapping and gave her a scathing look as he picked up the cup. With eyes closed, he brought it to his nose and inhaled its aroma. Then he sucked in a tiny sip, rolled it around in his mouth, swallowed. Maré held her breath while he weighed the flavor.

"This is... acceptable, Maré."

"Thank you, Sir!" she said in a rush of air. She allowed herself to experience a small thrill at the hint of a complement. After a pause she said, "Since Maré did well, may she use the bathroom, Mr. Breylin?"

"I believe I said 'acceptable', not well, Maré." he said, oblivious to her need. "I have changed my mind about breakfast. You may use the toilet after you have heated one of the supplements for me. One only, I will take the other with me when I leave."

After a brief moment of panic, Maré goaded herself mentally and kicked her actions into gear. She extracted one of the meal packets from the satchel, got a plate from the cupboard, opened the packet and emptied its thick, starchy contents onto the plate. The stew would smell much more palatable when hot, but cold as it was the chunks of congealed fat made it smell a little nauseating. Wasting anything was never *acceptable*, so she scraped out every morsel with the edge of a knife. She put the plate in the warmer, set the timer to sixty-five seconds and the temperature to medium-warm. Thankfully, the rations came shelf stable and fully cooked – only heating was required.

As Maré waited on the timer, Breylin said, "Let's go over today's schedule. It's nearly 5:45am. You may do as you wish until 6:15 – eat, pee, whatever. After that, do the dishes and clean the kitchen before eight. I want my laundry done and the rest of the place clean before two."

The timer on the food warmer issued two electronic tones. Careful to avoid touching the stew, Maré picked up the cool-to-the-touch platter by its rim. She turned and set it down in front of him, then got a clean fork from the utensil drawer and set it beside the plate.

"After two I want you to exercise for an hour. Aerobic exercises, I don't want you getting flabby. Between three and four, disinfect the exerciser, then wash yourself. *Clean*, Maré. And remove all of your body hair – I want you clean and smooth as glass.

Do you understand my wishes?"

"Maré understands, sir," she said quietly.

"Good, my things must be well in order. Anything else is *unacceptable*, right?"

"Yes, sir." She hesitated, but decided to see if suggesting the coffee had paid off. "Do you think Maré might be allowed to keep her hair on top?"

"Okay, Maré, call it a treat." He held up the mug between them. "For the coffee."

He picked up his fork, scooped up a bunch of the stew, and shoveled it in to his mouth. He chewed a bit, slowed, and then put the fork down. He swallowed with a wince, as if he was trying to choke down raw sewage. He said, "it's cold, Maré. The food." He paused, then continued quietly. "The food you just put down here in front of me, is cold. How am I supposed to eat this?" He pushed the plate away from himself.

Shock shot through her, and a small, terrified portion of her mind gibbered with mindless horror. *What just happened? Shit, I was doing so well!* She had to say something into the awful silence that followed, offer some explanation, but time thickened and froze around them.

Her heart rate doubled and pounded with the ferocity of the wind storm outside, and she nearly collapsed with the blood rushing through her cardiovascular system, black and silver flecks sparkling at the edges of her vision. She wanted to bolt, run somewhere, anywhere but there was nowhere to go and her feet remained welded in place. "I'm *so* sorry, Mr. Breylin! I don't know how —"

From where he was sitting, Breylin backhanded her, hard enough to stagger her into the counter top by the sink, leaving the red imprint of his hand large on the side of her face. The legs of the chair barked along the floor as he stood. Two quick steps, and he was looming over her. Maré nearly reacted by throwing her hands up to protect her face, but doing that always made the beatings worse.

"*No*, Maré." His face was close to hers as he leaned in. She could smell the stew on his breath mixed with the antiseptic wash he had used earlier. "Words like that are for people. You're not people, are you Maré?" he said terribly.

"No, Sir..." she said cringingly. The tears streamed down her face and dripped down onto the tops of her bare breasts.

He took her by the chin and turned her face up to his, their noses centimeters apart, but she kept her eyes averted and down. Direct eye contact could provoke a savage assault.

"You know what I want," he said as his fingers flexed and tightened on her chin. "Look me in the eyes and tell me, Maré."

She couldn't move except to tremble in his too-near presence. The blows would rain down on her any moment now.

"*Look at me!*"

She flinched at the outburst, but dreadfully she complied.

The level of his voice diminished to a menacing whisper as he let her go. "Now I want to hear you *say it*."

Anxiety had a tight grip on her chest, but she had no choice but to obey. Looking at him she timidly said, "I'm not a person, Sir."

"That's right, *Maré*, you're not a person. Why won't you listen? You've had to learn this lesson a few times, haven't you?" She started to respond but he laid his index finger over her mouth. "Shhh... There's nothing more to say."

He let her feel the fear and his breath for thirty seconds. The silence was broken only by her near-silent crying and the wind that ached to shiver the house to synthetic splinters. *This is it,* her mind told her as she screwed her eyes shut tight. She knotted her hands together so taut her knuckles were as white as bone, but her mind was racing, terrified, whimpering. *Any second now – the fists, kicking, pain, humiliation, the whip, something, something, SOMETHING, HE'S GOING TO –*

Silence. Sixty seconds.

She used the last tendon of courage to look into his dead lucid eyes, losing sense of everything else but the pressure building between them.

Unexpectedly, he stood up and smiled. Gently patting her cheek he said, "I'm feeling generous, Maré. Let's forget this happened. After all, your birthday is only a month away. I'll have to come up with something special for it."

Terrified at the thought of his special surprises, Maré began to sob, and the pressure finally gave way. Her bladder muscles buckled, she urinated down her legs, and a small pool collected beneath her, warming her toes and arches. The rest of her froze with crushing fear.

Breylin took a step back and whispered, *"now look at what you've done."*

Part 1 – Counterpoint

One

Joss Breylin Jr. had been born to a relatively poor but well-connected family. His father, Joss Sr., had been a medical doctor on staff at United Nations Headquarters in New New York. Although he hadn't been able to cure his wife's debilitating illness, he had nevertheless been quite capable of writing prescriptions of a dubious nature for anything the career politicians wished. The access that was provided by his usefulness had enabled him to secure a commission for his son. Although Joss Jr. had been fairly bright in tech school, he hadn't had the grades, nor his parents the money to get him into one of the better tech colleges. Since he had no enlistment waiver, he would have to serve in the Marines anyway. Senior had at least been able to use his influence by proxy to secure a spot in one of the middling universities and make sure the boy was an officer while he completed his military commitment. It was considerably more than most people hoped for.

There were dozens of freshmen at college orientation, but almost all of them were bound for the more glamorous sectors of astrophysics and bioengineering. Only he and Larissa Oralla-Sadler were going into geology, but even if the rest of the students had been going into their field, she still would have caught his eye as she sat smiling to herself and doodling in a small unlined pad through several inane but nevertheless required "alignment" sessions. Though the way her narrow glasses sat up high on the bridge of her nose somehow made her seem intellectual and demure, she was also drop-dead gorgeous with creamy, freckled skin, mischievous, emerald-green eyes and long, fiery red hair in a thick braid. She completely stood out in this crowd full of vaguely asian/spanish/caucasian people. *She's a sunburst of color!* he thought, and his mouth ran dry just sitting next to her. Frankly, she intimidated the hell out of him.

Still, there was something melancholy about her, and she seemed strangely focused. The sketch she was working on was abstract, but it was angular, conflicted, and somehow dark – and he couldn't take his eyes off of it.

"What is that, Larissa?"

"Just Riss," she said.

"I'm sorry?"

"My name – I prefer my friends to call me Riss."

His pulse jumped a few ticks faster as her words swirled around in his head, and he knew he needed to cement a connection to this girl. Feeling foolish at his own hesitancy, he lowered his voice and replied, "Are we friends, then, Riss?"

She showed him some narrow, white teeth with her smile. "I haven't decided yet."

He felt slightly flushed at her demeanor, but he smiled back anyway. "Okay... Riss, then. But you didn't answer my question – what are you drawing?"

"What, this?" She gestured at the drawing with her pencil. "I don't know... sometimes I just draw what I feel."

They quickly struck up a friendship and settled into a routine of mutual aid and study. Though he hadn't told her of the physical attraction he had for her, they'd spent a lot of time together working through the terse material, and their freshman year had flown by. Without trying, they had become good friends.

He didn't catch it at first, but near the end of that first year, he began to notice little things, kindnesses that she did for him. She would fold his laundry when she came to his room – she didn't want to be seen with someone wearing wrinkled clothes, she said – or she would bring him a special pastry from the cafeteria. It wasn't so much what she did, but *how* she went about it. She wasn't doing favors for a friend, she was doing things that just seemed to make him happy. Eventually, she made a gift of a small, framed drawing of the two of them as exaggerated characters holding hands amidst a bunch of impossibly huge flowers.

Dumbfounded, he wasn't really sure what to do. *Am I even reading the situation correctly?* His previous relationships had been about lonely people adding their loneliness together and hoping the sums came up in the black. It didn't though, and never could. Ultimately he was afraid to move, so he waited and tried to reciprocate.

As the weeks went by, and weeks turned into months, an unspoken understanding grew up between them. There was something special there in their relationship. Joss found himself doing little kindnesses too, and it wasn't to get Larissa naked; he did it because he could tell that their dancing around each other made her happy, and that made him happy. Before he knew it, he had quit caring about the shape of her rear end or how she filled out her sweaters with deep, sculpted curves. He could see enough pieces of the puzzle that was his life, and he knew that it would only ever be complete if she were in it.

It was in their fourth year together that the word Love was first used, but neither one could remember who had said it first. It would have been a milestone in their relationship but for one thing: they had felt the emotions long before the words had been spoken. In any case, once the word was loose in the air it became a frequent visitor, always in the room.

Larissa was content with where life had taken them so far, but Joss had an emotional need to make a plan. He would bring it up again tonight, but this time he would force the issue if he could.

—∧=∨—

She had made a simple meal of sandwiches in her room, and they had washed it down with cheap local beer. The good stuff was pricey, but this was better than recycled water. When the food was gone they reclined on the sofa and listened to music. As she worked an image of a castle with colorful sticks of charcoal, she could tell he had something on his mind, even in the offhand way he picked up his beer, sipped and set it back on the end table while staring off in the distance. Knowing that he preferred the absence of banter while composing his words, she gave him the space to figure out whatever had him ruminating.

At last he said, "Larissa, we have to talk about the future."

So, it's this conversation again, is it? "No, we don't, Joss," she replied. "It isn't yet time."

He was tempted to be irritated with her, but he decided instead to play it cool. "Can you help me understand why we shouldn't start laying it out?"

"I don't think I can."

"Why not?"

She sat up with a huff and crossed her arms beneath her breasts. "Because."

He sighed as he sat up, too. "Okay. Go ahead."

"We're still more than two years from graduating."

"...And?"

"*And* nothing. It's as simple as that."

"It's as simple as that, huh?"

"It's as simple as that."

He smirked, picked up his bottle and sipped his brew. "Well if it's that simple, I'm glad I didn't splurge on good beer." Then he said, "but you're full of shit, Riss. You're going to have to do better if you want me to buy it."

"Aren't you ever afraid of the future, Joss?"

He knew she was reaching into a part of herself she'd rather not, that he needed to pay attention; if he didn't he might hurt her. So, he considered her question carefully, looked at it from different angles, weighed the various ways he might answer. "No, I'm not, Riss. I can face what comes as long as I know we'll be together."

—∧=∨—

Exasperated, she got up and started pacing back and forth with her arms still crossed. *Why can't he just let this be until later? We're so young... What if we can't make it work?*

She sat back down and looked up into his eyes. "After school is done, we will have to figure out careers, let alone a great big Us. I love you, Joss Breylin Jr. I don't want to think about being without you." She hesitated. "I... just don't know if I'm ready for the big questions, let alone the answers. I need time."

"Okay, Riss. You can have whatever time you need."

—∧=∨—

Later the following year, Joss' mother gave in to her illness. Odessa Breylin had suffered for more than ten years with late on-set Tay-Sachs. Its rarity had made diagnosis difficult, but regardless, there was no cure – only treatment. She had needed canes, then walkers and eventually motorized assistance. She had struggled with self-worth and guilt over the pall she had cast over her husband's image. The final straw for her had been when the feeding tube had become necessary. She and Joss Sr. decided that medically-induced termination would not only be more dignified, but fitting. She had outlived both her usefulness and the mandatory conclusion of life that would have applied to most everyone else with a fatal disease.

"I've got to return to Earth, Riss. I want to see her before she passes."

"Okay. I'm coming, too."

"What? You don't need to do that, hon. I can't really afford it, anyway."

"I've been saving my pennies. I want to do it, to support you, and besides," she murmured into his ear as she put her arms around him, "this is my last chance to meet her."

"Okay, I'll ask my dad to get your name on the official request to the university. You know I love you, right?"

She laid her forehead on his, and he took comfort in feeling the warmth radiate off of her as she spoke. "I know, Joss."

To Joss' eyes, Mom looked thin, hunted and more than ready for the humiliation to be over. She had tried to make the auto-feeder work, but the affront to her person was too much and she had it removed two weeks earlier. It was no wonder her eyes were sunken and her clothes hung on her. Dad did the brave face thing, but Jr. could tell he too was ready for it to be over. In a private moment he had spoken of the need to move on. Joss did his best not to show it, but he couldn't believe the temerity of the man; Mom wasn't even gone and he was moving on.

Pissed about the whole thing, he told Riss about it later that night as they sat in bed and she began to fill in a pencil drawing of his mother that she had started in her hospital room earlier in the day. She was rarely without something of her art, and he might not have taken note of it this time except that this piece was quite realistic; normally she focused more on fantasy settings that were easily digested by children. Even at a trying time like this, he marveled at her ability to remember and capture the nuances of his mother's profile. Her use of shades, tones and highlights made her look as young and dignified as she had years ago.

"Cut him some slack, Joss. He's suffered too, and they're both prepared for an ending that must come."

"Wait a minute... Are you really agreeing with him, or are you trying to make it go down easy for me?"

"Maybe both. Of course I want to soothe your feelings... but I understand his, too." She set aside her oversized pad and pencil, then rolled her back towards him. "When you're watching someone suffer... or it's you going through it, a release from can be... darkly appealing."

Wait, what? Is she talking about my parents, or herself? Silence hung in the air for some time before Joss could speak, and when he did it was barely a whisper. "Have you felt that way, Riss?"

Her tresses rustled on the pillow around her head as she nodded.

This was new territory for him. *What do I say to a thing like this? How do I support her?* He rolled towards her and put his arms around her before speaking. "You can trust me with this. Why would you be suffering?"

"I don't know, Joss. It's just a thing I've had to struggle through sometimes."

This gave him something new to focus on. His mother's death no longer seemed quite so important, and he forgot his anger. He spooned into her and brought his hand up to stroke her face with the pads of his fingers. "I'm sorry. How often do you feel that way?"

"Only sometimes." She brushed the back of his hand. "I'm fine now."

How can I fix this? Can I even fix this? "What do I do to help when it happens? Will you tell me?"

"Just hold me."

He put his arm around her again and squeezed. "I'll get started now. Thanks for coming, hon."

She set her pad down and squeezed him back in reply. "Of course."

He gestured at her drawing. "That's really quite good, you know."

"I like her a lot. Odessa is a beautiful woman."

"It's a lot to ask, but may I have it? I'd like to get it into a nice frame and hang it in my room."

"You big silly," she said. "It's for you."

One quick push from a hypo-spray, and Mom's eyes closed

slowly. It was done. Joss tried not to let his emotional mask slip, but the old man sobbed. After the conversation the day before, Joss was surprised by Senior's show of emotion. *Maybe Riss was right after all...*

"I'm sorry, Dad. I know you loved her."

"Yeah... I'm sorry for you too, son." He seemed to be casting for the words before continuing. "There will never be another like her, and I can't live without her." His eyes were sad and far away, and as the contact stretched something in them helped Joss to begin to understand what his father was feeling – grief. Comprehension began to fill the void that had been occupied by his childish annoyance, and it helped him to finally see what his father had really meant by moving on.

"I'm glad you've found someone, Junior. Revel in each other while you can. Life is too short." He began to weep as his anguish took root.

After a few moments, Senior pulled himself together and turned to Larissa. "Will you take care of him, dear? Do you promise to cover him with the love he's going to need? You're all he'll have."

Larissa looked at Joss as she spoke softly. "Nothing can stop that from happening."

"I've got to go now, Joss, to be with your mother. We gave you all the love we could. Will you forgive me after I've moved on?"

He spoke as he moved to sit beside the old man. "It's okay, Dad – I think I understand..." He put his arm protectively around his father as they both wept.

—∧=∨—

One evening shortly after they had returned to Mars and resumed their studies, Larissa said, "I'm tired of the food in the cantina and I don't feel like cooking on the hot plate tonight. Will you go out and get us something?"

He put the book he was reading down. "Yep. Do you know what you want?" he said casually.

"Surprise me. And you'd better pick up decent beer with it." She began to hum something pretty he couldn't identify as she began a fresh sketch in her pad.

The door had closed behind him before what she'd said registered, and he stopped dead, dumbfounded. *Wow. Is she really asking what I think she's asking?*

Joss had found his equilibrium and a wide grin was splitting his face by the time he'd made it back to her room. Riss set her pad down and unpacked the food. Looking past her at the drawing that was complete enough for him to identify, he could see the picture was another illustration of the tree of life that the Celts of her ancestry were so fond of. His smile widened.

"Is this *real* meat? And real glass bottles of beer from Earth? I didn't quite expect this... You must have spent a fortune!"

"Nearly a month's worth of my allowance," he said with the mischievous voice of a little boy, but then he got serious. "Actually, it wasn't too bad. I hate dipping into my resources, but I wanted to make this something special. Sorry I can't do it every night. You're worth every penny, though."

"Gimme a break," she said and gave him a light shove, but she was smiling as she did it. "What took so long?"

"This stuff has to be prepared fresh. And I needed to pick a few things up from my room." Gesturing at her pad he said, "will you color this one in?"

"I haven't decided yet," she said in an airy tone that contrasted with her lidded eyes, and he warmed at her playfulness.

As they sat down to dig in, Joss said coyly, "So what's up?"

"Hold on there, cowboy. You may know what's coming, but if you think I'm going to roll over and give you the keys to the castle that easy, then you're crazy. Besides," she said with a very self-satisfied tone, "I want to savor the moment."

"As you wish, and I already have several castles drawn by you hanging in my room. What do I need with the keys?" he said with a snort, but then he got serious. "Will you tell me why you're ready now? I thought you wanted to wait until after graduation."

"Let's just say recent events have made me take a look at what's important in life. Focusing on grades and careers doesn't stack up like it used to."

Waiting wasn't exactly his cup of tea, so Joss sat and ate full of nervous energy in the expectant silence. If the feel of the atmosphere affected her, she gave no sign he could detect. In fact, he took the small smile playing on her lips as an indication that she was enjoying his squirming. *The nerve of her!*

When they cracked open the last round, she leaned in and whispered, "if you've got any questions to ask, now might be a good time."

He decided to give her the same small smile. "Maybe *I* want to savor the moment, too. Or... maybe I have to screw up my courage."

The time Joss had long anticipated had finally arrived, and he wondered if she was as nervous as he was. *I hope so, at least.*

—∧=∨—

Stars, he picks now to try his hand at my game? She gave in quickly; although she loved pushing him – and she knew he loved the pushing – now wasn't the time. "Do what you have to do, Joss."

"That's a very practical attitude you got there, lady," he replied nonchalantly.

"I think you'll find I'm pretty much all business," she said amicably.

So they sat on the sofa in the wan light of her room, listened to instrumentals broadcasted across the global nets, and enjoyed the rare treat of Earth-grown hops. She was flushed and nervous now, but she did her best not to let on. She reached for her pad several times – her art always had a calming effect on her – but left it lay in each instance, not trusting her hands to betray her tension by shaking.

Eventually it was more than she could stand, though. "Just do it, already!" she said after only a few minutes.

Grinning ear to ear – *the nerve of him!* – he drained the last of his beer, set the empty bottle down, and picked up his backpack from the floor next to the sofa. Unzipping it casually, he pulled out a holo-recorder, and set it down on the table. She knew he could feel her eyes watching him, and he was most definitely enjoying himself. *Will you quit screwing with that friggin' thing and put it down?!* He caught her glare *and smiled wider!* Finally, he turned it on, and a little blue light on top lit up.

Walking over to her, he took her hands and drew her to her feet, then dropped to his knees before her. He brought her hands to his face, closed his eyes and inhaled her scent deeply, then kissed the back of each one. When he looked up and they locked eyes, she could see that sweat was standing out on his forehead. He spoke in a near whisper. "Larissa Oralla-Sadler, you have been my colleague and confidant these past five years. You have been my constant companion and supporter in tough times." He smiled. "You have even been a competitor, making me be a better man to match you. You deserved nothing less."

Her lips parted, but she closed them. It was obvious that he had been practicing this, and knowing him, almost certainly he had many times. Though the anticipation was really working on her, she would wait and see what he would make of the moment.

He continued. "You are beautiful of form, but more importantly, your character is stunning. Shy and quiet, yes, but trustable and creative. Sometimes you seem completely oblivious to the power you have over me, but other times you know exactly what to say and how to say it and we both know I'll gladly give you whatever you want of me. You are self-effacing at times, yet perceptive where others are concerned, and possessed with a strong sense of value in the truth. You are," he said, "the best woman I have ever met. I have to ask myself if I can ever be worthy of such a creature as yourself."

The words hung for a few moments before he continued.

"You probably expect me to ask you to marry me, don't you, Riss?"

What? What did he just say? If he doesn't ask me to marry him, I'll kill him! Confused, scared, she slowly nodded her head yes, and tears began to well in her eyes.

He barked a brief laugh, and her confusion deepened.

"That may be the vulgar form of public expression... but it will never be an adequate interpretation. Larissa, I am taken by you.

What shall I do?" He paused to catch his breath while tears began to stream down his beautiful face. "When we are apart, the pain closes off my throat and I cannot breathe. When we are together, my heart threatens to smash itself against my sternum and my innards twist."

Unable to hold them back any longer, she began to softly cry, too, as his words resonated within her. She could feel his hot pulse racing in her hands. *Or is that my heartbeat racing?*

"My soul is yours, my dear, if you will have it." With one of his hands he withdrew a ring from his pocket, plain but with a solitaire diamond of fair size that flashed with the light it caught. "This was my mother's ring – Dad gave both to me before we left Earth. Please understand this, Larissa; I am not asking for your *hand*, because I don't deserve it. What I am asking you, Larissa Oralla-Sadler, is to be my true queen. If you would accept me, all of me, then I would be your subject, dedicated to your protection, well-being and happiness. My only wish is that my submissive love would be cool water on your parched days."

When he was done, she simply presented her finger, and he slipped the band onto her. She wiped her tears and took his up-turned face in her hands, mingling their water and salt, and bending down she gave him a long, chaste kiss that tasted like him. Nothing more needed to be said.

Two

Different areas of her brain stirred from the dark depths to break the surface of consciousness. She began to perceive the random waxing and waning of flaring phosphenes, but nothing else, and if they had any meaning or order it had utterly escaped her.

She became more aware of being. Vague impressions, ghosts of experience, swam through her mind, but try as she would nothing would solidify. Though her eyes were closed, she could sense the harsh glare of overhead lights. She gave up and tried to settle back into the quiet nothingness.

Still, she eventually became aware of the slight pressure of a mask on her face, and the muted susurration of air flowing from it. She began to hear beeps and ticks, and the low, dissonant music of electronic machines. Slowly but insistently, reality intruded.

Cracking her eyes open was difficult, as if the lids had been stuck to her cheeks with old glue. The glare worsened and forced her to squint, though its hard light was helping to bring her around.

A woman's narrow face framed with dark hair leaned down into view. The woman appeared to examine her, first holding a probe to her ear, then uncomfortably drawing back her eye lids. The woman stood erect but stayed mostly in sight, and she could feel pressure at various points on her body. Something about the woman seemed... familiar... but the vision wouldn't materialize.

She tried to lift her head, though it felt leaden.

"Please do not try to move yet," the woman said. "You will

need about another thirty minutes before you should, and you will need my help at that. I will raise the temperature a few degrees on the amniotic gel. Please try to relax."

She had no choice. *Amniotic gel,* she thought thickly. *What in the world is that? And where am I?*

A few mild beeps, and within seconds she could tell she was suspended or floating in something – the amniotic gel, she supposed – and that it had gotten a little warmer. She shut her eyes and tried to relax as she was bid. Time passed, though her alertness grew.

"I am going to try to get you into a sitting position. Are you ready?"

Without waiting, the woman got her hands under her shoulders and slowly drew her up, causing her posterior to sink a little deeper into the gel. The woman said, "I am now going to remove your oxygen mask." The adhesive on it pulled away, and the tangy, chemical smell of the stuff she was sitting in wrinkled her nose. As she looked around the white room, everything appeared to be strictly functional and severe. Down to the few chrome accents, there was nothing of warmth in this place. She looked down at her own cool nakedness and the clear plastic tank in which she sat and wished for a covering, or, failing that, an upward adjustment of a few more degrees.

The woman drew up a stool alongside the pod and sat down. She had mousy brown hair cut in a page boy, and a smooth, white, button-down lab coat. Oddly, she also had a thin, black choker on her neck that prominently displayed "183A" on the front of it, centered just above the dimple at the base of her throat.

"You now need to exercise your lungs a bit with some deep breaths," she said. "If you understand what I am saying, please acknowledge."

Acknowledge? But she croaked out, "Yesss," punctuated with a hoarse cough. It felt as if she hadn't spoken in a long time – or ever.

Holding a tube to her lips, the woman said, "please blow into this using deep, slow breaths. Try to increase the length of each one as much as you're able." Again she did as she was told, since there was nothing else to do.

"I am going to ask you a few questions to see what you re-member. Can you tell me your name?"

Her head was still packed with wool, but the question dumb-founded her. She couldn't remember. *Why can't I remember a thing like my own name?* She shook her head no, the confusion plain on her face.

"Please answer the questions verbally between breaths. It's part of the protocol."

"No... W-what is...?"

"You may be confused. Please be patient, and I will answer at least some of your questions as we go." After a few seconds pause to let that sink in, she said, "Do you recall what your job is?"

She had to think, but frighteningly, she didn't know that, either. Between breaths that were becoming less labored, she said, "No."

"Do you recall the man you dated in tech school? His name was Tyler," she prompted.

"No." She took a deep breath and pushed it out. After hesi-tating she said, "Can I... get out of this thing?"

"We can try." And with that, the woman began to help her to get up on her feet, then draped a sheet around her shoulders. She had to lean heavily on the woman; without help she might

have lost her footing in the gel, but more than that, her treacherous muscles felt like putty. Simply standing was almost beyond
her.

The woman turned her, nudged the stool with her foot to the
edge of the tub, guided her down onto it, and then helped pick
her legs out. The sheet plastered itself to the sticky gel all over
her frame. Immediately, the woman put the tube back to her
mouth, obviously expecting her to push through the heaviness in
her chest.

"What happened?" She took a breath, and rested for a moment. "Why don't... I remember anything?"

"Nothing? Surely you remember school from your childhood,
yes?"

"No... Impressions..." she said with a dispirited voice. "Who are
you?"

A small machine off to one side emitted a soft tone and said,
"please have subject 370 Bravo perform a stress breath exercise."

"Most of the people here don't use their given names. You
may call me 183 Alpha, or 183, if you wish. Please take two normal
breaths, then as deep a breath as you can. LabSys is trying to
gauge your condition."

She shook her head in confusion. *What kind of name is 183
Alpha?* As she went through the breathing exercises, she tried to
pull at the indistinct ghosts in her mind, but nothing would coag-
ulate. The machine made a few more beeps, but it was meaningless to her ears.

"183, why don't I remember... anything? Why do... you seem
familiar?"

She sighed. "Just a moment."

She moved over to a cabinet and drew out a white, tapered instrument. She opened a cover on it, inserted a small nodule, and slapped it shut with a click. As she walked back, she drew another small stool from the corner with her. 183 sat back down and said, "I'm going to give you a booster. It will make you feel more awake, and you will feel a lot less shaky, at least for a time. More importantly though, it will send something of a wakeup call to your body. Your heart will race, you will feel flushed as if you have just finished exercising, but it may also cause a headache. If it does, it shouldn't be bad. Otherwise, tell me and I will administer something for it. Do you understand?"

"Yes. May I stop using the tube?"

183 consulted a small screen covered with inscrutable codes on the wall beside her. "Yes, you may – for now."

After she turned back, 183 pressed the device to her neck. There was a hiss and twinge, and then she felt the sensations she'd been told to expect. As if someone had turned on a light, her system kicked into overdrive. As her heart began to pound faster than she thought safe, she got lightheaded, and nearly swooned. She reached out and grabbed 183's arm to steady herself. It did nothing for the dizziness that was washing over her, but at least she wouldn't fall.

"You will feel this way for fifteen or twenty minutes, and then it will taper off." She paused, and then said, "I have some time before a man will come in, Doctor Almeida. He will perform a thorough eval on you, and it is important you comply with him. He has a certain importance to your immediate future. Have I been clear?"

"Yes. And no. I don't know who I am, where I am, or how I got here." She paused as a series of wet coughs forced their way out. After she had wiped her mouth with the driest part of the sheet she could find she said, "How do you know anything about me?" She paused again to catch her breath and avoid more painful hacking. "Help me, *please.*"

"I know more about you than you realize," she said cryptically. "I will bring you up to speed as much as I can, but you may find that you're sorry you asked. I will start with your name: it is Maré."

Maré... she rolled the name around in her mind, trying to decide how it felt. *Mah-ray.* The pronunciation was a little strange, and yet somehow... familiar. *Right.* Yes, it definitely fit, and she knew the name was hers. *Maré.* She was disoriented, but this at least was a fixed point.

As she considered, something else crept up on her. She sensed the cords of her muscles... changing... somehow. Tightening, but not as if they were straining at some difficult task. Her breathing picked up again, almost panting now, and black flecks raced around in her vision. As she was considering the strange sensations, 183 drew another nodule out of the medical cabinet and loaded it. She pressed it to Maré's arm and gave her another twinge, but it was a very distantly sensed thing.

"Try to slow down, okay? I don't want to have to pick you up off the floor," she said with a laugh. "This last dose is medication. Physically, you have had a relatively minor case of viral meningitis. It is indirectly responsible for your memory loss. In the short term, you will need regular doses, but as long as you are here, you will be cared for."

She hesitated, choosing her words. "This will be hard to accept, but the truth is, that in any way that matters, you have just been born."

Silence held Maré's tongue as her words sank in. *That's impossible – I must have heard her wrong.* The seconds crawled through as she rolled the concepts around in her mind, but nothing made sense. Finally she said, "what did you say? I'm not sure I heard you correctly."

She smiled feebly. "No, I'm afraid you heard me fine. Worse yet, there's also more and stranger coming," 183 said. "You aren't human – you're a *memetic* being – though you were created by mostly copying a human pattern. They use a process known as *mimetiosis*. You're a human analogue. The commonly used word is 'simulant', and as you might guess there are several less flattering epithets."

183's bizarre statement hit Maré between the eyes, and the bottom fell out of reality. Here she was, covered with a mildly stinking gel that was slowly bonding a sheet to narrow her, and unable to recall a single event from her life beyond a few, short minutes ago. The whole thing was a tiny, surreal bubble that was threatening to burst.

"This has to be some sort of joke, 183." Maré looked up at her. "Isn't it?"

She shook her head. "I'm afraid not."

The sound of static intruded, followed by a man's curt voice. "183 Alpha, please ensure that 370 Bravo is prepared for my arrival in fifteen minutes."

"Shit," 183 said with a tired sigh. "We're running out of time."

Maré was still grappling with the incomprehensible terms 183 had been using before the broadcast. "A simulant? Is that what you said? And who was that voice?"

"Yes, a simulant. There's a lot to tell, though it will have to wait." 183 got up, took Maré by the elbow, and drew her to her feet. "We need to get you cleaned up before the doctor arrives. I know it's a lot to take, but try to absorb it as best you can. We have to move on for the moment."

The quickly drying gel was shedding from her skin and drop-ping to the floor as 183 brought her over to a circular shower stall in the corner of the room. *I wonder who'll have to clean it all up?* She unwrapped herself and held up the soiled sheet and 183 pointed to a bin. As Maré tossed it in and stepped into the shower, 183 handed her a small pair of goggles and said, "Put these on to protect your eyes, and keep your arms up, please." She slid the glass track door shut. "Try not to drink any, either."

"Why, what's in the water?"

"Not the water – the amniotic gel. Your hair is matted with it. It won't hurt you, but if you ingest enough, it will sour your stom-ach." After pressing a few buttons on the shower's control inter-face, its bland, androgynous voice said, "please specify tempera-ture."

Maré's head was spinning too much to think of something so trivial. "I don't know," she said. "Can you make it hot, but not too hot?"

Tones ensued. "A speculative temperature will be used, but it may be changed as desired." Nozzles sprang to life, whirling in tracks around her that pulsed soothing, warm water and slick soap onto her. She held onto the sides of the shower for balance as it stripped the mostly dried amniotic residue off of her. Over the course of a couple of minutes her tightened muscles loosened under the pressure of the water jets, but it ended far too quickly for her liking. As she stepped out of the heavy, water-laden air and into a pair of flimsy slippers outside the stall, 183 handed her a large, rough towel.

When she was passably done drying, Maré padded over to the stool, sat down and said, "can you give me something to wear? And maybe something for a headache?"

"The clothes will have to wait until after Dr. Almeida has done your examination," she said as she went over to the clinical sink, drew a small cup out of a drawer and put some water in it. As she walked back to Maré, she drew a small packet from a pocket in her lab coat. Handing it to her, she said, "take these."

As she took the wafers out and swallowed them, 183 sat down next to her on the other stool. "Okay. Simulants *are* copies of humans – blood, bones, neurons, DNA, the works. Most simulants have been gifted with perfect, distinctive looks, but otherwise you'd have to look down at the cellular level to tell the difference between one and a natural human. Most simulants have been enhanced in various ways to make them more useful, or desirable, beyond looks. Some are engineered to have greater intelligence, making them suitable for use in technical roles. Some are given increased strength and stamina, and are sent to serve in labor-intensive or military jobs. Form and purpose – they go hand in hand. With me so far?"

"I understand what you're saying, 183, but I've got a long way to go before I'll really be with it."

"Fair enough," she said as she put her hand on her arm. It was a simple thing, but as Maré look down at the familiar seeming touch, she was comforted. Still, the feeling posited itself against her yawning lack of personal history. *Familiar... I feel like she's... someone I've known... but where...?*

The sentiment wouldn't leave her alone.

183 continued. "Okay, so, some simulants are used in... domestic roles, like caring for the few who are allowed to become elderly. Some, such as yourself, are created for common purposes, requiring few skills. You were designed to be reliable and loyal, and disposed toward being generally happy in the mediocre chores required of you. You might even be feeling somewhat

deferential towards me, and that is no coincidence. We're all supposed to be that way, but few are as receptive to authority as the
simulants from your bloodline."

Maré wasn't feeling any of those things – she felt lost, and
though her imagination was threatening to run wild with the answers, she still felt on the verge of exploding with questions. She
felt like running. She felt like crying and screaming in frustration,
too. The one thing she definitely didn't feel was receptive to authority. But this woman, she was something else.

183 got up and went over to a different cabinet, drew out a
hand mirror, and came back. She handed the mirror to Maré and
said, "Here, look at your own face."

She thought about asking her why, maybe even aching to, but
now that she thought about it she couldn't remember what her
own face looked like, and she had to know. Looking at it, what
she saw was a fairly plain but not unpleasant face. Young, good
skin, dark complexion. Short, mousy brown hair, water-darkened.
But it was still foreign, like it belonged to someone else. As she
stared down at the mirror though, the face began to seem familiar
somehow. Maybe she *had* seen this face before... then everything
clicked – 183 had the same but slightly older face.

"You're a simulant too..."

"Yes."

"Like me...?"

183 nodded. "Yes, but a little different," she said. "The person,
the woman from which you were copied, lived nearly a hundred
years ago. *Her* name was Maré. It is now your given name, but
you are also identifiable by your designation, ten ten oh six dash
three seventy Bravo, or just 370."

"Is that why you go by 183 Alpha?"

"Correct. Around here, I am hardly unique. My unused given name is Luna."

Maré thought for a few moments. She tried to compartmentalize what she was feeling, but she completely failed. *She had used the right words a few minutes ago.* "This is... a lot to take."

She nodded and reached out to touch her arm again. "I can understand your confusion. Simulants almost never emerge from the maturation pod to be greeted by another from their own bloodline, and at that, never without experiential memories."

"What happened to me?"

"I'm getting there, but more background information would be helpful. The real Maré had a twin sister, and she was also used as a *premisant* —"

"Premisant? The person copied?"

"Yeah – sorry. Anyway, Maré's twin sister was named Luna."

"Are you my twin sister?"

"Sort of, but not exactly – I was grown in last year's crop. To continue... the simulant pairs of our bloodline are grown in the same maturation pod, in each other's arms. Your Luna, 370 Alpha, had gotten very sick with viral meningitis before it was detected about a week ago. We don't know how it happened – everything's been checked, and anything that comes into the facility is sterile packed to begin with. Anyway, she was immediately pulled and euthanized, but the decision was made to allow you to continue maturing."

"What does 'euthanize' mean?"

"Destroyed. That's what they do to anything or anyone who threatens something as valuable as a crop."

Horror blanketed Maré. "How can they just kill us? Who *are* they?"

"*They* are the conglomerate that owns this building, this entire facility, and every simulant in it. I'm sure they have a name, but I couldn't tell you what it is. And understand this – they can do whatever they want to anyone here – but most especially to us. We are simulants."

Maré shook her head. "You're losing me, 183. I'm over-whelmed and I don't understand any of this."

"When I said earlier that we were created for various purposes, I wasn't speaking facetiously. We are essentially property, and we do what we are told. The price of disobedience is sometimes repurposing, and often termination."

It was then that the door opened, and in walked Dr. Almeida.

Three

Almeida listed into the room trailing a small cloud of noxious, blue smoke from the cheroot he was smoking. He was a short, dark skinned man, and everything about him clashed with the pristine lab. He was old, and his tie was nearly undone and heavily creased. His dingy, grey lab coat looked as if it had been slept in, and he probably hadn't combed his halo of nearly white hair in some time. It had been a few days since he was clean shaven. A small bit of ash wafted down onto the clipboard he was studying, but he didn't seem to notice.

Troubled, Maré noticed that 183 had stiffened in his presence. It came to her that she had identified him by name, and her mind began to work. *He's got no collar either – I wonder if that means he's human*, she thought.

If he was a human, he wasn't completely, though; he had odd ocular implants that were either covering his eyes or had replaced them – she couldn't tell which. He also had tiny antennae sticking out of crusty, yellow holes in the skin below his earlobes, and he had a fine wire mesh embedded in the skin of his hands. *This man must see and hear everything*.

Maré wanted to say something into the itchy silence, but sensing 183's reticence she was unsure if she should. She decided to risk it. "Am I okay, Doctor?" she asked uneasily.

Without looking up from the clipboard, Almeida curtly held up his index finger. After a time, he looked over to 183 and asked her, "did you identify anything physical about subject 370 Bravo that I should be aware of during your initial examination?"

"No, Doctor. 370 Bravo is physically a little immature. Though she is still sick, the meningitis is responding to treatment. Also, she still has some fluid in her lungs."

"All of *that* I can determine for myself," he said dryly, and Maré wondered to herself what sort of answer would have satisfied him. As she was puzzling over this, he startled her as he addressed her directly for the first time: "It's time to examine you, 370."

He forced her go through several diagnostic exercises, like balancing on one foot and touching her nose with her eyes closed. He caused her extremities to jump with electrical jolts from probes connected to a small handheld device. He made her follow his finger with her eyes without moving her head.

Maré wondered that such tests were necessary in a place like this. "Don't the machines check these things?"

183 timidly but quickly answered, "The machines have already done all of the tests, 370, but the doctor appreciates the value of a good hands-on exam."

"LabSys, access diagnostic file for present subject ten oh six dash three seventy B."

"Done, Dr. Almeida," a directionless female voice said sedately.

"Have the automated neurological tests confirmed that there is no lasting damage?"

"Confirmed, Doctor."

He smacked a button on a wall-mounted panel, and a thin, padded slab quietly hissed its way out of a niche in the wall.

"Lay face down, 370," said Almeida.

She obeyed, uncomfortably resting the side of her face on one of her arms.

Almeida carefully put his cigar down on the edge of one of the stools. She watch a thin streamer of smoke curl away from it until he moved and blocked her view. He began by examining her head, separating the hairs and looking behind both ears. "Did you check her hearing, 183?"

"No Doctor, I hadn't yet gotten to it," said 183. She chewed her lip as Almeida turned to give her a withering look.

Turning back to Maré, he felt the vertebrae in her neck, checked the lymph nodes under her arms, and pressed on her lower back. To this last he asked, "Is that uncomfortable?"

"No. Doctor, what are you checking for?"

Standing just behind Almeida, 183 shot her a dangerous look and shook her head. *No!*

Impatiently, he said "I am attempting to determine whether or not you still retain value to my company, 370. Would you like to discuss it further?"

"I'm sorry, Doctor. I don't know what's going on and I'm just scared."

"Your confusion is understandable. Now remain *silent* unless something is asked of you," he said in an annoyed tone.

Feeling the palpable tension in the room, she decided that keeping quiet was better than trying to satisfy her curiosity, but he was callous and she wanted to answer him. *What the hell does he mean, retain value? I'm a person!* The thoughts churned through her mind, but he didn't seem like he was about to listen to anything she might say. If he wasn't convinced, she'd only make it worse.

He continued by running his hands over her skin and kneading her muscles. "LabSys, musculo-skeletal is within normal parameters. Close enough, anyway."

"Acknowledged, Doctor."

"Lay on your back, 370."

Maré turned over. Almeida told her to look straight ahead while he peered into her eyes. When he came close she could smell his cigar-rancid breath. After he was done, he stood up and said, "LabSys, spectrographic retinal analysis normal."

"Acknowledged, Doctor."

He felt her neck, performed a breast exam and reported no findings. He listened with his ear to her chest, telling the computer that some fluid was present.

He made her endure the shaming experience of having her legs spread apart and the folds of her sex peeled back. Almeida continued to act insensitively – *is he uncaring, or is he enjoying this?* – to her discomfort as he took his time to probe her internally, with a ghost of a smirk on his face.

"LabSys, pelvic analysis normal."

"Acknowledged, Doctor."

When he was done, Almeida picked up his cigar from the stool and sat down. As she covered herself with the towel 183 had given to her, Maré wondered if Almeida would bother to wash his hands at some point.

He smoked and appeared to be lost in thought for a few moments, and a tense silence collected around him. Maré and 183 looked at each other, one with questions and the other with anxious preoccupation.

He stirred, exhaled the noxious weed, and a short but violent battery of phlegmy coughs contorted his face and watered his eyes. Maré nearly clamped her hands over her ears at the din created by his expulsions. When he'd steadied himself, he wiped his mouth with the back of his hand and said, "Not great, but subject 370 is physically acceptable. The real question is the memory, though. 183, what did your tests show?"

Maré sat up on the edge of the table. 183 dithered, but under his stare she said, "very little experiential memory was successfully implanted, though 370 appears to have a functional vocabulary and age-appropriate practical skills."

"No experiential memory, huh?" He pondered. "You sound unsure. Should I order definitive testing?"

"It won't be necessary, Doctor." The words hung like a shroud in the air. Quietly, she added, "The testing would show you what I've told you."

As he stared off in no particular direction the muscles in his jaw flexed, and she could almost feel the gears in his mind turning. Eventually he said, "This was expected, but I had hoped for a better outcome." Holding it with the tips of his unclean fingers, he dragged on the cigar, then nodded his head. "It is what it is. I can't justify any further cost associated with this simulant pair. LabSys, close this case file as —"

Maré was afraid of what she was hearing. Something final was happening, and she had no control over it. *What is this? I should say something – but what? I should just –*

"A moment, Doctor, please indulge me." said 183 timidly.

"Quickly, please," he said irascibly. "I have spent enough time on this. I have other, more pressing matters to attend to."

Uncertainly she said, "I believe the organization could benefit from subject 370's repurposing as a lab assistant here."

"That won't be possible, 183. The four allotted slots are filled. You know this."

183 paused and shook her head, but then she squared her shoulders and stood straighter as she met his eyes. "She could

bed with me, and I would train her."

"And what about the rations? Will she share your rations as well? The budget is tight, and will already be strained by the loss of three previous simulant pairs, now four."

Speaking quicker now, she said, "Yes, Doctor – the cost will be mine."

"It *is* an interesting proposition," he said as he stroked the wisps of hair on his chin, considering. "As you wish, 183. You of course understand what it means if this goes badly, *si*? I will have to find another way to control the costs of the project."

"Yes, Doctor."

"LabSys? Strike last command. Mark this case as unresolved and release."

"Acknowledged, Doctor."

Almeida drew a thin black strap from the pocket of his coat, reached over and fastened it about Maré's neck. As he did, he said, "370, this is a behavior modification collar. It will display your moniker, but it will also discharge small doses of a number of compounds that interact with your nervous system. Your body will produce everything it needs; it simply leeches and stores a little at a time from the blood vessels under your skin. Using it, I can not only monitor your whereabouts and vital signs, but I can also reward good behavior with pleasant sensations and emotions. I do so on very few occasions, as you will behave or you will leave this place for somewhere far less pleasant. The collar can also be used to correct wrong behavior... which can also be quite unpleasant, but considerably more immediate."

Then he produced a small control from the opposite pocket. "LabSys, prepare for new collar linking."

"Ready, Doctor."

The collar produced several mild beeps when he scanned it with the small controller.

"Recorded, Doctor. Confirm when ready."

He pressed a button on it, and the band grew snug around her neck.

"183, you have one week to make this work. If she is to be punished, you will be punished twice as much. Get her remaining infection under control. She is not to be around the crop during that time. *Comprende?*"

"Yes, Doctor."

"Do not fail, you sentimental fool."

With that, Almeida left the examination room, snickering to himself and trailing blue smoke behind him.

Maré huddled in on herself and a tremor of anxiety that started in her gut shook its way up her torso. Events were outpacing her and she didn't know, couldn't understand the rules of the game. *"What just happened?"*

183 pursed her lips and exhaled. "For one thing, I just saved your life, Maré. We'll talk more in a bit, but first I need to clear your lungs. He's given me a week to make sure the job's done, and there's only one way to be certain. Please lie back down."

She wasn't happy about it, but Maré laid back and watched her dig around in a cabinet. When she came back over, she had a thin, black probe, a chrome canister, a bunch of tubing and a big bucket. Maré's eyes went wide. "What are you going to do to me, 183?"

"We're alone now, Maré – you might as well call me Luna.

This," she said as she held the jumble of equipment up, "is a med-ical vacuum, a specialized robotic one, and I'm going to use it on your lungs. I'm sorry, but we'll probably have to do it every day for the next week. The good news is you'll be essentially infection free head-to-toe afterward, meaning the meningitis will be gone, and anything else that might be lurking undetected. It's going to jack you up on so much antibiotics, antivirals and antifungals that you'll be about the cleanest person alive. The bad news is it's going to be uncomfortable, to put it mildly. It will become toler-able and you'll get used to it after a minute or two, but until then it'll feel like drowning."

Luna fitted various pieces together, put the bucket on the floor, and finally hooked the canister up to the probe. "You won't like this, but I'm not going to hurt you," she said as she sat down on the stool next to her. "Do you believe me, Maré?"

She was scared, but she knew that this woman was her only guide. "I'll trust you, Luna – I..." she said with tears on the verge of spilling down her cheeks. "I don't think I have any choice."

Luna grinned. "Not really, no," then she leaned over her. "I'll put this strap across your arms loosely. If you have to fight, fight against that." She fastened it, but not too tightly, and said, "Do you want to know the specifics of what I'm going to do, or would you rather just get it over with?"

The grave way Luna was looking down at her gave her pause. "I feel pretty blown away at this point, and I'm not sure it makes a difference." *Do I want to know? How bad could it be?* "Tell me, I guess..."

She sighed, and held up the black probe. "Okay. Using little articulated legs, this thing is going to open your windpipe, then –
"

"Wait! Stop! I was wrong – I don't want to know any more.

Just get it over with, please."

"That's a better call," she said with a pat on her shoulder. "Ready?"

Maré nodded.

"Open your mouth, please."

Trying to follow the probe with her eyes, Maré did as she was bid.

Luna put the tube into her mouth and close enough to her throat that her gag reflex nearly kicked in. She mashed a button on the box attached to it. Maré wanted to close her eyes, to will it all away, but she couldn't; the tube was picking its way into her throat, and it was far too real to pretend otherwise. *Stars, the damn thing feels alive!* From the corner of her now leaking eyes she could see a small light on the box pulsed red as the tube crawled deeper, and it flooded her lungs with a terribly cold fluid. It was all the excuse her gag reflex needed, and she almost vomited. Luna said, "try to breathe normally – as much as you can – the antiseptic liquid is oxygen-rich. And whatever you do, try not to cough or heave, or we'll have a huge mess to clean up. Getting it in your nasal passages will make it worse, too."

Maré made a grab for Luna's hand, but only managed the sleeve of her lab coat. Looking down, she gave her a smile. "Don't be afraid – I've got you. Hang on," she said, and moved Maré's hand so they could lace their fingers, and gratefully, Maré held on as tight as she could.

As revolting as it was, she did adjust slightly – as much as she thought she possibly could – to the pressure of the bizarre sensations in her lungs. A small, barely sane part of her mind told her that the fullness of the liquid in her chest meant that she was going to black out and drown at any moment, but somehow she gripped Luna's hand tighter and managed to fight through it. It *was* revolting, she was definitely breathing after a fashion. It was every bit as bad as Luna had warned her that it would be – and then some – but she'd also been right that she'd be fine, able to respire, if she just held on.

The liquid was pumped in, sloshed around, seeped through her innards and filled her with its cold, surging wake. Maré could just hear it making wet sounds as it fell into the unseen bucket on the floor below her over the sound of the blood rushing in her ears. She barely noticed it, though; what drew her attention from everything else was the sensation of the device's minute attachments picking through her lungs, separating her, sifting her, cleaning her. She had the crazy image in her mind of a sadistic swarm of miniscule robots, each with a mop and a bucket, scrubbing away at her bronchial tubes, pausing only occasionally to poke her for fun. The cure seemed every bit as bad as the disease.

The machine continued to go through its cycles and filling the bucket, and Luna gripped Maré's hand tightly with a tight but patient smile.

After an eternity, the light changed to a steady yellow and the sensations changed. Luna said, "It's almost done now... it just has to pull any excess moisture out and coat your lungs with aerosolized meds."

The light went green as the thick tube snaked its way out, collapsing into the canister as it went. After Luna dislodged the end of the tube from Maré's mouth, she helped her sit up. She disconnected the canister from the vacuum, and tucked it under her arm. She put the vacuum back in the cabinet, and the rest went into a receptacle in the wall.

Maré looked at Luna. "Stars, that was rough," she said a little hoarsely, as a nauseating medicinal taste was beginning to creep out of her heavy chest and up into her mouth. "We'll have to do that again? You've got to be kidding me – a whole week?"

"Yeah, I thought it was nerve racking, too."

"Why were you nervous? Haven't you done this *before*?"

"Nope. I've seen the training videos though, and I'm a fast learner."

"I'm glad you didn't tell me that before you stuffed that friggin thing down my throat!"

"*Relax* – the machine does all the work," she said with a dismissive shrug of her shoulders. "Would could go wrong?"

"Nice."

She held her hand up with a sickly smile. "I think you may have bruised a few bones in there, though."

"Sorry. I've got so many questions that I don't know where to start... My throat hurts."

$$—\wedge=\vee—$$

"Here," Luna said, as she handed her some scrubs from a cabinet. "Put these on. You can wash your mouth out if you like."

Maré got off the table, dressed, and walked over to the sink. She cupped her hands under the spigot to rinse and spit several times, but paused when she stood back up. Looking at herself in the mirror, Luna watched her hand stray up to touch the collar on her neck. *I'm sorry, Maré,* she thought with a pained heart. *You're property now, too...*

Luna turned from her and sat down, and tried to grapple with the implications. *What have I done? There are going to be some huge obstacles, but it wasn't like there'd been time to think it through...* She hoped she was successfully hiding what was going on inside – Maré had been through enough shocks – but she was uneasy about the situations that were coming at them. At least she could avoid introducing Maré to the others until the morning; the twins should be fine, but 85 would probably make trouble. *She always did, and that's not going to change...*

She shook her head to clear that line of thinking. *Whatever – it's done, and it was the right thing to do.*

Maré sat back down next to her and put her head in her hands. "Where do we go from here?"

Luna said, "let's start by showing you our room. I warn you, it won't be much."

—∧=∨—

Maré rubbed her temples between the tips of her fingers and squeezed out a few more forlorn tears, but she tried to pull it together as she looked up. Luna was still trying to give her what she prayed was meant to be a reassuring smile, but she wasn't terribly hopeful. "Believe me when I say that after this start my expectations are mighty small."

She proffered her hand, Maré took it, and allowed herself to be led from the exam room. What confronted her on the other side of the recessing door was one more thing to knock her off balance.

Four

Feeling lightheaded and shocked, Maré put her hand on the door frame, certain she was going to swoon.

Whereas the examination room had bright, powerful fluorescents that harshened every edge and drained what little color existed, the corridor beyond had warm, sepia-toned recessed lights along the ceiling that were almost comforting. They were evenly spaced between the door at her back and several more just like it. There were also a few couches along the wall as well, and part of her mind took note of the thinly cushioned carpet beneath her flimsy slippers, but it was the view that astonished her.

Opposite the exam room doors was a floor to ceiling wall of glass, exposing a view of the silvered roofs of many lower buildings. The swirls of the weather patterns of a large gas planet provided the backdrop to the whole scene. The view was quite severe, almost as if someone had turned the contrast knob on reality to maximum. Still, it was beautiful in its alien way.

Maré drifted over to the window and put her hands on the cool glass. Smooth. She could feel it leaching the heat out of her palms. The sensation was something she could believe in, something she understood. A tiny bit of condensation haloed between her fingers.

"Luna... where *are* we?"

"We are on Paradise Station in orbit around Jupiter," she said with quiet awe. To Maré's ears her voice almost seemed muted, clipped, as if sound didn't travel as far as it should in this place. "We are in a small medical wing adjacent to a crop building." Luna came up beside her, and stood there for a few seconds. "Off to the left," she said as she gestured towards a taller building sided with glass, "there is another medical wing, for that crop building. You can see its skywalk easily enough." She pointed at the roof of the building next to them. "That building down there – it's where we were both formed and grown. You, I, and all of the *chromanity* in our bloodline." Just a few meters below their point of view, it looked just like many of the other buildings, boxy and warehouse-like. As featureless and non-descript as they were, they surrendered no hints at the gestating lives they held within.

They stood there for a few minutes, and Maré's mind tried to wrap itself around the colossal scale of the view before her, redefining her understanding of distance... and of people being grown for a purpose.

"How many of us are there?"

A pause. "About ten thousand in our bloodline alone, give or take. We grow five hundred and twelve pairs a year. I'm not sure how many are in the other bloodlines. A lot, though."

Maré let her eyes roam over the lower rooftops, speechless.

"Compared to most of the other models, our numbers are actually pretty low." Her voice picked up a cynical quality as she continued. "I guess we go pretty cheaply in the market, but the humans want the better, more specialized models."

"I wonder if the real Maré and Luna would be proud of... this."

Luna took her by the shoulders and turned her so that they were facing each other, but she kept looking out, still trying to absorb the universe and her place in it.

"Look at me, Maré," she said. It took her a moment to drag her eyes from the view and back to the corridor, to the here and now, and to Luna.

"Thinking like that can be dangerously depressing, though

honestly, I've wondered, too," she said. "And you might not have your memories, but your perception shows through. You are who you are. In any case, it doesn't matter; our premisants are long gone, and we are here, Maré. We *are* real."

"How do we get by? I –"

Luna thought about it. "This *is* a bizarre existence, but we can be happy."

Unable to think how that might be true, Maré gave a short laugh. "I don't know, Luna." She looked out on all of the buildings that held their sleeping male and female chromanity. She tried to count the building pairs, but they were all the pretty much the same and she kept losing her place. *Chromanity*, she thought. *Another new word, and such a strange one for artificial people... For what we are. It's like the word used to describe humanity, yet just different enough.*

"How many thousands are out there?"

"Try not to swallow all of it at once, Maré. Give yourself some time to adjust, and it will get easier."

They stood in silence for a few more minutes.

Finally, Luna said as she tugged the sleeve of her tunic, "We should go for now, but we can come back here, if you like this."

Maré turned to her. "Wait."

Luna's eyebrows shot up with a question. "Hmmm?"

Luna watched her as she moved to her other side. Maré reached for her hand and laced their fingers. When she looked up and their eyes met she said, "I'm not sure, but it feels like that's how it should be..."

Luna gave her hand a gentle squeeze. "Yep, we always held hands," she said with murmured words, and started walking.

"C'mon now, it's very late."

Leaving the skywalk, Maré was drawn along sterile corridors between empty labs, down drab, concrete and steel flights of stairs, and even along the outskirts of a small set of cheaply carpeted office partitions. They saw no one else until they came across a nondescript looking man in green coveralls emptying the trash cans of the cubicles. If he took notice of their passage, he gave no indication.

As they had passed him, Maré noticed that he also wore a thin black collar, but it didn't display any markings like theirs. When they were out of earshot, she asked Luna about it quietly.

"You don't need to whisper – he won't think you're rude," she said with a shake of her head. "He is neither human nor simulant, but an android. Androids are like sophisticated computers – they are programmed and predictable. The ones kept around humans are usually imbued with a thin veneer of personality – it makes humanity feel more at ease – but they are just simple creatures, limited in their abilities to doing a narrow set of skills."

"So, like us, just not as smart?"

"Not really. Large parts of them can be thought of as fleshy machinery, but they definitely have gears and wires, and a large central processor. They can be programmed on the fly to acquire new skills as needed. Besides that, they don't feel like we do. Some *seem* like they do, but it's all a function of excellent programming."

Luna stopped and she and Maré looked back at the oblivious man. "I could walk back there and strike him. It would register, and he would probably look at me, but then he would go about his mindless work. If what had happened registered strongly enough, it would only notify LabSys. Security androids are capable of aggression, but not by much, and even then only within narrow parameters."

They descended further in the building, until they reached the bottom of a stairwell. They walked down a short hallway that opened up onto a small common room that had a few functional tables and chairs. Along one wall were several small appliances sitting on a counter top, above them a few cabinets.

"Welcome home, Maré. This is where we get to eat."

Down here at the bottom of their world, everything was smooth white and beige plastic, as if style and color were unnecessary luxuries that had been ruthlessly torn away, leaving behind cold, unrelieved industry. Even the appliances that had been provided for their use seemed like they had been engineered to numb the mind.

Luna walked over to one of the wall mounted dispensers and said, "183 Alpha, morning rations, please."

"You have drawn your quota for food today. Would you like to draw tomorrow's?" the machine tonelessly droned.

"Can't have me overfed, now can we, so yes, give me tomorrow's."

It made a couple of tones and a slot in the bottom of the dispenser clicked open. Luna pulled out four or five small, plastic containers.

"This way," and Luna walked over to one of the other doors that opened into the common area. As she approached, the door chirped and recessed with a small pneumatic hiss. Maré followed her in, and the door closed behind her.

"LabSys, code the door to this room for access by 370 Bravo, please."

"Acknowledged, 183 Alpha."

"Is that computer everywhere?"

"LabSys? Yes. It controls just about everything around here – door access, file access, ration allowances, sample processing, you name it."

Maré trudged over to the small bed and sat down on its wide lip, leaned over and put her head in her hands. She exhaled a big wind, as if she had been holding her breath and had to release the pressure. She followed it with a few scratchy coughs.

Luna put most of the containers down on a desk that was built into the wall, then she came and sat down next to Maré. She said, "drink some of this," and handed her a flask of brownish, orange liquid. It had the word "juice" helpfully stenciled on its side.

She sat up, took the container, and flipped open the top. She took a sip and looked at it. She was glad that the packaging displayed the nomenclature of its contents; it was a little sweet, and it seemed to quiet the rasp in her throat, but if she'd had to guess solely based on its taste and viscosity, then she might have mistaken it for machine lubricant. She thought about complaining, but it seemed so very pointless. Instead, she gestured with her chin towards the flask, she said, "so, how long is this supposed to last us?"

Luna smiled weakly. "About lunch time tomorrow." She dug out a couple of antiseptic wipes from a small box on a shelf next to the bed and used them to gently clean Maré's face. Her touch was light, and the pads left her skin feeling tight and cool. "Don't be too worried about it. The others might be willing to chip in a little bit of their rations. We try to stick together more than the humans."

"Others? You mean simulants?"

"Yeah, another alpha and a matched pair. We'll meet them at first call."

Maré nodded. "Wow, okay... so, why did he call you a 'sentimental fool'?"

"Well, you heard him refer to the loss of other pairs, right?"

"A lot was flying over my head, but yeah I caught that. I didn't like the sound of it."

"I wasn't involved – the others were – but destroying them bothered me anyway, and I sat by myself next to their empty pods those nights to eat my dinner." A pause. "It's been about a week since the last one – your Alpha."

A lot of undigested questions seemed to hang in the air. After a couple of minutes, Maré whispered, "Why did you do it, Luna?" She turned to her. "Why did you save me?"

"It's complicated, and I'm not sure I completely understand it yet myself." Luna looked at her. "Listen... you look pretty beat up. Do you want more answers now, or take some time?"

She shook her head. "I... I need a little time. Maybe some rest." Tears started rolling down her cheeks, but she didn't notice.

"We'll talk more when you're ready. And I'm a little wrung out, too." Luna put her arms around Maré and brought her close, and she allowed herself to be comforted.

"I'm overwhelmed, lost..." A nervous laugh bubbled out of Maré. "Hell, I'm freaked out, I guess!" She paused to process her feelings, to find a way to verbalize them. "I can't explain it, but the one thing that feels right is being close to you, Luna, as if it were normal. 'Thanks' seems like a stupid and small thing to say to someone who's thrown you a lifeline, but thank you, and I mean it."

Luna nodded. "I feel it, too. The truth is that chromanity, and our bloodline especially, were made to be in pairs, Maré. Like you, my paired chroma didn't make it. It wasn't detected until our inception." She hesitated before going on quietly. The room was dim, and it seemed right to speak softly, but her voice still carried quite clearly.

"My Maré, 183 Bravo, was brought out of sleep with an apparently severe emotional disorder. I guess the memory imprinting doesn't always take. She didn't recognize me – tried to tear me apart. I didn't know what was going on, or even that we were simulants. I couldn't understand why she was hitting me, flailing at me with her fists... Anyway, it made her 'unsuitable for intended purpose'," she said with air quotes, "and she was sent to the organ farm. I have been alone since."

She paused as she seemed to gather her thoughts. "Losing her that way was hard, but it wasn't the worst of it – that came later. Once I understood what we were, the hardest part was getting past that her existence was so short, so devoid of meaning. It wasn't long before I realized that my own life wasn't so different – short, pointless, *alone*." When she was done speaking, she snaked her arms back around Maré, drew her close, and laid her head on her shoulder.

Maré had been listening, and for a few seconds she had allowed Luna to pull her into the story, but that was done, and Maré found that it was just more difficult thing on the dog pile. She absorbed the words, but all of the words and concepts put together made an inscrutable avalanche. She felt her own identity, as miniscule as it was, subsuming beneath it. Into the silence she said, "I'm not sure I can make it, Luna. I'm really lost." Exhale. "I'm not even sure what it means to be me."

Luna pushed her away a bit so she could look her in the face. "You *can* make it, Maré. You weren't born with your memories, but I have all of the ones they gave me. I remember you from when we were little girls helping each other dress. I remember you helping me do my homework in school, and I remember you helping me understand boys because you had dated one first. Even if you don't remember, that's the kind of person you are, strong. You *are* my Chroma, and it's my turn to help you. But we have to do it together. Can you try?"

"Yeah. I'll try. I'm scared, Luna, but... I get that it's serious."

"Serious, yes," she replied. "I once heard our grandfather use the phrase 'where the rubber meets the road'."

"I don't know what that's supposed to mean, but it does sound serious."

"It means this is as real as it gets."

"Yeah... And I know that you've put yourself on the line for me. We're connected, right?"

Luna nodded.

"Tell me it's going to be alright."

"I'll hold you and stroke your hair until you believe it."

That night, the two of them slept the way they had come into existence, naked, and in each other's arms, wrapped in darkness and floating in the lowered gravity of their clamshell bed.

Five

After graduating from college, Joss would have to serve in the colonial Marines for a term of equal length to his schooling: six years, a long time to be separated from a part of yourself. They gave him six days – one for each year – to wrap his life up and get his ass up on the line for deployment. Meanwhile, Larissa would return to Earth to work for her father's company as a contractor in the South Pacific. It would be hard to be apart for so long, but hopefully between the meager estate his parents had left him, his small military salary and her wages they would be able to save enough to move to Greenland once his tour was up. The whole arrangement was an unfair inconvenience, and made him simmer with ire, but there was nothing to be done about it.

He'd never see it, but Joss had done the old man proud. Driven, he'd worked long, hard hours at his studies and achieved grades near the top, and it had been more than sufficient to guarantee that he wouldn't have to pay it all back to the military – assuming he survived his commission.

Except for the select few who filled highly specialized jobs, all young lieutenants were sent outside of the Terran system, and Lieutenant Junior Grade Joss Breylin Jr. wasn't any different. His first assignment was to quell a minor but potentially dangerous simulant squabble on Zarmina's World, a small planet in orbit around Gliese 581 some 20 light years out towards Libra. If the incident hadn't involved *gabachos*, the U.N. would have let the local corporate security wonks clean up the mess. As it was, the U.N. needed to protect the image of the simulant as a trustable perk to the off-world emigrant. So, they sent in the lads to keep things quiet and establish a small but important presence.

Breylin wouldn't know it for some time, but his first deployment would evolve to establish a new Marine post, and he would remain stationed there for his entire career. Even with faster than light travel, the transit times involved were still quite long, taking months to move between the stars. The enlisted ranks were moved around a little more frequently, but Command had found relocating the officers fewer times between duty stations made for better uniformity. He suspected that moving the enlisted around figured into the development of junior officers, too.

Zarmina's World, having been colonized nearly two hundred years earlier, was in a slow decline. Being relatively close to the system of human origin, it had been identified early on as a destination for dreamers and those looking for a fresh start. As it turns out, it had a few unusual qualities that made it seem more attractive to settlers than it actually was. First of all, it was tidally locked to its parent star, meaning that one face of the planet perpetually faced it. The current theories of the time had predicted that the natural properties of the planet might produce profound gas exhumation, most pronounced at the subsolar region, the point that received the greatest amount of solar radiation. A lot of it had depended on the thickness of the mantle and whether or not the planet still had a hot core. The first settlers wouldn't know until after they had arrived.

The other romantic notion that surrounded Zarmina's World was that, due to its tidal locking, it would have a narrow ring around it running north-south where the sun was seen to be perpetually rising or setting, depending on the viewer's disposition. People had fawned over that idea alone, and quite a few had placed themselves on the waiting queue for emigration.

In practice however, the U.N. had been reluctant to marshal the resources to mount an expedition for simple gas mining rights, particularly since it was expected that only a small segment of the planet would be truly habitable. Even at that, it was expected that there would be strong winds flowing nearly constantly from the subsolar region towards the opposite side of the planet, where it was always cold and dark.

Not only had there been nearly ceaseless wind blowing through the so-called twilight strip, there had also been a regular but very long pattern of thunderstorms that robbed the planet's inhabitants of the marvelous view most of the time.

The U.N. had punted: first rights had been given to a consortium of mining venture capitalists who would foot the entire bill and bear the entire risk. If it worked out, the U.N. would get its taxes; if not, then it lost nothing and the private corporations would write off the loses. Everyone wins.

LT. Breylin woke from hyper-sleep with the platoon he had deployed with only days before the transport had left Mars orbit. They were mostly a likable enough bunch to Breylin's eyes – even those that had opted for enlistment in lieu of lengthy prison sentences – but he hoped the sergeants were as competent as he had been told by his aloof commander. They would have to be if the platoon was to be successful.

Gunnery Sergeant Azul was what one might expect from most platoon sergeants: gruff and hard, he possessed a formidable combination of competence, confidence and boldness. He was dominant in a gathering, and his men were fiercely loyal to him. Right away, Breylin could tell he was entering a family, and that he was the outsider who would have to prove his worth before he would be made a member. Regardless of rank, Azul was the head of that family.

When he first met him, he asked Azul what he could do to contribute to the mission. "I'm just a geologist, Gunny. You've done this before and you know what works. How do I fit in?"

Gunny nodded his head in agreement. "A lot of times we get these kids in – begging your pardon, sir – that want to make a lot of changes and do things that sounded good in the classroom, but don't necessarily translate into operational fitness. If you're serious about doing things right and taking suggestions, then we'll keep our asses alive long enough to enjoy liberty." It was no slip of the tongue – Azul said what was on his mind.

"I get it, Gunny. I'm smart enough to know that if I trust you, stay out of the way and help where I can, then it will be all right."

He had earned Azul's respect – a thing not easy done with an experienced soldier.

Six

As it turned out, the local civilian authorities had exaggerated, and conditions on the ground weren't what they were told to expect. The disruptive simulants were only complaining about the conditions under which they worked; to be fair, the temperatures climb to nearly seventy degrees out in the star-ward side. Even though the engineered nature of the simulants reduced hot and cold to little more than annoyances, their labor was still intensely manual. What did they expect though? They were filling the jobs for which they were designed. And it wasn't as if they had a choice; if they wouldn't work, then the best they would be able to hope for would be abandonment and dealing with no food, shelter or transportation to a more hospitable area of the planet. The options quickly grew worse from there. Breylin didn't necessarily disagree with their viewpoint, but, as tough as their lives might be, they had it better than those who remained in many isolated and less habitable parts of Earth. They should count their blessings instead of bitching.

Since most of the foremen of the various gas tap crews – humans, all – didn't care if the simulants griped, everything was business as usual. Breylin's platoon enjoyed an easy assignment that essentially consisted more or less of basic police work, general security and providing a face for the U.N. Though the area of settlement was fairly large, most settlers – only about 2,500 of them yet remained – were living in Twilight City.

For several months, life for the Marines consisted of daily readiness drills and conducting unscheduled patrols, even among the outlying settlements, for no reason other than to be seen. Occasionally, the platoon – or at least the Marines that were on duty that night – would show up in the few watering holes and brothels in the city. The minor show of force was enough to deter serious issues.

There were very few incidents, and only one of consequence. LCpl. Styers, one of the grunts, had a little too much of the local moonshine one night, and made a pass at one of the males. A couple of the others tried to wave her off, things got out of hand, and she ended up pulling her Kabar on her squad leader. Sgt. Nakamura restricted her to the barracks for a week, but not before he thoroughly kicked Styers' ass. She knew she'd screwed the pooch royally, though, so she took the beating no sweat and didn't gripe once she'd sobered up. The jokes and harassment afterward were worse, anyway.

There were a few fights that grew out of boredom, stress and cultured rivalry, but the group was always tight knit. Azul knew his people and managed them well, leaving LT. Breylin free to do a little rock hounding in the mountains to the north. Everything was going well for the group. Even in the absence of a legitimate threat to confront, the platoon continued to focus on staying at peak readiness – and looked good doing it.

About six months after they arrived on world, five of the original simulant rebels had surprised their overseer, a woman named Ainsworth. Moving swiftly, they had apparently subdued her with a sizable electric shock. The gas taps were notorious for building up fantastic voltages as the gases were extruded from the ground. They had removed her environmental suit and tied her naked to one of the gas taps. The site was far out into the subsolar region, and she had died from exposure before anyone even thought to investigate why they hadn't returned. It was a horrible way to go. By the time the Marines were summoned to check out the site, the simulants had taken the cargo lorry and were long gone. The only thing that they had left behind was a note scrawled on the back cover of a technical manual, sitting next to Ainsworth's body and held down by a pitted rock. It had only three words: *We are People!*

The first thing Breylin had checked was the vehicle mounted tracker, but they quickly discovered that the rogue simulants had been smart enough to find and disable it. He had the Marines conduct a search of the surrounding area for ten clicks, but neither their eyes nor their sensors found anything. Unsure how to proceed, they returned empty-handed to Twilight City. Since they were trained as light infantry and not as true police, they didn't know the investigative procedures that might have helped them better. Even so, Azul took it as a personal challenge to get the situation resolved. It just made Breylin angry.

Twilight City wasn't large by Earth standards, but it was big enough to make it unlikely that if they had returned there that they would make it easy for the grunts to find them.

Of the five simulants, four were simple laborers of fairly normal intelligence. It was likely that the fifth, a technician's assistant named Tomas Ridder, was doing the thinking for the group. Even though they now had very limited resources, they would still be motivated by a sense of self-preservation. They wouldn't be much of a threat in a face to face confrontation, but they wanted their freedom and had demonstrated that they were willing to kill in its pursuit.

Many of Twilight's row home neighborhoods stood empty and rundown, or nearly so. Instead of wasting their efforts on a futile building by building search they sent a broadcast message over the global nets to be on the lookout for the bastards. It was the only way to reach everyone on world, including those few remaining settlements. After that, they then settled into a semi-constant pattern of patrols in the city's narrow streets. If they were there, then they would have to show themselves eventually. The grunts anger smoldered for a week while they waited for the *gabachos* to make the next move.

It came in the form of a comm from the last family still at Amity Canyon, a tiny remote settlement about an hour north and near the mountains. The settler claimed that his wife had seen a brief, intermittent light from within one of the abandoned houses down in the valley. He wasn't sure what she had seen, but he believed she had seen something. It wasn't much to go on in Breylin's way of thinking, but Azul pointed out that even if it was a false alarm, it was a good exercise for the squads. Breylin agreed, so they geared up and were on their way within the hour. Giving them something to do took the nervous energy off of his people and helped them keep a deadly edge.

When they arrived, they went directly to the settler's home overlooking the canyon. Oddly, there was no answer at the door, nor to hails from the tactical transport. They scanned with the movement trackers and looked for heat signatures, but found that the residence had been unoccupied for a little while. The whole thing was suspicious, and Breylin and Azul grew more pessimistic about the safety of the human family each time they came up with nothing. They would have no choice but to check the five or six houses down in the canyon.

The first two they approached were empty, but Nakamura picked up a large heat signature in the third. He ordered the squad cover the domicile from several points, and one of them found the cargo lorry sitting behind the flat, the turbine ticking as it cooled in the shade. Nakamura radioed Gunny, and since it was impossible to conceal their presence, Azul brought the transport forward.

There was no point in delaying the inevitable. Sitting at his tiny, utilitarian desk inside, Breylin had gotten the long unused comm codes from the global directory for the house and called. It buzzed a half a dozen times and the channel was opened, but whoever was on the other end refused to speak.

"Who am I talking to?"

No answer.

"Can you tell me what you want?"

No answer.

"Do you have hostages? What will you trade for them?"

Silence.

"How do you see this ending?"

The channel was silent at first, but after a few seconds, a voice came through: "with death, and I don't think either one of us can stop it..." The line was closed.

"We must act now, sir," said Gunny, "if those people are to have any chance."

"Send 'em in, Gunny."

He had Nakamura's squad enter from the rear and one of the other squads from the front. The stutter of automatic weapons lit up the shuttered windows, then silence. More gun fire, then nothing. Styers came running out. "Medic! It's Nakamura!"

Azul and their medic, LCpl. Headly, were running towards the house before Styers was done yelling. As Breylin followed them in, one of the privates carried a crying child outside.

Nakamura was gasping and turning blue as he thrashed on the floor of the kitchen in a pool of blood. Headly had Styers and one of the others hold him down while he set to work on him. "His windpipe is crushed! I'll have to do a tracheotomy!"

Joss was stunned; he'd seen the training videos, went through the simulations, practiced all of the maneuvers, but none of it prepared him for this room, for standing in the blood of a man for whom he was responsible. A good man at that – Nakamura was one of the strongest personalities in their unit. He was tough on everyone around, always demanding better performance, hammering away at the fact that lives depended on automatic actions. Even so, he was also usually at the center of their sports, chow, and whatever made them laugh. Breylin sweated as he begged the silent points of distant light above that Nakamura would still be those things after he left this house.

Headly dug in one of his packs with the speed of someone with moves so practiced he was able to take his eyes off his hands. He shredded a slim pack and withdrew a scalpel from its tatters as Nakamura's struggling was slowing down, his face turning purple. A slash, some blood, and he was shoving a tube in. He attached an Ambu bag and started pumping it furiously. Nakamura's chest was rising, but his eyes were closed and he was quiet. Headly held the tips of two fingers on his carotid. He readjusted once, twice. "Not good, he's got no pulse. Styers, pump the bag!" He moved a little closer and started chest compressions. "Somebody dig the oxygen tank out of my bag and hook it up while I work!"

Headly huffed and counted as he did everything he could to force Nakamura's heart to pump, pausing only to let Styers flood his lungs with precious O_2. As the activity continued and the tense moments ticked by, Breylin began to doubt Nakamura would make it.

Nakamura's eyes fluttered open, and Headly sat back on his heels. "You scared the hell out of me, Sergeant," said Headly as he wiped his face. "Don't do that again. LT, he'll probably be okay."

Breylin nodded. "Good job."

With tears in her eyes, Styers leaned in and said, "You got your blood on my uniform, Marine. I expect you to clean it." He was still pretty out of it, but he feebly grasped her arm as Headly gave him a shot.

Breylin looked around for the first time, and it was then that he noticed the dead simulant lying on his side nearby. Nakamura's Kabar was buried hilt deep in its throat. It must have been his blood all over the floor. Somehow it seemed odd to him that its blood should be red.

The little girl had been the only human survivor, though they had managed to capture the technician's assistant. Sergeant Pellegrino, the squad leader for first squad, had capitalized on the initial confusion and managed to stun the simulant with a hard butt stroke from her rifle. Judging by his misshapen appearance, Pellegrino must have broken the simulant's nose. The blood that had gushed down his face was already dried and black around the edges. It still hadn't been enough to knock him out, but it was sufficient to get the child out of his arms. The rest of the room was chaos and carnage.

As one of the privates was binding his hands behind him, Breylin said "You brought us here, *gabacho*. Why?"

The simulant merely looked up at Breylin.

After a few uptight seconds, Pellegrino said, "I speak his language, sir," and she slammed the butt of her rifle into his jaw.

"As you were, Sgt..." Breylin grabbed her arm before she could hit him again. He could tell that Pellegrino's blood was on fire from the angry look she shot the LT., but her muscles under Breylin's hand relaxed, so he let her go.

The simulant spit out a broken tooth and a wad of blood, then said, "I didn't bring us here – humanity did." He thought for a moment, then added, "You hate us – we get it. What we don't get is *why* you hate us."

"You bastard," Breylin said. "Look around you. We do hate you – for these deaths! These people never harmed you, yet they died by your hands!"

"You hated me and everyone like me before you even knew I existed," he breathed out.

Is he off his rocker, or do I just not understand what he's saying? he asked of himself. When he couldn't make sense of his words he said, "what the hell are you talking about?!"

"The only deaths here that matter to you are the *humans*."

"I heard enough of this bullshit," Azul said. "May I stow him, LT?"

"Go ahead, Gunny – this isn't accomplishing anything, and I'm not sure it makes a difference, anyway. Get him out of here."

After three of the privates dragged Ridder out, Mathias said, "LT?"

Breylin looked around at the bodies. The mother's and an older boy's neck had been broken. The father's throat had been torn out, the edges ragged as if he'd been savaged by one of the military dogs Breylin had seen on Mars. He wasn't sure if it was his blood sprayed on the wall or if it was the simulant's with the bloody hands. One of the grunts had stitched five or six shots across his chest. "What is it, Staff?"

Gesturing with his chin at door to the outside he said, "that one was different." SSgt. Mathias, the assistant platoon sergeant, was a tall man, and he had the darkest skin Breylin had ever seen. He was also quiet and observant, so if he had something to say it was worth listening to. He pointed to the simulants at their feet and continued, "these ones were ready to kill the family as soon as we rushed in. I don't think that tech assistant was."

Pellegrino bristled. "You saw him – he had her in his arms!"

"Relax, Sergeant. Getting the kid out alive was what was important and you did what you had to. If I'd been closer I probably would've killed him outright." He turned back to Breylin. "LT, he might have been shielding the girl. I thought you should know."

After his words sunk in, Joss stood up to leave the house. He paused in the doorway, and turned back to Mathias and Pellegrino. "You should have killed him."

They bagged all of the bodies – humans and simulants equal in death – and loaded them in the transport. When they mounted up, the child was still clinging to Pvt. Coohill, but thankfully she was quiet – probably in shock. The only sounds the whole way back to the city were intermittent static from comms and the whine of the transport's drives.

That night Breylin made his report coldly factual and sterile and sent it off to his superiors. He laid awake most of the night wrestling with the sight of blood and bodies etched into his memory, but it was the loneliness he felt created by Riss' absence most bitter and real.

The next morning, he had the simulant brought to his office and his hands restrained behind his back. Breylin locked eyes with him and clicked a pen in and out, in and out, letting the time stretch.

Eventually he said, "I have just received my orders from Command. Tomas Ridder, my priority one mission is to terminate you ASAP and do my best to secure the hatch on what happened out there as best I can."

Another quiet filled the room, broken only by the rhythmic ticking of his pen.

The *gabacho* shook his head, but spoke quietly. "Do you believe in God, human? Heaven and Hell?"

Breylin tossed the pen on his desk. It was the last thing he expected the bastard to say, and he had to think about it before it really sunk in. He sat back in his chair and pushed out a lungful in one long, exhausted rush. "Yes... I think so," he said guilelessly, in an effort to defuse his own tension. "I guess I don't like the idea of this being all there is. What's that got to do with anything?"

Tears started to flow. After a few moments Ridder lowered his eyes to the floor as said, "do you think He will let me in one of them?"

Breylin was again taken aback, surprised at the ability of this creature to feel, but he replied before he could think it through. "God didn't make you. We did," he said more flippantly than he had intended. He wasn't sure he understood why, but he began to hate him.

He laughed as he looked up at Breylin and said sardonically, "and where would *you* send me, O Creator?"

Breylin's animosity flourished, and he nearly lunged across the desk at the snotty little shit. He managed to restrain himself, though it was only by a narrow margin. "I'd send you straight to hell, you murderer," he said nastily. "But God will have to sort out your final destination. He only lets me book your passage."

Ridder laughed incredulously. "You're some piece of work, military man..."

Breylin snorted, languidly stood and walked past the restrained man, but he turned – whip crack fast. He grabbed Ridder by the throat, hauled him to his feet and drove him into the wall. His skull rebounded and the partitions shuddered with the impact. Official notices and the thumbtacks that had been holding them to the partition scattered around them unseen while a light dust sifted down from the darkness-shrouded rafters above.

"What's the matter, *gabacho*?" he said dangerously with his nose a couple of centimeters from Ridder's. "Can't you take me like you took that family?"

"You won't believe this, human," he replied in a croak. Spittle was collecting on his lips. "But that wasn't supposed – *cough* – to happen. We damn sure meant – *cough, cough* – kill that bitch Ainsworth, but not them. I – *cough* – just couldn't control the others anymore."

He began to get redder with each hack, but Breylin tightened his grip, closing his windpipe and putting an end to his weak expulsions. Ridder began to turn purple as his hands scrabbled over Joss' shoulders trying to push him off. "I should kill you right here, you satchel of fake cold cuts, but you know what stops me?"

Eye to eye, Ridder shook his head *No*, but only what Breylin's hands would allow.

"I'm not going to kill you now because I can't fucking *wait* to see your expression when you're staring down the business end of Marine carbines. You won't be quite so tough then, will you?" Breylin jerked him away from the wall and slammed him back into it, and more dust sifted down on their heads unnoticed. "I hope your hot piss runs down your legs before those triggers are pulled, too, but if you don't, you will once they drill you and you're dead. It's a shame we can't kill you twice."

After a few more seconds Joss let him go. His knees unhinged and he slid down the wall as he hacked hard and swallowed air as fast as he could. Looking down on the rasping mess, Joss let himself feel a thread of the black pleasure nearly squeezing the life out of Ridder had given him.

"You nearly killed me... didn't you?" he graveled out as he sat among the detritus of military notices their clash had torn off the wall. "Your capacity for hate... astounds me."

He was seized with a burning desire to shut him up by kicking his ribs in, but he turned, slammed his door open and stormed out of the office before he lost control. Two grunts who had been waiting outside came in, snatched Ridder to his feet by his arms and dragged him back to the seldom used holding cell.

Later that day, Ridder was executed by firing squad in the Marines' compound. He had refused any further attempts at conversation and walked to his own death with his eyes cast skyward.

Seven

There was a short series of unpleasant tones. "183 Alpha and 370 Bravo, first call. Please report for duty in seventy five minutes," chimed LabSys.

Luna opened her eyes and looked at Maré, and for a few seconds she marveled at their wonderful new relationship. *My Chroma...* She stroked her face and said, "good morning, Maré."

Maré came to disoriented and half startled at the tones, but then she realized where she was. She laid her head back down on Luna's bosom. "I'm scared to face this day, Luna."

"Why do you say that?"

"I don't know..." She paused." I know so little about what I am, what I'm doing. It's all happened so fast, and I have so little to begin with. Even our relationship has moved faster than I would have thought safe... but if not for you, I don't know where I'd be now. Maybe nowhere. I'm lost, Luna."

Luna could feel the tension in muscles under the skin of her back, so she continued to caress Maré's face. Delicately using her fingertips to trace its outlines, she gave herself a minute to enjoy their intimacy. Then she brought her hair near Maré's face as she whispered, "give me two minutes, Maré. I want you to forget last night and ignore what today might bring. Just breathe in the scent of me, your Chroma."

—∧=∨—

"Chroma. It's kind of a funny word," she said, but she inhaled deeply with the tips of her hair tickling her nose. She could faintly smell the antiseptics she had used the last time she had cleaned herself, and she could distinctly smell her night sweat. Stronger than both put together though, she could smell the musk, the natural smell that could only be Luna. The scent was so strong that she wasn't sure how she had been able to sleep. Somehow, it made her feel... something. Something almost familiar. She took the strands from her, brought them closer, and inhaled deeply again.

"Can you smell me, Maré?"

"Yes..."

"No other Alpha will smell quite like me. Every Alpha ever created was grown from the same genetic blueprint, but only I am yours."

"How can that be?" she said as she moved her head to smell the hair close to her ear. "Is it psychological?"

"I don't think so. Since we eat the same things it can't be diet. The best we can figure is that experience plays a role."

After a few moments of shared closeness, she continued. "We have a lot more to talk about, but it will have to keep until later. In the meantime, can you try to do me a favor?"

"Yes, Luna," she replied as her nose brushed her ear.

"I know nothing makes sense yet, and today will be more un-balancing events. Do you think you could try to remember my scent when you're scared?"

"You're the only friend I've ever had. I'll never forget the smell of you."

"Good. I get scared too – I'm scared now – but I will be doing the same thing, remembering the smell of my Chroma."

There were more unpleasant chimes, and LabSys said, "you now have sixty minutes to report for duty."

Luna reached up and turned on a tiny light and opened the lid of their clamshell bed, returning them to standard gravity. Just like that, reality barged its way in and the moment was broken.

"Now what?" Maré said as they climbed out.

"What now is you and I see if we can squeeze into that shower. We'll have to make some of my clothes work for you. Fortunately, you're physically only a little smaller than I am."

"Luna, that's not really what I meant."

She paused. "I know, Maré," and she sighed. "Once we get ready and eat what's left of our tiny breakfast, we will meet the others, at least for a few minutes."

As they climbed into the shower together, Maré asked, "what are they like?"

"Uhhh... well, you'll find that there's a surprising amount of variety for a group of genetically identical simulants."

"What does that mean?"

"Well, I don't want to color your judgment. You'll have to trust me and judge them on your own. We can talk through it in bed later tonight. There, your hair is done. Do mine, please."

When they were done getting around, Luna led Maré out into the common area. Two women were already seated with their backs toward Maré. She couldn't tell much from this angle, but she could see that they both had oddly bare heads, and they were wearing identical pale grey jumpsuits with a single pin stripe down the outside seam. Luna brought her around to meet them.

"216 Alpha, Bravo, this is 370 Bravo. Dr. Almeida had me bring her out of sleep during the night. 370 Bravo, these are the twins."

They looked at each other, then turned back. 216 Alpha said, "370 Bravo, it was expected that you would be brought to consciousness reasonably soon, but your presence here is a surprise to us."

"Very. The normal protocol would have been to repurpose you," said Bravo.

"You must be well, and that makes us glad," said Alpha.

"If we may be of assistance, you must tell us," said Bravo.

Maré didn't have a whole lot of experience upon which to draw, but the twins weren't what she had expected. At least they seemed friendly, if somewhat awkward. Still, Maré wasn't sure what to say. "Thanks... you can call me Maré."

The twins cocked their head in the same direction, but she doubted they were aware of having done it. They then looked at each other, and Alpha nodded to her match.

Bravo said, "Please take no offense, but that would be most inappropriate. Though I have never used it, my officially designated forename is also Maré."

Luna said, "Allow me to explain: it was discovered when 370 Bravo was brought out of maturation that her memories had not been successfully implanted. She has only the very little context I have been able to impart in brief conversations."

"This explains your confusion, 370 Bravo, but now I am more curious as to why you were not repurposed," said Alpha.

Maré took a good look at them, and Alpha in particular. She

had no hair, and though her smile and the angle she held her head seemed quite different, the soft curves of her face and her liquid brown eyes were definitely identical to Luna's. It was a little disquieting, strange. It occurred to her that Bravo was just as similar to herself, and yet not the same. *This is perfectly normal to them*, she thought. *I'm the one that's strange...*

"I am responsible," said Luna. "Dr. Almeida *was* about to re-purpose her, but I begged him to allow her to stay. He agreed, with the stipulation that the cost would be mine to bear."

"This will present problems. Have you paired?" said Bravo.

Maré looked to Luna, who answered. "Yes."

"Wonderful. May your happiness be completed in each other," said Alpha.

"370 Bravo, We believe you are in good company. We have found 183 Alpha to be both competent in the performance of her assigned tasks and compassionate towards our sleeping sisters," said Bravo.

"She is our friend, and we would be pleased to have your friendship as well," said Alpha.

Maré said, "thank you, both. I'm sure I'll need all of the friends I can get."

"Twins, there is a way in which you could help. If you could spare some food, it would be greatly appreciated," said Luna.

The twins looked at each other again. It seemed to Maré that something must pass between them when they look into each other's eyes. When they turned back, Bravo said, "we will have to work out a rotation."

"It will be easier to bear if we work together," said Alpha.

"And the training, as well," said Bravo.

Maré was touched at the kindness of these people. *Simulants*, she corrected herself. "I don't know what to say. Thank you very much."

Then the last bedroom door opened, and out came 85 Alpha. She was still buttoning up her lab coat when she noticed that there was a new addition to their group, stopping her dead in her tracks. "What's this?" she said.

"This is 370 Bravo," Said Luna. "Dr. Almeida ordered her brought out of maturation."

Bravo said, "370 Bravo has no memories, because they'd not yet been successfully implanted."

"I see," said 85 Alpha.

The moment seemed strained and tense, but then it mostly passed. 85 Alpha came over to Maré and extended her hand. "I'm very pleased to meet you."

Maré took her hand lightly and said, "So am I. Pleased to meet you, that is." She couldn't identify what it was, but something about 85's inflection was strange. *Something about this woman is... off*, thought Maré.

Their hands parted.

"You must be very out of sorts. Have... living arrangements been made? I could —"

Luna took a step so that she was not directly between them, but close to it. "Everything has been taken care of, as far as that goes. She is staying with me." The temperature of the room went up a few degrees as she spoke.

85 stammered with annoyance. "B-b-butt... it's so sudden..."

The Twins stood up. "85 Alpha, you have friends," said Bravo.

"You must find your center there," said Alpha.

She seemed to pull herself together. "Yes, well... very fine. Maybe we can catch up later, but for now, I must get to my duties." She rushed out with her lab coat still half buttoned.

Back in their room, Maré could tell that Luna was a little unnerved. "What *was* all of that?"

"*That*," said Luna, "was 85 Alpha. I expected a reaction from her, but not like that."

"I don't know what to make of her. Do we worry?"

"A certain amount of caution is wise, but I don't think she'll do anything to harm you, no." After a moment, she said, "But she is right about duty calling. I have to go, Maré."

"What, just like that?"

"Yep, and you must stay here."

Once again, life seemed to be outracing Maré. "When will you be back? What do I do while you pop off to work?"

"Listen, don't worry. I'll check in at lunchtime. In the meantime, you might as well start preparing for your new career. LabSys?"

Tones. "Ready, 183 Alpha."

"Please help 370 Bravo navigate to the training materials for maturation pod procedures."

"Acknowledged, 183 Alpha."

"The most practical thing you need to know is that LabSys is always present and monitoring. If you need me, you can contact me through comms over it, and you can always ask it questions. Otherwise, I need to go." As she moved towards the door, it swished open.

"Luna?"

She paused in the doorway and looked back.

"I'll miss you."

Luna came back and put her arms around her. "Maré, I would rather be with you than out there." She broke the embrace, and ran out the door leaving her alone.

The dreary day slowly passed with her watching some introductory lessons on simulant biological maintenance, punctuated only by a too brief visit from Luna at lunchtime. At dinner, Luna got the food and brought it back to the room. As they sat at the desk, Maré on the chair and Luna on a box, they opened the hot packages. Maré said, "So... tell me about your day."

"Ha! There's not a lot to tell. You look tired; did everything go okay?"

She paused with food half way to her mouth. "I guess I am tired – probably a combination of that booster you gave me wearing off and less than exciting training materials. And I'm serious about wanting to know about what you were doing. I only get to live through you for the next week."

Luna snorted again. "Don't forget the lung treatments... We have that to look forward to yet tonight."

Maré frowned. "Is it really necessary? I *feel* fine."

"You might be, dear, but we have to be sober about this thing. Dr. Almeida *will* get rid of you if he thinks you aren't in perfect condition."

"Almeida's really got it in for me, huh?" she said playfully.

Luna lightly smacked the top of the desk with her palm. "*Dr. Almeida, Maré.*" She shifted her eyes around toward the ceiling, then she whispered, "It must have been a long day – it has made you needlessly... talkative."

Maré was a little hurt at the slight rebuke, but she understood – everything they said and did was watched. "You're right, Luna. I'm not adjusted and I forgot. I think I'll try to take it easy."

"Good. As for my day, I drew sixteen samples of amniotic gel from several of the maturation pods and ran them through Lab-Sys' analyzer. Three of them required me to add hormones to the related pods."

"What were the hormones for?"

"Different things related to development. We'll show you everything you'll need to know once you're allowed to be around the maturation pods, but basically sometimes a set of twins will have lungs developing a little slower than they should, or a nervous system a little too fast, things like that. I also checked the pods around the one used to develop you, looking for signs of infection."

"Did you find anything?"

"Luckily, no. It shouldn't have been able to happen in the first place, and as far as I know, none of the test results have been able to show anything conclusive. Anyway, we normally spend a lot of time taking samples, running tests and keeping an eye on things."

Maré poured half the contents of their drink into yesterday's container and got up. "Do you want water in yours?"

"Yeah, but only fill it three quarters, please."

She padded over to the sink, and as the water ran, she spoke. "Doesn't it feel weird to you, taking care of the sisters?"

Luna's brow creased in thought. "I hadn't thought about it. I dunno, maybe it is weird – but we take care of them as well as anyone might or could. If androids or machines did it, there would probably be more problems."

Maré brightened as she came back and sat down. "I'm proud of how diligent you are, Luna."

"Of course. They are chromanity. Next week you are going to be just as diligent as you ever were."

"A good design, right?"

She nodded. "I remember how you were, Maré. I was a better kid because of you."

Maré shrugged and took it in without a word.

"Here's something. When the originals were born, Maré came out first. It was only a few short seconds, but you were the older."

"And now *you* are the older, sort of," said Maré.

"Sort of. And you know what else? We still bring Maré out first – at least the ones that wake up here, anyway."

As they were finishing up, Luna started to collect the wrappers. Maré said, "Leave that go a minute – I'll clean it up. Come look at this with me, please." And she went over to the bed and sat down.

Luna came over, and Maré turned to an old, faded holo that was fixed to the wall with yellowed tape. It was almost 3D, but it was so old that the illusory effect had faded somewhat. "What is this?"

"That's Mom and Dad, Maré, and us in front of them. I am on the left, and you are on the right." Luna reached out and gently smoothed one of the slightly curled edges at the bottom of the image. The whole edge was smudged, as if she had tried to flatten that edge many times.

"Really?"

"Yes. I don't know for sure, but we must have been about ten or so."

"How long has this been here?"

"I'm not sure. A long time ago, a previous occupant of this room hung it there."

Maré shivered a little. *A previous occupant. Will someone think of us that way someday?*

"It's okay, Maré."

She looked up at Luna. She threw her arms around her Chroma, and cried into her neck.

"Hey, it's okay, honey. Shhh..."

After she quieted down, Luna said, "What did you think of the twins?"

Maré broke the contact. "They're odd, I guess, but I think I like them."

"They are a bit odd, but it's because of their relationship. They were brought out of the same maturation pod, specifically to work here. They were grown together, and they've been together ever since. Their rapport is impenetrable."

"They do seem really synced up."

"Meshed is a better word. I think it has a lot to do with this environment, like it distilled them or something. 85 once told me that they have... relations, as well."

Maré appeared puzzled.

"Relations. Sex. You know what I mean, right?"

"Uh, yeah, I get it. I guess I wouldn't... expect that between sisters."

"With them it's less like incest and more like masturbation. And we aren't really *sisters*, we're Chroma, grown on demand."

"It feels a little weird." She paused and said, "Is this something that will be between us?"

Luna sat up stiffly. "It's *not* weird. I hope we'll be deeply close, Maré. I loved you before I pulled you out of that crappy gel, and I love *you* specifically now. But I don't think we can go there."

Maré sensed the thick wall around Luna's emotions. She had just run into it. "Tell me," she said.

"Not yet," she said with stormy eyes. "Let's go get the lung treatment over with," and she pulled Maré to her feet.

When they came back later, Luna got Maré a glass of water for her raspy throat.

"Thanks." After a couple of sips she said, "How did 85 know about what the twins have been doing?"

"They probably talked about it. 85 has been here a long time, longer than the twins."

"How long?" asked Maré.

"About eight years. The twins have been here about five."

"And you?"

"I've been here for a year."

"What was it like for you? I mean, living without your Bravo."

"Well... it was hard... and I was pretty lonely." Pause. "I mean, I had my memories, so it felt like my sister had died. I knew she wasn't the real one, and that I wasn't either, but the memories drove my emotions a lot more than my ability to think did."

Maré could tell that Luna didn't visit these feelings very often. Choosing her words, she spoke softly. "This is hard for me, and I have you. How did you get through it?"

"We're going to have to turn the lights out for that one."

They got undressed in silence, climbed into bed together and pulled the lid down into place. The darkness was deep, but it was intimate and comforting, like being in the womb.

Maré sensed her Chroma's trouble, so she pulled Luna to her. She wanted to say something, but she held her tongue. Luna would talk when she was ready.

"85 brought me out." She was trembling slightly.

"You don't have to, Luna. Forget it."

After a few seconds, Luna said, "No, I can't forget it, and you need to know what happened."

Maré waited.

"They'd known there was a problem with my Bravo from her brain chemistry, and 85 was there to do the initial assessment when the androids brought us out." She took a couple deep breaths. "To make a long story short, she convinced me to try to pair with her."

Maré could feel the drops on her chest, and she knew that Luna must be crying.

"She'd already been here. She'd been paired for her first two years here, but *her* Maré died. She'd been alone from that time until I came along."

Maré stroked her hair. "I was going crazy alone by myself for only part of a day," she said. "She must have felt... *forsaken*."

"Yes. The vacuum in her was vast. It still is."

Maré kept stroking her head while she waited for her to continue. It was becoming painful, wanting to soothe her and not knowing how. A need to fix things, to protect Luna, was emerging... She wasn't sure why she should feel challenged this way, but she quietly accepted the responsibility without looking back.

"She bullied me into it, Maré." She shook with silent sobs. *"She... forced herself on me."*

Understanding dawned. Maré was heartbroken for her Chroma, and she held her as tight as she could while they both cried in the dark womb of their bed.

Eight

Joss had become a different person by the time the fourth year of his tour was done. Extreme heartache and the rigors of military life had contended with the deep emotional attachment he had formed with his platoon, and the infrequent, asynchronous contact he'd had with Riss back on Earth over the interstellar nets. Azul had been reassigned the year before, but Breylin had been true to his word to let him have his head while they were together. In return, Azul had treated him with the respect he typically saved for the sergeants, advising him and counseling him on how to manage people who depend on each other for their lives. Breylin put it all into practice well – if not perfect – and the platoon respected him for it.

After Nakamura's trauma and while he recuperated, Azul had Styers step in during Nakamura's convalescence to lead the squad. Within a month, LT had promoted her to Sgt. She spent most of her free time with Nakamura, though; initially she assisted Headly with tending his injuries, but she quickly took over the responsibility. Before the end of that year, the two of them had come to Azul and Breylin to ask for permission to get married. It was against regulation, since this was technically a forward position, but Nakamura and Styers were high-speed low-drag grunts. Breylin figured he could take whatever little heat it might generate, if any. Once the news was out though, it became popular with the rank and file to call Nakamura Mr. Styers behind his back. The scuttlebutt got back to him anyway, but to his credit he took to wearing it like a badge. In the end, it was the name tag on his uniforms that had to change, not hers. When their tour was up though, she opted to leave the service, while he stayed on with the stipulation of staying on Zarmina's World. They rented a small, ratty apartment in the city, and stayed there a long time after.

There were other changes, of course. Some of the Marines earned rank, including Pelligrino who finally earned her rocker. First tours for the enlisted were four years in length, but for those who reenlisted they moved around on a two or three year cycle thereafter. The men and women came and went, but the unit cohesion stayed pretty much the same.

—∧=∨—

It was the Styers' union that got Joss to rethinking the plans that he and Riss had laid out. Moving to Greenland would provide them with fascinating geologic studies for the rest of their lifetimes, as well as keep them on Earth near her parents. But it had been so long since he had seen his queen that maybe, just maybe, Riss might also be willing to reconsider their plans.

Unfortunately, personal communications were relegated to the low priority bands on the interstellar nets. Transmission one way could take a month, and sometimes a month and a half. To avoid a whole lot of back and forth, he would need to be succinct, yet passionate and honest.

For hours that night, he wrote and rewrote his thoughts. He printed them out, paced and spoke them aloud with varied inflections. He balled them up and threw them on the floor. After midnight he was no closer, only exasperated with his own inability to trap the right words. He gave up and hit the rack.

The next morning after PT and chow, a tired Joss took a cup of coffee, the blackest stuff the synthesizers would make, to his office. He closed the door, sat down, and punched up the recorder. He knew what needed to be said, but he hadn't collected his thoughts and he was afraid he'd screw it up. It was best to just get it out. Nervousness was a feeling he wasn't used to, and sweat soaked his fatigues under his arms and sheened his forehead, but he was as ready as he was going to get. He took what he hoped were a few cleansing breaths, and he flicked the button to Record.

"My Queen... I love you, Riss, more than life itself." He exhaled forcefully through his moustache and continued. "These four long years that we have been apart have been hard on me, more than I can say, and yet we have two more to go. The thought crushes me," he said as he mimed squeezing something with his hand. "I know the distance between us pains you too, and I am sorry that I can't protect you from it. This may have been our plan, but it's had a heavy price – to use your words.

Riss, would you think through an alternative, if it would bring us together now? If we were to consider leaving Earth and build our lives here, we could do it. We would have to book civilian passage for you, which might bust a huge chunk of our reserves, but there's beautiful mountains to the north, and unused houses in little settlements that I think I can get for the price of signing up with the gas mining companies. Parts of Zarmina are desolate, but where we would live can be breathtaking. We will do as you wish, mistress of my heart, but I beg you to consider the idea." He pressed Stop, and thought for a half second that he should record it again. When his stomach protested at the notion with rumbles of nasty bile, he pushed Send before he could reconsider further, and as he bolted from his office towards the head, he just hoped it wouldn't be three months before he heard back. He was about to release the water his bowels had turned to, and very likely he would also vomit his breakfast between his legs, but he laughed anyway, knowing that the message was already speeding away on its journey across the interstellar medium, that the mission had been accomplished.

—∧=∨—

Nearly five weeks later, the platoon had mustered in environmental suits for cold weather training. It was three months past the start of the storm season, and the atmosphere was putting on a really spectacular lightning show. It wouldn't matter where they were heading, though; fifty eight clicks to the east it was expected to be white out conditions. The temperature was largely irrelevant – as long as they weren't training in EV suit failure mode; the real training was just getting use to performing in the suit with the visor in place.

Cpl. Coohill, who had charge of quarters duty, came running out to the grunts as they were mounting the transport. "LT!

There's a priority one message on the holocomm!"

Breylin's gut tightened. "Priority one holocomm? What the hell? You ever receive one before, Gunny?"

"Nope. We'll hold in place until you sort it out, LT," said Trastman, the platoon sergeant who took over for Azul.

"Thanks. I'll be back ASAP," he said as he dismounted and moved out smartly.

He brought up his comm panel in his office, hoping that it was just some crazy unit readiness test from Command, and not orders to respond to a real threat. Breylin was no coward – none of these people were – but he didn't want to be called upon to use deadly force. One of the few lessons he had learned as an officer candidate that Azul had confirmed was to avoid needing to draw a weapon, if at all possible. If that wasn't an option, then act with finality.

When Joss brought up the holo and the face materialized, his heart skipped a few beats – it was Larissa. "My darling Joss, I miss you. Every day I think the hole in my life, the one shaped like you, can't get any larger, but it is a hungry thing. It devours a little bit more of the world, and the color of what remains is a little more washed out. I long to cross this chasm between us.

"But... it is a hard thing you ask. It would probably mean that I would never see my parents again. We would miss Greenland too, though I think you were more in love with that than I was. I've talked it over with my Mom and Dad; she thinks it's charming that you would sacrifice so much for us to be together. Dad hates the idea that he wouldn't be able to spend time with our kids. You do still want to have kids, right? You'd better, Mr. Breylin!

"I don't know if I like the idea, Joss. I'm just not ready to throw that big of a switch.

"Now don't get too worked up... I do need you, my heart, so here is what I've decided and already set in motion: we'll try it out for a couple of months. It *has* put a big dent in our savings, but I've bought a one way ticket out to that rock. Just think, I am in hyper-sleep right now as you are watching this!

"I am coming in on a civilian transport, the Wunderkind. We should make planetfall in about seven weeks. You should see the ship, Joss! It's huge and shiny, and... oh hell, it's not like I'll get to enjoy the trip! I've got the good end of the deal – I'll slip into sleep and practically wake up in the arms of my knight and pro-tector... but you will have to stew on the anticipation... I'd like to be able to say that I'm sorry, but I much prefer the idea that you'll be more than ready to receive me. I am the queen, am I not? You'll probably have your way though, both with me, and where we settle. Don't count on it though – a queen will exercise her options.

"Now, I insist that you get everything done before I arrive, Joss Breylin Jr. You know how I'm all about business, and we've got plenty of it to get through."

Larissa blew him a breathy kiss, and the image faded.

He sat there stunned. *She was coming? Just like that?*

All of a sudden he felt a little nauseous, light-headed, and alive. It was if instead of racing, his heart had just started beating.

He let the thrill pleasantly chime through him for maybe another thirty seconds, and then he got his ass moving. Marines don't think about liberty until the mission was done.

—∧=∨—

Joss tried to contact some low-level administrator by the name of Cole in Twilight to find out how he might go about using a flat in one of the unused settlements, but the guy kept putting him off. After a week, Joss had had enough. He had two of his biggest people gear up, and the three of them drove in to see the guy in person. It's easy to blow somebody off over comms, but he might not be so brave with three grunts on his door step.

"I'm sorry I haven't been able to make time to speak with you... Lieutenant, is it?" he said as he mopped his brow with a damp, sweat stained handkerchief.

He was middle aged, balding, and so obviously bored that Breylin wondered if he might be in danger of slipping into a coma. The heat in his office was making him sweat profusely, and the languid overhead fan did nothing but push small, hellish puffs around. Overall, it was the sort of workplace no one could be happy in, and Cole was probably giving him a hassle just to make life interesting. "Yes, lieutenant. LT. Breylin – I command the detached platoon that keeps station at the edge of town. Surely you've seen our patrols, Mr. Cole."

With only a huge dollop of sarcasm he said, "you might think so, but I'm sure I haven't. Do you see much combat here on Zarmina, Lieutenant?"

Breylin ground his teeth. *The little piss-ant's going to make this as difficult as possible, isn't he...* "No. If we did, you would have noticed. That sort of thing tends to be spectacular."

"You're probably right," he said, sounding as if he was tiring of his own game. With a wave of his hand, he continued. "So what is it that you think I might be able to do for you?"

"I would like permission to use a house in one of the settlements to the north for a few weeks, maybe as long as two months."

"Did you have a particular settlement in mind?"

"Yes – Amity Canyon."

He appeared thoughtful, but then he said, "oh, I don't think that will be possible, Lieutenant..."

Joss began to silently pray that his back teeth didn't snap from the force of his grinding before he got out of this man's office. "And why is that, sir?"

"Well... you see," he said in the most patronizing voice he'd ever heard, "those houses are reserved for company-sponsored settlers. Quite honestly, young man, the company can't afford to have soldiers tearing them up," he said with another run at his forehead with that filthy rag.

"*Marines*, sir," Breylin said quietly, dangerously. "We are not soldiers."

One of the Marines spoke up. "LT, I'm not sure he understands who is keeping his streets safe."

"Oh, come now," he said in a tone set on full patronize, "I think corporate security is able to keep things under control in our little city."

"That bunch of candy-asses? I could —"

Breylin held his hand up and the grunt fell silent instantly. After a few seconds Breylin said, "Can you tell me what the plan is if you should have another simulant revolt?"

He faltered for a moment, as if the thought hadn't occurred to him. "We would call you, of course. Our people aren't equipped to deal with that sort of thing. But that has only ever happened once," he said dismissively.

"I know," said Breylin. "*I was there*. One of my men was seriously wounded trying to save your settlers. It's a good thing he isn't in the room, or worse yet, his wife. You might find their response... excessive."

Bored guy took a few seconds to blink while the words sank in, and then he sat back in his creaking, burdened chair, threw the rag on the desk and considered Breylin over steepled fingertips. "Well now," he said. "That's very interesting, Lieutenant... and maybe it changes a few things."

"Favorably, I hope."

"That depends on your perspective," he said with humorless eyes. He sat forward again and rested his forearms on the desk, clearly becoming attentive. "I might be able to use some of my authority to provide you with what you need..."

So, he can be pushed, he thought. *But only so far.* "What do you want, Cole?"

"Well, let's see. Is there any chance this arrangement might become permanent?"

"Possibly – I may opt to stay on world at the completion of my assignment, depending on whether or not I am offered a job with one of the mining companies."

He responded quickly. "I can help with that, too."

"All these favors," Breylin countered. "I'm guessing you won't be providing me with anything out of your generous, good nature. In fact, the cost'll be high, I'd imagine."

"I want something in return for my help, of course."

"What *do* you want?"

"I'll make sure you're offered a job when the time is right, and I'll guarantee you whatever residence up there in backwater Amity you chose are part of the terms. The rest of the agreement will be decided then. Whatever you're offered, you'll accept."

"You don't want much, do you? Those houses'll never be used again, and you know it."

"Maybe... but you get peace of mind knowing my company will definitely hire you," he said. "It's not just a house, is it? Security's what I'm offering you, Lieutenant."

Breylin sighed heavily, knowing the guy had him. "Fine."

"Excellent..." Cole turned to his console and banged away at it for a couple of minutes, and a sheet of paper whispered its way out of a slot below the screen. He took it and placed it on the desk in front of Joss with a pen.

"What's this?" Breylin said with a gesture.

"It's a promissory note between you and my company. You sign now, you get your house now."

"Sign it? No one does this anymore – everything's done with thumbprints."

"Call me quaint." He handed Joss the pen, eyes now full of life. "Sign it," he said lasciviously.

"You want me to sign it? Here's your quaint signature." Breylin rushed to his feet, drew his Kabar and with a massive overhand swing drove three quarters of its length through the sheet and the desktop beneath it. The blood grooves along its keen edge had whistled on its way down, but the impact had been like a thunderclap in his stale, hot office. Joss leaned towards him with his fists down on the surface and did everything he could to nail him to his chair with his eyes.

Cole looked up at him poleaxed and sweating twice as hard. "Holy shit! What the hell is wrong with you?" He shook his head. "You've ruined my friggin desk!"

"I have two other fighting knives at my disposal, Cole," he spat back. "Do you want anything else signed?"

"Whatever," he said trying to sound cool. He pushed himself back from the edge of the desk, Breylin, and his knife. "Have at it, Lieutenant. Pick a place and it's yours."

"Thank you, *sir*. You can keep the blade."

As the Marines were leaving the guy called out, "Make sure you don't destroy the place, will ya?"

Joss paused and nearly turned around, but he decided to let the door close between them instead. *Let him have the last word.* He'd gotten everything he'd come for, and maybe a bit more.

—∧=∨—

Joss had taken very little liberty his entire tour – only for a few rock hounding excursions at a couple of days a piece. He had even lost a few this past service anniversary because he had been over the maximum allowed. Even so, he was able to block out the two full months Riss would be on world.

The memories of what had happened at Amity Canyon weren't painful, but they were still quite vivid to Joss. Of the two houses at the top, he chose the one he hadn't needed to search. If the view wasn't quite as good as it was from the other, it would still be great.

Gunny made the whole platoon available to help get the place in order. The work got done, but since a break in the storms presented itself, it became more of a party.

The inside was old and dusty from long disuse, but it was still furnished. *The previous occupants must've died here*, Joss decided, *with all of the personal items scattered about the place.* He found quite a few holos on the walls, clothes in the drawers and toiletries in the bathroom. There was even food still in the cabinets. None of the stuff had been thought of in at least a couple of decades. All of it went into boxes that were loaded into their seldom used lorry. With the squads more or less rotating, everything was carted out and the house was cleaned fast, paving the way for the serious business of picnic-style chow and tossing a couple of balls back and forth. Everyone had a great time, and Breylin knew that a better platoon didn't exist.

He got food in the place, and he had salvaged the towels and sheets and the like. He let the water run for a couple of hours. As a final touch, he made a couple of 2D hard copies of holos of their parents and hung them up in some salvaged frames in the kitchen.

Time crawled, but eventually the day arrived. He received no-tification that the Wunderkind was in orbit, and once the crew was fully awake they would rouse the few passengers and ferry them down to Twilight City. It would be a couple of hours yet, but he waited for the shuttle to land in the terminal in his best dress uni-form. He had a few scraggly flowers and his palms were full of water. If he had thought time had crawled before, he had been sadly mistaken.

At last the shuttle arrived, and the hatch lowered with the sound of escaping compressed gas. Larissa shoved her way out, to the chagrin of a couple of the other folks who were disembark-ing, and ran to him.

She stopped just short of him, and they stood looking into each other's eyes. Her clothes were rumpled and her hair looked as if it had been combed with one of her shoes, but she was the most beautiful thing he'd ever seen. She was so radiant that he couldn't breathe. The seconds ticked by and the world receded.

As if drawn by gravity, she began to move toward him. Only centimeters separated them, and he caught the heady scent of her perfume in his nostrils. Careless of his uniform, he dropped to his knees, and as he put his arms around her, she took his face in her hands. His mouth hung open just a bit, awestruck and speechless at the sensation of the return of the missing half of his life. As the tears dropped off her cheeks and onto his, she said, "I'm here now, and I'm never going to leave you."

But she'd lied.

Nine

After Joss was decommissioned, he and Larissa plunged into the normal routines of life.

By then, Larissa had already been working in the research labs in Twilight City for two years as an assistant to one of the Ph.D's. Currently, they were taking the opportunity provided by Zarmina to study the effects of constant solar wind bombardment on the mantle. The whole region under the subsolar point was slightly depressed, most pronounced at the center, but gravity's constant pressure kept trying the force the shape back spherical. Minor quakes were a frequent part of life on Zarmina's World. Most folks blithely ignored them, but it was a source of wonder for a couple of geologists.

Joss, on the other hand, didn't have the pick of jobs his wife did. Although his grades had been quite exceptional, he hadn't had the time for practical application, given his service in the Marines. As a result, he'd had to take a job in the samples collection and maintenance group. At least it was supervisory, though only over *gabachos*. Still, it made him mad every time he thought of it.

Fortunately, his and Larissa's skills were useful to the companies that controlled Zarmina's capital interests, and that would afford them the opening to settle on world. But because of the method by which they'd found themselves living on Zarmina, as opposed to the normal immigration process, the companies were able to negotiate a more beneficial compensation package from the Breylin's for themselves. Desperate people in a monopolized market make fantastic customers.

The consequence of their position was that they made a little less money than their peers, their medical care was relegated to class B – adequate, but not top tier; they would have to continue to use the house they had initially chosen. Though the top of the ridge was always windy and the house was old and sand-scoured, it was sound, and the view from up there was often quite nice. If they had chosen something in Twilight, the best that would have been made available to them would have been a small apartment, as it was for virtually all other Twilight residents. In the city's hey-day, anyone who could afford a nicer place found it in one of the settlements. As it was, most had stood unused for decades, and could be had for the same money as something in town.

The last notable concession they had to make was to take a single simulant, even though settlers were afforded one for each working person who signed on. Joss didn't actually trust the *gabachos*, but mostly he could take them or leave them. Frankly, it didn't bother Joss if the laundry and the dishes were only done as they needed to be, but that was flatly unacceptable to Riss. And she had been the one to point out that they wanted to have children. Living remotely as they did, they would need simulants to care for them. Otherwise, one of them would have to stay at home, and it wasn't going to be her. Since the prospect of a permanent apron didn't appeal to him – even when posited against the job requirement of an EV suit – and it was clear where Riss stood, he quickly gave in.

Joss was glad he left the contract negotiations to her because she was a quick thinker – as she often kidded, all business – and it showed. At the bargaining table, she managed to exchange one exceptional model for two standard ones. Going through the promotional holos, they agreed on a set of twin females. The pair were only remarkable in how normal they were. Still, they should perform admirably in a home with children, and were rated to last about ten years. With a sample of Larissa's DNA, they could even be configured to produce breast milk identical to hers. Larissa, ever the queen, overrode his objections and ordered it done. They would be ready in about twenty one months, serendipitously close to Joss' exit from his Marine commitment. It was time to begin planning a family.

Two years later, Joss pulled the lift into the garage and cut the power to its plant. His own tears had long since ceased, but they sat there for a few seconds in a pained, turbulent anguish punctuated by Riss' continued sniffling. She was winding down now, but he wasn't so foolish to believe she was feeling better – quite the opposite; it would be a long night, and the worst of it would probably stretch for days.

He started to reach for her hand, to tell her that it would get better, something, anything, but she climbed out and ran into the house. He reached over and shut her door, then sat there trying to get his own emotions under control. If he went inside without having done that, then he wouldn't see straight enough through their shared pain to be what she needed. A failed pregnancy was *a lot* harder the second time around.

If only her doctor – *that useless bastard, I should have broken his scrawny neck!* – had been able to offer an explanation or provide some meaning, then maybe it would have been more tolerable. No such luck, though. *"You'll just have to keep trying,"* he'd said. *"If it was meant to happen, then it'll happen. You just have to be patient."* Joss' hands gripped the steering handles and shook with rage at the thought of those words that had fallen uselessly like shit dropping out of a dog's ass. *"Yeah, doc?"* Joss had replied with Riss crying into his shoulder. *"It* isn't *happening, so I guess it wasn't meant to be. Is that what you're telling us?"* And Riss had silently screamed, then.

After four heartbreaking years of failure, Joss and Larissa gave up trying to have children. Apathetic doctor after doctor had done pointless test after test, and they'd been unable to detect a reason for the failed pregnancies. *Nothing* they tried to do made the slightest bit of difference. Maybe if they'd been a little more interested – or intellectually engaged – they might have done a better job, *but it wasn't meant to be.* Remaining aloof might've been an emotional shield for all those contemptible charlatans, but to the Breylins neither truer nor more painful words had ever been uttered.

Larissa would sink into a pit of despair a little deeper and take longer to snap out of it each time. Joss had felt useless and black during each period, but he never gave up on her. He was fed up with the failures, but instead of becoming depressed he became murderously angry – though without a valid outlet for all that negativity he did his best to bottle and hide the pain inside.

The only option left to the Breylin's was to keep trying to have children, and so they did, but it had finally proved to be too mentally exhausting. Fulfillment would have to come from something else.

Their lives became fairly solitary. All of Joss' friends from his time in the Marines had moved on, including the Styers' down in Twilight City. He had opted to leave the service and had taken a corporate security job. He would be supervising an entire security detachment, but it meant that they would have to move to some new colony on the outer rim of human settlement. They would be in hyper-sleep a long time.

Between bouts of despair, Larissa had been working on her doctorate, spending time in the evenings with the Ph.D's. Their sponsorship meant that the university on Mars would accept the experience of her current role and apply it as credit instead of class time, provided she somehow demonstrated a contribution to the science of geology. It would be five, maybe six, years in the works, but it drove her professional satisfaction – as much as anything did, anyway. It meant that there would be less time for the two of them, but Joss was supportive. He was very proud of her, his queen, and in some ways he managed to live vicariously through her efforts. Anyway, if he couldn't successfully give her a child, maybe he could do this to make her happy.

Joss spent long hours out in the glare and heat of the waste-lands among the gas taps – any time spent in an EV suit was long – but he returned home each evening to Riss and their girls, Maré and Luna. Pleasant enough, the girls were, and though they were physically about nineteen years old, they had become sort of like daughters, and their presence added to the family atmosphere. It wasn't what they had planned, but it was maybe a little bit better than just good enough.

Joss hadn't lost his taste for exploring in the traverses, hillocks and crags to the north, and Riss and the girls would accompany him to some of his favorite spots on a few occasions. They were his favorite times, as they would eat food prepared by the girls, and Riss would read to them by firelight. Afterwards, they would bed down near wind-sculpted, rock-strewn fields or immense cre-vasses, the sun large and perpetually setting in the distance, turn-ing the sky and clouds a royal mélange of purple and orange. Overhead, the sky would be purple, fading to black towards the east. Sometimes the clouds would completely part, and the view of alien stars would be breathtaking. It was as if the universe had put on a show for them, its only inhabitants.

As they grew accustomed to the form of their lives, Riss decided to take the girls to work with her. She enjoyed their presence, and if they assisted her, the four of them would spend more time together as a family. It sounded good in theory, and seemed to work in practice, and if it made his queen happy, then so be it. The subtle change gave Joss a notion, and once he figured out how it might work, he decided to offer Riss a way to take their pseudo-family a step further.

In the dark that night, with his chest hair tickling her cheek and his fingers moving over the nape of her neck, he said quietly, "Riss, I've been thinking, and I have an idea. I think you'll like it."

"Tell me, my knight," she breathed.

"Maré and Luna may be simulants, but I don't think that plays a part in what we feel for them. Would you agree?"

"Um... I guess you're right. As you say, I hadn't really thought about it. We're just who we are."

"What if we removed their collars and had them call us Mom and Dad? You know that I used to mistrust their kind, but I've changed how I feel about them – at least our girls anyway. We could treat them like people."

She was silent for a few moments. "I'm not sure how to feel about that. You know they're supposed to be collared..."

He shook his head. "As long as we keep it low key, I can't believe it would become an issue." He paused to squeeze her to him. "There's no rush. Think about it. If... if it would give you something, then let's do it."

She pushed up, leaned across him and turned off the light. Laying her head back down on his chest, she listened to his heart beat and thought for a few moments. "We'll see," she said quietly, but he thought he could feel the gears of her mind working.

It took less than a day. Riss and the girls came home early

from work. She bid them to make supper, whatever they wanted, and while they were at it, she drew Joss into their bedroom.

"You were right, my love, they have become like our children. But... someday they will pass. Have you thought the conse-quences through?"

"I have, Riss. Their lives are temporary, but aren't ours too? Regardless of whatever plans we make, there's no such thing as a guarantee. I could die in a flaming lift wreck on my way home, or you could have an accident at work. All we can do is hold on and roll with what life hands us. And when their time came, we could get another pair just like them. Until then, we would make their lives happy." He held his breath before speaking further. "This could help make your life happy, too."

Stepping closer she looked up at him, and he could see by the set of her eyes that she was afraid, yet daring to hope. "It might be something of an illusion, but illusions can be real. As real as we make it, right?"

He smiled and delicately caressed her cheek with the back of his fingers. "Precisely, my queen."

—∧=∨—

Over dinner, Maré could feel the eagerness of their masters. They had been nice to them, particularly so recently, yet the un-usual tension at the table, the forced small talk, made her nervous. She could feel the bewilderment rolling off of Luna, too. Certainly the Breylin's had never given them any reason to be afraid, but their collars and the threat it represented was always there in the back of her mind.

It was Luna's turn to clear the table and straighten up the

kitchen. When she rose and began to pull their empty plates into a pile, Mr. Breylin spoke up.

"I'd like you to sit a moment, Luna. This is a special night, and I will clear the table. Riss, would you help?"

"Certainly, my love."

As Mr. Breylin removed the dirty dishes and started making coffee, Mrs. Breylin got out four spoons and small bowls and set them down in the center of the table. She dug out the last small container of Ice Cream, an expensive treat normally reserved solely for her consumption — not even Mr. Breylin would dare cross that line. Yet she divided it into the four bowls and set one down for each of them. Mr. Breylin made them each coffee, and set down a small, steaming cup at each setting. He had never done that before.

Something must be wrong, thought Maré.

Luna broke the silence. "Are we in trouble, Mrs. Breylin?" she asked fretfully.

The Breylin's looked at each other in confusion. Mrs. Breylin said, "No Luna. Why would you think that?"

"It's just... well, you've never allowed us to have Ice Cream and coffee. We know how *enormously* expensive it is. We were just a little scared that if you would waste it on us then maybe we did something really bad."

Maré's eyes were downcast and on the verge of crying, but she nodded her agreement. "You're getting rid of us, aren't you?" She didn't know what else to say.

Larissa got up and came around the table and knelt between them. She put her arm around Luna, but she hugged Maré to herself. "No dears, listen to me, it's much the opposite."

Joss reached across the table and took a hand from both of them. The girls were really crying then, but he couldn't tell from relief or fear, so he spoke up. "Girls, we have grown quite fond of you, please don't be afraid," and he gave them a small, comforting squeeze.

Riss took the ball. "We want to change our relationship. You know that we haven't been able to have children of our own."

"Yes..." said Maré, as she held onto Mrs. Breylin.

"We would like you to call us Mom and Dad. What do you think about that?" she said.

Luna looked up, as her eyebrows rose as high as they would go. "Really? Is that what you want?" Passively, she wondered if her face looked as surprised as her Chroma did.

"I..." Luna faltered. Maré couldn't think of what to say. She wasn't sure how this would go, but it wasn't anything like this.

"Tell you what, would you like to think about it?" said Joss.

"Yes, please."

"That will be just fine, girls – you go think about it for tonight. Joss, take off their collars."

Joss obeyed. For the first time, Maré and Luna didn't have a snug band around their necks reminding them of who and what they were. It was a stunning – and maybe scary – thing.

"What about the chores?" said Maré said as she wiped her nose.

"Don't you worry about that – we'll take care of it," said Mrs. Breylin.

Still fearful that this would be taken from them, Maré and Luna held onto each other as they left the kitchen.

Back in their room, the girls got undressed and crawled into bed.

"Hold me," said Luna, and Maré took her in her arms, laid her head down on her breasts and stroked her hair.

After a long silence of laying that way, they talked it over.

"What do you think about what they said?" Maré whispered.

"I don't know what to think, Maré. What would our *real* Mom and Dad say?"

"Real? I thought we were Chroma."

"I know you know what I mean. They're dead a long time, and they weren't *our* real parents, but we both remember them as if they were. How would they feel?"

"Okay, I give," Maré said with a sigh. "They loved us very much... I believe if they couldn't be here, they would want what's best for us."

"Yes... but what's best?"

Maré thought it over, then spoke up. "I think these people are serious. I don't know if they *love* us, but I think they care for us."

"They owned us an hour ago, Maré."

"Yes, they did," she said. "And then they took our collars off."

"I suppose they've never mistreated us..."

"No, they haven't. I guess this could be some kind of trick... but I don't think so."

"If you believe them, then I do too."

She hugged her tightly. "I love you, Luna."

"You're my Chroma – I love you, too," said Luna as she snuggled into her small cleavage. "Let's give them a chance."

"That Ice Cream was pretty good, wasn't it?" Maré said with a laugh, but dessert was quickly forgotten as Luna began to suckle.

Ten

Though the girls had trouble trusting them at first, the Breylin's had made good on their promise, and the next two years were happy for all four of them. They lived comfortably together, and though they had to be guarded about their relationship with outsiders, the girls often went to work with Mom. They kept on going on excursions in the hills and mountains as a family, even camping out in the dry season, all in the same canvas tent Joss and the girls had stitched together from old surplus equipment from his time in the Marines that he still had stowed in a box in the back of the lift port. Larissa had been after him to clear that old crap out anyway, and this seemed like as good a use as anything else.

The girls still did most of the chores, but Joss and Riss reminded them that, just as their memories confirmed, it was perfectly normal to expect the children of the house to do chores. Mom and Dad willingly took a turn each week, anyway.

To be sure, it was a strange family, but it *was* one. There were special meals; the girls' birthday was treated just as importantly as Mom and Dad's. There were times when the girls chose what to listen to on the radio. They were often allowed to pick the meals, and if there were no chores to do, they could go outside or read from Larissa's collection of books as they chose. There were times when the girls were a little withdrawn, but Mom and Dad gave them some room when they needed it. The girls were allowed and encouraged to discuss their feelings, even about hard subjects like the implanted memories of their "real" parents. Mom and Dad just treated those memories with respect and as if they were real.

Larissa often read to the girls, especially at night when they laid down in bed. She would read about the animals on Earth, fantastic, sprawling cities that gleamed like crystal in sunlight, and about mythical beasts and the heroes that slew them. Still, the times that she read of the old children's stories she had fondly acquired were what they liked best, and of those their favorite had been *Snow White and Rose Red*.

The first time they'd heard the tale, Larissa had come into their room carrying a book tucked under her arm, and holding two small roses, one red and the other a pale ivory, mounted on a thick display and covered by clear resin on its sides and top.

"Oh, *look*," Maré said with a small gasp.

Dad came into the room, and he was carrying his holo-recorder. "Don't mind me," he said as he walked over to their dresser. He set the recorder down, turned it on, and their eyes followed him as he left the room.

Smiling and shaking her head as she turned back to the girls, Mom held the case down at their eye level and close so they could see the flowers inside clearly. Their stems were crossed, white over red, and they seemed to be fashioned from delicate tissue paper, very like what the perfumed bits of soap were wrapped in that Dad would sometimes bring home for her. They were delicate and crinkled, and when Maré looked closer she could see that the colors were slightly varied in uneven tones that worked perfectly on the twisted stems and whorls of its petals. The white one almost seemed pure yet aged, while the red spoke of love and adventure. There were a few pictures of colorful flowers in some of their books, and Mom had some that she'd drawn in her art pads, but these had a tranquil beauty she'd never seen before.

Their eyes followed her movements as she silently walked

around their bed and laid the case on one of the shelves built into the wall above their heads, with the white bud pointing towards Maré's side, and the other to Luna.

When she sat down on the bed next to Maré, Luna snuggled closer, and Riss pulled the soft comforter up under their chins. She smiled broadly as she tucked them in, so very like the mother of their memories had when they were little girls.

Maré noticed that Mom had a faraway look in her eyes as she stared off at nothing, held the thin book, and the solemn silence stretched. Her fingers moved lightly over its textured pattern of a spreading tree on the cover, almost reverently, and Maré doubted she was even aware of it. It had sunk down the tangled tendrils of its roots nearly as large as the canopy, and etched into its bole was a simpler yet alluring knot perhaps made of heart shapes. It immediately brought to mind the stylized patterns Mom sometimes drew; perhaps this had been their inspiration.

Whatever else this book was, it was also art that had dropped out of time.

Coming back from wherever she'd gone, she took the book, opened it and flipped through the first couple of pages. They could see that the words were hand written on paper that had yellowed with age, the edges brown in places where it had been opened perhaps many times. Mom paused, used her finger as a bookmark and closed the cover again.

"This book," she said in hushed tones as she ran her other hand over it again, "was given to my mother by hers a long time ago when she married my father. The story, Snow White and Rose Red, is very old and it has many versions. This particular one was my grandmother's interpretation of it. It's about a mother and her two daughters." She paused with her eyes beginning to brim with emotion. Looking down at them, Riss moved to caress their faces. Maré fought to hold back tears at the tenderness in the light gesture, though she could feel Luna's making her shoulder damp.

"Before she gave it to my mom though..." She smiled a little sadly, and a few tears managed to slip down her cheeks as she continued. "My mother had a sister, and they had been very close, just the way you two are. When they were teenagers, my aunt had become ill, and she perished before her time. It happened years before I was born. My grandmother had died before then too, so I never knew her, either. I was an only child, but when I was a little girl, my mom showed this to me. I knew who my mother's mother was from the pictures of her scattered throughout the house, but this book in her handwriting was much more special to Mom, more real than anything else. It gave me... a sense of connection to the past. I don't know how else to explain it, but... maybe you'll understand in time on your own.

She let her words sink in for a few minutes. When at last she spoke, her smile broadened. "When she would read it to me, she would make it seem like I was Rose Red, so she was my favorite character. I remember wishing that I'd had a sister." She laughed a little. "It was a silly fantasy, but not having a sibling didn't take anything away from those sweet times she read to me. Anyway, when I left Earth to come here, my mom gave these things to me in the hopes that I after I married your father I would have a daughter." A few more tears slipped down her cheeks as she reached to brush the hair from their foreheads. "I was blessed with two," she said, and Maré finally let herself cry at the warmth spreading through her.

"I think," Mom said loudly, lightening the mood, "that Maré is most like Snow White and Luna is most like Rose Red."

"Hey! I want to be the favorite!" Maré said playfully through her tears.

"Quiet, you," said her Chroma.

"I'm afraid you'll have to settle, daughter," replied Mom in the same playful quality as she held the backs of her fingers to her forehead.

"And the roses?" asked Maré. "What about them?"

"My grandmother had fashioned a pair for my mother and my aunt and set them in two small plastic cases. They were smaller than these, and when my aunt passed away, my mother chose to have them placed with her when she was laid to rest, rather than keep them herself. It was her way of saying goodbye. But when she got married, she shaped a new pair in the hopes that she would have a daughter. When she had me and it was time to read the story, she put them both in one case and sat them on my dresser, where I could always see them. Those two that now sit above your heads are *those* roses. I thought it was fitting, to leave them in that one case for the two of you, as close as you are."

"They're beautiful," said Luna as she sat up and threw her arms around her. "Thank you, Mom."

"Yes, thank you," said Maré as she joined the embrace.

"You're very welcome, girls," she replied a touch breathlessly. "The case is quite special," she said. "When she had it made, my mom wanted it to keep its contents safe for the generations to come, and not just for the roses, but for the book as well. The resin top is shatterproof, fire resistant and airtight. Both may become slightly more aged looking, and the white may look more ivory-toned, but they will always be beautiful and recognizable. The base has a tiny hidden button, and when you push it, a compartment will open up. When we're done reading the book goes in there." She paused. "Shall I read the story to you now?"

They laid back down and Mom fixed the blanket again. Opening the book, she began to read. "There was once a *beautiful* queen who ruled from a grand castle. Near a fountain in the castle's courtyard was a bright garden, and at the center stood two *huge* rose bushes, one of which bore white and the other red blossoms. She had two daughters who were like the two rose bushes, one named Snow White and the other Rose Red..."

Eleven

On a Friday at the end of a long week, Riss had taken Maré and Luna to work. She had been running a complex but largely unvaried set of simulations on rock erosions and the related gas exhumations. The commute trips to and from contributed as well; she had been using the time to show Luna how to drive her lift. She wasn't sure which had donated to her exhaustion more – the pressure at work, or the apparent inability of her daughter to keep her damn foot from mashing the accelerator through the deck of the lift.

She had set up several large magnetic vats down in the basement testing lab. The simulants from several of the gas tap crews had brought in many different samples, lining the bottom of each vat with the material they had brought in, one type in each. Using a mixture of several common chemicals, each day she had soaked the rock samples, charting the emission results, having everything cleaned out and repeating the next day. The smell was awful; they had to turn the air processors up so high that it sounded like they were doing the experiments at the height of one of the wind storms.

Some of the results had been promising as sources of interesting and marketable propellants, but two samples in particular caught the attention of one of the other departments, the biologists. Normally they studied the simple plants that were indigenous to Zarmina, but these samples were interesting because the exhumed gases had shown a few, tiny traces of complex hydrocarbons. Contamination from the gas tap crews seemed unlikely, and they were fairly certain that they couldn't have been blown in by circulating weather patterns. Much more research would be required, but such might lead to the discovery of Zarmina's first extremophiles. If that happened, there would be no living with the biologists.

That afternoon, Riss was up on the catwalk above the tanks checking the samples, when she noticed that one of them inexplicably seemed to have turned into a bubbling, sickly yellow foam, filling the vat almost halfway up to the rim. *Very strange*, she thought. *What would cause that?*

She called down to the girls. "Maré, please bring me a couple of the special surgical glass vials that the biologists seemed to like, please! And a long fingers!"

"Okay, Mom!"

"What did you say, dear?!"

"I said, *I'll get it!*"

"Okay!"

Time to take some measurements. When she turned back to the vat, she leaned over the railing to get a better look at the graduated depth marks on its side, but the lighting was wrong and she couldn't see them properly. The light was just catching the sharp edge of the laser-made marks, but it just wasn't enough to quite make it out. *Shit, is it 370L or 375L?* Righting herself, she moved further along the tank and leaned in again. *Still not quite right... but almost...*

She went up on tippy-toes to lean out as far as she dared, and that did it – she could finally make it out, 375L. Just as she was making up her mind, there was a loud shriek and a shudder vibrated through the catwalk, startling her. The involuntary reaction caused her weight to shift, the lattice grille beneath her shifted in its frame and her toes lost their purchase. She squealed as she went over the edge. She managed to hold onto the railing, but she went into the froth almost to her hips. The stuff was warm for a few seconds, but it quickly turned to ravenous fire. That was when she *really* started screaming.

—∧=∨—

Maré was thinking about dinner later, that maybe she would make some of the thick stew Dad liked, when she heard Mom call for some supplies. She had put the glass vials in the lab coat pocket Mom made them wear, got the long fingers and had just started up the cat walk stairs when she misstepped. She went down on her knees hard. There was a loud squeal as metal gave way, and a few bolts snapped at the top of the steep stairs and pinged off of a nearby vat. The end of the catwalk dropped about ten centimeters, came to rest on the top of the vats, and the whole assembly jerked violently. Immediately, she heard Mom scream.

"Luna, something's wrong with Mom!"

Luna had heard though, and was already moving towards the bottom of the stairs as Maré reached the top. Mom was nowhere in sight!

Luna dashed up beside her. "She must have fallen in one of them!"

As they hurried down the cat walk looking in the vats for her, they heard her scream, worse this time, from one of the last on the right. They rushed forward. They found her dangling from the edge in some awful stuff, screaming hard enough to freeze their blood. It took both of them to pull her up and out onto the cat walk. Riss lost consciousness as they flopped her down over the railing.

"Luna, get help!"

She ran back the way they had come, crying as she went. Maré realized she was crying herself.

She had no medical training, but she could still see Mom breathing rapidly. What remained of her legs was a horrific caricature with the skin stripped back and much of the flesh eaten away, the smooth, wet extensions of bone showing through in places.

—∧=∨—

Larissa had survived the incident, though they'd had to amputate both legs to save her. There'd also been a fairly massive amount of injury in the pelvic region. It had taken some threatening, but Joss had convinced the primary doctor to destroy the relevant pain receptors. The trauma would make ongoing care necessary; there was no way he would ask her to endure debilitating agony too.

The night of the accident, Joss had been summoned to the small but sophisticated medical wing in Twilight City. The only thing they would tell him was that Larissa had had an accident, and the simulants that were with her had been detained. He raced his lift down so fast that he was afraid he was pushing it beyond its limits, yet instead of slowing down he pushed it harder. For all he knew she might die, and if that happened before he got there he didn't care if he were killed in a flaming lift wreck. If she died it would probably kill him, regardless.

When he arrived, she was in a medically induced coma and would be that way for at least the next twenty four hours. They said they thought she might live, but wouldn't make any better predictions until they did another eval at that time. As to what had happened they wouldn't tell him much, as if they didn't really know the circumstances. What they could tell him was that she had been exposed to some sort of super-base. Although the stuff had been extremely potent, it had been lowly concentrated. Had it been any less so, the damage might have been considerably more catastrophic. It was almost as if they thought he should feel lucky, the cold bastards.

He left in a daze and walked the streets for hours, his emotions all tangled up and his stomach churning. At first he was just worried and terrified that she would pass, and if she did he wouldn't long survive her.

His dark thoughts were strongly influenced by his erratic feelings, and he began to feel guilty for not having protected her from... whatever had happened. *I should have been there! Why wasn't I there?*

As he walked the unseen streets, he began to acknowledge that his guilt was irrational, intellectually at first, but then he really started to believe it. But that inevitably lead to blaming her coworkers... and finally the girls.

It was their fault! They were there! They were supposed to be helping her! Why?!

Then he remembered that he needed to pick them up from corporate security. It took a minute or two to realize where he was, but he had a general understanding of the lay of the streets and he walked back both briskly and more or less directly.

The security guys were a little better with much needed information. "As near as we can tell, your wife fell into a tank of some kind of chemical crap that burned her pretty badly. Your *gabachas,*" he thumbed at the holding cell in which they sat, "pulled her out when she screamed. One of them... uh..." he said as he looked at his clipboard, "Luna, it says here, called us – but if you can tell the two of 'em apart, you're better than I am."

"If they pulled her out then why were they brought here?"

Puzzled, the guy looked at Joss. "Huh? They're simulants – we couldn't just let them run around loose, Mr. Breylin. We put temp behavior mod collars on 'em and brought them here." He held his hands up. "What else were we gonna do?"

The two of them looked pitiful when security released them from the cell. Joss could tell from their puffy faces that they had been crying, and probably a lot of it. *Is that how I look?*

Maré asked, "how is she, Dad?"

"She's alive. That's all I know for now. C'mon, it's time to go."

It was a long, quiet ride home with him refusing to talk or look at them the few times they tried to ask questions. He could almost feel their apprehension and he let it build. As he piloted the lift over the contours of the land he set his jaw and brooded, hoping that their imaginations were going crazy wondering what would happen when they made it home.

When they walked in, Joss curtly told them sit at the kitchen table, while he went to his bedroom. He came out a few minutes later and got scissors from one of the drawers. He took the collar remote from out of his pocket, surprising them; it was a thing they hadn't seen since the Breylin's had made them their daughters and taken their collars off. He deactivated the temp ones they now wore, then used the scissor to cut them off.

The girls were relieved, but it was short lived. Once he had the temps off, he drew their old permanent collars from the other pocket and snapped them in place around their necks before they had fully realized what was happening.

"Dad...?" said Maré.

Joss used the controller to give her a mild pain jolt in her legs. She yelped, more from fear than actual pain. "Get in the living room, both of you." His voice was shockingly cold. They moved, eyes wide with surprise, but he used the controller to motivate them to hasten their gait.

They were both afraid and crying. "Strip off your blouses and lie on your stomachs."

Luna opened her mouth. "Dad —"

He held up the controller before her. "Talk if you like, but you'll be sorry if this turns into a discussion. I swear, I'll roll over top of you like a pyroclastic flow, Luna."

Maré was already stripping off her shirt. Luna looked at him past the small device, and whatever she saw made her rush to do as she was told.

"Now lie facing each other. Quickly, girls — I'm losing my patience."

They did as they were told, stark terror written large on their faces.

Joss tapped at the collar remote to tell their nervous systems to refuse to move, then showed them a stout length of tubing. Dragging it lightly down their backs, it didn't seem like it would take a whole lot to put them into a fear-induced shock. The whimpering it produced in them was a pretty good start.

"Tell me what happened tonight, girls, and you'd better make me believe it." Joss was still feeling quite a bit of shock himself, but his old Marine training kicked in and he conducted a very thorough interrogation.

The next day, Joss Breylin was still shaken to his very core.

When he called down to the medical wing for a status update, they told him that Larissa, his queen, had pulled through the night, though they were going to keep her in the induced coma a while yet. He had cried like an infant when the doctor on the other end of the comm told him that she would live. If she hadn't then his life wouldn't've had meaning any longer. He felt a lot of numbness and relief now, but his heart was shot through with betrayal and grief, and it was still wrapped in a dull shell of stoked rage. He thought back to the previous night, when Maré and Luna had come to a sharp understanding of what he'd felt.

He hadn't really had to hit them too many times. A few occasional swats — taps, really, no blood at all — had helped shaped the message, but he had used fear and their compassion for each other to get his point across. He didn't enjoy hurting them, but they needed to be punished and he needed answers; it was just a thing that needed to be done. Action, reaction.

Life had been forever changed for the Breylin's, and most definitely for their simulants.

—∧≡∨—

The night of the accident, Maré and Luna couldn't understand why Dad was so angry with them. It was a dark, terrifying side of him that they never knew existed. When whatever had happened to Mom, they had been down at one of the desks, nowhere near her. They had no idea what had caused her to go into that tank, but it wasn't them. By the time they'd been hustled off to the holding facility, they were as confused as they were frightened, and that was before they'd gotten home and the questions had started.

The first thing they learned that night was the value of holding their tongues until it was requested. Without saying a word, Dad would apply the lash more vigorously whenever they spoke otherwise. It was only the first lesson of the night, though.

He set their collars to allow them to move. Though he left the room, they suspected that he wasn't done, since he had said very little while he was about punishing them. They were still sobbing a little when he came back in and sat down. As time stretched, they could hear him taking a sip of a drink.

Luna was the first to grow quiet, but she could see that Maré was nearly done crying. The urge to wipe the tears and snot from her face was bad, but she wouldn't move until he told her she could. Maré seemed to be thinking the same thing; she just laid there trying to calm herself, catching her breath and waiting. Oddly, she became distracted with the way her Chroma's hair was arranged over her ear.

"Now that I think you understand your position," he said, as he dropped several coils of a beige rope on the floor between them, "it's time to get down to business."

Maré began to whimper, and Luna could tell that she was going to do something to get herself in trouble – unless she interceded. "Be quiet, Maré," she said, and Maré's eyes opened wide at her voice, but she clamped her mouth down.

Joss came over to Luna and kneeled down beside her. As he stroked the side of her face he said, "That's good advice, Luna. Would you like me to let Maré rest a bit? You and I can spend a little time together first."

It was up to her. She wanted to protect Maré, but it would mean that he would beat her and probably make Maré watch. Not only that – he was going to make her ask for it. She knew what she had to do, but it was an awful choice to have to make. "Yes, Dad – please let her rest."

"Okay, Luna." He stroked her cheek with something like tenderness a few more times, but it felt very threatening. "It's time I take a more hands on approach for the rest of the evening." With his fingers on her cheek, she couldn't imagine a more chilling comment. Maré clamped her eyes shut and began to whine in a way that Luna felt more than heard.

When he rose to his feet, he bent down, grabbed her by the back of the neck and forced her into a kneeling position. "I have a rule for you," he said. "This goes for you too, dear." Maré twitched as he nudged her with his foot in her side. "Open your eyes and pay attention – terribly important stuff going on over here." He paused, then spoke very slowly. "If you ever call me Dad again, I'll *really* hurt you. I am Mr. Breylin or Sir, and my wife is either Mrs. Breylin or Ma'am. I hope I've been clear, because you can't afford too many corrective lessons, though you can be certain that I'll give you as many as you require."

Maré started to whimper a little again, and Luna was losing some of her control on her own fear. She shut her own eyes tight and tried not to breathe so fast.

Dad – Breylin – leaned in close to her, implacable and threatening. He still had his large hand around the back of her neck. He whispered into her ear, "don't move – understand?"

Luna nodded.

Breylin let her go, bent down again and forced Maré into the same kneeling position she was in. He shoved Maré against her so that their bare chests were pressed together, and then he positioned them so that their faces were touching, cheek to cheek. He grabbed the rope and bound their hands up high in the middle of their backs. As he continued tying the knots, Maré laid her face on her Chroma's shoulder and cried. The terror was trying to consume Luna too, but she forced herself to be as strong as she could for Maré.

Breylin fed the rope through their arm pits, pulled it taut and tied it off tight. Maré was panting by the time he was done. Lastly, he pulled their slacks and underwear down around their knees, leaving their asses exposed.

"Mr. Breylin? Please, I thought you would let Maré rest?"

—∧=∨—

He squatted down in close to the two of them. "Quite so, dear," he said. "She will be the one answering questions first. You'll answer my questions, won't you, Maré?"

"*Yesss*," she cried pitifully.

"That's good, very good, Maré," he said with a quiet menace like a knife gliding through silk. "If you do well, then Luna won't suffer *hardly* at all. You *don't* want her to suffer, do you, Maré?"

"*Nooo*," she cried again.

"*Very* good." He let them go and sat back down on the couch. He took his time sipping his drink again.

He gave it a couple of minutes, letting their imaginations torment them, then he jumped up to his feet, startling them. He said, "how about some music?" He walked over to the entertainment center and put on something soft and instrumental. "There, that's nice," he said, "I think this is the station you like, Maré."

As the music played, he sat back down and said, "let's go over some more rules. The first thing: if you feel like you need to scream or cry, whatever, that's just fine. This is where we live, girls, and it's something we can share." He took another sip, then held his glass up to the light and appeared to consider it. "Next: if you feel hoarse or raspy, please let me know and I will give you some water. There will be lots of discussion, and I want you to be able to talk freely. Do make sure you express your gratitude afterward. A lack of appreciation is *very* rude. Next: *don't* give up hope. You can trust that I'll be here to help guide you through this difficult thing, okay?"

Maré was sobbing and clearly leaning into Luna. For her part, Luna seemed to be trying to keep her back straight and support Maré, but she was crying by then, too. He made a show of rolling up his sleeves.

"Never give up hope, girls, because there's *always* something more you can lose."

The next thing they learned was that it was best to answer questions quickly and directly.

—∧=∨—

Joss took his time with them. He asked them many questions, though a lot of of them were similar but reworded. But because he didn't want to break her, he'd plied Luna's back and rear with the improvised whip only so much. Since he didn't want to draw any blood he couldn't get much more than a grunt from her, and it just wasn't producing the results he wanted. She was obviously trying to stay strong for Maré, and he couldn't have that. It was a difficult line to walk. *Perhaps it's a good time to take another brief pause*, he thought as he sat down on the couch.

After puzzling it over for a few long moments, he decided to try something different. He took off her sandals and lightly pinched the soles of her feet. "Maré?" he said. "Did you know how soft Luna's feet are?"

After he began again, he found he could use a much lighter stroke on her feet than the rest of her, yet it was very effective, both in getting her to respond enthusiastically, and to motivate Maré. He knew he'd found the right combination after she'd tried to tuck her feet under her; the only way he could get her to put them back without doing it himself was to threaten Maré.

When it was Maré's turn at the whip he'd focused more on terrorizing her. He would flick her with it often – not to cause her any pain, but to let her know it was always near, always available. She was quite weak, and her fear had made Luna particularly eager to answer anything and everything.

Whenever they wanted water, he would pull their heads back by their hair and pour the water from his glass into their open mouths. After a few gulps he would let them go. Luna had been the first to ask, and had been surprised by the delivery method. She coughed more all over herself and Maré than she had drunk. Joss only gave her a few seconds of spluttering, then he harshly flogged her insteps for not thanking him. It wasn't an issue for either of them after that.

By the time he thought he had a pretty clear picture of their role in what had happened and that they had been punished enough, the two of them were slumped into each other, digging the rope encircling them into their flesh. Joss laid them down on their sides, untied the chest rope, then their hands. He decided to give them a couple of minutes to rest.

As he walked out to the kitchen to get himself another glass of water, he realized that he had nearly sweated through his shirt. He idly wondered, as the glass was filling, if the session had gotten a little out of control. He shrugged it off contemptuously. *At least they have their legs*, he thought. *Not like Larissa.*

When he returned to the living room and sat down, he found that Luna had rolled onto her back and was moaning. Maré was trying to murmur, probably something comforting to Luna, but she clammed up when Joss reappeared.

He used a softened tone when he spoke. "Can you two hear me?"

"Yes..."

"I can..."

He chuckled. "I think you both meant to say 'Sir', but I've had my fill of attitude adjustment for tonight. Consider this your warning."

Maré said, "thank you, sir."

"See Luna? Maré gets it. Make sure you follow her lead, dear," Joss said, but he thought, *I hope I didn't break that one after all. I didn't even go that hard on her...*

He continued again in what he thought was an even, soft tone. "You two probably think I'm a monster. I can understand that. But as you lie in your comfortable bed tonight, I want you to consider that Mrs. Breylin is struggling, right now, for her life, surrounded by strangers and with tubes running in and out of her. She has no legs, and for the rest of her life, someone is going to have to clean her when she defecates on herself. She took the two of you to her work so that you could be there to help, but while that shit was eating the flesh off her bones you two *were off fucking around!*" He stopped and swallowed before he lost control of his own emotions.

"I'm not sure what happens from here. I don't know if I'll be married or widowed tomorrow. What I do know is that the way we were, like a family, is over. I trusted you with the most important thing in the world to me, and you blew it. No more pretend, no more playing house. You two are *gabachas*, and it's time you were treated that way. You will do as you are told, and if you screw up there will be consequences, and I think you know what I mean by that. I will feed you and house you, but make no mistake, I don't owe you anything. Have I made myself perfectly clear?"

They were crying again, but they both responded.

"Yes, Sir," said Maré.

"Yes, Mr. Breylin," said Luna.

"Now get the hell out of my sight."

Maré got up first, and she had to help Luna limp into their bedroom.

As they lurched down the short hall towards their bedroom, Joss said, "you may use the bathroom, but no food until tomorrow. And you'd better pray that Mrs. Breylin doesn't die through the night; if she does, you'll watch each other die screaming."

Ever since the accident that had taken her legs, Larissa's mobility had been severely limited. The Breylin's health care benefits would have afforded them the opportunity to get prosthetic limbs for her, but Joss simply couldn't get her to buy into the idea. Simply put, Larissa didn't want to be seen as a monster.

After Joss brought her home, she mostly withdrew into herself. Though she would sometimes read or listen to music, typically she would spend her days staring out of the picture window in the living room. No matter how he tried, he couldn't get her to draw at all.

At times, she wouldn't seem to notice Joss in the same room, even when he would talk to her. Other times she would. He figured that when she returned to work things would get better, but unfortunately, the research held no interest either, and Larissa never returned. Joss gave her time to adjust to the changes – it was all he could think to do in the face of her worsening depression.

Joss had taken a week off to reorganize their life – it was all Harry and his superiors would allow. After it was over he returned to his duties out in the subsolar region, leaving the care of his queen to the ministrations of the twins. Though he spoke to them using guarded, quiet words in front of his wife, his tone was pregnant with dire implication, and they agreed that it would be best for everyone if they were quite attentive to her every want or necessity.

By the time he went back to work, Joss had noticed that her demeanor was starting to become expressed physically. First she denied him all but the most casual touches and refused to let him sleep next to her.

Her clothing followed; she refused to wear anything like pants or shorts, so Joss would lay out her sleeping shirts to wear during the day. They covered her well enough, and since it solved a few practical issues, he gave in to her desire to put on nothing else. Anyway, it seemed foolish to him to be concerned about the fact that she would exclusively choose the most shapeless pieces.

Within two weeks he began to notice other things, too, like her hair; in school she had worn her thick tresses long and loose, since they both enjoyed it when he would cafuné her. Here on Zarmina she had kept the length, though it had been pulled back into a utilitarian ponytail low on the back of her neck. After she had come home from the med center she had demanded it almost all roughly hacked off, and what yet remained was limp and lank, as if the simulants were neglecting to rinse the soap out of it. When he questioned them about it, they told him that Mrs. Breylin had refused to let them clean her.

Inescapably, he realized that something had broken inside her with the accident. He couldn't protect her in the past, but maybe if he loved her enough her desire to live would grow back in time. His hope was an emaciated thing, but it was all he had to hang on to.

It was about a half a year before Luna's and Maré's tenth inception anniversary, and therefore their imminent expiration. To Joss, it felt suspiciously like a looming storm of which he was becoming more aware.

He hadn't explained the implications to them when they had been a family – it had been too hard to think about their deaths back then – and after Larissa lost her legs he continued down the path of least resistance. It would have been so easy to keep doing nothing, and he thought about putting it off until some later time, but he knew that the longer he waited the harder it would get. Besides that, he had arranged for their replacements to arrive in another three months, give or take, depending on storm activity. The time had come to get it out of the way, so Breylin sat them down one night after evening chores to make sure that they understood what would be happening to them soon. He was uncomfortable with the task, but if he delayed it would only be worse.

"We've lived together a long time... some of it was good, much was bad. But a change is coming, and I need to explain it to you."

They anxiously waited for him to continue.

"Our lives have been pretty far removed from contact. No neighbors, no people... and no other simulants. If you had been around others of your kind, you would have learned about a normal part of the simulant lifecycle... look, the hard truth is in about six months, give or take, you will expire."

Luna didn't seem to comprehend, but fear bloomed in Maré's expression. "You mean...?" she said.

"I mean, you'll die. Slow at first, but once the pain and muscle cramping starts it will be almost over."

Luna blurted out, "why? *We've been so good!*"

"I don't think you understand, girl," he said in harsh frustration. "This isn't a matter of good and bad. It is a thing that's just a part of your nature."

"What can we do?" Maré asked. "Can you help us? Are you willing to help us?"

"Do? I can't do anything about this, any more than I can protect myself from my own mortality. I just get more of it."

"We're copies of humans. Why don't we live as long?" Maré asked.

"I don't know," he said with a wave of hand. "I don't have those answers."

Luna appeared shocked. *"It isn't fair!"*

"Life never is," he said. The hard edge in his voice said more than his words. "The good news is you don't really have to get used to it."

"Will it... hurt?" asked Maré in a whisper so low he had to strain to make it out.

"There will be a couple of weeks of cramping that will get worse. If it goes long enough, the body fights back and the pain stops right before the end. Also... it could come any time within about two months of your birthday. Chances are that you will go at different times."

They sat there stunned looking at each other than to him. He could tell they wanted him to fix this, make it go away, *do something*, but there was nothing for it. He could tell that this was scaring the hell out of them. *Maybe I should have found a way to avoid telling them, but it's too late to change now...* He nearly said he was sorry, but instead he crushed the tiny twinge of feeling he had for them.

"I can do this much for you. When your time comes... I will let you decide if you want to go easy. You may even go together if you want."

Maré was holding Luna as she began to sob. Since the accident she had grown a thick emotional shell, and she was trying to pull it over Luna. They had both changed, really.

Maré turned Luna's face up so that she could see into her eyes. "Pull yourself together, Chroma. Not here."

Luna gave her a wan smile and sat up, trying to compose herself. She kept a tight grip on Maré's hands, though.

Maré said, "if there's nothing else, may we go, Sir?"

"No, that's it," he said with a sigh that seemed to lift the pressure off of him. "Go to your room."

"Thank you, Sir," she said, and they left the kitchen in each other's arms.

Joss found his wife in the living room listening to music. "Did you finally tell them?" she said, as she turned the device off.

"Yes. They took it... well."

"It must have made you happy to see them twist over it."

His eyes went wide with astonishment. "No, I... I don't want them to suffer."

"Don't you?" she whispered.

"No... What the hell are you talking —?"

"Put me to bed, Joss. I'm tired."

"Yes, my queen."

—∧=∨—

In their room, Maré undressed Luna and helped her into bed. "Lie on your stomach, Luna," she said, and she complied. Maré turned out the light, stripped, got onto the bed and straddled her Chroma. She began to massage the muscles in her neck and shoulders, kneading slowly and firmly. Along her spine she lightly used her elbow to press and twist. Working her way down, she kneaded her lower back with greater pressure, then her buttocks. She turned around so that she was straddling the other way, and proceeded to press her fingertips firmly along the edges of the muscles first in one leg, then the other. She moved to sit lower alongside her so she could massage her feet. Luna's feet always ached, so Maré took the time to carefully do it the way she liked.

When she was done, she pulled their soft, heavy blanket over them, then laid down on her back next to Luna. "Come to me, Chroma."

Luna rolled and put her head on Maré's breasts, her hand up on her shoulder, and Maré put her arms around her. "I love you, Luna," she breathed.

"*I love you tooo...*" she said, now crying.

Maré smoothed her hair, just as they often did for each other, humming soft noises. She knew that Luna enjoyed the soft vibration in her chest as she did it. It mixed pleasantly with her heartbeat. Luna began to nurse at Maré's breast. Maré smiled at the sensation, knowing that Luna would nurse her afterwards. No matter what else happened, they would always have each other's love.

Twelve

After a few weeks of hard study and diligent effort, Maré had become a contributing member of the staff. There was a certain amount of satisfaction in that, as if her accommodation represented something of a minor victory in stretching past her limitations. It would be a stretch to say that she enjoyed the situation, but she had made peace with it. Certainly she wouldn't have been able to come so far without Luna. Her Chroma had not only saved her life, but had helped guide her to find a measure of comfort and purpose.

Looking out upon the still sleeping pairs of their sisters, Maré had the strangest feeling of observer and participant. *Crazy, I could yet be out there among them...*

Luna took her hand, leaned into her and whispered, "We *are* among them."

In confusion, Maré turned to her. "How did you know...?"

Luna smiled and squeezed her hand. "We all think the same thing when we really look for the first time."

The Crop, as she had heard Dr. Almeida refer to their bloodline, was about three and a half months from maturing. No other pairs had contracted meningitis, and both the doctor and the crop's simulant care takers were grateful – though for different reasons. Whereas the simulants cared for the growing pairs almost as if they were extended family, all Almeida was concerned with was efficiency and results.

Maré quickly came to understand that he was a small man, and

not so different from them, for all his humanity. His attitude generally ranged from curt to surly. His incessant smoking had
stained his fingers and teeth, making him seem even older, and
the mildly sickening stench clung to his clothes. He often pawed
the girls carelessly under the guise of "examination". He must
have enjoyed the demonstrations of power, since the only evident
purpose seemed to be to make them uncomfortable. To her way
of thinking, humanity wasn't all that special, if Almeida was any
indication.

And he had played a direct role in Luna's abuse.

It had taken some time that night for Luna to tell her everything. In the beginning, Luna and 85 had had a friendship. When
85 had brought her awake, she didn't have the complication of
memory loss that Maré did. 85 had emphasized their sameness,
and that it could be a place from which their relationship would
proceed. It had seemed to work at first; there was a honeymoon
period where 85's loneliness was temporarily dimmed. Luna
could have had her own room, but 85 had manipulated Luna's
feelings into thinking that they would be better off as a pair, that
she could better help her navigate this unknown and scary new
environment. It had been nice to face the darkness together, but
nearly from the start she could tell there was something wrong
under the surface of 85's demeanor. Not long after waking up,
she began to try to get Luna to call herself Maré, even refusing to
talk to her at all when Luna openly defied her. It had gotten better
for a time, but then her emptiness returned worse than before,
and that was when the pressure to have sex started. Finally, 85
intimidated her into yielding completely. She had given in, both
to the fear of abandonment and from physical violence. Luna
spent the rest of that night lying next to her softly snoring abuser,
crying and wracked with shame. Unwilling to risk another epi-
sode, she went to Almeida the next day.

"Why should I be concerned about it? Is it going to influence your responsibilities?" he replied with mild indifference and a lot of annoyance at the disruption. "Otherwise, I don't care."

Luna goggled incredulously. She was still new to all of this, but couldn't believe him. If something was going to change, she would have to deal with him on his level. There was no way she was going to sleep with 85 again.

"Doctor, this will affect me. I can't stay in her room!" She paused to get a hold of herself. "We have an unused room. Please let me have it so that I can rest at night – it's the only way I can maintain my productivity."

"Fine." Almeida sighed and nodded his head. "It may take a few days to get to it, though. You'll have to make the best of it until then."

Luna had tried to sleep in one of the chairs in the common room, but before the night was though he himself had come down to rouse her. He even brought two security androids with him, as if she might dare attack him.

"Let's go, 183 – you cannot make the common room a place to crash!"

Terrified, she said, "but Doctor, what am I supposed to do?"

"You're going to get in the room assigned to you, that's what!"

Out of options, she complied and went to the room. 85's smile was both triumphant and cruel. She spent that night and the next five sleeping on the floor, listening to both sharp insults and 85 pleasuring herself up on the bed where she'd been raped. All she could do was cry herself to sleep after 85 finished, fell asleep and was snoring.

During that time, Almeida would sometimes stand and watch her work during the day with a smile that for once seemed to light up his eyes. He had known what was going on in the room at night, and he had enjoyed the voyeurism. She tried to internalize the humiliation, but she still withered under his smug gaze.

The worst came the day before Almeida had the androids re-configure the rooms. He had taken both 85 and Luna into one of the examination rooms and had them strip. First he forced Luna to hold 85's limbs as he performed a detailed internal exam. It was a preview for her own. 85 had laid there motionless and impassive during hers, but Luna could tell that she enjoyed help-ing Almeida when they switched places, as if he were violating her with 85's fingers. All Luna had been able to do is lay there and wail noiselessly in utter shame.

—∧=∨—

Maré listened to the instruction that Luna and the twins gave her each night. She asked questions and she tried to take initia-tive – until the others discouraged her. Do well, was the message she got, but not too well.

Sometimes she would stare at the twins still encased in the iri-descent gel of the transparent pods. They were physically com-plete now. They looked so peaceful, sleeping in each other's arms, row after row after row. She wondered if they ever dreamed.

85 kept to herself, eating at off times and working in the sec-tions away from the others. Luna hadn't asked her to participate in the food sharing plan, but they would sometimes find some left on one of the tables in the common room. The twins attempted to talk to her and console her a few times, but she mostly spurned their efforts at conversation. It seemed best not to push her, so the others left 85 to her self-imposed isolation.

Within a week, Maré would occasionally feel like she was being watched while she worked, but whenever she looked around she wouldn't find anything. It happened a few more times though, so she asked Luna about it in bed afterwards.

"Well," Luna said, "you're probably just sensing LabSys. It's everywhere in the complex, and it nothing escaped its notice. Besides, it can sometimes feel that way out in the crop surrounded by our chromanity, if you let your mind wander."

It seemed like a reasonable enough explanation. Maré let it go, and the feeling became a part of the background noise of life.

Maré and Luna *were* quite happy in each other, just as the twins had wished. They ate and talked together, they shared laughs and held each other in the night when they were scared. Still, Dr. Almeida was always around, with his odd proclivities. Maré learned that life – their life, at least – was cheap. It hadn't happened, but if something went wrong with one of the pods, then its entire contents would be rendered for any value it might contain. It really didn't matter that the contents were living, thinking – albeit unconscious – beings, because they were merely simulants. It was a crushing realization to learn that one's worth could be established with simple buying and selling transactions.

She also learned deep love from her Chroma, written large in her caresses and caring eyes. Perhaps the intensity came from the distilling nature of their situation, as Luna had put it. With no frame of reference and as inexperienced as she was, it took a little bit to figure out, but she discovered that no matter what anyone thought, meaning was found in the eyes of loved ones. If you had that, then it was enough.

There were many such soft lessons, and she was hungry for them, even desperate.

A few nights after she had woken up, she had slipped from Luna's arms, gotten out of bed and, as silently as she could, padded over to their desk and turned on the small light. She held her nose close to her upturned arm close to the light, studying. As she watched, she could see the delicate heartbeat pulsing in arteries that were a shade or two darker than her complexion. Flexing her forearm, she could feel the muscles contract and see them writhe under the skin. Turning her arm up, it seemed she could sense each of the tiny hairs as she watched them stand on end as the skin beneath them pebbled in the cool air that seeped into her nakedness.

She heard Luna stir and rise behind her, then join her by the light. She went to her knees and moved her face close to study the same arm. "Is everything okay, honey?"

"What are we made of, Chroma?" she asked, sounding like a small child in her own ears.

The words lingered for a few seconds, as if she was deciding on an answer. "We're flesh and blood, Maré," she said. "*Real* flesh and blood."

She turned to her slightly and held the limb out between them. "That's what it *looks* like," she countered nearly soundlessly, "but how can we *know?*"

"Hold still and close your eyes," Luna whispered. When Maré nodded and her lids fell, she felt Luna touch just the tips of the hairs on her arm with her fingers, against the direction they were angled, and the electric sensation of the intimate contact coursed around Maré's body. She gasped and surrendered an involuntary tremor. "That's how we know, Chroma."

It was a soft lesson she'd always remember, and fondly.

Sometimes they would read to each other, or Maré would ask her about their parents and what growing up was like.

"Tell me about our room, Luna."

"Actually, we had separate rooms."

"Really? Why was that?"

Luna pursed her lips as she considered the question. "Well, I don't know, really. I suppose because they could give 'em to us."

Maré smiled. "What was yours like?"

"Ha! It was pink, lots of ruffles and stuffed animals. You hated it."

"I wouldn't have guessed you for a girly girl."

Luna belted out a big laugh. "That's because you've only seen me in scrubs. Well, that and nothing I suppose. I should see if I could fashion a few ribbons from the medical supplies tomorrow. What do you think?"

"I dunno, it's hard to picture; we can try it and see. What about my room?"

"Guess!"

"Oh, C'mon. I have no idea, Luna."

"Guess, anyway."

"Um... green?"

"Nope, but close – yellow. Green would have been better though – I didn't like the color of your walls."

"Books?" she asked tentatively.

"You had *so* many books, Maré. You always had your nose in one."

Maré was fascinated by those stories; seeing it through Luna's eyes made her feel even closer to her. It also made her feel less two dimensional, more real.

Still, she wondered if previous occupants of this room had had the exact same conversation.

Occasionally, they would take their dinner to the sky walk overlooking the roof tops. As Jupiter royally dominated from the background, they sat on the floor with their backs to the wall and fed each other, just as the twins often did elsewhere. Though they hardly spoke during those hushed times, they often made a game of playfully nipping at each other's fingers and laughing if they scored a hit. Sometimes they would just sit holding each other, staring out into space, mesmerized at its stark serenity.

But Maré's feeling of being watched returned scalpel-sharp. When she looked around the first time, she spotted 85 staring at her. 85's eyes went wide for a single heartbeat, but then she composed herself, gave Maré a small smile and backed away. Maré had been silently loathing her for what she had done to Luna, but it still made her a little anxious. She could feel that 85 was capable of doing something dangerous.

It continued to happen. Every couple of days, she would find 85 watching; each time, she was a little closer, a little less surreptitious about it. Finally, Maré went towards her, but 85 eluded her. A confrontation was probably a bad idea, anyway; as long as 85 only watched, Maré would let it go.

It didn't take long to test her resolve – just one day. When Maré pointedly refused to acknowledge her, 85 surprised her by coming up to her. It was a bold, unexpected move that, despite Maré's best efforts, managed to set her teeth on edge.

"Hello, Maré."

Her resolve cracked and she responded with a snort. "*You don't get to call me that, 85. What do you want?*"

"Why, I want to be your friend. Would you like to be friends, Maré?"

"No – you and I will never be anything to each other," she said flatly. This game was 85's, and she knew she shouldn't be playing it, but she was committed now and her blood was surging.

"Why would you say such things to me, *Maré*?" 85 invested just enough sarcasm in her name to push her buttons.

"I know what you've done to my Chroma, *you bitch*, and I will never forgive you for it."

That got her thinking. 85 tapped her chin and waited a moment before replying. "I don't know what you think I've done, *Maré*," She paused again before continuing. "but you don't seem to mind eating the food I leave behind."

"Not any more. I don't want anything from you, and neither does my *Chroma*." She hissed the last word, unable to stop herself from responding in kind.

85 feigned a light laugh. "*Really*? Well, perhaps the twins will take a more practical approach. They so *hate* confrontation."

Maré wanted to pummel her with her fists, but instead she shoved her hands in the pockets of her lab coat. "What do you want from me?"

"Nothing, *nothing*!" she said brightly. "I just wanted to talk a little and get to know you better. We've all been so busy," she said with a casual wave. "And I can see you're busy now, *Maré*, so I'll say so long and leave you." She gave her an exaggerated wink, backed away a few steps, turned and walked off. Maré listened to the soles of her shoes make tiny scritches as she retreated, until the white noise of the air processors working overhead drowned them out.

That night, as they lay in bed they talked about what had happened. "What do you make of it, Luna?" she said nervously.

"I think 85 and I are going to have to have a little chat about her attitude," she said in cool tones. She remained thoughtful and preoccupied until Maré fell asleep.

The next day, Maré was taking samples in the pod farm when she noticed 85 again. No matter what she said this time, she wasn't going to let 85 get the best of her. She turned her back on her, and climbed up to the top of the pod, then opened a small sampling hatch and got to work.

85 walked up without saying a word. She just looked up at her and watched, the intensity of her stare boring into Maré. Taking a perverse pleasure in ignoring 85's presence, she smiled and let the uncomfortable silence stretch. The only sound was the tinkling of the little vials as Maré took samples.

Unexpectedly, 85 said, "I may have upset you a little yesterday. I wanted to apologize." She spoke softly, actually sounding as if she might be contrite - for a wonder.

Maré opened her mouth to say something acerbic when Luna came around the pod behind 85. She grabbed her arm and spun her around so fast that the two of them nearly collided. With steel in her words, Luna said, "I suggest you move along, 85. 370 Bravo is *my* mate, and if I catch you near her again I'll —"

"You'll *what*?" 85 said as she looked between Luna and the ceiling. "You can't do *anything* to me, and you know it. Besides, my work has been done. How's yours coming along? Bad things can happen when we fall behind."

"Don't worry about my work, 85. Just mind your manners and I won't feel like I need to protect my Maré."

"Protect her? You couldn't care less about her, 183, only your own needs. You always were so selfish! Did you even tell her she had options, that she could pick another for a partner?"

Luna let go of 85's arm. "No I didn't, 85," she said calmly. "You're reckless, and that makes you a danger, not an option."

85 seemed to have forgotten that Maré was there, up on the pod. To Luna she said, "It should have been me protecting *you*, but you just wouldn't do it. We could have been happy, but *nooo!* Now I'm not going to let you have any happiness!" As she spoke, her voice climbed until she was practically screeching. Now that she was finished she stood there with hate for Luna in her eyes. She was huffing with the emotion and her face drawn up in a rictus, but after a few edgy moments she must have realized that her reaction was over the top. She moved her gazed between Maré and Luna, straitened her lab coat and stilled her breathing. Finally, she walked off.

As 85 retreated, Maré climbed down the rungs and went to her Chroma. Luna returned the embrace, but Maré could feel the tension in the muscles beneath her scrubs. "Don't let her upset you... I'm not ever going to leave you, and certainly not for that *thing*."

Luna broke the embrace, and pointed with her chin behind Maré. "It's not that."

Maré turned around and saw Dr. Almeida standing at a distance, quietly watching the simulants torment each other and fingering the collar control pad.

Luna was quiet the rest of the day, and later that night in bed. It's not that she wouldn't talk, exactly, but she spoke as if any spare words were a waste she couldn't afford.

"You're awful quiet tonight."

"I'm just thinking about the argument with 85."

"We've only been together for a little over a month, but I can read you pretty well. I know you're thinking about her, but don't dwell on it, hon. Don't give her any power over your emotions. It will be alright."

"What if she was right, though, Maré?" She sat up and stared into the darkness. "What if I didn't tell you that you could pair with her just so I could keep you to myself?"

Maré eased her fingers along her spine, then her shoulder blades. "I don't think either one of us believes that."

"No, I guess I don't – but I'm troubled by her words." She huffed. "That's probably what she wanted..." She turned, laid back down, and whispered in her ear. "Though I do wonder if the good doctor's presence meant something."

"Shhh... don't worry about that..."

Luna laid her head down on her shoulder. "I'm not worried, exactly. Concerned, though; it seems like something's got to change."

Maré murmured soft words of comfort, and Luna responded by caressing her arm, but she remained pensive regardless, and after a while, Maré could feel the somber mood infecting her own attitude.

The next morning, Luna was still guarded. They washed and dressed each other as usual – Maré liked the way Luna tied the string in her waist band, and enjoyed combing the knots out of Luna's fine hair – but there was still very little talk between them. The air was just too... preoccupied.

Just like every other day, they fed each other crumbly bits of protein cake and dehydrated fruit substitute for breakfast at one of the tables in their common room.   The twins had just taken the table next to them and started eating when 85 exited her room. Without saying anything to anyone, she walked over to the dispensers and requested breakfast, pulled the packets out of the slot and sat down at a table by herself. If her presence registered with the twins they gave no indication from inside their private near-spiritual commune. The only sounds in the room were shifting chair scrapes and the occasional crinkles that came from food wrappers.

Anxious minutes later, the chimes for the ten minute reminder jangled about them, and each got up to throw out their trash and leave. 85 stuck her elbow out as Luna passed her, brushing her arm. She paused, and Maré thought that the situation would erupt. Luna took a deep breath, then took Maré's hands, and they walked off.

By choice they kept close to each other through the day. When they still hadn't seen 85 before they were done with lunch, they began to relax and they returned to their duties.

Out in the crop, Luna was handing a tray of hormones up to Maré, who had climbed to the top of a pod. A flurry of movement, and 85 rushed out from behind a bank of storage lockers and plowed into Luna. Startled, Maré had to grab the edge of the pod to keep herself from falling, but she managed to regain her balance and scramble back down the ladder as Luna and 85 fell in a shrieking, grappling heap. Warning blats came from overhead speakers adding to the chaos.

They were rolling around on the floor, but 85 came up on top with her hands on Luna's throat. She started slamming her head against the floor as Luna rasped and struggled to push 85 away. Maré screeched as she crashed into 85, slamming her head against the locker. Both of them were grappling and screaming wordlessly as Luna rolled on her side, coughing. Blood was leaking out of 85's ear.

85 turned towards Maré, thrusting her hands like claws at her throat, but Maré was faster. She thrust the palm of her hand upward into her chin, slamming 85's head back into the locker again. Stunned, 85 let Maré go, giving her the opportunity to get a proper hold on her. The screaming continued as Maré rammed 85 against the locker, over and over, until Luna pulled her off 85. "Let her go, Maré! Let her go!"

The two of them sobbed and rocked as they held each other. 85 was slumped over next to them, with blood slowly leaking from her nose and both of her ears. They didn't notice when the twins ran up, nor did it register when they pulled them to their feet with something like sadness in their eyes. They only saw each other as 85 was carried off a crude litter made from her lab coat, and their only reaction was to comply meekly as the security androids and Almeida led them away.

Thirteen

Joss retrieved their new simulants from the spaceport in Twilight City after he had finished working for the day. Androids loaded them, still asleep in their stasis transport pods, into the back of his lift and he sped home. When he arrived, he had Maré and Luna help him unload them in the lift port. They quietly did as they were told, but they were obviously affected by the presence of another pair of simulants identical to themselves. They were sullen and quiet; the skin of Maré's face was stretched over stone, but Luna's eyes leaked steadily.

With a sigh, he stopped them from going back into the house. "I won't wake them until after, girls."

"Yes, Mr. Breylin. You don't need to worry about us," said Maré.

"I'm not worried. I was just being... kind."

"Of course, *Sir*. We know how kind you are," she said, regretting it instantly.

Breylin didn't feel like having it thrown back in his face. He grabbed her by the arms and pulled her in close. "Maré, do we need to have a discussion about the way to speak to me?" She just glared up at him.

"Please, Sir, leave her be!" Luna pleaded.

The moment stretched as Maré and Breylin fought each other with their eyes. Luna was crying and gripping the sides of her pants.

Breylin half snorted and let her go. "This doesn't need to be an issue, I think. You two go on about your chores before it becomes one."

Luna said, "thank you, Sir." She grabbed Maré by her arm and led her out of the lift port, but not before she shot him a wordless, defiant glare.

It may have been his irritation talking, but Breylin had a pretty good idea on how to prevent it from becoming a problem.

When he told her about it, Larissa didn't seem to care one way or another that Joss had brought the new simulants home. "It will give us a fresh start," he told her.

"Yeah. I guess."

"I'll make sure these two will take care of you, Larissa," he said with thick urgency.

"You haven't called me by my given name in a long time, Joss. I thought I was your queen."

"You are," he stammered. "You'll always be that. You know I am nothing without you."

"I'm a legless freak, and I wish I had died when it happened," she said. "But I think you *did* die, Joss. Inside, at least."

Her words were ragged, deep cuts. He sat down on the floor at her feet and rubbed his temples with his hands. "I can't go back, my love. I can't change it. I'd give *anything* to put it all back together. All we can do now is be together."

"Yeah!" she laughed mirthlessly. "Look at the two of us!"

He buried his face in his hands in a vain attempt to shut out the world. "I know I'm not good enough, but I'm doing the *best* I can. Why can't that be enough?"

"It doesn't matter how hard you try, Joss, and it never did. We're broken."

"I'm sorry, Riss. I wanted more for us." He wished he could have cried, but all he could feel was hollow, like an old husk.

She did give him a real smile then, the first in some time, as she reached down to touch his cheek. "Don't torture yourself, Joss – it's not your fault. It's like they told us - it just wasn't meant to be." Looking towards where they were in the kitchen, she paused before continuing. "When will you..."

"Soon. They're quite upset at seeing their... replacements."

"Make sure you send them off peacefully. I know you've blamed them, but I think they... were just the instrument the universe used. Maybe they were just there when it all went wrong. Anyway, I won't have any more pain in this house."

"It will be as you say. They won't feel anything at all – I promise." He held up the collar controller. "One touch and they will just slip off."

"Do it while they sleep tonight, husband."

"Yes, my queen."

"Send them to me now, please. I'm about to piss myself again."

That night, Joss sat up in the living room until quite late. As he had promised Riss, he would put the girls down while they slept. What he was about to do had him all churned up inside, and it was beginning to express itself physically in the form of nausea. No matter how he tried to examine his feelings though, all he could discern was a sense of... awful expectation. Cast about as he would, he couldn't put any other words to it. Regretting the waste, he eventually threw the coffee that had grown cold and bitter in his hand down the drain, but it was better than retching it back up. Just the thought of vomiting set his guts to roiling.

Persevering, he waited until he thought they were likely to be out cold. About halfway through the night, he cracked the door to their room and peered in. He found them in each other's arms with the blanket tangled around them and their hair soaked with sweat, as it was so often when they laid together. They were out, just as he'd hoped.

He stood there for a few moments, possessed by the strange sensation of the moment. Maré was laying down with her head on Luna's chest, and he could see her back rising and falling with each slow breath. There were three lives in the room, but in moments there would be only one. It had been many years since he had been forced to kill, but he found being on the cusp of it once again a little darkly compelling. He found the reaction disturbing, and he had to lean against the door frame and breathe slowly until he was sure he wouldn't puke. When he felt he had it under control, he entered the room and eased the door shut behind him.

Wanting to delay the inevitable, he decided to look around, peruse their belongings, and perhaps get a sense of what they now were. Looking at the shelves above their bed, his eye was drawn first to the frame he knew held the holo of the parents of their memory, though in the darkness the illusion wouldn't solid-ify. There were also a few books... but then he noticed the case with the small paper roses that years ago Riss' mother had given to her, and she to their daughters. He quickly turned away; he didn't want to see any more of the loss that the things on that shelf represented.

He slowly ghosted over to the chest that contained their things and kneeled down. Gently, he lifted the lid and began to sift. On top were a few bits of clothing, sweaters and thick socks mostly, that they had long ago stopped wearing. He recognized them from the patterns, and though they appeared to be dark and greyscale, he knew they were quite colorful. It was the first time he had noticed, but all they had worn since the accident were drab smocks – practical work clothes, really. *If they wouldn't wear them, then why the hell would they keep them?* Setting the question aside as unfathomable and ultimately unimportant, he moved on. Somewhere in the back of his mind he knew he was searching for anything that would distract him, and maybe assuage what he was beginning to think was guilt.

Digging further down, he found some amateurish drawings of hills and sunsets one or both of them had doodled on some unlined sheets of paper. There were a few children's books that Riss had given them early on, thinking that they might enjoy reading them as she had. Lastly, he found a holo frame at the very bottom. When he pulled it out, he brought it close to his face. It was too dark for the dimensions to pop out, but he could just make out that it was a holo of the four of them on one of their camping trips. *We were so innocent then...*

As he was plumbing the image for better detail, he became aware of eyes on him. When he slowly looked over, he saw Maré staring at him, and watching him go through their things.

With their belongings on the floor around him, Breylin turned and put his back against the chest and slid into a sitting position. Only a couple of meters apart, their eyes were once again locked on each other. This time Maré's were moist with what he supposed was fear, or maybe loss. At times, their emotional complexity still surprised him. This was one of those moments. Though he was glad that his anger had wicked off, it left him matching her sadness with only his own regrets.

Time stretched as they held each other's gaze.

"Will it hurt?" she whispered.

"No – nothing."

Something in him said the time was right, and he pulled out the controller. She followed the movements of his hands carefully with her eyes.

"Dad?" she said, and hesitated. "I'm afraid."

He looked at her as placidly as he could, but the knots in his gut were coiling tighter in on themselves. He wanted to stop this, fix it, somehow work things out, but there was nothing for it. None of them had any choices. He almost moved, crawled over to her, to put his arms around her, to murmur some stupid word of comfort – *do it, Joss! Be a fucking human!* – but he was afraid to touch her, to feel her touch. The ropes of his muscles wanted to move, flex and bunch of their own accord, but he fought it back and stayed where he was. He'd pay for it with more wearied regrets later, but right at this moment he just couldn't stand letting any more of his emotions loose. "I don't know what to say, Maré."

"What will it be like?" she whispered.

"I – I don't know." He could feel his eyes beginning to well, and he covered his face. "I just don't know, Maré."

"Dad," she said plaintively, "we're sorry about Mom."

And then the tears did fall. He dropped his hand so they could see each other, but his attention spun away with grief. *End it, now, push the button, push the BUTTON –*

"I am too."

He thumbed the little black chit on the pad, and Maré closed her eyes, stopped moving. Her back no longer rose and fell. He sat there a few seconds half distracted, half in an emotional retreat. In an odd, unfocused way he wondered why tears were slipping down his cheeks and onto his shirt.

When he mostly came back to himself, he got up, fixed Maré's hair, and then eased the blanket up around them. When he backed out of the room, he used two hands to keep the door from making any noise as it shut. It would be wrong somehow if he made any noise.

He needed to do something with them, but there would be time enough after a few hours of sleep. He went to the couch and curled up with his despair, and thought *let them have this last embrace.*

Fourteen

The next morning, Breylin marveled at ever having felt guilty about the passing of the simulants. It was part of their nature, and he made their deaths painless. *Hell, I did them a favor.* It was a comforting thought but he wasn't sure he believed it, so he didn't examine it any closer.

Breylin called in to work and explained the situation to his boss, and that he would pull a double shift later. Harry reluctantly agreed. He disposed of the simulant carcasses down at the processing station in Twilight and headed home after a long morning of paperwork, brooding the whole way about how the bureaucratic nonsense that all governments and corporations seemed to like to inflict on people was nothing short of gleeful sadism.

Larissa was in one of her non-responsive moods, so he left her alone in the living room staring out the window at the eternal sunset. He went into the lift port and maneuvered the heavy transport container that held their next pair of twins, then he keyed the activation sequence that would start the cycle that implanted their final memories and bring them out of hyper-sleep. The lid unlocked and popped open a couple of fingers with a hiss. He locked it back in place, then used the couple of minutes it would take for them to come around to put their obedience collars on their necks and key them to his controller. Then he sat down on the fender of the lift and waited.

It didn't take very long until one of them, Luna, stirred, picked her head up and looked around. After she spied him through slitted eyelids, she lay her head back down and shut her eyes. She used her hand to massage her brow, as Maré started to come around, coughing.

He stood up and came to the edge of the container so that they could see each other more clearly. After regarding one another for a few moments he asked, "How are you coming along?"

"Still a little out of it," Maré replied, and she coughed a few times. She reached across and took her twin's hand.

Luna croaked, "Are you our owner?"

"Yes. You may address me either as Sir, or by my name, Mr. Breylin. Can you tell me your names?"

"Maré, Sir. This is Luna."

The idea was for you to answer each for yourselves," he said dryly, "but you seem well enough. Stay here, and I will get you some water."

He left the lift port for the kitchen.

When he returned a couple of minutes later, they were sitting up. Maré was touching her collar, but when she saw him she dropped her hand from the band.

He handed them the glasses and sat back down on the lift fender. They gulped it down, as if it was the first they'd had in a long time. When they were finished, he took their empty tumblers, set them down on the lift's hood and asked, "Are you ready to climb out of that box?"

Luna said, "yes, Sir," and she looked around, trying to figure out how she might do that.

"You're going to need some help," he said, and lifted her out. Next he offered Maré a hand, who went to him willingly.

Once they were both out, they stood there and looked up at him, ready for what comes next.

"Before we go inside, we need to go over something. There are several rules in this house, but first thing you need to know is that my wife, Mrs. Breylin, is your mistress. You will have many duties here, but her needs are your highest concern. I will explain everything to you later, after I have fed you the meal you need after a long hibernation, but first I will take you to meet Mrs. Breylin."

They looked at each other, and Maré said "we understand, Sir."

They followed him into the house.

Larissa was still sitting by the window staring out. "Honey," he said gingerly, "I would like you to meet Maré and Luna."

When he touched her arm, she startled, but she turned towards them, her eyes starting to come into focus. "What...?"

"Riss, this is Maré and Luna, our new simulants," he repeated.

She shook her head and came back to her surroundings. "Of course they are."

They stepped forward, still holding hands. "We're very pleased to meet you, Mrs. Breylin," Maré said.

"Of course you are, dear," she said vacantly, and turned back to the window, and perhaps to wherever she'd been moments before.

The girls looked at Joss, puzzled.

He jerked his head towards the kitchen. It was going to take a long time to explain the way this house functioned.

Life with the new pair had been going as well as might be expected. On their first night, Breylin sat them down to a carb-laden meal and explained their duties as the keepers of the house and caretakers for Mrs. Breylin who was, as far as they were concerned, the very center of the world. He was specific, without being too graphic, about what sorts of behavior would earn them correction, and what the possibilities for correction might include. Breylin told them if they followed the rules, then there wouldn't be any issues, and that he would take care of them fairly. He told them nothing of the accident, except that Mrs. Breylin had lost her legs and an implication of it being the fault of their predecessors. Striking the right balance was something of a challenge; he wanted them to know enough of the past so they'd know what to avoid, yet little enough to keep them a bit uneasy, on edge.

They took it quietly, but he could tell that wide-eyed Luna was at least nervous, maybe closer to nearly scared. Maré seemed less so, but it overall seemed he'd struck the proportion of tension he wanted.

"Your day will start when I rise at 5AM," he told them. "One of you should try to be near Mrs. Breylin whenever she is awake."

"We will do as we are told, Mr. Breylin," said Luna quickly.

"This is a lot to take in; do you have any questions?"

"No, Sir. I think we've got it. We'll try not to disappoint you or Mrs. Breylin."

"If you think of anything, let me know. It's better to ask questions than to be punished for misbehaving. I'll show you to your room now. I want you to get some rest and be ready to face tomorrow."

—∧=∨—

That night in their room, they stripped and showered together, and then they got into bed. Without a thought, Maré drew her Chroma to her and stroked her hair.

"Are we going to be alright, Maré?"

"We're going to be fine, Luna. We don't have any choice so we'll accept it. And we're going to do as we're told."

"I guess..." she started. "I guess it doesn't seem too bad. I guess you're right."

"That's a lot of guesses," she said as she tweaked her nose, but she continued in a more serious manner. "Nothing is going to go wrong, and no matter what happens, we'll be together."

"You're right, but... I'm still scared of him," said Luna.

"We should be scared of him. I think he's dangerous, but... I think we can believe him when he says he'll take care of us and treat us fairly."

"What about Mrs. Breylin?"

"I don't know. She doesn't seem... too good. We'll just have to see."

After a few moments, Luna said, "Maré?"

"Yes, dear?"

"I miss Mom and Dad."

"So do I, Luna." She hugged her tight, and kissed her on the top of her head. "We're going to have to stick together."

Time passed. The pair learned how to do their jobs, ignore the stress between the Breylin's, and most importantly, how to follow the sometimes-arbitrary seeming rules. There were very few minor incidents, and only one that warranted more correction than a direct talking to; Luna had been late getting dinner started, and as a result it wasn't ready when Mr. Breylin got home after a particularly stressful day at his job. He'd whipped her feet over the course of an hour using the short, thin length of plastic tubing he kept over the door of their room. He took his time, almost making a ritual of it, and he'd forced Maré to watch, locked in place by her collar and unable to speak. He'd even repositioned her a few times to make sure she had a proper view. He was careful not to break the skin, but the bruising was deep and he'd left Luna's feet entirely purple and black. She'd limped for four days afterward. He'd done such a thorough job that it made Maré wonder how he'd become so skilled – though she'd kept the question to herself. In any case, it was a hard lesson well learned, and it was the last time they risked dinner not being on time. As bad as Luna had been punished, they were certain that if they made the same mistake twice it would be far worse.

Their days started early with Mr. Breylin. When he got up he would wake them, and they tended to his needs until he left for work. They would take turns sitting with Mrs. Breylin and doing the chores, which consisted of things like cleaning the house, doing the laundry and preparing the meals.

The days were boring and long, but they had been cared for, fed and housed as promised. It took time, but Maré and Luna started to trust their owners, despite their idiosyncrasies and strict code of conduct. It was a very small world that just the four of them lived in, there in the solitude of their home overlooking the peaceful canyon, with its eternal sunset and beautiful rust brown mountains further north.

Though they did take care of her and spend time with her, Mrs. Breylin continued to grow more oddly disconnected. The weeks turned to months, and then their first birthday passed. As his wife's demeanor deteriorated, Mr. Breylin became more distant from them, then cold, and eventually, outright surly. He would question them for the list of things they had done during the day, sharply if they had difficulty remembering details and times. Most especially, he wanted to know how their interactions with his wife had gone. They learned to pay close attention to those particulars, and they told him everything, but regardless he still grew angry with them, as if they had somehow been the source of her difficulties.

Mrs. Breylin began to look gaunt and hunted. In addition to cleaning her, they started feeding her or risk her not eating. Fearing his reaction, they went to Mr. Breylin panicked and begging for help. He was clearly upset, but it was as if he understood on some level. Though the extra attention made them apprehensive, they were also relieved that he was now watching their interactions with her. For the first time in their recollection, he admitted that he could see it wasn't them. It was a very bittersweet realization; they regretted her appalling state, yet they were also guiltily comforted that Mr. Breylin wasn't blaming them for it.

Later that night, he took his wife into their bedroom to talk to her. He used hushed tones at first, then heated tones. That was when she began to respond, and she did so with even more heat. Quickly, their discussion turned into an ugly argument, and Maré and Luna hid in their own room with the door closed. The last thing they heard was Mr. Breylin slamming the door on his way into the lift port, and then the whine of the lift's engine as he sped off to the south. When they checked on their mistress, they found her distraught and refusing assistance for the clothing she had obviously soiled. Fearfully, they obeyed her and went back to their room, where they spent a long, sleepless night holding each other and listening to Mrs. Breylin wail through the walls.

After that terrible night, things seemed to improve. Mrs. Breylin appeared to be much more alert to what was going on in the room around her, and even talking with them occasionally. At times she would even smile unbidden, as if she were reliving some pleasant memory. She would direct them to get her nicer, more colorful tops to wear, so long as they were long enough to cover her diapers.

The change in his wife was immediately noticeable to Breylin. He was quite expressive in his apologies for their fight the night before, and within just a couple of days the shell of his nasty demeanor dissolved, revealing the nice man he must have once been. Within a week, the Breylins were almost doting on the girls. One Tuesday night, Mrs. Breylin had Luna dig out a container of Ice Cream from the back of their cold storage chest in the lift port. Chocolate, the label said – and it was delicious as it was ostentatious.

Later, after the kitchen was cleaned and the preparations for the following morning were complete, Maré and Luna went to their room. They washed and dried each other as usual, but they deviated from their routine to look through a book they had found in their room. It described animals from Earth, most of which, the book said, were now extinct. Many of them had once long ago been kept in great zoos that people would walk through. It was strange to think that people had had things like dogs, cats and other small animals as pets. Why would they want to? With such undeveloped brains, the animals must not have been able to obey very well.

After they read for a while, they became tired, so they stripped, closed the window shutters and laid down in each other's arms. The only sounds in the quiet room was the sighing of their blanket. These were their happiest moments, when they held each other close in their nakedness. Luna laid her head on Maré's chest and listened to her body. After a time, she said, "Maré, you know those pets?"

"Mmhmm. You mean the cats and stuff? What about them?"

"Do you think they ever beat them?"

Maré thought about it. "Probably some. I imagine it was a good way of training them whenever they would break things or go to the bathroom where they weren't supposed to."

"Do you think... Are we pets?"

Maré was struck by the thought. *Could she be right?* "I don't know, hon," she replied. "What made you think of such a thing?"

"I don't know... It just seems like we're creatures they let stay in their homes."

"Maybe you're right." It was an ugly line of reasoning to Maré. "We're of more use to them, but we don't even live as long as the dogs they used to keep." She considered where that thinking led, then continued. "Are we real? How would we even know?"

Luna eased up on one elbow so that their faces were close. "We aren't human, but we *are* real, Maré. Do you love me?"

Maré reached up to caress her face. "You know I do, Chroma," she said with a warm smile.

"That's right, I'm your Chroma," she said with velvet in her voice. "Can you feel your Chroma love you?"

"Yes, I can."

"That love is real, Maré." Luna glided her hand up her stomach and gently squeezed her breast. "Tell me, what is in your breast?"

"My milk."

"And when I nurse at your breast;" Luna bent down and drew her nipple into her mouth, and Maré gasped at the pressure of her Chroma's suckling. "Is it not pleasing?"

"Mmm... yes... very."

Luna slid up higher to offer Maré her own breast. "And when you nurse at mine, doesn't it thrill you just as much?" Maré's reply was muffled as she latched on, and Luna clasped her in closer. Maré's hands danced along Luna's skin, and she whined as her Chroma drank deeply and parted the folds of her womb with her fingers.

"We *are* real, Maré..."

The next morning, Mrs. Breylin got up with the rest of them and saw her husband off to work. It was strange but not unpleasant to have so much activity in the kitchen at this time of their daily cycle.

After Mr. Breylin left for the morning with lunch and coffee in hand, Luna helped Mrs. Breylin into her shower, while Maré began cleaning in the kitchen. Somewhere around midmorning they would exchange duties, with Luna working on the laundry in their small processor and Maré tending their mistress while cleaning the living room. It promised to be a busy day.

When it was time to get started on the laundry, Mrs. Breylin stopped them.

"Girls, I want to prepare something special for Mr. Breylin's dinner. In the cold storage chest in the lift port, please find a small, blue container of food. I think it must be towards the bottom of the chest."

Luna answered for them. "Okay, Mrs. Breylin – I can get it."

"Maré, be a dear and go help her."

"Yes, Ma'am."

They searched for a couple of minutes, pulling things out one by one and stacking them in front of the chest, but they couldn't find exactly what she had described.

"Wait, is that it?" asked Luna, pointing a purple container.

"Wrong color, doofus," Maré spat playfully.

"Oh, of course. Just pull out the blue one, then..."

"Okay, fine, maybe you're right. She might've forgot - the stuff at the bottom's been down there a long time." She pulled it out. "I'll just ask her. You can start putting the rest away."

"Fine by me," replied Luna. "But if you're wrong, you're pulling this crap back out."

When Maré tried the door, it wouldn't budge. "Hey, what is this?" she said. "We're locked out."

"What? Why would she lock us out here?" Luna said while picking up the last of the frozen parcels.

"I don't know... maybe we pissed her off."

"Are you turning it the right way?"

Maré smirked at her. "You're kidding, right? Try it for yourself."

Luna came over, jiggled the lever, and frowned. "That's not good."

"Mrs. Breylin!" yelled Maré as she pounded. "The door's locked!"

But there was no answer.

They tried to get her attention for a few more minutes, and got the same result each time.

"We might as well sit down and wait," declared Luna. "Whether we upset her or not, it's all we can do..."

"I guess," said Maré. "But you know he's probably going to beat us for it, right?" She walked over to the freezer and put the purple container inside, closed the lid and hopped up to sit on it. Then they waited in anxious silence.

After a long while, they thought they could hear odd scraping and bumping noises in the house, and when it became crashing and breaking, they were sure. Luna decided to try pounding on the door as hard as she could, when she put her hand on the latch. "Maré, the knob's hot! What does that mean?!" But dread was already dawning on her face.

"It means the house must be on fire!" Mare began to beat on the door harder. "Mrs. Breylin! Mrs. *Breylin*! We have to get out!"

"She can't get to it, Maré! If the door's hot that means the fire's near it! We'll have to try to get in from the front!"

As they bolted to the front of the lift port, the overhead track lighting strobed, winked out, and the darkness solidified around them. Only a sliver of daylight seeping under the massive door oriented them as to where they were. Maré's heart began to pound as Luna stumbled her way over to the console beside the door and began mashing its buttons. "Shit! With the power out it won't budge!"

"We'll have to force it!" Maré screamed. "Help me lift it!"

The two of them grabbed a reinforcement rib that went across it and began to strain at moving it upwards. After several seconds of groaning, Luna said. "It's no use! We'll never budge this thing!"

"Wait," said Maré, and she began to rummage around in the dark along one wall. Sweating profusely and searching blind, she began to panic, afraid that it was getting hotter in there. "Here it is! One of Mr. Breylin's old shovels!"

She hurried back and scraped it under the door. Working it

up and down and kicking the top of the blade, she managed to move it a few more centimeters out. Shrieking as she used it as a fulcrum, she applied all her might to lift the door. Slowly it moved one, five, ten centimeters, and more daylight flooded in.

"Luna!" she said through a grimace of gritted teeth. "It'll slam shut if let go and I can't hold it for long! Wriggle under and get the hell out!"

"Ae you crazy?!" she replied as she ran over to where Maré had gotten the shovel. "Just hold that damn thing while I get something to hold it up!"

"Hurry, Luna! I can't hold it! The hydraulics are trying to force it back down!"

A few precious seconds later, she rushed back with another shovel and one of the toolboxes. "Okay, hang on, Maré. I'm going to get this one under further and lift it higher. You get the box under as quick as you can!"

Luna got in position, began to pull up on the makeshift lever, and managed to move it a little higher. As soon as Luna had taken the weight off of her, Maré dropped her shovel and began to try to get the toolbox under the door. "Luna, you have to give me a few more centimeters!"

"*Rrrr!*" With the ropes of her slight muscles knotting, Luna cried out as she struggled to nudge the door higher. It edged up a tiny bit more, and Maré pounded the box under it. "Let it go!" Luna nearly fell over as she unclenched and the box took on the weight of the door. Immediately its lid began to protest loudly as it kinked and buckled in the middle.

"C'mon!" said Maré as she began to shimmy her way under. Luna followed as the hinges on the box squealed and snapped off, and the lid crushed down further. Standing behind her, Maré grabbed her by the arms and hauled her out as the lift door finished the box's demolition. The door was held with only five or six centimeters of clearance, but the box had done its job and Luna had gotten her legs out in time.

Luna climbed to her feet, and when they looked they found that the house was all but fully engulfed. Windows in the front and around by the kitchen were beginning to burst from the heat, one by one, leaving shards of clear glass littered in semi-circles below the gaping maws they left. Lurid reflections were flashing with flame twisted by shadows inside the structure, and fire driven by wind was beginning to jet from the roof line. Horrified, they realized that there was no way Mrs. Breylin could have made it out.

—∧=∨—

It was a tiring day, Joss mused on his way home, *but a good one.* Harry had brought him a hunk of cake that his wife had made, and it had gone down well at lunch time. Most of it, anyway – he had kept himself from eating the last little piece so that he could bring it home to Riss. He had nearly left it in their work truck, but at the last minute he remembered and went back for it. Now it sat on the seat beside him in the lift. *Cake at 150 kph.* His mind wandered with odd thoughts, only half paying attention to how the gusts were moving the lift side to side as the pressure varied.

The two of them, and their simulant workforce, had spent the day moving a set of gas taps from one part of the mining field to another a few hundred meters off to the south. Depending on the deposits, they might not have to move a particular set for a couple of weeks. This last one had made it a little over that, so the pipes were tough to extract from the dense rock layers. Regardless, the day had started out well. It had been full of honest labor, and even though he was dirty and his clothes were stuck to his sweat-soaked body, he was determined to carry his light mood home.

He navigated between the low, rocky hills that fanned out before the mountains, using them for cover in the windstorm. He crested the last ridge before the canyon in which their settlement sat. The black plume of smoke rising from where the house had once stood dominated his view. His guts sank and fear tightened its grip on his frame, and he thought he would swoon. He ignored the sparks dancing in his vision as he floored the accelerator. He flew down the last stretch and screamed the lift to a halt sideways in front of the house, bouncing it off the unfinished surface of the road. Getting out, he could see that most of the house had already fallen in on itself; the fire was all but over. The girls sat on the ground, holding each other and covered in the soot and ash that had been thrown off the house in its death throes. They had been crying at one point – he could see the runnels the tears had made in the grime on their cheeks – but now they just sat there stunned, looking at him vacantly. Riss wasn't there.

"Where the hell is my wife?!" he screamed at them. He grabbed Luna, yanked her to her feet and yelled at her as he shook her. *"Where is she?!"*

"She's... in the house, Mr. Breylin," she said detachedly.

Breylin threw her to the side and ran up into the house. "Riss! Riss!" He was running around, over and under the remains of their house. *"Riss!"* But she was gone. He sat down in the remains of his life as squalls whipped ashen cinders and sparks around him. It was all gone.

Breylin had no idea how long he'd sat there, but he'd had time to grow hungry. The burned plastic stink of the fire was heavy on him, and when he looked down at himself he was covered with smoke grime and ash. What remained of the outer walls was still smoldering, though part of the back of the house had partially caved in on itself. Idiotically, his mind wandered to the cake back in the lift. On some level he understood that his mind had withdrawn from the horror of what had happened, but he had no wish to fight it for control.

He got to his feet and looked around. This used to be the living room. He could tell where the furniture had been.

Not wanting to see any more of what was around him, he got out of the house. The girls were asleep on the ground. One of them had her arms around the other, but at the moment he couldn't tell them apart. He walked by them, and kept going back down the road. He stopped in front of the other house at the top of the canyon, tried the door and found it open. He walked inside, roving from room to room. When he found himself in a bedroom, sleep beckoned him, and his body relented. He laid down on the bare mattress and passed out.

His bladder woke him up. His muscles felt like soft polymer, but he pushed himself up and stumbled to the bathroom. As he was peeing, a wave a nausea rolled over him. He stumbled into the wall and he pissed all over his filthy pants and the floor. He crumbled to his knees and vomited noisily in the toilet bowl. When he was done heaving, he lost his loose grip on the commode and fell down. He smacked his face on the floor, and quickly urine started to seep through the shoulder of his jacket. He couldn't have cared less if he'd tried.

After a couple of minutes, the feeling of nausea and weakness waned, and he opened his eyes. Laying there, he felt numb and stared out at nothing, but gradually he became aware of a familiar shape. He focused in, and realized that it was a thin, plastic water pipe. It snaked its way out of the floor and up into the tank at the back of the commode. It was white, and though it appeared smooth, it looked like it had dark fibers ringing it for reinforcement. It was pretty narrow as pipes go, but it was still a little bit thicker than the tubes they often used with the drilling rigs out in the zone. It might have even been made in the same facility.

He pushed off the floor and took a couple of minutes to let his head clear as he lean against the wall. The urine on his clothes had turned cold, but he barely noticed it. He just didn't care; it was all he could do to fight off the miasma that was threatening to make him lay back down.

Once he had nearly reasserted his self-control, he decided that the time to go find the girls and get some answers was long overdue. Unfortunately, he didn't have any of those pressure tubes handy.

When he walked outside, the wind was starting to kick up, stinging his face with the cold rain it drove sideways. He walked towards the burned out shell of everything he ever cared about. As he got closer, he could see that the two of them were sitting on the ground, huddling over by the lift for the shelter it provided from the squall. As he walked over to them the storm plastered his hair to his head, and he wondered if he looked as sorry as they did. *Probably worse*, he thought.

They watched him as he walked in their direction, and stood holding each other when he got close. They were soaked to the bone, shaking and miserable. "Tell me what happened," he said.

They just looked at him.

"*Tell me what happened!*" he shouted into the storm. They

flinched as if he had struck them.

Maré was closer to him, and she said, "we don't know, Sir."

Luna said, "Mrs. Breylin locked us in the lift port."

They started talking over each other, and Breylin held his hand up. When they quieted, he pointed at Maré.

"We thought we must have done something wrong, when we found that she had locked us in the lift port. She sent us out to get something from the cold storage chest."

"Then what?"

"I don't know. We sat there a while, and when we tried the door again, it was hot. We could hear noises in the house. We went outside and saw that the house was all on fire. That's all we know."

With his eyes down, he seemed to be thinking about it. All of a sudden, Breylin's fist exploded against the side of Maré's face, and she went down like an avalanche. Luna had no time to react before he was on her. The storm raged on, oblivious to the dance of violence. He had his hands around her throat, squeezing, squeezing, and he drew her in close so that he could look into her eyes. She started hitting him, trying to push him off, but he had her tight. Scrabbling, she tried to pry his hands loose as her face was getting so hot, but her hands were wet and she couldn't find the purchase she needed to dislodge him. She started to grow weak, and the edges of her vision were turning, fading. As she fell down a deep hole, the blackness swallowed her completely. *Why am I falling? Where's... Maré...? She was... here...*

And then, nothing.

—∧ = ∨—

Maré woke to a blinding pain in the side of her face. There was something wrong with her jaw; it felt... wrong. She was lying in ashes. *I must be in the house,* she thought, *but I can't move.* Looking around she saw Luna lying next to her, with her face slack and eyes closed. Her mouth was open, and the rain was bouncing off her skin. *"Luna... wake up, please, honey!"*

"She's not going to wake up, Maré," Breylin said. She looked, and Breylin was sitting nearby in the rubble looking at her. "I used my hands to wring the life out of her."

"Nooo... Why?!"

He moved to kneel next to her. "Now you know, Maré," he said, barely audible over the violent oscillation of the wind. "Now you know what loss is like."

She was crying hysterically and trying to scoot closer to her Chroma. *"Luna!"*

"Here, let me help," he said, as he got to his feet. He picked her up by her lashed arms and laid her across Luna. "Is that better? Does it help, to be near your dead twin?!"

"Why? Why?"

"You know, I've been sitting over here next to what's left of my wife's burned corpse, *and I thought you might like to do the same!"*

Maré was moaning Luna's name when he started to pour the hydraulic fluid he had stashed in the lift port over her and her Chroma's corpse. When he got it in her hair, it ran down into her face and she spluttered at the noxious stuff. As she was coughing, he bent down to her. "Can you hear me, Maré?"

"What do you want from me? You've killed my Chroma, you

bastard!"

"I did, Maré, and pretty soon I'm going to kill you too, but I wanted you to know how it felt first."

Breylin stood, backed off a couple of meters, lit the waterproof torch and threw it on them. He closed his eyes and stood in the rain. Her screams did nothing to satisfy the utter poverty that pierced his soul; after they wound down to nothing all he could feel was wet and a vast emptiness inside.

Fifteen

There were no holding cells in the facility, so Maré and Luna were made to stay in their room by the dim, stoic androids positioned outside their door. The guards would tell them nothing – indeed, they wouldn't say anything at all; even their look was vacant. The twins brought them their food, and though their manner was compassionate, they weren't allowed to talk, either. Even LabSys had gone silent. They had no choice but to wait in fear for whatever would come. At least they had been allowed to stay together. All things considered, it was a great comfort.

After they had been forced into their room, they lay together in their bed without even having taken off their clothes. Maré still had some of 85's blood on her fingers, but she and her Chroma were too numb to notice. They simply held each other in the meager illumination cast off by the light over the desk. Eventually, they slept.

Luna woke sometime later to find her sitting on the edge of the bed, staring at the holo of their parents. Maré heard her Chroma stir, and she turned. When she saw her eyes open, she gently reached over to stroke her hair. Luna could smell the antiseptics she had used as she leaned into Maré's tender touch. In better times she might have nipped her fingers, but she couldn't summon the cheer to do it now. Instead she sat up, moved behind her Chroma, and put her arms around her.

Maré held onto Luna's arm with one hand as she turned back to the semi-flat image. She lightly tapped its edge a few times, and though it flickered, the illusion wouldn't pop out as it should. Perhaps it had hung there for a long time.

"Tell me more about our parents, Luna..."

"What would you like to hear?"

"I don't know – something... sentimental."

Luna pondered. "Well... There was an occasion when Mom and Dad took us to see our grandparents for the first time. I'm pretty sure they were Dad's parents. I guess we were about... maybe five or six. It felt like we had spent hours in the lift." She thought for a moment before she continued. Maré could tell from her voice that she was a little girl back in that lift a long time ago. "We were in the back, and we were on a grand adventure. Sometimes we watched the scenery – actual trees, Maré! None of that stuff grew in the city, not the real stuff, at least. The big, green leaves on them, the bushes and tall grass, and small explosions of colorful flowers along the edge of the road..."

"It sounds delightful."

"Mmhmm, it was..." She laughed, saying, "we got to romping around on the bags in the back, and Dad hollered that we'd better stop or the jumping around would crash the car!"

"Really?" Maré said incredulously.

"Oh," she said as her laugh was winding down. "As little as we were, I can't believe we were in any danger. Dad was ticked, but Mom laughed, anyway."

"And our grandparents? What were they like?"

"Gramma was heavy, but she hooted when she saw us. She smelled like the food she was cooking, too, and she wouldn't stop hugging us. Pap was so serious, but he sneaked us candies when he thought no one was looking. Mom saw, but she just winked at us and stood so Dad wouldn't see us eating before dinner."

Luna's tears were on Maré's neck. For once, they were the

tears of happy memory.

"What else? Tell me more, Chroma."

"Lay with me and I will," she whispered.

Maré got up, padded over to the desk and turned off the light. She stripped, dropping her things on the floor and crawled into bed. With their cheeks and their breasts touching, they lay there with their arms around each other and their legs weaved. Though she had the tang of old sweat, Maré loved her Chroma's smell, and she inhaled it deeply.

After a time, Luna let her go and pushed up on one elbow. "We stayed a week in that big house. The time flew by... Pap took us fishing on the second day, just long enough for him to catch one. The thing stank so bad in the bucket in the back of the lift, but it was *wonderful* that night after Gramma cooked it."

Into the silence Maré said, "I wish I could remember it."

Luna slowly pushed out a breath. "Yeah... I do too, Maré."

"What are they going to do with us, Luna?"

"I... I don't know, honey," she said as she tucked Maré's hair behind her ear.

"I'm afraid, Chroma." She might have shook with it, giving in to the immense fear, but she was tired way down in her soul, and she just didn't have anything left to sacrifice to it.

"I am too."

Luna laid back down and instinctively they braided.

Two days later, the androids took them by the arms and brought them to what they supposed was Dr. Almeida's office. It was the first time they had ever been there, or that they had ever seen such warmth in this place. One wall to the right was dark glass, but the other three were burnished wood paneling of a dark brownish-orange hue. Almeida sat behind a desk at the back of the room. Reluctantly, they navigated the occasional, comfortable-looking furniture and stood before him.

He wasn't smoking the weed he normally did; the one he now had smelled strangely festive, maybe fruity, and oddly pleasant. He was just pouring himself a drink of something viscous the color of the walls out of a cut-glass decanter, the implants in his fingers ticking against its sides. "I'd pour you two some," he said as he replaced the stopper, "but I only have the one tumbler."

He closed his eyes, inhaled its vapor then sipped the liquid. He made a small, satisfied face at the taste. "More expensive than drugs, but worth every penny." He looked up at them, sat back and propped his worn shoes on top of a stack of papers that was being vomited out of one of the desk drawers. "Well, you might as well sit down." He waved his hand at the two leather chairs arranged in front of his desk. "Enjoy those, it's unlikely you'll ever sit in anything like them again. Hell, most people never do."

They were extremely plush, hugging their contours as if they'd been designed for their use. Luna said, "Doctor, is this real leather? I read about it in one of the archives."

He laughed. "Hell, no – are you crazy? I can't afford *real* leather."

"I'm sorry, Doctor – I don't mean to offend."

He waved again as he coughed a few times. "It's nothing. I guess you couldn't know."

Maré spoke up. "What happens now, Doctor?"

"You want to get right to it, eh? Fine." He put his feet on the floor, took another sip, and punched a few keys on a panel on the desktop. A light came up in the room behind the smoky glass in the wall to the right, revealing a bed, machines, and 85. She had several tubes and wires connected to her and a mask over her nose and mouth. They could just tell that her eyes were open, periodically blinking, and staring upward, but vacant and sight-less.

"She will live, but you did quite a number on her, Bravo. She had a subdural hematoma. Her brain scans don't look promising, but the techs were able to drain off the blood. We have to wait for the swelling to subside, but once that happens we should be able to get a better sense of the extent of the damage." He let that sink in. "I think you can probably tell just by looking at her that it's probably extensive."

"I'm not going to tell you I feel awful, Doctor, or that I'm sorry. This is the result of her own self-destruct, and she got what she deserved."

"You may be right, Bravo, but consider this: you weren't sum-moned here to talk about her fate, but yours." He looked over at Luna and said, "and yours, too, Alpha."

Luna hung her head a bit and said, "I'm not sure we could say anything that mattered at this point."

"Just so," he said. "I'll let you in on a little secret, though. The damage this situation has caused was really quite minor, all things considered. 85 was the best worker we'd had here in a long time, but she was less than two years out from expiration. I'd probably let the two of you stay on as you are, except that my superiors have decided to take this gift-wrapped opportunity to rap my knuckles. I've been ordered to make the two of you go away."

"Expiration?" Maré said.

He stared at her, considering. "Perhaps you don't know. Why

don't you explain it, 183?" he said slightly amused.

"I haven't told you... it's a thing we don't like to talk about." Her brows knit in thought. "The difficult truth is that we only live about ten years, and then we expire," she said quietly.

"Expire? As in die?"

Luna averted her eyes and nodded her head.

Maré took it in. "So you have, what, about nine years left?"

"Something like that, yes," she quietly murmured.

Maré sat there stunned, not sure what to say. She had to say something though. "Well," she said uncertainly. "At least it's a long way off."

Almeida spoke up with a dry chuckle. "I'm afraid it's not going to work out like that. You *might* make it, 370." He pointed at Luna. "But not her."

"How do you plan to repurpose me?" Luna said in defeat.

"I probably would have considered selling you off as a cheap pleasure model, but you really haven't the looks, and your sexual dysfunction makes you even less ideal. There aren't very many options left. I thought maybe I might keep you on; 85 is going to need a lot of care, and it might have been interesting to have kept you on to do it."

She leaned forward and stammered, "Please Doctor, I —"

"Relax, it isn't really an option. I probably could have kept your endorphin levels high and would have kept you useful, but then what fun would that have been? Actually," he said as he hunted for a pen and started making notes on his blotter and muttering to himself. "If the damage to 85's brain is extensive maybe it might be amusing to push her chemistry to orgiastic levels."

Maré exhaled noisily at his callousness.

Luna sat back. "Is it the organ farm, then?"

"Maybe some of you – I still have to figure it out. The good news is I've decided to grant you a minor boon. When I terminate you it will be painless."

Maré said, "if a quick termination is the good news, what's the bad?"

"You've a bold streak, 370, I'll give you that. The bad news is we don't waste good protein around here."

The girls sat there horrified.

"Take it as a lesson, 370. Boldness is dangerous for a simulant, and asking questions can always bring awful answers. I recommend you learn to keep your curiosity to yourself in your future endeavors."

He tossed back half his drink, looked at the glass and tossed back the rest, then he carefully refilled it.

"What will those endeavors be, Doctor?" Maré said.

He shook his head, and said, "Some have to learn the hard way." He began to croup again, this time easily as hard as when he'd first examined her. He scrambled to pull a few tissues from one of the pockets in his lab coat. When he was done, he threw them on the desk, then used another one to wipe his eyes. Maré noticed the wad of tissues on the blotter had specks of bright red blood in them. Curious.

When he had himself under control, he finished his thought. "Actually, there isn't really a lot I could do with you, now that you've killed another simulant and I'm forced to get rid of you. I probably would have sent *you* to the organ farm, but I have just received a special request for a pair from this bloodline. Some poor and desperate colonist out there on some corporate world wants two of you in the worst way – too bad he'll only get one, though. I was able to recoup the normal price for you; you're damaged goods, but the client doesn't have to wait. Once you're asleep, I will have the necessary hormones to develop your physical characteristics administered, at least as much as possible. You'll never be voluptuous, but your new master should be able to look at you without too much trouble." He paused. "Call it another boon."

"You're a monster, aren't you?" Maré asked, doing nothing to mask the terrible awe in her voice.

"Am I?" he grunted as he scratched his ear absently. "I guess it might look that way to the likes of you. It's what you were born to."

She shook her head. "I don't understand."

"I mean you were just sold by some remote, faceless corporation to some nameless dirt farmer on a particularly uninteresting rock somewhere out beyond nowhere. Life is cheap for the best of us, and so much less for your kind."

"*Why* are we so worthless, Doctor? *Why don't we count?*"

"On the contrary, you have value, and you do count. If it weren't for you specifically," he said putting the cigar between his teeth and dragging on it, "I would have taken a much larger loss in the budgets."

Maré was stunned into silence by the sum of his cruelty.

"Will you let us have some time to say good bye, Doctor?" said a desperate Luna.

"I'm afraid I'm all out of boons for today, 183." He punched a few more keys on his desktop panel. Their collars exuded chemicals into their spinal columns, and the world went dark for the two of them as they slumped into the plush faux leather chairs. "LabSys, have workers sent to my office. Please close the case files for 370 as resolved, and mark 183 as abrogated."

"Acknowledged, Doctor."

He mulled it over for a few seconds as he chewed on the end of the cigar. "Strike that, LabSys. Mark both case files as resolved. Maybe we can still get something out of 183."

"Acknowledged, Doctor."

Almeida settled back into his chair to suck down another draught from his glass. "Damn, that's good scotch," he mumbled.

Part 2 – Crescendo

Sixteen

Though he could only manage six short steps, Harry Westport paced his tiny office in concern when Joss didn't show up for work, the intervals between consuming hand-rolled cigarettes shortening as the number of turns he made added up.

This was really out of his character – the guy's always on time. I just hope something else hasn't gone wrong at home.

He and his crew were already running forty five minutes late, and the simulants were clearly getting impatient when he checked in on them. Yet he delayed them from moving out with a stand-in supervisor while he went into the office and punched up the contact for the Breylin home and hit Connect. There was no answer, but Larissa might have returned to work. Joss had mentioned something about how he had been hoping she would at some point. There wasn't any answer on his mobile, either. Strange. Harry sat there a few more minutes twirling a pen around his fingers, dragging long and hard on a cigarette, and trying to figure out if he should release the crew or wait a while longer.

When there was still no sign of him at the turn of the hour, he asked one of the other guys to take the crew out to the Zone and get started. Doing it last minute like this would make it impossible to keep the others from noticing Breylin's unexplained absence – the rumor mill was probably already in full motion – but Joss had been a model employee, and he'd earned a little latitude. If anyone didn't care for their friendship then they could take it up with him; between his unease and heavy intake of nicotine, he was in just the right mood for an argument.

Comms still produced nothing but mildly warbling static by the time the second hour had crawled by, and Harry was done sitting around. He decided to take a lift out to search along the route to where the Breylin's lived. Hopefully he wouldn't find anything, but Joss might have had an accident and could be lying somewhere unconscious – or worse.

He did his best to quickly stitch back and forth over the dry, rocky terrain surrounding the primary route of access between Twilight and Amity Canyon. *I'd forgotten how remote it was...* He was glad at first that he hadn't found anything, yet his anxiety grew as the kilometers added up and he neared the settlement. When at last he got to the Breylin home, he found Joss' abandoned lift next to the burned out remains of the house, the driver side door still open in its up position. The fire had guttered out in the storm, Joss was nowhere in sight, and Harry's breakfast his wife had made him hours earlier was threatening to pay his lap a visit.

Harry pulled his lift right up into the yard and he killed the power. He sat stricken while the acid in his gut churned, and he had no idea what to do next. Either the house had no automatic sensors or they'd failed, and as remote as this settlement was, no one had intervened. *I should just call Emergency Services*, he thought, but he knew the time of their limited usefulness had long since passed. Joss and his wife were dead, nothing would bring them back, and a dark cloud of morose futility settled on his shoulders. His friend was gone.

Where do I go from here? But his only answer was the patter of the rain hitting the glass around him.

He lit another cigarette and cupping it against the rain, climbed out. He walked over to the rubble and looked around, afraid to look, that he might see something horrific, but unable to stop himself regardless. From his point of view he could see nothing among the desolation, except the occasionally hissing construction foam beams that were still producing wisps of greasy, black smoke. Thankfully the breeze was at his back and it kept him out of the stink. He couldn't see much... *but I'm certainly not going to walk around in their ashes*.

He was stunned; the situation was obviously much worse than he had imagined what he'd find. Standing there, loss washed over him, and the rain pelted the scalp under his thinning hair. There was nothing here, and he forced his legs to get him away from the carcass of the house.

Returning to the shelter of his lift, he slammed the door shut and shook the rain from his hair. "Dammit," he muttered in frustration under his breath. He used a rag from a small compartment in the door to wipe his face off as he tried to think of what to do. Sitting there drying his face and doing his best to suck down the end of his smoke, he puzzled over that the way Joss' lift sat with the door still up. *He must have gotten to the scene* after *the fire had started*... A small hope bloomed, and he punched in Joss' mobile one last time. If he didn't pick up, he'd call the authorities – for all the good it would do.

After three tones, there was a crackle and hiss as the connection opened, and Breylin's tinny voice came through. "Harry?" he said groggily.

"Joss? Stars! Where the hell are you?"

"I'm... still in bed."

"What? What the *fuck* are you talking about? I'm outside your house, and it's burned to the ground!"

"I'm in the house next door. Is that your lift out there?"

Harry let the silence hang for a moment, then sighed and said, "thank the Stars you're all right. You want to tell me what happened? Where the hell is your wife?"

"I've been a mess. Just... gimme a minute, Harry. I'll be out." There was another burst of static, then the line went dead.

"Shit!" he said as cold rain continued to drip out of his hair and down the back of his neck, but he allowed himself to feel a little relieved. Fire was bad – the Breylins had probably lost everything – but it was a thing you could recover from.

A couple of minutes later, the passenger side of the lift opened and in climbed the wretched figure that used to be Joss Breylin. His skin and clothes were filthy, and though the horrible smell of the fire still clung to him, it was the stench of piss and body odor that made Harry recoil. He could see the whites of his eyes as he sat there blankly staring out the front window towards what was left of his house with his eyebrows climbed halfway to the top of his forehead. It was hard to believe that this was the same person who'd left for home on Friday evening. Harry was a pretty stunned himself.

"Holy crap, Joss. You look like shit."

"Do I?" He looked down at himself, then shook his head. "I guess I couldn't care less."

"Joss... what happened, man?"

"It's all gone, Harry. All gone." Breylin said in a flat whisper. He reached up and scratched his nose, streaking the dirt on his face even worse.

"Everything?" he said, then quietly, "Larissa? Your simulants?"

He turned and looked at Harry as shadows crossed his eyes as they unfocused. "Yeah. There was a fire, and Riss... she's... moved on." Breylin squeezed his eyes shut and sobbed with emotion.

Harry rubbed his eyes as he tried to think of what to say. There really weren't any words for it, and he began to cry at the immensity of his friend's loss, too. Some things are damn hard to recover from.

Two weeks later, a thinner, hollow-cheeked Joss Breylin returned to work with his new, green coveralls hanging off of him.

"Are you sure you're ready to come back to work, Joss? If you need more time... You look like you could use more." He looked up at the ceiling, pursed his lips, and blew out a stream of grey smoke. "We'll manage fine. Whatever you need, take it."

There was a dim, layered haze from the smoke, making the cramped office seem closer than it really was, and Joss wondered if Harry had been smoking more today in anticipation of his return to work. He would rather just get out and get *to* that work – away from this office and Harry's questions – but he didn't want to offend his friend and boss, since he'd been really accommodating over the past couple of weeks. "Uh, yeah – thanks mate. You've been really accommodating, and I can't say thanks enough, but I'm done sitting around the house looking at the empty walls and thinking about her." Breylin coughed and shifted uncomfortably. "Thanks for the clothes, too."

"No problem," he said with a dismissive wave that trailed smoke from his cigarette as he did it. "I've got another box in the back of my lift. You look like you've lost a couple of pounds, but they'll do well enough. Did the housing people give you any crap about the house, or did you get everything squared away?"

"Nah, they were fine. I just had to fill out a shitload of paperwork. They actually seemed relieved that I was willing to just take the place next door – they didn't have to arrange anything, I guess. They weren't even going to send anyone out there to look at... the house."

"Ah. What about the simulant registry?"

"It was another paper drill, but I got through it quicker. The people over there couldn't've cared less about the ones I'd lost, as long as the paperwork for the replacement was filled out to their liking."

Harry hedged, but he went on quietly. "Did you send something to Riss' parents?"

He nodded. "Yeah. I haven't heard back yet, and I don't guess I will. I'm sure they still blame me for the accident. The first one, I mean, and hell, they'll probably blame me for this one, too." He shook his head. "Oh well, fuck 'em."

"Wow. They've lost a daughter, Joss. You might go easy."

"What? Listen, I loved Riss, but she had issues that went way back. If they'd done their jobs, things might've been different."

"Harsh, man."

"Cry me a river, Harry" said with a shrug. "How about we change the subject?"

"Ooo-kay," he said, and decided not to dig any deeper. "Listen, Sirvon and I wish you'd come to stay with us for a while. You still can, if you want."

"Uh... thanks, man – I know you mean it, but to be honest, I just don't really want to be around anyone yet." He smiled at Harry then looked away. "I just don't want to have to pretend I'm fine. Let me take the crew out by myself and get the work done. It will give me something to focus on besides... everything else."

"Well, I guess. If that's what you want..."

"Yep, that's what I need. I want to get back out there."

"Okay. Did you say you want to do it by yourself? I thought you said you didn't like being around the simulants."

"I *don't* like the *gabachos*," he said emphatically with narrowed eyes. "And I don't care what they think of me. But around them I don't have to paste a smile on my face. It might be a good thing too; we can just dispense with the bullshit of seeming to care about each other and focus on getting the work done."

Given the huge stress of losing his wife, the changes in Joss' personality were understandable, but Harry was still troubled; occasionally a tight darkness would creep into his eyes, but then it would pass. As he sat now, he wondered if he'd actually seen it. "It's probably nothing," he muttered under his breath.

"Huh?" said Joss with a puzzled look on his face.

A sharp, hot sensation broke through his distraction, and when he looked down, he found that the cigarette he'd been smoking had burned down close to his fingertips. "Damn," he said as he ground the butt out in a nearly overflowing ashtray.

He shook his hand as he looked up at Joss. "Sorry, I was distracted for a moment there. Take the crew out if you want, Joss."

He started to move, but Harry held his hand up, stalling him. "Hey, would you do me a favor though?"

He looked back at his boss. "What do you need?" he said with impatience.

"Would you have dinner with us? Or maybe you and I could go hit a bar. Whatever – I think you need to spend some time around people. It isn't good for you to be up at Amity all by yourself with no one but the ghosts of the past to keep you company."

"No promises, but I can probably come to dinner – just say

when. I guess I could use a good meal." He thought for a moment, then stood straighter as he continued. "And you're right, I could use the company. Hopefully I'll get a *gabacha* or two to keep me company soon."

There was that damn slur again, the friction of it grating on Harry like course sandpaper. He grimaced, but he let it slide; the way Joss had been flexing his hands into fists as he'd spoken was an obvious sign of unspent energy and unresolved issues, but Harry doubted he was even aware of what his hands were doing. Still, he wasn't getting a sense of where the tension was coming from. Unsure if it was a good idea or not, he decided to probe him further. "Didn't you tell me you've always had twin simulants?"

"We've – I've – had a pair of twins for years, since I left the Marines. I was hoping I could get a different model this time, but no such luck – story of my life, though. Still, it's something to look forward to, right?" He dismissively waved his hand in front of his face. "I gotta go, Harry – I'll talk to you later. How do you *breathe* in here?"

"Later," Harry said to his retreating back, but then something offbeat struck him about what he'd been saying. There was a conflict somewhere in there, but Harry couldn't pin it down. *What's going on with him? Maybe it's time to get him in front of the company shrink...*

—ʌ=ᴠ—

After work on Friday, Joss got cleaned up in the locker room and put on a set of new clothes that he had gotten in the city. He still didn't have a whole lot of personal things, but he didn't want to show up to dinner in Harry's clothes. He hated handing over the money, but he'd be damned if he'd give Sirvon a reason to feel sorry for him.

Having met her only one time at work when she had stopped by to bring Harry his dinner, Joss felt a little strange. He wasn't sure why, but he got a strange vibe from her that time. It was eating at him a little as he followed Harry to his apartment in his own lift, and when they got there, Harry picked up on the way he was feeling.

"Sirvon, Joss." He waved his hands back and forth between them and tried to keep the mood easy. "You guys remember each other, right?"

"Sure. How are you?" She stuck her hand out to him, and Joss took it.

"I'm really good, Sirvon. Thanks for having me."

"I hope you're hungry and you like pasta." She turned to her husband. "You," she said sternly. "Loose that cigarette, or you get nothing to eat."

"You and Amber always make too much, babe." He opened the front door and threw the butt outside. "If you don't feed me you'll feel awful for wasting it and starving me."

"Don't test the theory, husband," she said in a quirky accent he couldn't place. She was hiding a small smile as she turned from him, but he turned to Joss and said, "you saw that too, right?"

"Who's Amber?" Joss asked.

Harry spoke up. "She's our daughter. Aaron is our son. Amber does most of the cooking." He lowered his voice. "Are you okay around kids?"

Joss thought about the kids he and Riss had had – Maré and Luna – and unpleasant memories flooded back. It was too late to back out of dinner, so he swallowed the uncomfortable lump in the back of his throat and spluttered out, "ah, no. It's ah, it's fine."

Over dinner, Harry kept trying to bridge the silences that Joss would lapse into. "So, how was it out in the region with the simulants this week?"

"Mmm..." he said around a mouthful of food. "The *gabachos* don't give me any trouble."

Sirvon flinched, and Aaron sat up stiffly. Amber seemed to be pointedly ignoring the conversation around the table.

"Uh, but how did you feel, being around them?"

"Me? I felt fine. Never better."

Harry had been hoping Joss would express some reluctance or difficulty out there. If he had, he would have started going back out there with them. As it was, he didn't want to push him on the point in front of Sirvon, but he knew that the work crews were saying that Breylin was starting to get pretty nasty towards them. He would have to keep an eye on his friend, and on his interactions.

Sirvon became quiet herself after that, and Harry knew he'd get an earful later in bed, if it took that long. He guessed he would probably get some tension from Aaron and Amber, too. *Holy shit, I need a smoke.* It wasn't to be, though. He sighed into his pasta and willed the night to be over. *And this was all my idea...*

—∧=∨—

Joss wasn't sure how or why, but somehow Sirvon and Harry had become uncomfortable. She kept shooting looks at Harry who was trying to stare at his food a little too intently. He replayed the short conversation in his head, but he couldn't see what went wrong. The silence was beginning to make him uneasy, too. It was time for an exit.

Joss finished his food quickly and sat back, thinking of what to say to get out of there without being rude.

Amber came in from the kitchen. It was amazing how much she looked like her mother. Looking at him, she clipped her words as she said, "Have you finished, Mr. Breylin?"

Staring at her, he said, "Ah, yes, thanks."

As she picked up his plate, she turned to her parents, and her tone softened as she spoke. "Mom? Dad? Can I get you anything else?"

Sirvon smiled at Amber. "I don't think so, dear. Please sit and finish your own meal." With a suggestion of an edge she said to Joss, "Are you sure you're done? We have some desert, if you can stay. I know it's getting late."

That was the opening Joss needed. "Actually, I think I should get going. I have a long drive home yet, and I need to get up early." He made a short laugh. "There's still a lot to do in the new house."

Harry wiped his mouth and tossed his napkin on the table. "Sure, we understand, Joss. Thanks for coming over."

Joss gulped down the last of his juice and stood up. "Well, thanks for dinner. I really needed it."

Harry got up with him, and walked him out. "See you Monday morning, right?"

"I wouldn't miss it, Harry. See you then."

The two men shook hands and Joss left, pulling up his collar against the infiltration of wind. As he was walking back to his lift he tried to figure out what went wrong over dinner.

Seventeen

On a Tuesday afternoon nearly eight weeks after the fire, Joss was notified that a shipment was due from orbit addressed to him — his new simulant. He had been nervously awaiting this, and now that the moment was here, he was full of anxious energy. He was glad that he would have a few hours to work through his feelings before picking her up back in Twilight; at least she would still be asleep.

After work, he took his beat up, old lift to the spaceport. On the way over, he had the strange sensation of Déjà vu, but he shrugged it off, having done this a couple of times before. Twice, in fact, though this time was a little different, since he was only retrieving one of the twins. He shrugged it off, chalking it up to pent up stress and shot nerves, broken sleep and easy but unhealthy meals. *On the plus side*, he reasoned, *at least I didn't pick up Harry's habit of smoking*. Just thinking of it instantly made him regret the distance that had crept into their relationship.

The dock foreman's name was Jones, according to the name plate picked out in red stitching on the blouse of his uniform. "Can I see your credentials and your invoice, please?" he said. His hair had become more salt and pepper since the last time Breylin had seen him.

"Here," he said as he handed everything over.

When Jones saw the holo on his ID, he said, "You look familiar. Have you picked up cargo here before?"

"A couple of times. Twin simulants usually, but just one today."

"I thought so," he said with a grin as he held up the ID so he could see it and him at the same time. "You've gotten older since this holo was taken!"

Gesturing at the top of Jones' head, Breylin said, "we all do."

"Yeah, I know it. And now that you mention it, I remember thinking how odd twin simulants were... Didn't know they came that way."

"I guess." he said noncommittally. "We – I" he corrected himself, "picked them because they were cheaper. Uh, is everything in order?"

He frowned. "Oh, sorry – I get talking." He thumbed at the androids standing idly nearby. "Not many people around here."

He compared Breylin's ID to his invoice and handed them back, then scanned down his shipping manifest and found the right container markers. "You," he pointed at one of the androids. "Find shipment 456.34 BCH and load it into this man's lift."

The android shuffled off toward the various stacks of odd sized boxes and containers, tubes and shrink-wrapped pallets. *How does anyone find anything in that immense pile?*

"Thanks."

"Don't mention it. Good luck with the simulant," he said with a wave over his shoulder as he returned to his cluttered desk.

"Oh, I think it will be fine," Breylin said in a quiet voice that belied his anxiety, but he doubted Jones caught it.

After Maré's shipping pod was loaded into the back of his lift, he took off at a leisurely pace towards home, arriving just before nine. The clouds had been steadily clearing, and as he was climbing out of the lift, the clouds parted almost completely, allowing him the rare, full view of the sunset. Instantly, he thought of Larissa, sitting by the window and staring out, and grief took a hold on his chest. *I miss you, my queen...*

When he finally pulled himself out of thoughts of the past, his hair was a mess from the wind and he was bone weary. The sun sat in exactly the same place. Not wanting to deal with Maré – or anything else – he pulled the pod out and clumsily stuffed it in the back of the lift port. Just having his hands on the huge, coffin-like container made him uneasy. Once he was done, he wearily trudged into the house.

Without turning on the lights, he dropped down onto the couch still in his dirty clothes, hungry and tired, drew his knees up and shut his eyes. As he opened himself to the embrace of sleep, he let his past and future recede. The weekend would be more than soon enough to deal with what needed to be done.

Knowing that Maré lay sleeping in the lift port made the rest of the week progress by millimeters, particularly since he did more thrashing than sleeping at night. Breylin wasn't sure why, but he was almost afraid to face her. Every time he allowed himself to think of their next meeting, he felt as if something was lurking unseen outside of his field of vision – something sinister. Each time it happened he forced himself to let it go, but the strong desire to avoid the situation inevitably returned.

In the intervening weeks since the fire, Joss had replayed the scene of the final moments of his family, how he had lost everything in a single afternoon, and how he had then killed Luna with cold rage and Maré with hot, angry hatred. It seemed as if those events had happened to someone else, that he had been merely a ghostly witness. A couple of times the comforting fantasy almost seemed real, but then he would remember the sight of the burned husk that used to be Riss, and the anger would flash into his mind like a white hot bar of steel left to carbonize in a forge.

It seemed like that had gotten better. Though he did his best to avoid thinking about his losses, he was able to with a certain amount of detachment, as long as he didn't try to swallow the whole thing at once. He hadn't yet been able to shake off the anger, but at least now he kept it in a cage of thick iron bars with formidable welds and banding.

As he sat thinking in the driver's seat of the cargo lorry that Friday afternoon, one of the *gabachos* approached and startled him.

When his heart stopped racing, he said, "what do you want?"

"Ridder, Sir. We're having difficulty getting the bit pipe to shake loose."

"So? Do I need to stand over top of the lot of you bastards, or do you know what to do?" he spat.

"Of course, sir, we know what to do, but it's getting late in the day. We don't think we'll be able to finish before the end of the shift. I thought I should tell you as soon as I..." Ridder's words died on his tongue as he watched Breylin's eyes darken with animosity.

He spoke, not bothering to disguise the heat in his voice. "You get your lazy ass back there and finish your work yourself, or I'll join you and provide whatever motivation you require."

Ridder flinched. "Yes, sir..."

Ninety minutes later, the pipe still wasn't completely dislodged, and Breylin was fuming.

He punched up the dispatcher back at base camp on comms. After he connected, the woman asked impatiently if they were nearly done for the day.

"Nearly, but this lousy crew is taking its time!" He paused to bring his tone down a notch. "I'll be another hour or two," he said more reasonably.

"Leave it go until Monday, will ya? You're over an hour away and I'd like to get home."

"Let me see if I can wrap things up quickly, okay?"

"Fine, do what you have to do, but make it quick please."

"Okay, Janice." After he stowed the mike, he walked out to the crew, certain that he could get their asses moving. They just needed to be appropriately inspired.

—∧=∨—

They pulled in back at base three hours late. As the *gabachos* carried one of their number to the infirmary, Harry came out from the offices, slowing as he passed the simulants laboring to get inside.

"Joss... can you tell me what the hell is going on? Where have you been? And what happened to that worker?"

"Yeah, well..." He swallowed. "He was giving me a lot of non-sense about getting the work done and –"

"And what?!" Harry said, struggling to light a smoke with a shaking hand. "You beat him half to death?!"

Breylin hung his head. "Look, Harry, I was just trying to finish... I may have let it get a little out of hand."

"What, are you kidding me?" he said. "Get the hell out of here, Breylin. When you show up to work on Monday you had better hope Ridder is able to work – otherwise, *your* ass is going to do his work!" Harry paused to let his breath out slow and suck in another lungful of smoke before continuing. "Alright, look. Joss, as your friend, this isn't healthy. You have to let this anger towards them go, or it will destroy you."

Joss' anger flared. *I can't believe my ears!* "What? Until you've been there yourself, you don't know the first thing about my anger! You can kiss my ass!"

"We're done here, Joss," he said, exhaling smoke. "Go home and get some rest."

He started to reply, and Harry held up his hand. "Let it go, Breylin, before anything else gets out of hand."

Fuming, Joss stomped off for his lift at the edge of the motor pool.

—∧=∨—

Back at home, Joss saw Maré's container as he passed it on the way into the house, and it was enough to make him feel apprehensive. He knew his mood was nowhere near where it needed to be to bring her out. *After the week I've had, tomorrow might be too soon. I'll just have to see... But I'm starting to look forward to our reunion, Maré.* He had the uncomfortable feeling he was lying to himself, at least a little, as he retreated from it with each step towards the door. Leaving her in the dark, he hastened his steps and went inside to get cleaned up and something to eat.

It was nearly midnight when he had finished bringing the work-week to a close, but Joss was in a much better mood, so much so that he decided to break open a bottle of wine he had gotten some time ago. He sat down, cracked open the top and took a long swallow.

By the time he shook the last black drops of it into his mouth, he was pleasantly drunk. Staggering into the bedroom, he laid down and was out before he could even manage to pull the sheet over himself or draw the shutters closed.

The next morning, Joss woke up with a terrific pounding some-where behind his forehead, made worse by trying to open his eyes in the sunlight streaming in the front window. Stumbling his way into the bathroom, he relieved himself, then rummaged around in the cabinets looking for some pain killers. When he located a blister pack that was still intact, he tore three wafers out, stuck them in his mouth, then leaned over and drank from the faucet. The water tasted flat, but he didn't care as long as it got the tablets past the cotton in his mouth and down his throat.

He dropped his clothes on the floor in the bathroom, stepped over them and into the shower. At first he let the water run so hot that it created billows of steam and reddened his skin, but he needed to wake up, so he tweaked it until it was nearly cold. Since he was the only one drawing on the cistern under the house, it was virtually always full, so he let it run over him much longer than usual. When the pain in his head eased off, he finished, got dressed and combed his hair. Now it was time to get the day started, and that meant dealing with Maré. No matter how he felt, there was no sense in delaying the inevitable. He gathered the few things he would need.

In the back of the lift port, Breylin checked her vitals, then looked through the tiny port at her sleeping face, studying her seemingly bloodless features – pert nose, mousy hair, delicate mouth and lashes. He could just make out her earlobes poking out under her hair. *Such a placid girl... If you didn't know any better, you might mistake her for a real person – though dead...*

He opened the packet of documents affixed to the side of the coffin-like container. The top page was the title to her, the second was the mandatory lifetime registration. There were several bits of marketing enclosed, a certificate of authenticity, blah-blah-blah, all of which he dropped on the floor. Finally he came to her bill of sale disclosure statement, the only thing in the whole wad of papers with specifics pertaining to her. From it, he read that she had been woken up a couple of months earlier than normal, and that had left her a little undeveloped physically. Peering at her again through the window, he could now see a trace of youth in her features that only a just a couple of minutes earlier he'd identified as delicate.

Reading further down, the document said that she didn't have the memories that were always given to her bloodline. Evidently there had been some extenuating circumstances that had caused them to pull her early. Idly, he wondered what those details were, but he couldn't say that it really matter to him one way or another. Her memory loss was hardly important – as long as she did as she was told.

He also saw that after being woken up they had kept her at the facility where they grew her kind. *I wonder what she did during that period...* He was also curious if it would affect her personality, or if she would act like the others they'd had. He couldn't say if he hoped she'd still be the same or changed.

Breylin paused with his fingers over the controls, and the seconds ticked by.

Finally, he grinned at his own foolishness, and he punched up the sequence to wake her. When the cover cracked open, he pushed and locked it up in place. Next, he withdrew her collar from his back pocket, put it around her neck, and calibrated it with the controller.

He stood looking down at her sleeping form, and he began to feel somewhat remote. Almost of its own volition, his hand moved, and he found himself brushing her cheek lightly with the backs of his fingers. Chilly. Satin. *Alive again. How could she be alive?*

He shook his head to clear the vision, bringing himself back to the present. Using the same hand he had to touch Maré's face, he massaged his brow. When he pulled it away, he was surprised to find that his fingers were damp with sweat. So were his armpits.

A twitch ran through Maré, and it contagiously echoed in him. It seemed as if she were lying in a coffin, and he knew he had to get her out of there.

Scooping his arms under her shoulders, he flexed and hauled her torso upright. As he brought her close, her head rolled back and she moaned softly, the muscles in her neck working. Rushing, he thrust one arm under her legs and picked her up. He had to juggle her a bit to get the door, but he managed it. He maneuvered her inside, kicked the door shut and laid her down on the sofa.

She cracked her eyes half open and said, "What...?" She swallowed, then said, "Where am I...?"

"You're still pretty out of it, Maré. Just relax, and I'll get you something to drink." He stepped into the kitchen and began filling a tumbler from the tap. Coming back into the living room, he found her with her eyes open. She watched him with a drowsy, unreadable expression as he came closer.

Sitting next to her legs he said, "How are you feeling?"

Immediately, she drew her knees up to her chest, groaning with the sudden reaction.

"Breylin," he said. "My name is Breylin. You can call me Sir, if you prefer."

She stared at him blankly.

"Maré, it's okay. This is your home now."

"I... was somewhere else," she rasped. Her head swam with disorientation in these new, sudden surroundings.

"And now you're here with me. Would you like some water?"

She nodded yes, and he handed her the tumbler. She pinched her lips at the taste after a couple of sips.

"I'm afraid the water here is reprocessed. It rains often enough, but the mineral contaminants have to be removed before it's safe to drink."

She took a few gulps of the stale water. "Where is here?" she said.

"You're on Zarmina. This is one of the settlements near Twilight, the planet's only city."

She took another swallow and reached to set the cup down on the table. "Who are you?" she probed timidly.

"I'm Breylin. I own this place..." His voice dropped to a whisper. "And you, as well Maré."

Her eyes went wide as tears started to brim.

"Oh, don't worry, dear. I'll be here to help you through the difficult times."

Eighteen

After he had administered her hormone treatments, Doctor Almeida had 370 Bravo shipped out to Zarmina fairly directly. With an existing order to fulfill, that was the easy part. The difficult part was trying to figure out what to do with 183 Alpha.

He had been a rising star among the young biogeneticists, but in the middle of Almeida's career, he had made a serious misstep. He had introduced a brand new experimental mitosis agent of his own design, in the hopes that it could further reduce the time of crop maturation down to two thirds, and perhaps as little as one half. Had he been successful, he could have revolutionized simulant production and certainly propelled his company far ahead of its competitors. The hard profit margin dollars were enough to convince senior management to allow him to put his theories to a serious test, and was given control of one bloodline of simulants grown for their analytical powers. None of that had mattered to Almeida; he was only indulging his near obsession with efficiency. He would squeeze each bottleneck in the process into something better-faster-stronger, until a new bottleneck appeared. When it did, his focus would shift, and the squeezing began anew. He was fully driven, and it seemed to be going according to his plan.

In his rush to push the limits of his ideas however, he had not fully vetted one of the steps invented by a colleague as an exercise in thought. As a result, most of the bloodline he controlled had developed at substantially faster rates – far exceeding his own expectations – but the process that arrested the accelerated mitosis had failed, causing them to continue to experience accelerated growth after maturation pod extraction. The few that had made it that far had died from several flavors of previously unseen cancer. In short, the entire crop was ruined, which was bad enough, but it also created a shortage of simulants needed for planned sales. Into that vacuum their competitors had rushed, deepening the failure of the project. The colossal blunder sent his career into a scorching freefall; all of Almeida's future experimentation had been cancelled, and he been relegated to managing the relatively unimpressive crop of simulant pairs. He'd been there ever since, decades, and in the interim new biogeneticists had perfected the technique. *His* technique, but because he had developed it under the auspices of the company, they owned the intellectual property rights, effectively rendering his desires irrelevant. It had been a spectacular failure for all concerned, but it was his own marginalization that consumed him and turned his thoughts inward.

His corrosive attitude toward his superiors had helped to fuel his professional setbacks, but he didn't give a damn about that – or if he did, the collective intelligence of mankind had yet to design a device capable of quantifying something so profoundly small. The bitter twist that had kept him awake at night, however, was knowing that he'd never be afforded the opportunity to prove them all wrong. He *knew* he'd never recover, and *that* effectively made him indifferent to everything else, including bioengineering. He just didn't care anymore. As he grew colder and withdrew further from everyone, his wife left him and his children stopped returning his emaciated attempts at contact. Eventually, even his bitterness left him, and all that had remained afterward was a husk of a man and the minutiae of the work assigned to him. That, and whatever little diversions crossed Almeida's path.

Some of *those* really did pick up his spirits.

85 Alpha had made a fair recovery in the months that had passed since 370 had nearly killed her. She was now awake, and though she was largely responsive, she would never have the same cognitive abilities. *Too bad, she was a good worker,* he thought with a smirk. *And she never failed to add interesting dynamics.*

Certainly her availability meant that he had diversions aplenty to keep his interest now. He would have to deal with 183, but at the moment, he was trying to decide what to do with 85. *I wonder what would happen if I over-steered her emotions in different directions? That might be fascinating.* It was an idea with possibilities. *Maybe I could bring a male into the mix. An aggressive one would really push her buttons. Force them together and ramp up their libido, then start pitting them against each other.* That had even better possibilities.

But... a great idea just wouldn't crystalize. *Ah, I'll keep her around a while longer; something'll come up.* He dropped the stylus he had been chewing on and sighed. He pulled out a cigar, sucked hot butane fumes through it, and decided to let 85's fate go for now. Business before pleasure, as they say, but before he could put any thought into what to do with her, a screaming tickle caught in his throat and sent him into a spasm of coughing. He could feel his face heating up and turning purple, and it caused so much pressure in his ears and temples that he was afraid he'd rupture something. Ignoring the red flecks he was expelling onto the rubbish and reports that covered his desk, he scrambled for the hypo-spray in his coat, pulled it out and jammed it into what little meat he had in his thigh. He depressed the actuator once, twice, three times in rapid succession, and prayed to the god he'd never believed in that he wouldn't keel over dead before the suppressants did their mean work. He wound down, ceased, then decided to break his own rule about mixing the powerful drug with which he'd dosed himself and his beloved scotch. He pulled out the bottle from one of the locked drawers and unscrewed its cap. Instantly he smelled its siren aroma, and nearly gave in to the urge to take a slug directly from it. Instead, he poured two fingers into the tumbler and quaffed it all in one go. He nearly put the bottle back, but he was feeling pretty mellow and he decided a bit more would hurt. He poured a finger and a half, looked at it, then ran it up to the full two fingers. He licked the threads, capped the bottle and put it away.

Swirling the glass, he decided to turn to the problem of what to do with 183. Reviewing the notes on the different divisions he had contacted in trying to find a home for her would be useless; instead, he went to the sheaf that contained the responses themselves. It was pretty unlikely, but he wanted to make sure he hadn't missed some vital clue, and he began to glean.

Because she was more than a year old, the brokers over at organ farm management were only willing to bid a value of ten percent standard *at consignment*, making it hardly worth the paperwork. Almeida hadn't really expected much better, so the offer to them was only cursory, anyway. At ten percent, he was better off losing her in the shuffle of paperwork and having her clean his office.

Psyche Services was *vaguely* interested, but they had capped their offer at a measly fifteen percent. The shrinks could always use new lab rats, but what they really wanted were simulants without implanted memories – they were currently offering 103% market value – so they had cut their offers for everything else. If only he had known that before shipping 370 out; he would have sent her to them and 183 to Zarmina, killing two birds with one stone and wrapping up the whole damn mess with a tiny profit as a bow. As he reviewed the files, he mentally kicked himself again at the missed opportunity. *Maybe a sale from the current crop would fall through.* It would still be a few months before he'd be able to pull a pair out of maturation, but the thought managed to give him a small glimmer of hope.

Moving past the outright rejection letter from Entertainment Services, he pulled up the offer from Warfare Research and Development. Theirs was the strangest of all, since they didn't make a formal submission, only a suggestion that they might be willing to take the simulant, since she was in hyper-sleep. Almost as an afterthought, they requested contact if a large supply of *dead* simulants became available. *Curious. What good are* dead *simulants?*

There were other divisions, of course – Sanitation, Mining Services, Animal Care… but none of them had ever held any promise before. They just weren't as well funded as the bigger divisions.

None of these options are good, he thought in frustration. *It's time to try something novel. But what?*

He decided to let his mind wander loose around the edges of the problem. *What makes a profit?* Obviously, the most direct route to a profit was sales. *How can I sell a damaged simulant with ten percent of its lifespan already consumed?* That was the brick wall, right there: you can't. No one wants a slightly used, slightly damaged simulant.

But wait, he realized. *That dirt farmer on Zarmina wanted a pair. And I had negotiated it to one at full price.* Apparently, what Almeida needed was someone else like that guy. Again, there was that brick wall.

Then, an idea occurred to him. *What if I just sent her to Zarmina with an invoice? I could put in a letter explaining that there had been a mishap and she had gone to the wrong place. The worst that could happen is the guy won't pay, and if that happens, so what?*

It had been about seven months since he'd delivered 370, making the story ridiculously thin. The buyer would have to be an idiot to swallow it, but he decided he had nothing to lose. It was time to roll the dice.

"LabSys? Access the resolution details of previous resident 370 Bravo."

"Acknowledged, Doctor."

"Prepare current resident 183 Alpha for shipment to the billed owner of 370 Bravo and mark the case as resolved."

"Doctor, there are no active requests from that entity."

"On my authority, LabSys. Do it anyway."

"Acknowledged, Doctor."

He was already feeling pretty good, but having settled on a course of action regarding 183 made him feel *positively capital,* so much so that he decided to see what fun he could conjure for himself with 85. *Perhaps a chemical dependency...*

Nineteen

Difficult times? What does he mean by that? Still groggy, Maré wasn't sure if she was getting what Breylin was saying. Maybe he said something important and she missed it. Still, the way he spoke of owning her was unnerving. *Luna... I need you, Chroma...* But Luna wasn't here. The lonely thought of her Chroma being gone left her hollow, and tears welled up in her eyes. "How long was I unconscious?"

"Well, I'm not exactly sure, but I'd guess you could have been asleep for about two months." He looked at her expectantly. "Are you hungry, Maré? You should eat something after a long hyper-sleep. I haven't eaten yet today myself." He raised his eyebrows in question. "If I make us both something, will you join me?" His cheeks rose up as his smile curved warmly.

Maré was still waking up, but her head was starting to clear. What she needed was some time until she understood what was going on and adjust to a new life. "Uh, yes. I should eat something."

He got up and was moving toward the kitchen, but he paused and turned around. "Please," he said. The smile disappeared beneath slack muscles as he looked at from under a lowered brow.

She thought she must have missed something again. "I'm sorry...?" She tossed her head in an effort to knock more of the cobwebs loose. "I'm not sure if I'm getting everything yet."

"*Please*," he said again. "I'm sure you meant to say please, right Maré?"

Understanding dawned. "Yes, I'm sorry. Please."

A change rippled through him and he smiled again. "Of course! I know you're just coming around. I should give you some time to adjust." He winked at her. "I'll be back in a few minutes." When he moved into the kitchen, Maré could see him opening a cabinet and taking out a few packets and plates. He started to hum softly to himself.

It was all too much. She laid her head down on her knees and tried to slowly think through the situation, but all she could think of was *Luna*. A sob escaped her chest, and she hugged herself and cried.

"Shhh... It's okay, honey." Breylin had sidled back into the room and sat next to her on the couch before she'd noticed. He tried to put his arms around her, but something about him was unsettling, and she jerked away from him. He dropped his arms and waited for her to settle. "Listen," he said quietly. "We'll get some food in you, I'll explain how things work around here... everything is going to be fine. You'll *see*."

"I... I'm sorry. My Chroma −"

"Luna, yes. She used to live here, too. I remember her very well... and I remember how the two of you were together."

It took a minute to sink in, but she realized that he must have meant others from her bloodline. "I mean *my* Chroma. Look." She sighed heavily and continued. "I'm really tired, Breylin."

He held up his index finger. "*Mr.* Breylin."

"Mr. Breylin, right. May I go lay down for a little while, Sir? I feel like I need to rest and get used to this before I take on any more."

He sat up straight and stabbed at her with his gaze, and right away she knew what was strange about him − his eyes; they were a cool blue, and liquid, and wild with too many emotions beneath the surface. As she looked at him she had the feeling that something dangerous was staring back at her through those eyes. She had to look away, and after a moment he spoke firmly. "I'm making food, Maré. I want you to eat."

"Please, Mr. Breylin, I'm not doing so well," she pleaded, hoping he'd be reasonable if she conveyed her distress. Her stomach was starting to knot.

He got to his feet. When he spoke, his tone stropped her with its edge. "We're done with this discussion. I've made food. You will eat it, Maré."

She started to cry as her insides began to roll, sweat popped out of every pore and her mouth filled with saliva. She got up as fast as she could and nearly toppled over, but thankfully her rubbery legs held. She was seconds from vomiting. "Where's the bathroom?" she said, and clamped a hand over her mouth.

Breylin pointed toward his bedroom, and she unsteadily made her way as quick as she could by running her hands along the walls. Seconds later, Maré was noisily retching up the water she had drunk. When the heaves stopped, she rested her head on the rim of the white, plastic toilet and tried to slow down the pace she was gasping for breath. She wiped her mouth with some toilet paper, tossed it in and flushed. Then she noticed that he was standing in the doorway watching her with his arms folded.

"That was quite a show. All finished now?"

What does he want from me? she thought. "I'm sorry, Mr. Breylin," she said as she forced herself to stand. "I feel dizzy... Can you show me where I can lay down, please?" she said as she steadied herself by holding onto the edge of the sink.

"You seem to have difficulty understanding. I said you were going to be eating the food I've prepared."

Baffled, Maré looked at the toilet, then back at him. *He can't be serious!* The taste of bile was thick in her mouth, and she couldn't possibly think of eating now.

He took her by the arm. "Let's go." With that, he steered her back out to the kitchen. Stopping abruptly by the table, he said, "Sit down. *Now.*"

Afraid to disobey him, Maré sat down. He pushed a couple of buttons on one of the appliances. There were a few tones and the machine whirred to life. Seconds later, he opened its front panel and withdrew a couple of plates. He put one down in front of her, then at the chair across the table. Next he dug out forks, handed her one, and then sat down. He dug in with gusto, but after a few swallows, he put the utensil down.

"Pick up the fork, Maré. If I have to feed you, we're going to have a bad day."

She did as she was told, scooped up some of the lumpy, beige goo and put it in her mouth. Thankfully, it was nearly tasteless – or maybe it only seemed tasteless compared to bile. She swallowed carefully, then repeated the process until the plate was nearly clean. Her stomach was still doing backflips, but she compartmentalized it away, along with the loss of Luna. There was nothing to do about either of those things now. *Stars, where am I?*

Breylin paused between sips of whatever he was drinking when he saw that she was done. "Very good, dear. Don't you feel better now?"

No – This is worse than Almeida! "Yes Sir... mostly."

"Would you still like to go lay down?" he said sympathetically.

Hope dawned. "May I, Sir?"

Standing up, he smiled and said, "sure. I'll just show you where the cleaning supplies are first."

"I don't understand, Mr. Breylin," she said as her hope began to falter.

"Well," he said while spreading his hands. "You puked in the toilet, and now it needs to be cleaned. You don't expect me to use it like that, do you?"

Holding onto the back of her chair for balance, she looked at him and tried to keep up with the pace at which he changed gears.

"*Do you?*" he said, piercing her with his aggressive eyes and raising his voice. The edge in his words was growing keener.

Compartmentalizing again, she kept her eyes down and bit back the tears. "Uh... no, of course not."

"Better," he said amiably. "You'll get the hang of this, Maré. I suppose this could be the first thing you need to keep in mind – everything around here needs to stay very clean. If you make a mess and don't clean it up, I'll become quite cross."

"I think I understand, Sir."

"Do you?" He patted her shoulder. "I hope so, Maré." He strode from the room, and she followed. She just wanted to catch her breath and come to terms with Luna being gone, but she would have to play his game first.

Breylin supervised while she cleaned the commode. Except for on old ring of mineral deposits around the edge of the water the hard material gleamed, but it looked the same to her afterwards. She didn't care, though - it had been something to just get through. "All done, Sir," she said as she dragged the back of her forearm over her face and climbed to her feet. She stood there on her treacherous legs looking at him through a few strands of sweat-darkened hair that had fallen across her eyes, though she couldn't summon the care to do anything about them.

"This appears to be acceptable, Maré."

"Thank you, Sir," she said as she stood there waiting, his eyes drilling into her, but she couldn't imagine what was making him tense.

It filled the air though, as he looked back at her from where he stood by the sink. "Well?"

"May I *please* go lay down, Mr. Breylin? I can barely stand."

"Your muscles can stand you up just fine, my dear. You tell them what to do, and they obey. You have to want it to happen though."

"I..." She took a couple of calming breaths. "Sir, I did what I was told to do."

"But what about the rest?"

"The rest, Sir?"

Breylin shook his head as he withdrew the controller and thumbed a few buttons. Maré felt her muscles lock up and she went as rigid as a post. It was too much for her. The room started to spin at crazy angles and she felt her cheeks flush. Every pore on her body threw itself open again and sweat poured out.

"See, dear? Your muscles just needed to be told what to do, and they obey."

He grabbed her by the arms and dragged her roughly from the bathroom, through the bedroom and into the living room, smacking her taut frame against furniture and the doorways along the way. He shoved her, the room yawed out of alignment and the floor rushed up to meet her as she toppled over. The acrid taste of copper was in her mouth, and darkness crept inward from the edges of her vision until black ink covered everything.

A grunt escaped her lips as pain seared her back, and her eyes banged open.

Breylin grabbed her by her neck and pulled her up enough to see her eyes. "Ah, there you are, dear." He let her thump back down to the hard plastic floor. "You're going to have quite a bruise on your cheek from where you fell on it. One of your front teeth seems to be a little loose too, but it should be fine in a few days. Assuming nothing else happens, that is. I'm getting the feeling you're going to require a lot of retraining. Time will tell."

She could move now, and her back felt as if it was laced with fire. Disoriented and crying, she slowly got her hands under her. When she started to push up, her tunic fell away from her in tatters. *He must have torn it down the back*, she thought thickly. *Why the hell would he do that?* She made a grab for it to cover herself, and out of the corner of her eye she saw a quick movement. She heard a swishing sound, and another sharp, thin line of fire stretched across her back, and instantly she went prone again as the shock of it made her arms give out. "I didn't tell you to get up, Maré," he said so quietly that she almost missed it, hidden by the blinding pain that filled the world.

"Look up, dear. Do you see this?" She forced herself to lift her chin, and he showed her a slender piece of tubing in his hands, about a meter long, white and narrowly ridged. He flexed its semi-stiff length into a curve, straightened it, and then curved it again. When she saw it, and the mad gleam it produced in his eyes as he considered it, she became terrified. The urge to flee screamed its way through her synapses, but there was nowhere to go, and fear kept her rooted in place.

"We use tubing like this at work. It's flexible – as you can see – but it's quite strong. It has to be, because sometimes it has to endure some pretty intense pressures." He watched, with an almost fascinated look on his face, as he flexed it a few more times. "None of that is terribly relevant to its use here, Maré. No... I'm afraid this particular piece of tubing has a much more domestic use."

He looked down at her. "Let me explain. I could use your collar to punish you – I guess that's how most people handle their *gabachas*. And I'll use it sometimes as an aid... but this," he said as he held out the improvised lash, "this is what I will use to get your attention. Do I have your attention *now*, Maré?"

Through her dread she husked out an answer: "yes, Sir. Please Sir, don't hurt me anymore."

"Hurt you?" he said sounding almost offended. "I'm not hurting you, dear. I'm *teaching* you. There's a difference." A sadistic edge crept into his voice. "Trust me, I know how to hurt someone."

A fresh wave of panic flared in her skull and she cried, harder now. "Sir, I don't know what I did. Tell me and I'll never... do... it... again!" she wailed as she stared into the floor.

When her crying subdued, he touched her face with the end of the tube, and she flinched. He caressed her with it, back and forth, around her neck, and down her back. It caused fresh agony as it touched where he'd already welted her with it. She trembled, scared that he might bring the terrible thing down on her again.

"Maré, I told you that any time you make a mess, you must clean it up, didn't I?"

"Y-yes, Sir."

"And yet you insisted on laying down when you knew there

were dishes to do."

The dishes. "I'm sorry, Mr. Breylin! I'll go do them now if you let me!"

"No, Maré. You needed to lay down, so now you're going to lay down, *right there.*"

She laid there crying for a long time, but with only the dull torment of her thudding heartbeat to mark its passage she couldn't guess how long. Breylin stroked her gently, back and forth, with the lash the whole time. Eventually her eyes stopped leaking, and the only sensations she could perceive were terror and the agonizing trace of the tube's edge as it played lightly over her exposed skin. Her attention seemed hyper-focused on the pain each time it touched one of the welts. She didn't dare move or speak.

He stopped touching her, and for a few agonizing heartbeats she knew he would begin welting her with the tube, but he merely sat down. Time froze as she continued to lay there, but at last he spoke. "You may now go do the dishes, Maré, then come back when you are finished."

She got up and tried to hold the ruin he'd made of her clothing to her breasts, but he spat at her, "leave that. You can wear shirts again when you've earned them."

A few sobs escaped as she dropped it and went into the kitchen.

When she was done doing the few dishes, she returned to the living room and stood to the side of him with her arms crossed, covering her chest. She saw that he was staring out the window, evidently at the sunset.

He ignored her for a few minutes, then without looking in her direction he said, "Maré, come over here and kneel down."

She hated the thought of getting any closer – he still had the makeshift whip laying across his lap – but she knew she didn't have any choice. Wordlessly, she moved and went to her knees.

"Closer, Maré. Put your hands on my leg."

The tears fell as she moved in and did as she was told. The worst of it was not knowing what he would do next. Her mind invented all sorts of dreadful things – anything but what he did.

He leaned forward and put his arm around her, then spoke. "Look at that, dear," he said as he pointed out the window with his other hand. The fiery edge of the sun simmered above the edge of the horizon, radiating dust-soaked bars of sunlight in all directions. His hand moved lightly on her hair, and they sat like that together for some time in silence.

He sat back, but he kept stroking her hair. "Your mother used to sit and stare out like this," he said, sounding hollow and far away – and maybe crying. She couldn't look.

What the hell is he talking about, my mother? Why did he pun-ish me if he was going to become nice? Is he playing a game? Oh the Stars, she thought as she realized what must be happening. *He must have me confused with some other simulant!*

Breylin gave no indication if he noticed her internal struggle. "I miss you so much, Riss..." he whimpered.

The air thickened as she held her breath and wished she could get away from him. His arm around her, touching her hair, was revolting. Even so, she was surprised to find that she had a tiny pebble of pity for this wreck of a man living in his own hell.

A tremor went through him and he withdrew his hand. From the corner of her eye she could see that he was studying her. His scrutiny was as fiery upon her as the edge of the sun was on the

land. Eventually he spoke. "Take this, Maré," he said as he proffered the lash. When she made no move he grabbed her hands
and enclosed them tightly around the thin tube. She could feel
the texture of its ridges digging into her fingers and palms.

"Now that your work is done, I will show you your room." He
stood and took her by her elbows, bringing her to her feet. "Back
this way."

He guided her down the hall towards the back of the house,
stopping before a closed door at the end. He gestured above it
and said, "see that hook up there, dear?"

"Yes, Mr. Breylin," she said in a quiet breath.

"Put your lash up there, Maré, so that you walk under it whenever you go in or out of your room."

Timidly, she obeyed and reached up. As she balanced it in
place, its edges dipped into a frown, and for an instant she
thought maybe even the house was looking upon her with tight
disapproval.

"Don't *ever* touch it, Maré," he said leaning in so that his lips
were brushing the hair over her ear, "unless I *tell* you to get it. If
you do, I'll know, and then I'll break you with it."

She started to snivel in gibbering fear again as she tried to shy
away from him.

"You will do as you are told, won't you, Maré?"

She nodded her head, and his grip tightened on her arm. He
leaned in closer still and spoke softly in her ear. "Use your words,
dear. I want to make sure you understand."

"I understand, Sirrr," she slurred through her tears.

"Okay, then." With that, he opened the door to her room,

shoved her inside and slammed it behind her. As his heavy footfalls retreated she heard him say angrily, "get some rest. I'll be back for you in a few hours."

She crumpled onto the bed and sobbed without tears, as much for grief as for her own seemingly-unending plight.

Maré woke to Breylin shaking her by the shoulder.

"Get up Maré. I have something *special* for you."

Her head started to clear as she looked around and realized where she was – her room in Breylin's house. She didn't remember falling asleep, but she must have been deep under. She wanted to lay back down, but that wasn't going to be an option. She swung her feet down to the floor and stood.

"Come with me." He said as he turned from her and left the room.

She resisted for all of two seconds. She didn't want to follow him. She was lonely and tired, her muscles ached, and where he had whipped her earlier was yet dull agony. But not wanting to follow him had nothing to do with any of those things – or not much, anyway; what seized her thoughts was anger – at life, at going from one hell to another, at *him*. There had been pleasant moments since she'd left the maturation pod, quiet times with Luna, but she been controlled and tormented and used on Paradise. She was sure life would be every bit as difficult now, compounded by being bereft of Luna. Yes, coming out of sleep had been mindless and rough, but she now felt awake, and the resentment tingling her scalp was sharp.

Breylin was still receding from her room. Sighing in resignation, she laced her arms over her breasts, stood and followed him out. She willed herself not to look back at the lash above the door, but it was there, she could just feel it, and the knowing made the skin on her arms pebble.

He walked over to the door in the kitchen, turned to face her. When she stood directly before her he said, "Turn around."

Fearfully she obeyed.

He dropped a cloth around her face and knotted it in the back, scaring her near to panic.

He dug his fingers into the skin of her arm and said, "I will guide you. All you have to do is listen." With that, he opened the door and walked her outside into the teeth of the wind.

It was the first time Maré had ever not been inside a building or a facility. The sensation of the fast moving air across her skin was strange. It was gritty, though, and dust was beginning to coat her throat. The air smelled... fresh. Not recycled. *Cold. Strange.* But not being able to see such an open space made it a little unnerving, and though she knew there was nothing but sky above her, it still felt like the ponderous bulk of the roof of the world was weighing down on her. It was just enough to dull the edge of her fear for the moment.

She leaned into his grip as they walked for a couple minutes over uneven ground, but how long she couldn't be sure. It was hard to concentrate between the surreal sensations of the swiftly moving air that was pebbling her skin, the texture of the rocks she could feel through the thin soles of her shoes, and the bits of light that crept in around the edges of the rough cloth on her face. Eventually he stopped her and said, "two steps up."

Carefully, he navigated her up the steps. She began to notice a slight but sharp stink of burned plastic over the air currents. Faint though it was, it was still bitter... and wrong. Its tang cloyed at her tongue, her throat, and as she moved blindly at his guidance it began to creep beneath the blindfold and sting her eyes.

Walking a few more steps he stopped her and said, "here we are." When he took off the cloth, she saw that she was standing in a burned out building of some kind. It was wet, desolate and black, and seeing it made the acrid, plastic stink worse.

"What do you see at your feet, dear?"

She looked down. There were odd, blackened sticks lying around. They were mostly connected, like a strange tree... but then she noticed a burned, cracked sphere lying next to it. To her horror, she recognized them to be bones, charred remains. *A body! What has he done?!* She started to emit a panicky whine of terror as she backed up and looked away, but his grip on her arm tightened, arresting her retreat.

"No you don't, dammit. Look!"

She mashed her eyes shut and struggled to turn away from the grisly sight. "I don't want to see it, Mr. Breylin!"

He dragged her into himself and whispered dangerously in her ear. "Look, Maré, or I'll become angry."

She stared at the awful things and began to cry. "*Why* am I here, Mr. Breylin?" she whined.

He spoke into her ear again. "Those bits of bone used to be my wife. She died right here a couple of months ago. Death by fire is... a hard way to go."

"Please, may I turn away, sir?!"

"Sure," he said. "By all means. Let's go look at something else." He dragged her to a different part of the ruin and pointed. "See those bodies?"

Maré let the horrific sight wash over her as she started to go into shock. "Yes, Sir – I see them!" The wind began to dry her tears on her cheeks.

"Those two were the Maré and Luna that lived in your room before you did."

Maré started making a noise somewhere in her chest. She wanted to stop it but she couldn't.

"They didn't die in the same fire, Maré. I killed them afterwards with my bare hands."

Stark terror at what he had done was making her adrenal glands pump out their juices and her pulse race, but all she could do is stand there horrified.

"I wanted you to know what can happen, Maré. Death is always nearby."

A wave of dizziness made the world swivel as she fainted.

Twenty

Over the course of the next seven months, Maré spent most of her energy trying to anticipate and read Breylin's erratic moods and behave accordingly. Keeping track of the seemingly unending lists of what was *acceptable* and what was *unacceptable* was exhausting. On those times she got it right, he would almost dote on her lovingly. When he did, she was positive he had deluded himself into reliving pleasant memories of past pairs. Regardless, it didn't make a difference what he believed; whatever it was, it made him happy, and that meant he wasn't hurting her.

As she learned to slip into the role and encourage the memories, she found that it bizarrely made her happy too – a little, anyway. At first she thought that maybe she was living vicariously through her long dead chromanity, and there might have been an element of that, but the house was a long way from everything else on world, and mostly she lived for the periods of his affection; there was nothing and no one else. She wanted to hate him – she did hate him – yet she craved what tender warmth he would occasionally dole out. As terrible as he could be, he was the only other person in her world. She still felt a yawning loneliness, but he kept it from being complete.

Unfortunately, there were many *difficult* times, as well. During those times, Breylin was all too lucid and very much in the present. He was quite proficient at working her back and legs with the lash, but he would also make her go for days without clothing or force her to sleep on the floor. Sometimes he would roughly shave her head and then make her say degrading things to her own reflection in the bathroom mirror. On one dreadful occasion he had locked her in her hibernation pod and used her collar to fill her with terror.

He was almost entirely closed on the details of what had brought him to his current state, but when he would relive his memories he would occasionally give up some of the particulars. He spoke with great love for his beautiful wife, Riss. Their first Maré and Luna had been special to him and his wife, but there had been some sort of accident, and Riss had lost her legs. Evidently, he blamed the twins. It was a long time ago, as near as she could tell.

Their second set of twins had been present at a fire that killed her. She would never forget the night she learned that; it had started out pleasantly enough, but once he thought of the fire, Breylin had plummeted out of his delusion and beaten her with his fists so bad that she had trouble seeing through eyes swollen nearly shut the next day. Worst of all, he had viciously kicked her in the ribs a few times, and for a week every breath she took, every movement she made, drove needles of torture into her left side. The sensitivity didn't go away for weeks.

After that incident, he had also forbidden her to use words like I, Me or My. She could only speak in the third person, as if she was an object. At first it made her feel ashamed, but in time it became just another thing to get past.

She wondered why he would keep acquiring the same simulants when they were the source of so much pain in his life, especially since he often seemed to be shunning contact with her. The only thing she came up with was that having her nearby must be what keeps him connected to happier times.

No matter what else happened, she never stopped mourning for Luna, her chroma. When she would lay down to sleep, she would think about how they used to wash and dress each other. She got through Breylin's difficult times only by remembering how her scent made her feel, and the way her fingers leeched the tension out of her.

—∧=∨—

He let her feel the fear and his breath for thirty seconds. The silence was broken only by her near-silent crying and the wind that ached to shiver the house to synthetic splinters. This is it, her mind told her as she screwed her eyes shut tight. She knotted her hands together so taut her knuckles were as white as bone, but her mind was racing, terrified, whimpering. Any second now – the fists, kicking, pain, humiliation, the whip, something, something, SOMETHING, HE'S GOING TO –

Silence. Sixty seconds.

She used the last tendon of courage to look into his dead lucid eyes, losing sense of everything else but the pressure building between them.

Unexpectedly, he stood up and smiled. Gently patting her cheek he said, "I'm feeling generous, Maré. Let's forget this happened. After all, your birthday is only a month away. I'll have to come up with something special for it."

Terrified at the thought of his special surprises, Maré began to sob, and the pressure finally gave way. Her bladder muscles buckled, she urinated down her legs, and a small pool collected beneath her, warming her toes and arches. The rest of her froze with crushing fear.

Breylin took a step back and whispered, "now look at what you've done."

Maré sobbed hysterically. After a few seconds, Breylin realized that he was close to losing control, and he had to get out of there.

If that happened, he might beat her to a pulp again – or worse. Without picking up his lunch or processing the situation any further, he dashed to the lift, fired it up and took off to the south, leaving the door open.

On the ride south, he tried to examine his own conflicted feelings towards Maré. *Why did these situations keep happening? Why won't she just behave? And why can't I reign in my anger?* So many questions... When he came up with nothing again, he put it aside for later. It was time to put on his work face, in case he ran into Harry.

Ever since dinner months before, his relationship with his friend had been strained. He still didn't understand what had happened that that night, but based on Harry's attitude since he knew that he had done something to piss off either him or Sirvon. Whatever it was, Harry wouldn't discuss the personal aspects of their relationship. Instead of being friends, they were now strictly boss and subordinate. It was Harry's call to make, but he missed his friend. He would just have to keep trying.

As he stood in the yard separated from both the other humans and the *gabacho* workers waiting for dispatch to bring him his assignment, his thoughts drifted back to how he had terrorized Maré this morning, and a pang of guilt echoed through him. He knew that his response had been out of proportion. *Maybe I should let her have her clothes and go back to her room. Maybe –*

Someone was shaking his shoulder, and he snapped back to where he was. It was Harry. He had a look of concern in his eyes, and a reflection of his friendship showed though. "Geez, man. You were a million miles away. You okay?"

"Yeah... Just a rough start to the day, I guess. I'm fine though.

Uh, how are you and Sirvon?"

Harry's mask fell back in place as he stiffly said, "Everything's fine for us. Listen, a note came in last night. There's a package to be picked up at the space port."

"Thanks. I wonder what it could be – any details?"

"No idea. About today – there's a shortage of supervisors." His voice lowered enough so that no one would overhear. "I'm going to let you take a crew out by yourself, Joss. It's been months since your incident, and I'm going to trust you."

He considered his friend and boss, who for once wasn't smoking, though the smell of it still hung on his clothes. His words were a real surprise. "Really? Thanks, I guess, but maybe you want to give it to someone else. I've got some things on my mind and I'm not sure today is the best day."

"No, it's you – you've been here the longest."

"Okay, I'll try not to disappoint you, Harry."

Harry stood straighter and took a more official tone. "Don't, Breylin. I won't cover for you again." When he finished speaking, he turned his back on him and strode off towards the offices.

During the day, Breylin couldn't stop thinking about the delivery he needed to pick up. *Maybe someone sent something of Dad's?* He had no clue. Whatever it was, he hurried the crew to finish up a few minutes early and rushed them back to base so he could get over to the terminal.

When he arrived, he went right to the foreman on duty and presented his ID. As the guy compared it to his manifests, Breylin noticed that his name was Lamereaux. "Where's Jones? He's usually here second shift."

Without looking up from the paperwork he said gruffly, "off today. I had to pull a double."

"Tough break, I guess."

"Huh? No, I appreciate the money. I'm saving up to head back to Earth."

"As young as you are, I'm surprised."

"I was a dreamer coming here. But the only way to find a woman is to look among the loners and widows. Too much baggage for me." He nodded his head. "Here it is." He called over one of the androids sitting on a nearby bench and gave her the container markers. As she got up, the others scooted down to fill the spot she had vacated.

Breylin signaled with his chin towards them. "Ever make you feel funny working with them?"

"The androids? Nope, they're quiet. I don't even notice them until there's something to be done."

A couple of minutes later, the android trundled back dragging a cart holding a hibernation pod.

"What the hell?" Breylin said.

"Isn't this what you expected?" said Lamereaux.

"No... who's it from?"

"Hang on, let me check." He rifled through the papers again. Holding one up to the light he said, "Looks like it says Paradise Station. Huh... must be a simulant." Looking back at Breylin he said, "didn't you order it?"

"No... at least I didn't think so," he replied as he moved to look through the narrow window on the top of the pod. Clearly, this was one of the twins. "I'll be damned," he muttered in surprise.

Lamereaux went to the container and tore off a packet that had been affixed to the side of it. Handing it to Him he said, "here are the documents. You may want to take a look at them and see if this is legit." He gave him a smile. "If there's been a mistake, it's a lot easier for you to clear up and less paperwork for me if you don't accept delivery."

Looking the stuff over, he found a letter apologizing for the late delivery of the Alpha model due to the confusion in orders, that this was the one that he should have received, and a promise of a minor price break on the next order. *Very strange.* He teetered on the edge of sending her back – his funds were low and it would consume nearly all of his emergency credit – but seeing Luna, he knew he had to have her.

"It seems in order. I guess I misunderstood."

"Fine by me." He thumbed toward the androids. "You want to pop the back of your lift open and I'll have them load it up?"

Arriving back home, he backed into the lift port, got out and popped the rear hatch. He decided to go inside and gauge how Maré was before pulling Luna out. This would be the perfect way to try to make up for his reaction this morning, but he figured that he'd better know how she was doing beforehand.

Entering the house, he found her on the living room carpet on her knees and her face all puffy from crying.

As soon as she saw him she said, "Mr. Breylin, Maré is sorry for this morning! Please don't punish her!" She spluttered and sobbed, and from there he couldn't tell what she was trying to say.

Guilt tore a hole inside him at her condition, knowing that he had caused this. "Maré, I'm sorry too." He knelt down next to her and put a hand on her shoulder, causing her to shriek and recoil. Trying to speak over her noises he said, "Maré, I'm not going to punish you. I'm *not* going to punish you!"

She looked up at him, not understanding, but then she tipped over and rolled onto her back. Though she continued to cry, the tears running unnoticed towards her ears, she appeared to begin to settle down.

Breylin left to retrieve some of her clothes from her cabinet in his bedroom. When he returned, she seemed to be sleeping, and when he bent down to give her a small nudge, he found that she was. He picked her up and carried her into her room. He laid her down, pulled the blanket up onto her, and left the clothes at the foot of the bed. Now obviously wasn't the time for a reunion.

In the morning, he gently woke her. She was disoriented and startled, but she said nothing. She held up her blanket slightly and looked at him with a question on her face.

"It's okay, Maré. Get showered and dressed quickly – I have a special surprise for you."

When he saw her eyes go wide and she started to back away he said, "Nothing bad, dear – it's a good surprise."

She seemed to let some of her fear go, but she still pulled the blanket up around her neck and huddled under it.

"Just get cleaned up and come out," he said a little harsher than he had intended, but he pulled the door shut behind him and went into the kitchen to make some coffee.

After a while, she timidly emerged clothed from her room to stand before him with her eyes down. He had never seen her so dejected. Keeping her eyes on the floor she said, "What's it to be today, Mr. Breylin?"

"I wanted to say that I know I contributed to the problem yesterday morning, Maré."

She laughed mirthlessly. "You contributed to it, huh?"

"Your sarcasm aside, I have something I think you'll appreciate."

This time she spoke quietly. "It's just something else you'll take from me."

"I'm trying to be civil and you're being difficult, Maré. Would you like to go back to your room and think about your attitude before we continue?"

She sighed and looked at him. "What do you want me to do?"

He had to give her credit for the guts she was showing. As afraid as she had been last night, her mettle hadn't left her. If she was afraid now, he couldn't tell. Maybe, but he doubted it. Tired, yes, or maybe weary was a better word, but definitely not afraid.

"Come with me, please." He got up from the table and walked towards the lift port, and she dutifully followed. When they got to the lift, he pulled the pod out enough so that she would be able to see through the small window. Pointing towards it he said, "have a look."

She had to climb up to do as she was told, but when she peered inside her eyes went wide. Without stopping to look away from the glass she said, "I don't understand, you got another simulant?"

"No – don't you see?" he said triumphantly. "She's not just any simulant, or even any Alpha from your bloodline. According to the letter that came with her, this is the Alpha you were with on Paradise Station."

Finally she did look at him with tears welling in her eyes.

"Luna?" she breathed.

"That's right. Help me get this out and we'll wake her."

"I don't know what to say," she said as they worked. "Did you bring her here?"

"Not exactly. I tried to get the two of you at the same time, but I was told only you were available. I don't know what changed, but here she is."

"It was probably one of Almeida's games," she said to herself, though angry and loud enough for him to hear.

"Almeida?" he asked.

"It's nothing, Mr. Breylin. He was just the last bastard in our lives."

He took note of the oblique slight, but he let it slide. Instead, he got the pod out of the lift. When it was sitting on the floor, he keyed up the cycle to wake her, and the lid popped open. He said, "She's been asleep a long time, Maré. She'll need to drink and eat as soon as it can be managed. We have a few minutes – why don't you get some water for her?"

"Yes, Sir," she said with happy tears – the first such he could remember – and she moved quickly into the house.

When she came back she knelt next to the container, leaned in and smelled Luna's hair. She smelled musty and unwashed, but Maré was sure now – *Stars above, this is her!* She was painfully aware of Breylin's presence, but she put her arms under and around Luna anyway, crying into her neck and awkwardly rocking her.

Luna made small noises down in her throat. When Maré heard it, she whispered into her ear over and over, "Luna, it's me. I'm here, honey."

After a minute, she said with a throaty voice thick with sleep, "Maré...?"

"That's right, Chroma, it's me."

Feebly she moved one of her hands up but let it fall back into her lap. With her face in Maré's hair she took a deep breath, and her eyes fluttered open. "Maré?"

She moved so that they could see each other. "That's right, dear. We're together again." She drew her back into her embrace, and this time Luna did get her arm around her mate.

—∧=∨—

Breylin stood there uncomfortably while the two girls held each other, the one crying with relief and the other drowsily. He decided to let it play on without interference. Still, it was affecting him – to his surprise. They obviously loved each other, somehow. From what Maré had told him, the two of them had been put to sleep together, meaning Luna had been asleep for nine long months. She would be out of it a long time, but even so she was clearly responding to Maré's presence.

Her reaction was much more pronounced. For months she had believed Luna to be dead, but now she was in her arms, and her relief was palpable. It got him to thinking about his parents, and then Riss... *No.* He fled from thinking about those things.

His mind came back to the girls, and how happy they were. *Are they really as happy as they seem*, he thought, *or are they acting according to some script? Is it possible?* He was baffled to find that he couldn't tell the difference. That line of thinking made him nervous, too, if less so.

He was feeling quite strangely now, and a tear slid down his cheek. Not wanting them to see him so vulnerable, he quietly turned away and went into the house. When he sat down heavily on the sofa, the tears fell freely. It bothered him that the tableau in the lift port moved him, and he tried to figure out what was going on with himself. A memory started to surface, but once again he recoiled from it. *What the hell is wrong with me?* His pulse started to race, and he felt like he was starting to panic.

He vainly fought it, but the memory that had started to tug at his consciousness was an insistent thing, and unbidden he remembered the night he had had to put his first set of twins down. Guilt coiled his insides into a tight knot, and he nearly emptied the contents of his stomach right there. It didn't matter that their deaths would have happened in a worse way if he hadn't intervened; they had been his daughters at one time, and he wept bitterly for the loss he had caused. *Dammit, I thought I was done with this...*

He gave his emotions free reign for a few minutes, but he knew that Maré and Luna would be coming into the house at any time, so he pulled himself together. It took a couple of minutes of intense struggle, but once again the façade was in place.

When Maré finally brought her Chroma in on unsteady legs, Breylin stood up, allowing her to stretch out on the couch. She laid down on her side facing into the room, and she was looking at him without expression. Maré sat on the floor next to her, and he wondered what she might have told him out of his hearing.

"Hello, Luna – I am Mr. Breylin," he said feeling better, but still out of sorts. "Welcome to my home. You were a long time in coming here."

"Yes, Sir," she said. "Thank you for bringing me here and giving me back to Maré."

He turned to her, who was staring at Luna and smiling. "Maré," he said. "You need to get some food into her right away."

This was one time she didn't seem to feel like resisting him. "Yes, Mr. Breylin." Turning back to Luna she said, "I'll be back in a couple of minutes, honey," and she went into the kitchen.

Breylin said to her, "since we have a few moments, I'll need to put your collar on you, Luna. I'll be right back." He withdrew into the bedroom and retrieved it. When he came back into the living room, he found that she had propped herself up on the cushions.

Wordlessly, she held her hair up and out of the way. He moved close, slipped the thin black strip around her and fastened it, then he took the controller, tuned the collar and put the device away. She let her hands and hair fall.

Hesitantly she asked, "Mr. Breylin? I know I just got here, but could I ask you for a small favor?"

Curious now, he said, "what would you like?"

"Could you retrieve a few holos of our parents?"

He thought for a moment. *Are they sentimental too?* There wasn't anything he could do about the past, but maybe he could work towards a better future. "I don't know what's available, Luna... but I'll see what I can do."

Twenty One

Maré brought Luna some hot, carbohydrate-laden cakes from the kitchen. She knelt back down on the floor beside her on the couch, split them with her fingers and offered her a piece. As she opened her mouth and wordlessly took the bite, she laid one of her hands on Maré's shoulder.

Breylin sat in a chair off in a slightly shadowed corner of the room and watched them interact without words, only touches. Something was conveyed even in the contact they maintained with their eyes. They didn't break it, even when Maré would delicately place the small wads of nourishment on Luna's tongue and she would lay her head down on the cushion to chew. Seeing them like this, alive, against the memory of the deaths he had caused... it was a strange contrast.

They continued to amaze him, that they could be so natural, so lifelike. *And these two, even more. They look just like the real Maré and Luna, but they're more connected*, he thought. *Maybe it's possible that they actually love each other.*

Ultimately it was his own reaction to the way they seemed to be acting that made him feel out of sorts, even with Luna's muted responses. Maré used her thumb to slowly tuck a few tiny crumbs on her lips into her mouth, and it was gentle, intimate... maybe even romantic. In a way he couldn't explain, he didn't like the added complication. It would be simpler if they were more machine-like. Still, he had obviously made the two of them very happy, and he did like that. Outwardly he was passive, but the conflicts pushed back and forth inside. This was a thing he might not be able to control, and he wasn't sure if he wanted to.

"Maré," he said, surprising her, as if she had forgotten he was in the room. She had stopped with a piece of cake in her hand halfway to Luna's mouth.

"Yes, Sir?" she said nervously.

"I'm going to make myself something to eat. Please clean up the kitchen before the two of you go to your room, but you don't need to deal with anything else tonight."

"I understand, Mr. Breylin."

He spoke softly. "You'll need to show Luna how things are to be done around here. I've decided to try to be patient, but I'd like things to be back to business as usual quickly."

"Yes, Sir. Mr. Breylin?"

He paused and turned back. "What is it, Maré?"

"Thank you, Sir," she said with brimming tears as she laid her hand on Luna's leg. "For my Chroma."

He hardened himself, turned and spoke as he walked into the kitchen. "You can best show your appreciation by making sure that your work is taken care of."

—∧=∨—

Luna was still muzzy headed and had to lean on Maré as they walked into the bedroom. She sat down on the bed and looked around dazed. "It still seems like we were just with Almeida."

Maré snorted from their bathroom. "It seems like a lifetime ago to me." Naked from the waist down, she came out stripping off her shirt, wadded her clothes together and threw them in the corner. She walked over to her, and started tugging her shirt up.

Luna held her arms up and let her do the work.

Maré pushed on her shoulders lightly and Luna went prone so Maré could pull the rest of her clothes off. Tossing them on top of the rest, she switched off the light and padded back to the bed, eased her way next to her Chroma, and drew her close. "I've missed you, Luna."

As she squeezed her, she could feel the tension in Luna's muscles. "What is it?"

"Just hold me."

"I won't let you go. Now tell me."

Luna rolled to lay her head on Maré's chest, feeling the light sheen of sweat in her cleavage. She cupped one of her breasts. "You're much larger than you were. Do you like them?"

"To be honest, I haven't thought much about it. What do you think?"

"Looks good on you."

Maré hugged her tightly again in reply.

She craned her head up so she could whisper in her ear. "Does he hear or see us in here?"

"I don't think so, but keep quiet just the same."

"There's a darkness in him."

Maré breathed her answer out. "Yes – he can be terrible. Sometimes he's nice, a little tender even, but he's whipped me a few times with a tube he keeps above our door. Yesterday I thought he'd kill me."

"He's definitely off, but he doesn't seem *that* bad now."

"He goes back and forth. He nearly apologized last night. It can be difficult to read his moods, and his treatment of me – now us – will follow those."

Luna laid back down and breathed her Chroma in, listened to her rhythms. "What matters is we're together now."

She reached down, took Luna's hand and put it back on her breast and covered it with her own. The gesture was a little strange, but she let it pass.

Maré rolled slightly into her and used her leg to pull Luna closer. She said with a laugh, "you know I'm a little older than you now, right?"

"Shit," she said. "I liked being the older one..."

—∧=∨—

The next morning, Breylin stood in the doorway of their room at five, and called out. "5AM, girls. Time to get started." When they stirred, he walked out.

Maré showed Luna where everything was before wrinkling her nose and dragging her into the shower. "Let's go, Chroma. After being in that box for months, you need it *desperately*."

She made a face. "I'm exhausted, Maré," she whined with ex-aggeration. "Wash me?"

She smiled. "Of course I will, and I'll dress you, too." She hugged her fiercely. She did smell, but it was *her*. "I'm so glad you're here..."

Afterwards, as they passed through the living room, they could hear him in the shower. "Go into the kitchen and start looking around so you can get the feel for where things are. I'll go find out what he wants for the day."

"Okay. Um, wait," she said as she looked around. "Notice anything strange in here?"

Maré looked around herself. There was the sofa with a glass top coffee table in front of it, the chair by the large window facing out front, the electronic consoles. The floor was the white, textured plastic that was everywhere else in the house. Another seldom-used chair in the corner. There were places where pictures had once hung...

"Not really. You mean the nail holes where there must have been pictures hanging once?"

"No – look at the furniture. You really don't see it?"

"Nope, a couch and two chairs. What am I –" She stopped, looking at something she hadn't noticed before. "That chair is out of place."

"Yeah. The rest of the stuff faces inward, but that one faces out."

Now that Maré could see it, it gobbled up her attention. She'd never walk through this room again without seeing its oddity. Still... "I guess it isn't that odd. I mean, yeah, it's out of place, but he likes to sit and stare out the window. He probably moved it at some point so that it was more to his liking. In fact, I'd bet on it."

"Huh... I guess you've had other things on your mind than the furniture."

Maré nodded, but she was picking at the idea in her thoughts. *What does he see when he looks out? Is it that horizon, or something else?* Luna had spotted something important, something that sailed completely by her, but try as she would she couldn't quite identify it standing there. There was something about how the chair had become the focal point of the room.

"Okay, let's get a move on," she said to clear out her mind. "Head into the kitchen and I'll be out in a minute."

Suiting her own words, she went towards his bedroom while Luna went in the other direction – but she made sure to skirt around the chair wide.

—∧=∨—

Luna began to look through the cabinets, trying to take note of where the plates and cups were, the bland food packets and containers – *does everyone everywhere eat out of these same generic packets?* – and everything else. Pausing to go over things in her mind, she noticed the light coming through the window and decided to grab her first real look at the outside world. There were windows in their bedroom, but they'd been shuttered last night, and she didn't have the chance to check the view. What she now saw surprised her.

Everything was shades of burnished copper and hues of tan, even the scant tufts of desiccated grass in front of the house. Rocks of all sizes and low hills to the horizon. But the sunrise dominated everything, and it was breathtaking. Luna knew that stars were massive balls of nuclear powered light, but knowing the physical process was wholly unlike seeing it up close. The sunlight streamed through the air, catching the dust, and it looked as if it was making its triumphant entry into their world. *I am here*, it seemed to be saying to her. She'd seen the star of their home system, but because the station had been so far out by Jupiter, the star had only appeared to be a big dot – little more than an oddity when compared to the massive, colorful gas giant that periodically churned its surface and threw radio signals that filled the comm systems with uncanny, almost intelligent sounding static –

but this was something else; though she could only see a small crest of it poked up above the hills, this sun was colossal, a thing not to be denied, master of its own domain. Its fiery, too-bright edge etched ghostly afterimages in her vision. Its appearance was the most magnificent thing she'd ever seen, pushing its way through a break in the clouds and hazing the air red with the fingers of its rays, and it came to her that she'd understood nothing at all of importance about them. It looked hot, primal, and forced an aridness so bleak as to be death for anyone unfortunate enough to labor beneath it, but it was also completely outside of her limited experience, giving it a surreal quality. *And this must have been how Maré felt when I woke her up*, she mused. *This place is so... unexpected.*

Luna heard the soft pad of Maré's feet behind her. She came up beside her, put her arms around Luna and laid her head on her shoulder. "What do you think of the view?"

After a few seconds she said, "It's pretty desolate out there, but it's beautiful in a stark way. The sunrise is... I don't have the words to describe it. It makes me feel something, though."

"I suppose. It never changes, you know."

Luna turned to look at her. "What do you mean?"

"The sunset. It's locked like that, so it's always going down."

"Wow. I thought it was coming up. How do you know it isn't?"

Maré wrinkled her brow in thought. "Huh, that's never occurred to me."

"Well either way, this is my first look at one, and it's pretty spectacular. Earth's sun is so far away from where we were that it's just a bright spot with a lot of glare."

"I guess," she said. "I don't give it much thought. These walls are pretty much my world, and it's often more than enough."

Luna nodded. "Do you think he'd let us go outside?"

She felt Maré tense up against her. "I'm not sure."

"What is it?"

"I didn't enjoy the one time I was taken outside," she murmured softly.

Luna turned to her. "Tell me what happened."

"I will," she said. "But it's not a talk for the light of day."

"Okay." She turned back to the view of the outside world. "Maybe beautiful isn't the right word, but I still think it's... I don't know – stunning I guess. It might be mixed with something else, but I'm not sure. And I think I'm beginning to understand how you felt when you woke up and saw Jupiter for the first time."

"That night was a blur of startling revelation, so it's kind of hard to separate it all out, but I think I was more bewildered by the crop buildings. The implications of them, I mean, but I don't think I'd been able to grasp it at the time."

"I see what you mean, Maré. I'm a little overwhelmed just now myself, but not so much that I can't appreciate the view."

"Well, try to enjoy it while you can," Maré said with a dry laugh as she broke the contact and walked over to the kitchen counter. "Before it gets old and the wind seems be trying to blow the place flat. I swear, sometimes at night the gusts seem alive and offended."

"Don't be cynical, Chroma," Luna said reproachfully. "It isn't like our skywalk, but it's striking and something to look at besides the walls."

She turned back and tried to meet her gaze. "Alright, but be patient with me, Luna. It hasn't been easy here, being alone and without the only friend I've ever had – alone except for *him*. I may have hardened, and I'm sorry."

Luna nodded. "I know. Maybe I can be soft, for the both of us."

Maré gave her an even drier laugh. "We'll have to see about that – 'soft' will be something of a change for you. It would probably be a lot easier if I could see you in a pretty dress."

She arched an eyebrow. "You remembered..."

"Oh, yeah. We might be able to manage a few ribbons, anyway." She thought for a moment, then continued. "You know you mean everything to me, Chroma, but you'd still be pretty amazing if you weren't."

Luna wrinkled her forehead. "I don't know what you mean."

"What I mean is," she said with a huge grin, "that in the span of just a couple of minutes, you've spotted two things I completely missed. I know I'm *engineered*," she said with something of a verbal sneer, "to be rather average all around, but I wouldn't have thought I'd miss those things. You didn't though, and I find it, well, amazing."

"Ha! Well, let's call it a draw. You had your focus elsewhere."

"I guess," she said, stretching her arms towards her. "C'mere and hold me, Chroma."

When Luna went to her, she expected the usual delicate embrace of their bed, but Maré gripped her with her arms, tight in, and full of feeling. This was a hug that spoke nothing of love, but cried of unity, need, solidarity, and as she pressed Luna in even tighter, it felt like Maré was trying to shell her with protection. *Yes, you are my dear Chroma, Maré, and I yours*, echoed her heart, *but you've definitely toughened up in this place, and it was you who were never soft to begin with...*

Maré let her go and said, "as nice as this is, I need to draw your attention to more immediate matters." Maré got out the canister that held the coffee powder, then pointed at one of the drawers. "Please reach in there and get out the small scale. I know you're used to medical equipment that *tell* you what to do and do half of it anyway, but pretty much everything is manual around here. Whatever else you do, make sure you get the coffee right. He doesn't get much..." She lowered her voice. "And wasting it is a sure way to earn punishment."

Next, she had Luna dig out a plate, a fork and a packet of spaghetti, and then she showed her how to work the food warmer. "You'll get a feel for how long to heat the food as you practice, but he likes it hot. When I said I thought he was going to kill me, it was because I served him cold food."

Breylin stepped into the kitchen, startling them. "To be sure, it's a situation best avoided, Luna."

With her eyes down, Maré spoke softly. "I'm sorry, Mr. Breylin."

"Think nothing of it. I told you to make sure Luna knows how my home works." He looked to Luna. "It's best to understand ahead of time."

After he left for work, the girls set to cleaning the house at a casual pace. More than anything else though, they continued to reconnect. When they sat down to eat at lunch, Luna wanted to talk.

"Tell me about what's happened to you since we went to sleep."

Maré laughed humorlessly. "There isn't much to tell. You're the only person I've seen except for *him*."

Luna looked down. "When you say it like that... I'm sorry I

wasn't here, that you went through it alone."

Maré reached for her hand. "I wasn't alone. My Chroma was always with me."

Luna smiled and said, "you've also gotten sentimental as you've gotten older."

Taking a serious tone, she said, "do you remember what you asked me to do whenever I got scared?"

"Refresh me."

Maré got out of her chair and slid into her lap. She took a pinch of Luna's hair, bend towards it and inhaled. "You asked me to remember the way this smells. It was enough."

She laid her head on Maré's chest and tears flowed. "I wish... I don't know."

"Hey, it's okay. We're together."

"Tell me about him and what to expect."

"I'll tell you what to expect. The difficult details we talk over later with the lights out."

"Fair enough," she nodded. "We've got a lot to discuss in the dark, don't we?"

"On this thing, there isn't much to tell, really. We cook. We clean. He's gone most days, comes home at night. From time to time he's nice, occasionally he's monstrous. When it's good it almost feels like love, other times I think he loathes me. Well, not just me but all chromanity."

"Whoa, wait a minute." Luna held up her hand. "Back up to the 'monstrous' thing. I guess you said something like that yesterday, but I wasn't much with it – still not I guess – and you're scaring me."

"I don't know what to say. He can be a monster."

"Why?"

"He used to be married, but she's dead now. She's –" Maré shook her head. "Too close – a topic for later. She died, and he blames us."

"I might have hoped we left this behind." Luna exhaled and rubbed her scalp. "But we never get away, do we?"

"Um, I'm not sure he's worse than Almeida was. He can be, but the mood swings are what make him tough to take. Definitely different, though."

She looked down at her plate. "I'm not sure I can eat this now."

Maré got up. "I'll reheat the plates. He's right about one thing – you need the nourishment."

Luna's face went pouty. "I don't want to eat..."

She nudged her shoulder. "What's with the whininess?" Maré said. "You weren't like this before."

She sighed. "I'm still a little out of it, I guess."

"Well, *eat* this," Maré said as she set the plate in front of her. "Then go lay down. I'll finish the housework."

"Are you sure?"

"Yeah, it's fine. I've done it by myself for months."

"No, I mean are you sure you don't mind if I go lay down?"

Maré stroked her cheek. "It's fine, Luna. I'll call you when it's dinnertime."

Later in bed, she snuggled her head into Luna's arms. "I need you to hold me."

She adjusted Maré so that they fit together better and laid her cheek on the top of her head. "Is there anything you want to tell me?"

"Not particularly, no. I still can't believe you're here – I never expected to see you again."

Luna gave her hair a plaintive kiss on her crown and tightened her embrace. When she loosened up, Maré rolled away from her so that they could spoon.

Luna said, "you've changed."

"What do you mean?"

"You're different. Less off balance, more confident."

Maré placed Luna's hand on her breast. Her muscles tightened, and she nearly pulled away, but she checked the movement.

"This is different, too," she said quietly into her ear.

"Does it bother you?" Maré queried. "You've had your hands on me lots times when you've washed me."

"Yes, I have." Pause. "But I think we both know this is different."

"I like your hands on me, Chroma."

"Maré... you know why this makes me uncomfortable."

She rolled back towards her. Faces close, she spoke quietly, sadly. "We'll never see 85 again, but she still has a hold on you, Luna." She laid her hand along the curve of her jawline. "You need healing from this."

Tears began to well behind her lashes. "It's isn't that simple, Maré. I was violated."

"I know. You *know* I know." She traced the outlines of her face while she spoke. "It's not the same, but I've learned something of violation. The day before yesterday Breylin made me tell him I wasn't a person. There were plenty of times he would make me say hurtful things while staring at my own reflection in the mirror – or face his whip. For months I wasn't allowed to refer to myself in the first person."

"You're so strong to have survived, Maré."

She stretched to put her mouth by Luna's ear. "I did it by re-membering my Chroma, and by fixing in my mind that *I am* a person, no matter what he thinks. He controls our bodies, but he can only control our minds if we let him. It's the same with 85."

Maré moved back so that they were once again nose to nose, eye to eye. As they looked into each other, Maré could feel her seeing the truth in what she was saying.

Luna nodded ever so slightly. "You've become more domi-nant, too – protective."

"I'll do what I can now, just as you did for me before," she said. "There's been a lot of grief in our lives, and there's more to come, but not in this bed."

She rolled back and deliberately put Luna's hand on her breast, covered it with her own and squeezed. "Now hold me because I like it. We can take our time, but we are going to heal, Luna."

—∧=∨—

Breylin made a conscious effort to be reasonable towards the girls. He had been afraid things would start to fall apart, but he'd been wrong – so far. He would just have to keep an eye out for issues, and deal with anything that came up. Action – reaction.

Within a few weeks' time, he noticed that as they had opportunity they would be in physical contact more and more. There could be no denying that they loved each other. Slowly, he accepted the change to his perception.

When Maré's birthday came up a month after Luna had arrived, he decided to allow them a special meal. "Pick what you want, and I will bring something small home for dessert. As I recall, your predecessors appreciated chocolate." he told them. "Luna, we've missed your birthday by a week. We'll just have to use the one occasion for both."

Maré sounded genuine when she spoke. "Thank you, Sir. We know you don't have to go out of your way to make us feel appreciated."

"Well, things have been going well with both of you. Showing appreciation seemed like a good response."

That night, Luna heated enchiladas and refried bean paste for dinner and served it to them. He kept himself reserved, but allowed them to laugh and have fun. It was a nice time. *This reminds me of happier days...*

"Your mother always enjoyed these dinners," he said.

Continuing as if nothing had been said, Maré laughed and pointed at Luna. "You have a smear of food on your nose! Here, let me get it." Luna held still while her Chroma reached over and wiped it with her index finger. At the last second, she nipped at her fingers, causing Maré to yelp. Breylin's eyebrows raised up at the silliness of it, while they fell into a fit of joyful giggling.

"Luna, why don't you get out the two pieces of cake?"

Luna got up. "I've never had any – I hope it's good," she said.

"Didn't you get one for yourself, Mr. Breylin?" said Maré.

Luna got a couple of plates out, then the small box from their tiny fridge. When she opened the box she said, "Wow, look at that." She carefully extracted the first piece and gently laid it on its side on a plate, then repeating her actions for the second one.

Responding to Maré he said, "nope – I didn't want one at the time – but based on Luna's reaction, I may regret it."

She carried the plates back to the table, set hers down, then the other in front of Maré. As she got close, she leaned in to her and said, "happy birthday, Chroma," and then she tucked her hand under the hair at the back of her neck. They closed their eyes as Luna drew her in and gave her a too-warm kiss. When they parted, Maré seemed breathless.

Breylin could feel the electricity that crackled between them, and it made him feel stunned as if someone had thrown a bucket of warm water on him. *What the hell just happened?*

After Luna sat back down, the girls noticed him looking at them and must have read something unpleasant on his face. They finished their desserts in silence and downcast eyes.

Without saying a word, he wiped his mouth, got up and left the room. As he walked back to his own space, he wondered what else was going on between them, especially in their room at night.

Twenty Two

For weeks now, Harry had noticed that Joss seemed to have turned a corner with his attitude, especially towards the simulant work crews. He had been making informal inquiries among them, and what he heard was that out in the region he still kept his distance from them, but he was much less surly. Apparently, trusting him once again with his own crew had been good for him.

It was tempting to think that his friend would be okay after all, but just this week he had started showing signs of slightly increased aggression again. No real problems – yet – but maybe it was time to offer him some direct encouragement. Maybe if he noticed Joss' efforts it would help him stay the course. It was worth a shot, anyway.

The next morning, Harry found him standing off to the side, waiting for his assignment. He smiled when he saw Harry walking towards him, and said, "morning, Harry."

"Hey, good morning! How's it going, Joss?" He pulled out his small satchel of tobacco, extracted a hefty pinch of it and put it onto a thin square of paper. He put the rest of it away while he expertly rolled the cigarette with his other hand. It was the first time he'd ever seen Harry roll one of those things.

"Mmm, doing pretty good." He shifted his feet. "What's up?"

"Well," he said as hit lit the smoke and sucked on it, causing its end to glow and lighting his face with its bright orange glow. "I wanted to tell you that from what I hear, you're doing well with the crews."

He smiled again. "Thanks, Harry. I appreciate it."

Harry exhaled, nodded and smiled back – as much from Joss as the exquisite taste of the warm smoke. "Sure. Keep it up and I'll make it permanent. It would mean a raise." He held up two pinched fingers. "A small one, anyhow."

"Wow, that would be great."

"We haven't gotten together lately. Would you want to?"

"Yeah, sure. What did you have in mind?"

After the way it had gone last time, Harry wasn't about to invite him back to spend time around Sirvon. She still shot daggers at him with her eyes every time Joss' name came up. "We could go hit a bar if you like."

He tensed up his face. "I guess I'd rather save that for when I get that raise." He thought for a little bit and said, "what if you came to my place for dinner? You can bring Sirvon."

Harry grimaced. "Ah, I don't know, Joss. She can be a little... touchy."

"You know, I'm... not sure what happened the last time."

"Honestly?" said Harry as he pulled air through the cigarette.

"No clue." Joss held his hand up. "I swear."

Harry dropped his voice. "Well... I wasn't going to get into this, but it was the 'gabacho' comment. Sirvon... Well, there's things you just don't understand about our home."

He couldn't imagine what Harry was trying to tell him. "I don't follow. What's your family got to do with this?"

Harry raked his fingers through his hair and shifted his feet. He took a last pull on his smoke, dropped the rest of it on the macadam and ground its embers with his shoe. He hesitated when he met Joss' eyes, but he took him by the arm and quickly drew him a little further away from everyone else. When he spoke, his voice was so low that Joss had to lean in to hear him. "Sirvon isn't what she seems to be, and neither are the kids."

What in the world was he talking about, they aren't what they seem? Then it clicked, and Joss understood. "You mean they're *simulants?"*

"What the hell is the matter with you?" he said as he tried to covertly look around. "Will you keep your voice down?! Yes, dammit, they're simulants!"

"This is crazy, Harry. How could you marry a *simulant?"*

His brow drew down in anger. "Watch your tone, Breylin. Don't piss me off."

"No, man – listen," he said, moderating his voice. "I'm just a little shocked. We're not allowed to inter-marry. They aren't people as far as the government is concerned. How'd you get away with it?"

The tension left Harry. "A long time ago I was a test pilot for ships with prototype interstellar drives. She was one of the units they gave me, a specialized tech model suited to the work, really intelligent."

Breylin nodded. "Okay..."

"She's... well, she's also really funny, and caring, too. I treated her with respect, and I got to see those sides of her. There was an unspoken understanding around others, but on board it was just the three of us. She and I became friends – only – and it worked. Hang on, I need another smoke." He smiled. "I have to have all the smokes I'm going to while I'm at work – she won't let me do it at home."

Harry paused to roll another one, and as he lit up, he began the story. "I was allowed to have two simulants because of the job I was doing – it would be too much for just two. Anyway,

Steven was his name. He and Sirvon were mated –"

"Yeah – chromas, I guess."

"Yes. Like I was saying, they pretty much did all of the inflight repairs. Well, on the last run we made, the drive malfunctioned and locked itself into a runaway process that just kept dumping fuel into the core. Once it completely saturated the chamber, we would have dropped out of hyperspace at full tilt. It could have happened at any moment. The ship wouldn't have been able to withstand the inertial forces, and we'd have been torn apart."

"Okay, I guess I follow close enough."

Harry drew in a deep breath, and sweat began to stand out on his brow. He looked away as he continued to describe the scene, and his voice took on a faraway quality as the visceral memories pulled him back to that place. "There was only one way to stop the runaway process. Someone was going to have to crawl behind the shielding on that damn drive and pull the plug on the fuel manually." He inhaled a lungful of smoke and let it out slowly, the cloud of it enveloping his face. "He didn't even think about it. I mean he *knew* what would happen, what it meant, but Steveo went in there anyway. Once he got in there he could tell that there was enough fuel in play that it didn't matter, so he scrammed the drive instead of killing the fuel. It was risky as hell, but he made the right call." He gave a little laugh. "Steveo was the best engineer I ever knew! And he was my friend, too."

Harry sighed. "Exposure to all of that raw radiation killed him fast... but not fast enough. I could tell the moment he died." He turned to Joss. "The screaming had stopped, but I don't know, maybe thirty or forty seconds later he gasped out his last death rattle. He might have been trying to stop the fuel by then, but I couldn't be sure. Sirvon was shrieking at the top of her lungs, but I could hear his breathing over the comm anyway, and then it stopped, and I *knew*... She got away from me and went in part way after him before I could grab her again. The ship was safe from being slammed into real space, but the fuel kept dumping into the intermix chamber and it exploded. She was hit by chunks that had spalled off the drive, and she was torn up pretty bad."

He paused to drag on his smoke again.

"Anyway, we still dropped out hard. The inertial dampeners couldn't keep up with a deceleration that rapid, and it felt like we'd collided with something. The jolt tossed me like a sack of laundry into a bulkhead, and I cracked a bunch of ribs and a collarbone. Nasty concussion, too. The shoulder still aches sometimes." He squeezed his left shoulder through his light jacket. "But I sealed her wounds as best I could and managed to get her into their hyper-sleep pod. By the time I got the emergency beacon activated, I was coughing up blood. I crawled into the pod beside her and shut us down until we could be rescued.

"Holy shit," said Joss.

"Yeah, I know," he replied. "But you see where this is heading. I got out of piloting after that, and took her with me. I was tired of the loner in space thing, and she was desperate for some companionship. They say simulants adapt better in pairs. So, our friendship became dependence on each other, and I married her nearly fourteen years ago." He took another pull of smoke, finding that it had stopped satisfying him. With a look of disgust, he dropped nearly a third of it on the ground and ignored it.

"What about the lifespan? How did she survive?"

"A lot of the high end tech simulants are engineered to live normal lifespans. It's just too expensive to let *them* expire in ten years. You'd never know it to look at her, but she's a hyper drive specialist, and a really good one at that. Anyway, we moved around and got lost in the crowd for a few years after the accident. I got her a legit-looking ID from a friend of a friend of a friend, married her, and we settled here. Been that way ever since."

"And the kids? I thought they were all sterile. Oh, wait –"

"yeah, simulants. We special ordered Amber as a prepubescent duplicate of Sirvon. No tech skills. We got Aaron to keep her company."

"Do they know... what they are?"

"We had to tell them. They've got real ID's, but they'd always need to be careful. Anything more specific than a blood test and the situation would be blown wide open."

Joss was reeled with the info. He'd heard more about his friend in the last few minutes than he'd ever known. "Holy shit – this is crazy. Who else knows?"

"Just you, now. My parents are gone and I haven't seen my brother in more than twenty years; don't even know where he is. I'm telling you because we're friends and to maybe give you some perspective, maybe help you see that however they're made, they're still just people. I don't give a damn what the government says."

"I'm not as down on them as I used to be, but they aren't human, man. Doesn't any of that register with you?"

"Most people would agree, more or less, Joss, but no, I don't." Harry took the edge that had crept into his voice out. "I'm not asking you to change everything you've ever felt, just giving you something to think over. On the job, sometimes I'm not sure you get how to work with them. If you treat them decent enough they'll just do their jobs. They know they aren't human, but if you make them feel like garbage, there will be problems."

Joss held his hands up. "Okay, I guess I'll think about it. In the meantime, I'll... try harder to get along with the crews, man."

Harry smiled. "That's all I'm asking for." He waved his hands. "Let me think about dinner. I'll talk to Sirvon, okay?"

On Thursday morning two days later, Harry got back to Joss. He had a peculiar look on his face as he spoke. "Okay, here's the deal. I spoke to Sirvon, and she suggested we do dinner at your house. We'd be glad to bring the food."

"Well, that doesn't sound so bad."

"Yeah, well, there's a small catch – two really. We can't just leave the kids by themselves, so we'll have to bring Aaron and Amber."

"You know my place is kind of small..."

"Smaller than mine, smartass?"

"Alright, I get your point. I just haven't spent any time around kids. Are they like regular kids?"

"Are you kidding? Of course they are."

"Okay, when?"

"Tomorrow's Friday; how about then?"

Joss stuck his hands in his pockets. "Okay, see you then."

Not sure what to say to the girls, he was nervous as he went home that night.

Their kiss the night of Maré's birthday was still upsetting him. *Sisters shouldn't act like that.* He knew that his history with previous pairs was affecting his view of them, that they weren't really like a family, but he was starting to remember how things had been. Sometimes it seemed like the timeline was a little jumbled around, but he didn't dwell on it. In any case, it would be nice to have love in the house again – Riss would have wanted it that way for the kids – but the kiss had changed everything. So he had kept them at more than arm's length. Now he needed to pretend that everything in the house was okay.

But there had been a not-so-subtle change in their behavior, ever since their not-so-subtle show of affection. He supposed that they must have sensed the change it had caused, because he hardly ever saw them touching each other now, and they kept to themselves whenever they were allowed to.

He decided he was going to have to bring up both subjects over dinner.

Except for the occasional clink of utensils on the plates, they ate in mild tension. He had trouble finding the right words to get started, and his gut was churning over it. Their world was very small; the present tension aside, it *had* been good, maybe even pretty well. He didn't want to ruin it. He decided it was best to just say what needed to be said, so he broke the silence.

"Girls, we need to discuss a couple of things."

They looked up from their plates. "Are we in trouble, Sir?" said Maré nervously.

"What? No – something special is happening tomorrow night."

Luna looked at him with curiosity, but he read fear in Maré's face when he saw the whites in her eyes. He held his hand up towards her in a braking gesture. "Easy, nothing to be defensive about," he said, though if she relaxed it wasn't visible. He plodded on. "A friend of mine from work, Harry is coming to dinner to-morrow night. He's bringing his wife and their two kids, Aaron and Amber. Sirvon and the kids are simulants."

Maré froze with her mouth part way open as if she were going to say something, but then forgot what it was. Breylin couldn't help smiling as he thrilled a little to see her reaction to his words. Looking at her he said, "close your mouth, dear, you look foolish."

Looking back at him stunned, she clicked it shut.

Luna spoke into the quiet that followed. "Neither of us has ever met a simulant from another line, Mr. Breylin."

"Don't stress over it. Everything will be fine."

Maré spoke quietly. "I haven't met anyone else on this planet..."

Luna took her hand and squeezed it. To Breylin she said, "What needs to be done? What do you want us to cook?"

"Actually, they will be bringing the food. You girls only need to make sure this place is very clean."

"We won't displease you, Sir," Maré said softly.

"I'm not concerned about that... but there is one thing that does give me pause – the other thing we need to talk about."

"What is it, Mr. Breylin?" said Luna.

"It's the nature of your... relationship."

Maré sat up straight and looked directly at him, surprising Breylin. "We haven't done anything wrong, Sir."

Looking between the two of them, he spoke. "I don't know that you have or haven't. I simply want to caution the two of you in front of my company. If they see anything inappropriate happen, I'll become very cross. Maré, have you explained what happens to Luna when I become cross?"

"I understand, Sir."

"Very good. It's been very quiet around here, and I'd appreciate it if we could continue to avoid any issues," he said lightheartedly as he stood up. "Make sure the kitchen is clean before you retire for the night."

He started to leave but he paused and turned in the doorway. "Good night, girls." Then he left.

—∧=∨—

In bed, Maré had her body pressed up against the gentle curves of Luna's back. In an effort to relax her, she was using the pads of her fingers to lightly smooth the outlines of her ear, neck, shoulder.

"He scares me, Maré."

"He should. It seems like he's been okay these past few weeks, but he's still capable of terrible things."

Luna rolled over. "Aren't you scared?"

"Yes, I am, but I'm not going to worry about tomorrow." She reached down to knead her breast as she spoke. "We have now, my Chroma."

"I know... but I'm still getting used to this place. And that was the first real taste I've had of his dark side."

"I think I can make you forget about it for a while." Maré moved over her, first kissing her lips delicately, then beneath her ear, then down the contours of her throat. Downward she traced, finally taking the taut peak of her breast into her mouth. She sucked, drawing as much of it into her mouth as she could while she dragged her tongue around the sensitive areola in slow, easy circles.

"Ahhh... that's nice, Maré," she said as she laced her fingers through her hair.

—∧=∨—

Breylin stood transfixed staring at the vid screen in his bedroom that showed what was going on in the other bedroom. For long minutes he had been unable to stop watching, but now he just couldn't watch it any more. Reaching over to its lower corner, he stabbed at the button turning the unit off. He slowly angled to the rest of the empty room. Wiping his brow without thinking, he mechanically moved to the bed, then sat down.

He ran his hand through his hair, and tried to figure out what he was feeling... *but I'm all confused. This isn't my bedroom. Where the hell am I?*

He shook himself. Reaching onto the bed behind him, he spoke with a muddled voice. "Riss, help me. I don't know what's happening..."

When his wife didn't answer he turned and saw that the bed was empty, and still made up. He was all alone. *What the hell is going on around here?* "Riss, dammit, where are you...?"

Then the horror came back to him, and he remembered where Riss was.

Forgetting about the girls, Breylin's mind began to retreat as he rolled onto his side and protectively curled into a ball. His last thought before the darkness took his was *Who the hell is crying like that? I hope they'll be okay...*

The next morning, Breylin's confusion of the night before was a distant memory that he was only partially aware of. What remained real to him was the bitter loss of Riss being gone. He had forgotten how helpless it had made him feel for a time, but then he'd remembered it all at once. Now that tired feeling of uselessness had returned to sit heavily on his shoulders, giving him the sense that once again he was unable to stop the train of consequences.

The other thing that remained with him was the sight of the girls engaged in sex. He had very mixed feelings about that.

He understood at an intellectual level that Maré and Luna weren't sisters, or even human. More importantly, they weren't those he had called daughter, the ones he and Riss had taken on camping trips and listened to music with in the living room. These two hadn't drawn crude pictures of the sunset. They were also far less innocent.

But they looked a lot like his daughters, and that's what was crawling around under his skin. Their lovemaking had been darkly erotic.

At a quarter after 5, he found himself hesitating before their door with his hand on the latch. He knew he wouldn't find them fooling around, but seeing them in their bed with his own eyes would make it more difficult to detach from what he had witnessed the night before. Uneasily, he wondered how Riss would have handled this.

Shaking himself out of such foolish notions, he scowled and jerked the handle. Inside, he found them asleep in each other's arms, naked but covered with a sheet. "Girls," he said a bit less harshly than he had intended, "it's nearly five thirty. Time to get up and get started." As they began to stir, he turned and retreated, telling himself that he wasn't rushing to avoid seeing their slender, bare frames.

Normally he would let the girls get his things around for the day, but he was interested in getting out of there once he said the things he intended to. He had already packed the food for the day and was pouring his coffee into a portable carafe when the girls came into the kitchen.

"Okay, so here's the deal," he said as he brushed his hands off into the sink. "This place is to be spotless when I get home."

"Yes, Mr. Breylin. Everything will be perfect," said Maré.

"Okay..." He wiped his face. "Sit down, the both of you, for a minute."

Uncertain what was going on, they sat at the table. Maré looked at him, while Luna looked at her with a question on her face. Maré must have felt her gaze on her; without looking at Luna she reached across and took her hand and squeezed.

He sipped his coffee as he leaned against the kitchen counter and nervously considered how to begin. Looking at the ceiling and then the floor, anywhere but towards them, he spoke. "I've been thinking... about how this house has been for a long time."

He could feel both of them looking at him now as sweat began to dampen his armpits. "Sometimes I'm... confused. I speak as if my wife was still here." As he paused he had to step on some unpleasant feelings that were trying to ooze their way up to the surface. When he had himself more under control, he continued. "Sometimes, I even get a little... belligerent, hurtful."

"Please, Mr. Breylin," said Maré as she started to rise. "We don't want you to become upset over it."

He motioned for her to sit down, and she slowly complied.

"You mean *cross*, don't you Maré? No, don't answer. Look." He wiped his face again. "It's best you just let me get it out. This is hard enough."

He raked his fingers through his hair and sat down opposite them. "There was a time here when my wife and I had a pair of girls just like the two of you. Maré and Luna." His tone continue to soften as he spoke. "We called them our daughters, and they called us Mom and Dad."

Luna was clearly studying him across the table, hanging on his words. Maré just goggled at him. He'd never opened up nearly this much before.

"It was a long time ago, before... before my wife died. It may seem hard to believe but we were a family." He wet his throat with a slug of coffee while he let that sink in.

"I've seen the two of you together, and I guess I've had trouble accepting that you two could love... but I've been wrong. I know that you do, now. I'd like there to be love in this house again."

They looked at each other. The small smile on Luna's face was tender, but she raised her eyebrows in silent question. Maré replied with a tiny shrug. "We do love each other, Sir," she stated. "But we're not sure what you mean."

"Ah. I'd like it if we could put the past behind us and maybe we could try to be a family again."

They just looked at him. The only sound in the room came from the wind sighing around the house.

"Do you think you could... I don't know, think of me as a father?"

Maré let a short laugh escape before she could clamp a hand over her mouth. "Forgive me, Mr. Breylin."

Their silence to his question had started to make him feel awkward, but it was her reaction that caused his brow to furrow as he spoke. "Did I say something funny? I didn't realize."

"I didn't mean it, Sir. It just slipped out," she said.

"Why don't you explain it to me, Maré? It seems like an odd way to respond to a serious question."

"Please, Sir," Luna quickly interjected. "We don't want to be – I mean, we don't want to upset you."

"I feel like my question is being avoided, and that very much seems like an answer."

Maré paused and shook her head slightly before she spoke cautiously. "Mr. Breylin, families are built on trust. I'm not sure we have that."

"I'd like you to acknowledge that I've been very patient lately. Do you have anything to add, Luna?"

Avoiding eye contact, she spoke carefully. "You haven't beaten us since I've been here, Sir, but... you do scare us sometimes."

Maré showed more of the courage she'd found, meeting his gaze directly. "We don't know what you're capable of," she said.

"So that's it, huh? *Fine.*" He pushed away from the table and stood up. "Make sure the house is clean when I get home tonight. Anything else will be *unacceptable.*" He grabbed his stuff and moved to leave, but paused and turned around. He bored into them with his eyes from under a lowered brow. "The love of a family can cover many wrongs, but it looks as if we won't have that. We'll have to see how things go this evening, but I fear I will become cross later."

Then he stormed out to the lift port.

—∧=∨—

"I think the time of it being quiet around here may be over," Luna told her in a tremulous whisper.

Maré squeezed her hand again, and she thought of the music that she had listened to on a few occasions. There had been two times when she'd pleased him enough that he let her turn it on for herself, but mostly she had been a vicarious listener. Breylin would sit in the living room, sit in that chair of his and stare out, and she was sure that whenever she had to edge past him as she was about her chores that he must be rather unaware of the hollow, constant thrums of the wind, but every once in a while he would look up as some particularly fierce gale would rattle the window shutters. On those times, he would get up with barely focused eyes and turn on the music, what the announcer had declared to be classical pieces that were ancient yet still pleasing to the attentive ear. Breylin had never given any indication as to what he thought of the sometimes long and epic music, but she had certainly appreciated them – though she had been careful to avoid letting him know. They were tremendously varied in composition; the individual tracks were usually like segments in a larger story she could almost visualize, but sometimes the movements stood alone and were like marches, or slow, hauntingly beautiful piano solos. *There was a lot of variation in those songs,* she thought, *but one thing almost all of them did have in common – you could always tell when they were ending.*

She could see the truth of it fully for the first time; either the music slowed, or seemed to recede back and down, or occasionally it would build to a dramatic cataclysm. The form it took really didn't matter – you could just tell in some hard to understand way. *And now our lives are like all those musical stories – winding down. You can just tell.*

"I know, Chroma," she replied. "We're going to have to be very careful now."

Twenty Three

Nervous about having company later, Joss gripped the steering handles with white knuckles and pushed down harder on the accelerator on his way home after work. Knowing he wouldn't have a lot of time to fix anything that was missed, he rushed so he could arrive first, and hopefully have just a few minutes to look around. On the other hand, maybe the girls would get it right and he was worried about nothing.

Walking in from the lift port, he found them sitting on the sofa in the living room when he arrived. "You two look relaxed. Is everything done?"

"See for yourself, Sir," Maré intoned.

Her comment sounded a bit smug to his ears, and he stopped in his tracks. "I'm not sure I heard you correctly, Maré."

"We did as we were told, Sir. You can look around if you don't believe me," she replied.

He didn't care for the implied push she was giving him. He walked over to the sofa, grabbed her by the arm and hauled her to her feet. "I don't need you to tell me that I can look around my own house, and I shouldn't have to. You want to try again?" He spoke quietly, but as close as they were she could feel the breath leaving him as he pushed each word out.

Luna jumped up at the same time and carefully laid her hand on his arm. "She didn't mean anything, Mr. Breylin! Just that we think you'll be happy with our work," she pleaded.

"Right," he said, and shoved Maré back down onto the couch. "It better be. One last thing – no affection or touching between you two."

"What's the problem, Sir?" said Maré. "We're not doing anything wrong!"

As the pressure in the room thickened a few atmospheres, he shrugged Luna's hand off his arm and backhanded Maré with about half the force he would have like to use. "You always did have a smart mouth, and it keeps getting you in trouble."

Maré righted herself and glared angrily at him as the faint outline of his hand started to show itself on the side of her face.

"Please, Sir! Your company will be here soon!" Luna said urgently.

He paused, and looked at her while he forced his tempter down. "Yeah, the company." He squatted down in front of Maré where she sat and looked at her closely. Without breaking eye contact, he pulled out the collar controller, held it between them and ran his thumbs over its tiny buttons. "Maré, you and I are going to address your attitude later."

They heard the whine of a lift's drives swell as it pulled up outside. "Shit, they're here. You two had better be right about the place." He stood up and moved to the front door, and a warm, moist breeze that spoke of recent rain blew in as he opened the door to the first guests he'd ever received.

He could feel that there was a tension present as Sirvon's eyes found his, but it passed as he spoke. "Hey, I'm glad you guys could make it. This is Maré and Luna, my girls." He spoke evenly in a hopeful attempt to hide anything he might be feeling. "Girls, this is Harry and his wife, Sirvon, and their children."

The girls came forward at his words, wide eyed at meeting new people. Maré had her mouth partially open again, and Joss had to suppress the smile that wanted to put in an appearance.

Sirvon decided to bridge the gap. "Luna, Maré, it's nice to meet you." Holding up the box in her arms, she said, "can you show me the kitchen so I can get things heated?"

"Sure, I can," responded Maré somewhat unsteadily. "It's nice to meet new... faces."

As they walked towards the kitchen, Luna asked, "hi – can I take your coats?"

"Sure," said Harry. "Kids, can one of you get your Mother's?"

"I will, Dad," said Amber. To Breylin's eye, she appeared to be stiff, uncomfortable. He wondered if it was the new environment or his presence that made her feel that way. *This is going to be a long evening...*

Luna took their things and spoke to Harry's son. "My name is Luna; what's yours?"

Smirking to her, he said, "I'm Aaron."

"It's nice to meet you, Aaron," she responded. "Would you like to help me carry the coats inside?"

"Yeah, sure." His father shrugged out of his jacket, and he took it, then his mother's from Amber when she came back with her arms full. He looked back at his father with a smile as he followed Luna into her room, and a thought flashed into Breylin's mind. *I wonder if he thinks she's attractive... I suppose it's a normal enough response from a young teenager, but from a simulant?*

He recovered quickly and called to Luna as she and the boy retreated down the hallway. "Please help your sister and Sirvon in the kitchen when you're done, dear." To Harry he said, "why don't we sit down while the girls get the food around?"

—∧=∨—

"You seem nervous, dear," said Sirvon to Maré as she put the box on the kitchen table.

"Do I? I don't mean to. It's just... new, I guess."

She brushed her arm. "What do you mean?" she said sweetly.

"I don't have a lot of experience to draw upon." She looked back towards the living room. "I need to be careful in what I say – forgive me for upsetting you."

Sirvon gave her a sad smile. "I'm not sure I'm the one who's upset, dear," she said as she gently stroked her fingers over where Breylin had just struck her.

Maré smoothed her face. If she gave away too much to this well-meaning woman she could get herself and Luna in serious trouble – the painful kind – and it might not be avoidable already. "No really, everything's okay. My Chroma and I just aren't used to new people." She thought perhaps she should try to lighten the mood. "Anyway, we've never met anyone from another bloodline. It's a little strange."

"I think I see what you mean. I guess it must be at first, but try not to think of us as simulants. We're just people, Maré. Different, maybe, but still people," she said, echoing nearly the same words to her that she had used to Luna. "And it might be our circum-stances, but I think the chromanity are more sensual, more feeling than most humans."

"Really?"

"Like I say, it might be just my perspective, but yes. Most of us only ever get to truly live in our heads. And not all humans are heartless, of course." She smiled. "Harry is a terrific man."

"What's it like, being married?"

"It's not so different from having a Chroma – usually far less connected, but it can become pretty close with time and work," she said. "The syncing up that comes natural to us takes a long time with humans. We are much more like family to begin with, and that closeness makes a good foundation for our relationships. And like I said, I think our status gives us all a certain amount of gravity for one another, but most especially for our Chromas." Her eyes became foggy. "Chroma... I'm sorry, I just haven't thought about it in a long time..."

"Did you have one once?" Maré asked reverently.

She nodded her head. "Harry saved me from the accident that took mine. It was a long time ago." She refocused on Maré, and cleared her throat. "Are you happy with each other?"

Deciding that she liked Sirvon, she drifted a little closer to the older woman so she could speak in a confiding but guarded tone. "Life has a way of helping you figure out what's important and what isn't; I'm not sure we could survive without our love."

Sirvon nodded and looked towards the living room past her as she spoke. "I understand. It's one of the ways we really don't differ from *them*. He may not be my Chroma, but I'd definitely die without his love."

After that, they dug the food out of the box and prepared it in a surprisingly easy silence.

—ᴧ=ᵛ—

It was a fairly large kitchen table, but with seven people it was still crowded. "So," said Joss around a mouthful of chicken gumbo. "How old are you kids?"

"We're both fourteen, Mr. Breylin," said Amber.

"They grow up fast," said Harry as he tussled his annoyed son's hair.

"You can just call me Joss. 'Mr. Breylin' reminds me of my father too much."

At his words, Luna shot Maré an incredulous glance, who gave a barely perceptible shake of her head as if to warn her off.

"Thank you for having us," Sirvon said to Joss carefully.

"Sure. It seemed the least I could do, especially since you guys brought the food. The girls did the most, cleaning the place to within an inch of its life." He surprised himself by lifting his glass to them, nodding to each in turn. "Thank you, Luna, Maré."

Maré spoke with obvious happiness. "We were glad to do it, Sir. We're excited to meet new people."

"It must be pretty lonely out here at times," said Sirvon. "What do you girls do while Joss is at work?"

Breylin was beginning to get a little uncomfortable. He didn't want the girls talking too much and risk saying something unfortunate.

Luna answered. "Mostly we take care of the house. Other than that, we exercise or read. Sometimes we listen to music."

"Aaron, Amber, how do you like school?" Breylin asked in the brief silence that followed. With their kids being simulants, it seemed like an absurd question to him, but he needed to shift the conversation, and keep the peace with Harry as well.

"I like it a lot – I have great grades," said Aaron with a smile.

"*I* get pretty good grades, too, but I hate school," Amber grumped. Looking at her father she said, "I wish I didn't have to go."

"I wish I didn't have to send you," said Harry with a wicked smile of his own. "But I do, pumpkin."

"You know, Joss," said Sirvon, "you might bring the girls down to see us sometime. Maybe they could help Amber and I cook another big meal."

"Ah, that would be a big change for them," he said nervously. "Let's just see how this goes and take it from there."

"Please, Sir. We would really love that!" Maré implored.

Breylin silenced her with a look, and she put her eyes down on her plate. The kids began to fidget in the silence that followed. He felt trapped, like things were getting out of his control.

Sirvon shot Harry a look, and he cleared his throat. "Joss..." He said. "We think it would probably do you some good, too. You know, to be around other people."

Breylin's mood darkened. *Why is everyone pushing me?* He punctuated the discussion by loudly dropping his fork on his plate. "That's an interesting idea, Harry. I'll give it some thought, and maybe you and I can discuss it away from the others, instead of putting me on the spot. Would that work for you and your *wife*?"

The awkward silence that followed was thick with tension. Sirvon exhaled in a rush like someone threw open the valve on a cylinder of compressed gas, but Harry stilled her by laying his hand on her arm, without taking his eyes off Joss. "This is your home, and we don't mean to upset you, Joss."

"Oh, clearly. But since you did, maybe it's time to pack things up," he replied in the same even tone.

The muscles in Sirvon's jaw started to tighten, and she spoke angrily. "Man, what is your issue –!"

"Please," Maré said, cutting her off quietly. "It's best if you just go."

Sirvon swallowed the rest of her comment. There seemed to be nothing more to say.

"Let's go," Harry said with defeat in his voice. "Luna, would you get our coats, please?"

After Harry's family left, Breylin stalked back to the kitchen. Standing in the doorway, he silently watched Maré and Luna clean-up. They worked quickly and did their best to hold up their end of the silence. When they ran out of things to do, they turned to him. Maré had the sense to keep her eyes off him, but Luna made eye contact. Then he noticed that they were holding hands.

He held up his right thumb and index finger nearly touching and said, "I'm this close to punishing the two of you. What stops me is that Maré had the sense to ask them to leave."

"Thank you, Sir," she said. "May we go to our room for the night?"

"Just a second." He moved over to one of the drawers and pulled out a long, slotted spoon. He walked back to them with an air of indifference, but then he lashed out with the utensil and smacked their joined hands – hard. Luna squealed and clasped her hand to her chest as blood began to well out of a cut on her knuckles. Maré yelled too as she drew her hand back, but if he'd cut her he couldn't tell. As they recovered from the initial shock they began crying.

"I thought you two understood where I was on the subject of your affections," he said. "You can either confine it to your room entirely, or I'll put an end to it. I'm warning you – if you upset your mother I'll be very cross with you."

Luna was sobbing and staring at her wounded fingers. Maré

got a disposable cloth, wet it in the sink and took it to her. Once she had it covering Luna's hand, she said, "you *don't* have to hit us, Sir. It was an accident."

Breylin struck her in the face, hard, with the flat of the spoon, and immediately welts from the pattern of the slots rose up angry and red. "I did promise you a discussion about your attitude, Maré." He threw the spoon in the sink. "Consider yourselves on probation – the tiniest screw up and I'll strip the hides off of the two of you! Now get in your room!" As he spoke, he drew the collar controller from his pocket and used it to give them several welts each on the backs of their legs to hasten them as they ran wailing from the room.

—∧=∨—

"Harry, you have to do something. You can't just let him..." Sirvon let her words trail off as she looked at her own kids in the back seat of the lift as they sped southward. They were sitting there quiet, but they were taking it all in.

"I know, dammit, I just don't know what yet. Let me think... Fuck, I need a *smoke*!"

When they got home and put the kids to bed, Harry paced the bedroom.

"Just call corporate security, Harry."

"And tell them what? That we think *maybe* he's hurting the simulants he's legally allowed to do whatever the hell he wants with?" He sat down on the edge of his bed, put his elbows on his knees and his head in his hands. "I'm not angry at you, but we have to think of something better than that, hon."

She thought for a moment. "What about the Marines? You said he used to be one of them."

"That was a long time ago. I don't know if they'll be any better, but it's worth a shot. I'll call them in the morning."

"Let's hope he hasn't killed them by then!"

"It's Friday night. Unless you want me to go hunt through the bars looking for them, there's nothing I can do tonight."

"Why didn't you say something to him while we were there?!"

"With our own kids standing right there? Think it through, Sirvon. The guy's wound tight as a spring – suppose he snapped? I care what happens to them as much as you, but the kids come first."

"I know, dear," she said as she sat next to him on the bed and stroked the side of his face. "I'm not angry with you, either, just scared for them."

"Yeah..." he said with a tired sigh. "Look, if the Marines won't help, I'll drive back out there. I don't know what I'd do, but I'll try."

"Gimme a break, Sergeant," Harry said the next morning. "He used to be one of yours. Don't you give a damn?"

Harry winced as the comm channel exploded with the duty sergeant's response. "No, sir, like I told you! We're busy doing our jobs, not worrying about what some guy is doing when he hasn't done anything wrong. I assume you know that, or you'd be talking to CorpSec. Look," he said as he began to relax a little. "I'd like to help – since he used to be a Marine – but the LT. nixed it when I asked the first time you called this morning. I can schedule some routine patrols that would include his settlement in about two weeks. That's the best I can do."

"Well, I'll take what I can get, but don't walk away thinking that's good enough –"

The Marine cut off what he was about to say by closing the channel.

"Rotten bastards!" Harry bitched as he rubbed his eyes. Looking at the set of his wife's chin, he knew what he had to do. "Alright, I'll be back in a few hours."

"You're not going anywhere by yourself. I don't care if he is your friend – suppose that whack job really *does* snap?"

"Well, you're certainly not coming with me, woman! Or do you want to bring the kids, too?"

She exhaled loudly in exasperation. "Fine – but you comm me when you get there and you keep the channel open."

"Okay, that's a good idea. Hey," he said as he touched her face. "I'm sorry I let us get dragged into this."

"Don't be sorry, for doing the right thing Harry. If we don't get involved no one will."

He pulled her to him and held her tight.

Harry threw the end of a cigarette out the window and punched up the channel for home as he was cresting the ridge right before the settlement. "Are you there?"

"Yeah, I'm here. Leave the channel open when you go inside, okay?"

"I will. Okay, I'm pulling up out front. 'I'll probably be a few minutes, so you won't hear anything, but the freq'll be open."

"Alright, just be careful."

"*Now* you want me to be careful! Thanks..."

He killed the power plant, got out of the lift and scurried to the front of the house to get under the tiny roof over the stoop. It was a meager covering in the wind-driven rain, but it was better than nothing.

A few seconds after he knocked on the door, he could hear the ratcheting of the tumblers in the old style lock. The door opened, and Breylin stood across the threshold. "Harry... I wasn't expecting you. Come in." He said coldly. He receded into the house, and Harry followed, shutting the door behind himself.

"How are you today, Joss? You still sore about last night?"

"Honestly? Yeah, a little, but I'll get over it. Sit down. You want some coffee? Maré, put some water on and get us a cup."

Harry watched her as she came through the room and went into the kitchen. "What happened to her face?"

Breylin gave a small laugh and said, "I think she fell. Not too sure." He hollered out to the kitchen. "Maré, come show Harry where you fell and hit your face!"

Harry could hear her getting things around, but she stopped and came back as she was told. Her face was perfectly impassive as she stood before him. He could see three long, bruised welts below her left eye, purple, sharp and even. Harry got off the couch and examined her injury closer. "Is that what happened, Maré? Did you fall?"

She shot Breylin an involuntary, furtive look before her eyes met his. "Yes, it happened just the way Mr. Breylin said it did. I fell." She almost managed to keep her face expressionless except for the tears that were beginning to collect on her eye lashes.

Harry could see that she was lying through her teeth – and terrified.

He heard the soft movements of feet on the carpet behind

him. When he turned around, he saw Luna standing just inside the room. She had a cloth stained with dried blood tied around her left hand.

He turned to Joss but spoke to Maré so that he could watch his expression. "Where did you fall, Maré? What did you hit your face on?"

"Harry? I..." Maré stammered out. "I fell inside. In my room. I forget what I hit."

Breylin, sitting with his feet stretched out in front of himself with the ankles crossed, was the picture of indifference. His expression was one of boredom. When Harry looked up at Luna, he saw a tear slide down her cheek that she rushed to wipe away.

He looked back at their abuser. "You wanna try the truth this time, Joss?"

Breylin got to his feet whip-crack fast and stood before him, muscles in his face and neck tightening. "What's the big deal? She decided to shoot her mouth off to me one too many times and I gave her a minor attitude adjustment."

"Yeah? And what about her?" he said as he pointed to Luna. "What did she do?"

"It's none of your damn business what she did!" Breylin pointed to the front door. "Now you get the hell out of here!"

Breylin went to shove him but Harry threw his arms around him, and they both toppled onto the couch and rolled onto the floor. Maré shouted, "stop, it was my fault! Please don't fight!"

They continued to scuffle and yell wordlessly. Harry got one arm free and brought his elbow down on the top of Joss' head, slamming his teeth shut audibly. It had cost him, though. A split second before Breylin's jaws slammed shut, he punched Harry in the midsection, throwing his weight into it, and all of his air left him in a rush. Tiny motes of light danced in Harry's vision as he struggled to catch his breath.

Luna had run over to Maré and now they were both holding each other and crying.

They rolled apart, but Breylin was on him in a heartbeat. He dragged Harry to his feet and shoved him towards the front door. "I'm really starting to regret ever having invited you over, Harry!" He jerked open the door and pushed him outside, sending him sprawling in the muddy sand of the front yard. "Get the hell out of here, Harry! And mind your own friggin' business! You and your *wife*!" After he was done shouting, he slammed the door shut.

Harry got his feet under him and staggered back to the lift. When he shut the door, he could hear Sirvon's tinny voice through the comm system.

"*Harry? Harry! What the hell's going on there?*"

"I just got my ass handed to me is what happened," he wheezed. He spent the next couple of minutes telling her the details and letting the pain in his solar plexus subside.

"You're lucky he didn't kill you!"

"I don't think he'd have done something like that. He was angry as hell, but the sarcastic asshole was in control." He dug his hand in his pocket to get his key FOB and tobacco. "Shit, I think he tore my lousy jacket," he said as he drew the pouch out and rolled a cigarette with long practiced moves.

"Look, just come home, and be careful!"

"Except for my pride, I'm fine now," he lied; his chest still hurt. "I'll be home in an hour." Firing up the engine and his smoke, he took off to the south using too much thrust.

Twenty Four

As Breylin was throwing Harry out the front door, Maré held Luna tightly to her in the living room. She was too afraid to move, too afraid of what might happen when he came back to them.

Through her tears, she noticed something black sticking between the couch cushions. When she focused on it, she could see the small, square buttons of the controller Breylin kept. *It must have fallen out of his pocket during the scuffle.* Quickly, she bent over, snatched it up and stuck it in the waist band of her underwear.

A low, fearful moan was coming from Luna's chest. Maré went to her, put her arms around her and hugged her as tight as she could. "Shhh... it's going to be alright, Chroma." As comforting as she tried to sound, her heart seemed to be thrashing at an alarming pace, and her temples throbbed in anxiety.

There was angry words and the front door slammed. Breylin stalked back in, looked at them and said, "What are *you two* doing? Go to your room!"

They nervously edged around him and ran back to their room and shut the door before he could change his mind.

Once inside, Luna hissed, "Quick, hide that horrible thing, before he catches us with it!"

"I'm trying to think... where?"

"I don't know!" said Luna in an urgent whisper. "Somewhere!"

"Yeah, I got that..."

"Don't get snarky! What the hell were you thinking?"

"I was thinking that one of these times he's going to kill us with it, maybe even tonight like he promised," said Maré. "How about in the chest?"

"No, that's the first place he'll look!" she replied.

"What if I roll it inside a pair of socks?"

"He's crazy, but he's not an idiot, Maré!" Her head swiveled as she looked for a place to hide the device. "What about the bookshelf?"

"Yeah... let me see." She started looking at the few possessions of theirs on it. There were five or six books, about a dozen pretty rocks, and a few wooden vehicles badly in need of a paint job that had been sitting there since before Breylin had woken Maré up from hypersleep. Then she spotted the framed holo of their parents.

"How about behind Mom and Dad?"

"Fine, just do it!"

Maré climbed up onto the bed and slid the little device behind the frame. "That's as good as it gets. We'll have to get it into the trash disposal as soon as we can."

Now that the crisis was passed, at least for a little while, Luna was starting to calm down. "If he finds it, Chroma, he really will kill us," she said wearily.

Maré sat next to her on the edge of the bed and laid her head on her shoulder. "I don't think so. If he kills us, he won't have anyone to torment."

Luna pushed her off her lightly and said, "Is that supposed to make me feel better?"

"Look, I'm sorry. Maybe I didn't think it through. I just acted.

I hate that thing!"

Maré pulled her back into her arms as she stifled a deep sob that was like an aftershock. "I know – I hate it, too."

—∧=∨—

In his bathroom, Breylin stuck his head under the faucet and let the cold water run over his hair and into his face, hoping that it would crush the anger he was feeling. He was going to have to make this right somehow with Harry, or risk losing his job. Right off the top of his head, he had no clue how he was going to do that after throwing the man out of the house and down onto the ground. As the water poured over him, he tried to ignore the sick feeling that something else was about to go miserably wrong. Again.

He shut the water off, grabbed a towel and started pushing his hair around with it. He draped it around his neck, sat down on the commode to relieve himself and rested his head on the wall behind. There was an annoying drip sitting on the end of his nose, but he was too wearied to care enough to do anything about it. Just sitting there, he shut his eyes and tried to think of nothing at all.

Despite his halfhearted attempt to remain a blank slate, the image of Larissa as she was back in college picked its way to the front, until he could think of nothing but her. Softly, he began to cry and pound his fist on his thigh. He noticed neither tears nor the dull ache in his leg, only the memory of a distant time when the sun's rays had created a thousand diamond splinters in his lost love's hair...

When Breylin came to an awareness of his surroundings, he didn't know how long he had been sitting there; since the sun was covered with storm clouds – and it never moved, in any case. The only signs that marked the passage of time were his numb legs, dry hair and an immense fatigue, as if he had been hard at labor working with the gas taps. His watch told him that nearly an hour and a half had disappeared while he had blacked out. With stiff movements and sore joints he got up and made himself presentable.

As he left the bathroom, his stomach complained about its empty condition, and he realized that he'd missed the noon meal. As he took a seat in the living room he called out while he massaged his calves. "Luna! Maré! Lunch needs to be made."

They emerged from their room cautiously and went into the kitchen. From where he sat, he listened to them opening cupboards, drawers and containers and working the stove. He was gazing out the picture window at the storm when he was startled by Luna standing next to him. He thought he'd been paying attention, but he hadn't seen her approach. When he turned to acknowledge her she said, "everything's ready, Sir."

He got up and followed her into the kitchen, where he was greeted by a familiar, old smell. He sat down at his place and immediately began to scoop the food into his mouth. "Spicy potato casserole – we used to eat this all the time. My daughters loved it." he muttered into the plate. After a short silence, he shook his head and looked up at them. "You aren't them, are you?"

Maré paused with her fork halfway to her mouth and shook her head no.

A single tear slid down his face. "Too bad."

When the plate before him was empty, he wiped his mouth,

got up and left the room without saying another word, leaving them staring at each other in bewilderment.

He was having trouble focusing. *Something about this house... it's not right. Riss must have moved the furniture again. No, that can't be it – Riss is gone. They're all... gone...*

Breylin sat down on his bed to try and sort things out. His eyes were sore, and when he rubbed them he realized that he was really tired. Maybe he just needed a nap and then everything would seem okay. He dragged himself to his feet, drew the shutters and turned off the light, then laid down. *Things will have to make more sense after I get some sleep...*

—∧=∨—

"Did he just cry?" asked Luna, when they heard the door to his room close.

"Yeah... he does that sometimes when he misses his wife."

"But he was asking about his daughters. Is it me, or was that eerie?"

Maré nodded. "Oh, it definitely was. I'm starting to wonder if we shouldn't have played along with his fantasy."

"Maybe it isn't too late," Luna said staring down at her own empty plate. "We could tell him we thought about how it might be nice to be a family."

She sighed with resignation. "Maybe that would be better, if we can keep him pacified."

—∧=∨—

Breylin came to with a start, with a strong feel — almost like a memory — that he had *something* thrashing against him as he held it close in his hands. Whatever it was that he had been dreaming about was fading fast, though, and the image wouldn't form. As he sat up in the dark and his thoughts cleared, the sweaty clothing that was all stuck to him was beginning to irritate him. He stripped off his shirt, dropped it on the floor and reached for the light. He was still a little irritated, but at least his head felt clearer. *Small mercies...*

It was nearly time to eat again. As he changed out of his clammy things, he noticed that the controller wasn't in his pants. It must still be in the bed somewhere. *Screw it, I'll find it later.* He went out into the rest of the house.

When he hit the living room, a startled Maré was jumping off of Luna's lap. It might have been innocent, but the look on their faces gave him pause. *It might be time for a little refresher course on household etiquette*, he thought. He reached for the collar controller in his pocket...

Of course, it wasn't there. "You two look guilty as hell. What were you doing?"

They were both wide eyed with fear. "Nothing, Sir. Just sitting," said Luna.

"Together, it would seem, and testing my patience." He allowed an edge, thin and sharp as a knife blade, to creep into his voice. "Was I unclear somehow?"

He'd found that tension was an extremely useful tool, so he let it linger in the air as he pierced them with the intensity of his stare.

Luna was actually beginning to quietly whimper, but not Maré;

she had the spine to glower right back at him. "We understood what you wanted, and we haven't disobeyed. We were only sitting together, *Breylin*."

The way she said his name caused one of the belts in his mental machinery to slip a little, and before he knew it, he was looming over her lithe frame with has left hand drawn back. She faced him not with resistance, but with an inner calm that he could easily read on her smooth face and defiantly upturned chin, and it was enough to pause him from delivering a blow that would likely heave her over the couch and across the room. Luna was kneeling at his feet, holding on to his leg and wordlessly wailing, but her actions barely registered.

She's going to push me, is she? This was something new, and though he didn't like it, he wasn't about to let her make him lose control. His arm *ached* to uncoil its tension at her, but he knew that if that happened, he'd probably kill one or both of them, and he didn't want that. He let his hand drop to his side, and when his hand brushed something, he looked down. It was Luna. He looked back to Maré and smiled while he lightly brushed her hair with his fingers. Her calm faltered, and he knew he'd found her weakness.

Obviously, he was going to have to help them through one of the difficult times tonight.

"That was too far, Maré." Using the backs of his fingers, he brushed the welts on her cheek. "Go make dinner – something with a lot of carbs. I think we're all going to need our strength tonight."

The tears were slipping freely down her cheeks when she hung her head and started to move into the kitchen, but she hesitated looking at Luna.

"Luna," he said harshly. "Go lie down in your room – now."

When she didn't move, he picked her up by her arms and gave her a shove in the general direction of their room. She turned the stagger into mechanical motions as she shuffled down the short hall. He turned back to Maré and said, "Well? What are you waiting for? You can either go make dinner or I'll have Luna come back with the lash. Your call, Maré."

This time she obeyed.

While Maré was in the kitchen, Breylin went back to his room to find the controller. A casual feel for it in the covers of the bed revealed nothing, and he ended up stripping it entirely. When he found nothing, he searched the bathroom, again finding nothing. He got down on his hands and knees and examined the entire floor. Zilch.

Its disappearance was odd. He went to the vid screen in the corner of the room. "HomeSys," he said. "Display the location of the collar controller."

The screen displayed a finely detailed floor plan of the house in white lines on a blue background, with a small, red reticle along one of the walls in the girls' room. "So," he said under his breath. "That's where it went, huh? HomeSys, deactivate it."

The old terminal made a few tones, and the reticle faded from the schematic.

Since he was sure he'd put it in his pants this morning, he couldn't imagine how they had gotten it from him. Then it occurred to him that he had that scuffle with Harry, and that it could have easily slipped out of his pocket while they were rolling around. It must have been then.

It didn't matter, of course. He got the spare controller out of the back of one of the drawers. Instead of using it though, he decided to let them dig the hole they were in a little deeper.

He sat down at the kitchen table as Maré was finishing the preparations. "Go get Luna," he told her when the stove alarm emitted its final tones. She looked at him with dry but puffy eyes as he spoke, and left when he was done.

When they came back, Luna sat down at her place. He could tell she was intentionally avoiding meeting his eyes. Indifferently, he wondered if it had been her who had secreted the controller in their room.

Maré took her seat after she sat a plate of spaghetti in front of him first, then theirs. Immediately they began to eat.

He broke the peace. "Thank you, Maré. This seems quite hot. I think I'll enjoy this," he said with a mirth that was completely at odds with the strain in the small space.

"Um, thank you, Sir," Maré replied uncertainly.

"Sure, dear. You know," he said to no one in particular around a mouthful of food. "I seem to have misplaced your collar controller."

Luna's head shot up to look at him when he mentioned the object. *Yes, it was her that took it. Maré must know, yet she manages a straight face...*

"It's a funny thing, isn't it? I normally keep it near;" he laid his hand on Luna's forearm and smiled at her as he continued. "I never know when it will be needed. Can you two keep an eye out for it, please?"

Luna's tears were dripping onto her plate.

"Oh, don't be upset, dear," he said to her. "It's such a minor thing, and I'm sure it will turn up soon."

Without taking her eyes off her plate Maré said, "We will bring it to you if we find it, Mr. Breylin."

"That's all I ask." He picked up his fork and ate a mouthful. "Mmm, it's gotten a little cold..."

"Can I heat it up for you, Sir?"

"Thanks, Maré. That would be great – but why don't we let Luna do it?"

She jerked at the mention of her name, but she got up, wiping her eyes and nose with her sleeve. She put his plate into the warmer, hit a few buttons and stood there while it worked. At its tones, she took it back out and set it down at his place.

He grabbed her arm tightly and pulled her so that she had to lean down close to his face. "Thank you, Luna," he whispered to her, and immediately she began to emit a soft whine. He let her go and said, "please, finish your dinner."

She sat down hard, put her head in her hands and quietly sobbed.

"Eat, Luna," he said. "I haven't fed anyone in a long time, but I assure you I remember how it's done. It's an experience *you* won't forget, either."

She began to wail as she slowly picked up her fork.

"May I help her, Sir?" Maré asked plaintively.

"As you wish, but shut her up."

She got up and kneeled down next to her, then put her hand on her shoulder. "Listen to me, Chroma, you have to eat. C'mon, I'll help you."

Luna looked at her and nodded, and Maré began to feed her.

Once Breylin had emptied his plate, he pushed back from the

table, walked around them and left the room.

—∧=∨—

When she heard his door shut, Maré stood up and looked in the living room. When she saw that he wasn't there, she returned and whispered to Luna, "keep eating. I'll go get that damn thing and get it into the disposal unit."

Luna nodded, and Maré went back to their room.

—∧=∨—

Breylin went right to the vid screen and switched on the cameras throughout the house. The top left quadrant showed the kitchen, just as Maré was turning from the doorway to the living room. She bent down to Luna and whispered something to her. Breylin tried to turn up the gain on the mike but it was over too fast for him to catch it. She was already turning and leaving the room.

She came into view in the top right quad on the cam in the living room. He watched her steal across and down their hallway while keeping an eye on his door.

On the cam in their room, Maré was climbing onto the bed and moving a holo frame. She took something small – obviously the controller – and tucked it into the back of the waist band of her pants and was climbing off the bed.

He went to the door of his room and waited. When he thought he heard the tiny click of their door, he gave it a few seconds, then quickly jerked the door open. She was in the living room halfway to the kitchen, obviously startled.

"Mr. Breylin, I –"

He advanced on her fast, grabbed her by her arm and twisted it up behind her back, causing her to yelp with pain. "Shut your mouth!"

He shoved her into the kitchen, past a horrified Luna and down onto the top of the table. Maré's plate crashed to the floor. She was screaming now, and flailing around for purchase with her free hand as Luna was rising and backing away. Immediately, he grabbed her clothes, and felt the device through the fabric. "What do we have here, Maré?! Something we're not supposed to, isn't it?!"

"I'm sorry, Sir! I'm sorry!"

Luna was hugging herself and screeching, too.

He picked her up by both arms and slammed her back down, hard, causing the rest of the things on the table to jump. "I told you to shut your mouth!" He rifled around and brought the controller out. Laying his torso over hers, he showed it to her and spoke softly. "You're going to pay dearly this time, Maré."

"Sir, stop! It was me! Please don't hurt Maré!"

"No, Luna, don't –!" cried Maré, but Breylin tightened his grip on her arms and she cut off. He stood up and looked at Luna for a few heartbeats. "Well, what do you know?"

He pushed off Maré and came around the table while Maré stood up. He held up the controller to a frightened Luna. "Here, you wanted it – take it."

She just looked at him.

"No, really – go ahead."

When she hesitated he shocked her by snatching her hand and

thrusting the small device between her fingers. "For all the good it will do you. It's been disabled." He reached into his pocket and pulled out the other unit. "This one's active, though." He pressed a few buttons, and they went rigid. "See?" He pushed a few more button to release their legs, then grabbed them both by the hair and dragged them screaming into the living room.

He shoved them around so that they were facing each other in front of the window, then pushed more buttons on the controller, freezing them in place. "There we go." He produced scissors, showed it to them, open, close, open, close. Luna mewled while he cut her clothing off of her. Her skin pebbled up with each piece that came off. "Hang on, I'll be back in a minute," he said as he moved to the lift port.

When he came back, he had a long, thin strap that he hung on Luna's shoulder. He roughly shoved Maré up to the window, then he produced the controller. He pushed buttons, and Luna could move. He grabbed her by the neck and she screamed and struggled against him, but with their size difference it was no use. "You wanted freedom from the collar, Luna – let's give it to you." He dragged her to the front door and out into the storm.

Outside, the wind-driven rain lashed them as he hauled her over to a large stone sitting in a field across from the house. He shoved her into a sitting position next to it, back first, then he tied the strap first to one of her wrists, around the rock, then the other wrist. She wailed the whole time. He bent down so she could see him deactivate her collar, then he cut it off her and dropped it in her lap, followed by the defunct controller.

"There you go, Luna, you're free!" he yelled over the wind. "Have a good night!" He turned and walked back to the house.

Inside, he found Maré with tears streaming down her face. He used the controller again to allow her collar to release her.

Immediately, she went to her knees. "Sir, I'm begging you, please bring her back inside! Please, Mr. Breylin! She didn't take the thing – I did!"

"Maré," he said as he took a knee next to her. She was cringing and weeping with her face buried in her hands, but he lifted her chin so that their eyes met. "I don't really care who took it – it's not important. *Now stand up.*" He took her by the arm and guided her back to the window. "Stand right there – don't you move."

From the corner of her eye she could see him go down their hallway. When he disappeared from view, she looked out at poor Luna, naked and soaked, and obviously crying in anguish – though from this side of the glass, Maré could hear nothing but the squall as it rushed around the house, and the staccato of rain striking the glass centimeters from her face.

Breylin returned, and he held up the lash so that she could see it. "Maré, you stand there all night and watch your *precious* Chroma. She stays there all night, and you stay right here. That's your punishment. If you move from that spot, I'll know – just like I knew about the controller – and I'll strip the skin off you using this. Don't test me, because I promise you'll regret it."

He shut off the lights on his way into his room and slammed the door.

—∧=∨—

Maré continued to cry while she watched Luna long after Breylin left the room. Unable to do anything but stand uselessly, she felt like her insides had been torn out. Luna appeared to be sleeping; at least Maré hoped she was. Her chin was down and her thrashing had ceased. A cold fear gripped her heart as she did her best to avoid thinking about the alternative. She began to mewl, wishing she could just do something, anything.

Since the sun never moved – with the cloud cover it couldn't be seen, anyway – she had no way of telling how long she had stood there, nor how long it would be before that bastard Breylin would go bring her Chroma back inside. *Hold on, Luna!* But watching her was intolerable. She started flexing her knees and shifted her weight from one foot to the other.

Next she tried leaning on the window sill for support, and then she just leaned her forehead on the glass. When the cold of it began to seep into her, the memory of that first touch after waking up as she stared out at Jupiter back on Paradise Station flashed into her mind. For a while she tried to focus on the happy memories of those times, but the spell broke when she noticed Luna had raised her head and was looking right at her. She was crying again. Maré realized that Luna must be able to see her standing at the window, and she began to cry a fresh round of her own tears. She couldn't take the sight any more, and she sank to her knees and buried her face in her hands.

A high whistle pierced the darkness and a white hot line of fire stretched itself across her back. The terrific pain of the lash broke the disorientation into which she had lapsed, and she screamed. *Stars, Breylin is here in the room!*

She didn't have long to think the implications through, because he grabbed her by the neck and jerked her back to her feet. He shoved her head back to the glass and said, "I warned you, didn't I? But I'm a good father, always willing to patiently retrain his children when they need it."

"Please Sir, I'm sorry I disobeyed – I just couldn't watch anymore. We're both so sorry, please bring her in, Mr. Breylin ..."

"She's staying right where she is and so are you, Maré. And I've told you before – you just have to tell your muscles to obey, and they do. Maybe I should help, since you have nearly five hours to go."

She couldn't see what he was doing, but in a few seconds she felt a slight tingling from her collar, and from the neck down her muscles went rigid.

"That should do. And don't worry about falling asleep – if your collar senses you going under, it will feed you some adrenaline. I would try to avoid it if I were you; too much of that and you'll really be miserable."

She heard him pad out of the room and shut his door, much more quietly this time, and unwanted, nervous laughter bubbled out of her.

Looking out, she could see that Luna had once again lapsed into unconsciousness, and her tittering died in her throat. Her mind retreated from the sight, pulled back from what Luna was going through, and how she had failed to protect her. Bitter tears replaced the nervous laughter, it almost seemed like someone else was shedding them.

Twenty Five

Breylin's vibralarm woke him up at 5AM, just as it did every morning. He silenced it and rolled over, but his mind began to hum with dull and indistinct thoughts, and sleep wouldn't return. Exasperated, he sat up and turned on the light. When he had collected himself somewhat, he threw the cover back and swung his legs out. As he began to rub the slumber from his eyes, he remembered the condition he'd left the girls in. *It's mornings like this*, he mused as he rubbed his eyes, *that I wish I hadn't given up those damn expensive stimpacks.*

He relieved himself and got dressed quickly. Walking into the living room, he found Maré with her head pressed up against the window, moaning softly. If she were aware of his presence, she gave no indication. There was a huge smear on the glass in front of her, where the tears and snot had streamed from her eyes and nose. It had clearly been a long night. Coldly, he wondered if she'd learned anything.

He pressed a button on the collar remote, and she dropped bonelessly to the plastic floor in a miserable, whimpering heap. Now standing over her, he could hear her trying to form words, but he couldn't decipher what she was trying to get out. It didn't matter. He bent closer and nudged her with his hand, but it made no difference.

He scooped her up and carried her sideways down the hall to her room, elbowed the lever and shouldered the door open. Inside, he clumsily laid her down on the bed. He reached for the light, and when he turned back to her to take her shoes off, he noticed the holo frame that they had used to hide the collar controller. Forgetting her shoes, he moved around the bed so that he could reach the thing. It was an image of their false parents. "*I'm* your father..." he whispered. Jealousy welled up inside him, and he had a notion to smash the image, but he checked himself; now wasn't the time. *I'll address this issue later.* Instead, he put it back on the shelf, face down, then he left the room to go get his other daughter.

Outside it was still raining, but the bluster had mostly died off. Luna hung loosely by her wrists, lifeless. He got scared that he'd gone too far and killed her. He felt for a pulse on her neck. Panic began to thrash itself in the back of his mind when he couldn't find it, but then as he moved around a bit, he discovered the slight twinge. She was alive.

As the rain began to seep through his hair and down the back of his neck, he undid the knots on her wrists. Her arms felt cold and rubbery under his hands. Leaving everything else behind, he picked her up and brought her into the house.

Maneuvering Luna into their bedroom, he found Maré watching him from half lidded eyes. She had more or less rolled onto her side. "Move over," he said, "so I can lay your sister down."

"She's not... my sister..."

"She *is* your sister, until I say otherwise. Now move over."

She winced, as if she regretted her words, but she shifted closer. Slower than he liked, but she got there. "Now, strip back the cover, she's cold."

She grabbed the cover and did as she was told. As Breylin laid Luna down, Maré made the effort to sit up and reach for her. "Stars!" she said when she felt her shoulder. "Is she still alive?!"

"She'll be fine, but you might not be. I'm going to jack up the heat, so it's going to get pretty warm in here."

"How long before we know?"

"Know what?"

"If she'll be alright or if you've killed her."

He fought down nagging guilt and his flaring annoyance with her. "Watch your tone... and I told you, she'll be just fine. We just have to get her warm."

Maré began clumsily stripping off her own clothes, then slid under the blanket and covered her with her body. Maré began to shiver herself, but she huddled closer to Luna. Maybe being left outside all night must have been far worse than he'd imagined. He wished it hadn't been necessary.

"If it isn't too much trouble, do you think you could get me a pain killer?"

His expression darkened at her comment. He said nothing as he looked at her, the seconds ticked by, and she crumpled a bit under his stare.

She sighed and looked up at him. "Please... Dad?"

Mercurially, he smiled and stroked her hair. "Sure. I'll be right back, as soon as I turn up the heat." With that, he left the room.

By the time he came back, the infrared panels under the floor were already warming the air. She sat up a little, and he handed her the wafer and a tumbler of water. When she was finished she laid back down with Luna.

"I'm sorry I had to punish you both last night. Are you hungry?" he said sincerely.

"Yes, Dad, but I want to stay with Lu– my sister a while longer."

"As you wish. Come out when you're ready." He turned and left the room, gently shutting their door.

—∧=∨—

As Breylin left the room, Maré tried to get closer to Luna, to put more of their skin in direct contact. She kept listening to her breathe, stroking her face and whispering soft words of love to her in a steady, unending stream. She knew it was irrational, but she had the strangest feeling that if she stopped, her Chroma would slip away. It was silly, but she didn't want to stop, anyway – it was her job to protect her. She was just so cold...

After a little while though, as her head was pounding noticeably less, she began to notice that Luna was warming up, and she redoubled her hopefully soothing efforts. Her breathing became less shallow, and she made a few low sounds.

Maré maneuvered her so that she laid more on her side, and she scooted in to spoon her. As she did, she noticed the scrapes that covered her back – scrapes made by the rock to which Breylin had tied her. When she looked over the rest of her, she found that her arms, her chest, her legs were also marked, and she was filthy where the storm had caked now dried filth onto her. A deep sadness came over Maré, filling her, for the ordeal that they had both suffered. All she could do was hug her close and emptily hope for better times.

A slight tremble passed through Luna and transferred itself to Maré, and she felt her fingers move just slightly under her arm. "Chroma?" she said, praying she was starting to come around, but there was no reply.

She continued to warm up as Maré caressed her, and eventually, she started to wake up. "Maré...?"

She hugged her tightly. "I'm here, honey."

"What...?"

"Shhh... don't talk. I'm going to roll you towards me, and I'll hold you."

Maré worked at positioning her. It took a minute or two, but by the time she was done, Luna's eyes were open and she was holding onto Maré's hip.

"I've been holding you for some time, Chroma. Truth is, you had me quite worried." She picked her head up so she could look her in the eyes. "You were quite cold when he brought you in."

"It was horrible, out there..."

"I know; he made me watch you all night – or at least until the pain in my head made my vision go out of focus." She laid her head back down on Luna's shoulder. "I'm sorry he did that to you."

"I hate him, Maré."

"Shhh... he's in his family fantasy pretty deep," she said as quietly as she could, "but he's still lucid. Listen to me, we're going to have to play into it, at least until he comes out of it. We'll be safer if we can keep him in it anyway."

"Just now I don't care – I feel like shit."

"Yeah, I get it. Listen, I'm starved. You want something?"

"I just want to sleep..."

"Okay, I'll get you something after you've rested. Will you be okay for a bit?"

"Stay with me until I fall asleep, please..." and she shut her eyes.

Maré watched her for a couple of minutes. Her breathing was even, normal – just sleeping. Except for the scrapes, nothing she could see spoke of the ordeal she had endured last night. Moving slowly, she slid from under the cover, climbed off the bed and put her clothes back on. She slipped from the room, eased the door shut behind her, then leaned against it with her eyes clamped tight. *Sleep for now, Luna, get what you can. It's up to me to try to protect you, but I can only do so much... and I think we're running out of time...*

Out in the kitchen, she found Breylin sitting at the table, drinking coffee. *Showtime*, she thought; she just hoped she could be convincing.

"How is your sister?"

"She woke up briefly, but she's resting now, Dad."

"And you? How is your headache?"

"I'm okay. I thought I would get something to eat. I'll make something for Luna when she wakes up."

"Sounds good. Listen, I need to run into the city to get some food. Maybe I'll even get something special for us. Will you and your sister be okay for a bit?"

Another crazy mood shift! Last night he tortured us, but now he's almost kind. I don't understand... why the hell does he keep changing directions? In any case, a thought had occurred to her while he was speaking. Leaving them alone for a while might present her with an opportunity. "We'll be fine, Dad. When are you leaving?"

He held up his cup. "Now that you're up, I'll just finish my coffee and head in. I'll only be a few hours. Please plan on making dinner later, okay? Enchiladas – your mother always liked those."

"I'll take care of it, Dad," she said softly. She didn't think he realized that she meant something other than dinner.

After she heard the lift port door close and his lift speed away, Maré checked in on Luna, who was still sleeping with her mouth open. Their room had gotten quite warm, and she had begun to sweat. She went back to the tiny display mounted on the living room wall.

"HomeSys," she said to it, and it acknowledged her with two tones. "Lower the temperature in the small bed room to standard." Again, it made two tones, a few meaningless icons flashed on its tiny screen, then it went dark.

So, it takes my commands, she thought. *I wonder how far it extends.* "HomeSys, deactivate the simulant collars." In reply, it made two discordant tones, and a red X flashed twice.

Evidently, certain functions were either locked out or inaccessible from this panel. *Of course it wouldn't be available here, only from the terminal in his room.* And she wasn't going to touch that.

She padded over to the entertainment system and activated its screen. Its comm functions were rarely used, but it was to those that she turned to now. Unfortunately, she'd only ever seen the menu options on those few times she'd been told to activate the system's stored music. She found herself stumbling now to figure out its operation.

After a few minutes, she managed to find the stored connections list. There wasn't much in it. Skimming through the items, she saw entries for "Larissa's Parents", "Joss' Parents" and a few for various places in Twilight City, but nothing that obviously identified Harry. She selected "Work", and looking through its properties, she spotted an entry for "Supervisor". She couldn't be sure, but she would have to take the chance. She highlighted it with her finger and pressed the Go button at the bottom.

The screen flashed, went blank, and then came back with a large, red X. At the bottom, it displayed *Unauthorized Comm System Use. You may proceed only under emergency conditions. Continue?*

She paused with her finger over the Proceed button. If she did it, the system might notify Breylin or send a separate signal elsewhere. She had no way of knowing what would happen, and there would be no going back. The seconds sweated by as she wrestled with the choice and the black consequences.

Fuck it, she thought, and mashed the button forcefully.

A red light began to blink on the front of the entertainment center. The screen went blank, then it slowly showed small, green concentric circles pulsing outward. After five or six pulses, the face of a woman appeared, and she breathed a sigh of relief.

"Hello?" said Sirvon.

"Hello... this is Maré."

"Harry!" she called out over her shoulder. "Maré's commed us!" Turning back to the screen she said, "of course, dear. I didn't expect to hear from you. Are you... okay?" Harry appeared at the side, wiping his hands on a small towel.

"Maré! I'm sorry I couldn't help yesterday."

"Hello, sir. Thank you for trying to help us. And yes, Sirvon – we're okay for the moment. *He's* left us and gone down to the city."

"What happened after Harry left?"

"It wasn't too bad at first, but later on I did something foolish and managed to provoke him, and it got really ugly." She quickly gave them a rundown of the night's events. Harry's face got redder as she spoke, and by the time she was done, his wife appeared to be on the verge of tears.

"How's Luna now?" said Harry.

"She was terrible when he brought her in this morning, but she woke up briefly a little while ago. She's sleeping now."

Sirvon shook her head. "I'm sorry it happened, Maré. For both of you."

"Yeah... Can you help? Breylin's mind is going, and he's spending more time living in the past than ever before. On top of that, he's very volatile. I don't think it will be long before he kills one or both of us."

"Let me figure something out, Maré," said Harry. "I'm not sure what to do yet, though."

She sighed. "We'll be okay for a while, unless he finds out about this comm connection. Will he know?"

Harry and Sirvon looked at each other before he responded. "I don't know. He will if he looks at the logs."

"He hardly ever comes over to this thing."

He nodded. "Good. You'd better stay off it and not risk contacting us again."

Sirvon chimed in. "Sit tight, dear. We'll figure something out."

"Okay, thanks."

"We'll talk soon – be careful," she said as she started to reach for the screen.

"Wait," said Maré.

"Yes, dear?"

Tears sprung forth. "I... don't want you to go yet," she said.

Sirvon's expression softened and she stroked the screen with her fingers. "Be strong – we'll be there as soon as we can."

Maré touched the pixels of her after-image just as the connection was broken. Wiping her tears away with her shirt sleeve, she noticed that the little red light continued to blink on the front of the device, and panicked. She knew that there was no way he would miss it as soon as he entered the room. She had to do something about it.

It was a small thing, and sticking out just a tiny bit, but it wasn't a button – so pushing on it did nothing. She got a black marker from the kitchen and tried to paint over it. It did a lot to hide the light pulses, but it wasn't good enough. Finally, she jimmied it with one of the kitchen knives, breaking it, and the light ceased. If he inspected it, he would know immediately that someone had tampered with it, but she couldn't do anything about it now.

She decided to go back to their bedroom to check on her Chroma instead of satisfying her immense hunger. As she reached for the lever, fear and nausea clenched her insides over everything so hard she felt like throwing up. She huddled in on herself and crouched against the wall outside their door. Tears streamed down her face. Rocking, she thought but she wanted to scream *this is so unfair!* Her mind cast for some meaning, something that made sense of it, but all she could come up with was a memory of a time Breylin had wept and asked the same *why?* of the sun. He'd been staring out the window, but he saw nothing as his mind had wrestled with it from deep in a fissure of despair. *Is that all there is for us? Despair and pain, the monsters gleefully screwing each other over and over? Eating each other when they can get away with it and sometimes when they can't?* But there were no answers, only the wind under the eaves of the roof.

Okay then, she resolved. *Somehow we'll make our own answers.*

Her mind had become clear with a new purpose, but her gut was still churning with acid and morose dread. She forced herself to breathe slowly, deeply, measured. They might pay for what she'd done, *hell, probably,* she thought as she stood back up. *But it had been the right thing to do.*

—∧=∨—

"Now what?" said Sirvon as she broke the connection with Maré.

"I don't know..." said Harry as he raked his fingers through his hair, then he let out a big sigh.

"I knew that bastard was mean to those girls, but I didn't guess he was capable of what he did," she said.

"Tell me about it. He's a lot worse than I suspected, too. But if I had known, I would have fired him, and we probably wouldn't know what was going on in the house now."

"Do we tell the corporate security people know?"

"We've been over this – CorpSec doesn't care if he's doing what he has a legal right to do. Same goes for the Marines," he said with wearied frustration.

"We have to help them!"

"I get it, honey. Dumping extra pressure on me is not helping me figure out what!" he shot back.

"Okay... I'm sorry. I just want to keep him from hurting them."

He sat down heavily in a chair, letting out a big sigh on his way down. "Me too. Let me think. You know... as hard as it's probably going to be to get them out, that won't be the most difficult thing."

She sat down opposite him. "What do you mean?" she said with raised eyebrows.

"I can't just seize the girls – his property – without giving him the chance to bring in the authorities against *me*. Keep in mind he knows things about us that would be bad if they came out."

"Oh my stars..."

"Yeah... If I can get them out –"

"*When* you get them out!"

"Okay, *when*. When I get them out, I'm going to have to give him a reason to not go after them."

She thought about it. "Could you hold his job over his head?"

"I can do what I want there, I just don't know if that'll be enough. Maybe I can threaten him with contacting his family back on Earth. They're all distant, I think, and they're too far away to really help, but maybe he'll want to keep what he's done secret. It's worth a shot. It might depend on how deep his delusions run."

"You won't be able to go to him by yourself..."

He put his head in his hands. "Shit, I hadn't thought that far ahead, but that's another issue." He started going through their coworkers, one by one, trying to think if any of them would be motivated enough to get involved. The problem was that Breylin had kept them all at arm's length, and none of them were particularly motivated about dealing with the simulants outside of the work. Even Janice, the dispatcher who sometimes talked to Joss, wouldn't be much help because she was on in years.

Then he realized he'd fallen into the same thinking that almost every other human was guilty of – only considering the humans. *Of course, that's it! Someone from the worker crews would be willing to help!*

Getting up he said, "I've got an idea, honey..." He rushed around and got ready to head into work as he explained it to her.

"Harry," she said, and he paused halfway out the door. "Have you thought it through if he won't cooperate?"

"I don't see those girls any different than anyone else, honey. I'll go as far as I have to in defending them." He turned and walked out into the breeze as it was picking up and blowing trash around in the street in front of their house.

Sirvon threw the door open and hollered after him, "Please, be careful!" As he moved down the block towards their lift, the wind gusted and blew her hair into disarray, and she shivered.

Because it was Sunday, his presence at work would be conspicuous. Harry hoped it wouldn't matter. From his office, he opened a comm channel over to the simulant barracks complex. A young woman – a simulant from the support staff – answered.

"Can I help you, Sir? I'm sorry it took so long to answer your call – we rarely ever get commed on Sundays."

He tried to sound official when he spoke. "It's nothing. I need Tomas Ridder from Breylin's crew to come to my office. Please have him bring any notes from last week's activity out in the subsolar region."

"Right away, Sir, but it may take him a few minutes."

"Understood – as soon as he can without breaking his neck."

He chain smoked while he waited, and it seemed like Ridder was taking forever. Nearly twenty minutes and about ten smokes later, he was just about to comm the barracks a second time when he knocked on the open office door.

"Sir? You wanted to see me?"

"Yep, come on in, Tomas."

He walked in hesitantly and stood before the desk. "Sir? I'm not really sure what you're looking for... I don't have any notes – "

Harry held up his hand to forestall any further uneasiness he might be feeling. "Hang on, Tomas. I'm afraid I asked you here under a pretense."

"Whoa – what happened to your face? And were you burning something in here?" he said as he coughed a couple of times and waved his hand in front of his face.

"Ignore the smoke, and we'll get to what happened to me in a bit. Can you sit down for a minute? I need to ask you a favor, and it won't be an easy one."

Ridder sat down, and Harry laid it all out for him. Before he was done speaking, Ridder's mouth had gone dry.

"I can't believe it..."

"I know. I knew it had gone bad with you, but it seemed like it was a fairly isolated incident. That is, until I found out about what was going on in his house."

"Sir? Can I ask you a question?"

Harry realized he'd been leaning forward, and he sat back and tried to relax. "Go ahead."

"Why do you care what happens to them? After what Mr. Breylin did to me, it seemed like he got away with it."

"You mean like I *let* him get away with it?"

Ridder put his eyes on the floor. "Well... yeah. Didn't you?"

Harry gave a tired sigh. "To be honest, Breylin *is* my friend, and he's had real crap in this life. I thought that's all it was, and that I could control him. If from where you were sitting it looked like he got away with it, then I'm sorry."

Ridder's smile dripped with cynicism. "Forgive me if that doesn't count a whole lot, Sir. He beat the hell out of me for nothing. But you still didn't answer my question – why do you care what happens to his simulants?"

"I'm sticking my neck way out here, Ridder. The truth is, no matter what you might believe, I don't think what he's doing is right, and I need your help to get those girls away from him."

He idly scratched his forehead while he thought about it. "I'll help, but you'll understand if I won't stick *my* neck out to help him, or you. I *will* do it for my own kind, though."

The two men were quiet on the way out to Amity Canyon, until Ridder spoke up. "I assume you think this could go bad – right?"

Harry looked over at him. "It's certainly one of the possibilities, but I hope it doesn't come to that."

"What do you plan to do with them, once we get them out?"

Harry studied the road a bit. "I haven't gotten that far in the plan yet," he said uncertainly. The thought instantly made him wish he'd rolled a few smokes before leaving.

Ridder sat looking at him for a few seconds. "You really are putting yourself on the line for a couple of *gabachas*. That surprises me."

Harry took his eyes off the road to meet his gaze. "I'd appreciate it if you didn't use that expression."

Ridder snorted. "Fair enough. I guess that was something of a cheap shot."

They crested the rise, and the canyon opened before them. "There's the house," Harry said as he pointed at it. "Alright, look. You stay off to the side while I knock on the door. As soon as he opens up, I'll barge in, and you follow me up. I want to overwhelm him fast, threaten him, get the girls, and then get out of there before he has a chance to think."

"Sounds good – let's see if it works though."

"Yeah. Breylin once told me 'no plan of battle survives first contact.' Let's hope he was wrong."

They pulled up out front, jumped out and moved into position fast. Harry wrapped on the door hard enough to make it rattle in its frame. He stood with the straps of his muscles laced tight over his frame as he waited for what seemed like years for the door to open as the wind tore at him. *Today was obviously a day made for tense waiting*, he thought, and it pissed him off.

Twenty Six

Just as the door started to crack open, Harry gave it a hard shove, banging the door against the wall, and he forced his way in. He found himself face to face with a startled Maré, and she was reeling from his sudden entry. She yelped, and it pushed his internal tension even higher. *Shit, it was supposed to be Joss!* Joss had been right; the plan went right out the window. It was too late to reconsider now though, so he shouldered past her into the living room.

Standing up, Breylin yelled, "what the hell is going on?! Harry?!"

Everything happened at once. Harry was advancing on Joss with Tomas at his back, but when their eyes met, he could see Breylin's understanding bloom, and he began to stride in their direction with his teeth bared in terrible rictus. They met somewhere in the middle and filled the air with the noises of predators trying to ward each other off. Harry swung a hard right at his jaw, but Joss backed a little out of reach, then replied with the heel of his foot, driving Harry into Tomas. By then Maré had backed into the corner, stunned.

Harry recovered quickly, and he and Tomas had grabbed Joss by the arms. "Don't fight us, Joss! We've got things to say and you're gonna listen!" They thrust him backwards until they had him up against the sofa.

"Let go of me, dammit! Or I'll kill you both!"

"Stop making this hard, you lunatic!" Ridder hollered as he dug his fingers into his arm. "Or I'll even the score between us!"

"Let *go* of me, you piece of shit! No one will even miss you when you're gone!"

"Stop fighting us, Breylin!" yelled Harry. "It's the only way out!"

Joss managed to jostle Ridder off balance and get his arm free from him. While Ridder was trying to grab him again, Breylin slammed Harry's ear with the flat of his palm.

"Ow, you bastard!" His vision filled with angry fireflies, and he let Breylin go. Dazed, he stumbled back. The edges of his sight turned black, and he could only watch with detached interest as they continued to swear at each other and scuffle back and forth, arms flailing all the while. On the other side of them, he could see that Maré had her hands over her ears.

Breylin threw a big uppercut but it only glanced Ridder's jaw. He answered with a wild swing of his own, missing him completely.

The scene was total chaos. Maré and Luna added their own yelling to the din in the room as they pleaded for Ridder and Breylin to stop fighting and tried to pull them away from each other. Dimly, Harry wondered through the ringing in his head where Luna had come from, and why the two girls would interfere. As they broke contact, Joss managed to shove the girls to the side and turn back.

Ridder was on him though; he connected a brilliant left hook, and Joss' head snapped back as blood ran from his mouth and nose. His hands went to his face, and Ridder used the distraction to drive his shoulder into Joss' midsection. They both went over the sofa in a tangle of limbs and guttural snarls. They were still clawing for purchase and the better hand as they staggered to their feet.

Joss' nose was bleeding freely, and he was spraying droplets of it from his mouth with each enormous exhale. Ridder's shirt was striped with it, but he didn't notice; Joss had one hand in his hair and was pulling it back, lifting his chin to an optimal angle for the heel of his other hand. When he connected the two, Ridder's eyes rolled up and he reeled away, leaving Joss standing there with murder in his eyes and huffing arterial froth on his lips.

—∧=∨—

Maré had stood shocked, watching the fray, and holding on to Luna. Things had moved fast, and once started there had seemed no way to stop this confrontation that had quickly careened into a war for survival. Fear had been enough to keep her and Luna from wading back in, but a small, hopeless part of her mind had been chittering the idea that there was no way two tiny women would be able to do anything other than get in the way. For better or worse, this would have to play on without their interference. It was a bitter conclusion to give in to.

She continued to watch as Harry lurched around the sofa to confront Joss, but he was moving slow, way too slow to Maré's eye, as if he were wading through water. She could see from the look on Joss' face and the way he stood to meet him that he was sizing up how to take Harry down. *No! No!* she thought. *If he wins this then he's not going to stop until he kills us all!* She looked at Ridder as his eyes began to flutter, but he would never be in time to intervene, not by a long shot. The whole damn thing teetered on the edge, and Joss was about to push them all over it. She could see how it would happen, as if they were all following a memory only she could recall. The music was definitely picking up its pace and building to the end.

Something shot through her, jolting her, flushing and dizzying her, an almost ecstatic perception that she was somehow above, outside, independent. Rational thought began to drain away, but she had the sense that the others were now becoming aware of her. She could feel Luna's gaze at the back her neck as they broke contact. Ridder regarded at her as if she had become something utterly incomprehensible. Harry didn't seemed to have noticed anything odd, but in a weird, crazy way she perceived that in a future context Breylin had already noticed her. Maybe all of the Lunas and Marés that ever were stood watching, too. She nearly laughed at the insanity of it, but there was no time, none. There had been some, a little, while her jumbled thoughts were jostling each other, but it was gone now, slipped away, and all that remained was the sense that doing something *now* was right. Rationality was quickly receding, and its last trickles were that giving in to that floaty, disconnected impression was linked to protecting Luna. *"Fuck it,"* she muttered, but even she couldn't hear it.

Movement. It seemed as if now she was the one pushing through water, but she wasn't. The rock hard, crystalline buffer of her fear, what had moments ago welded her fast in place, was now developing an infinitesimal flaw somewhere deep inside. It spidered out, shattered and fell away, and through its gaps she was rushing at Joss without thought or consideration in a paroxysm.

As she crossed the room she let out a wordless, high-pitched shriek, and she collided into him as his head snapped around, eyes wide with surprise. His awareness registered, and it gave her a warm echo of satisfaction at having seen it beforehand. At the very instant of impact, the steel bands of every muscle and tendon in her knotted around her joints. She dug her straining toes into the rough texture of the floor, and she did everything she could to lever him over. Though Joss easily outweighed her, he'd only been prepared for dealing with Harry, and it was just enough for her momentum to alter his center of gravity. Though it felt like the trip to the floor took forever, she was on top of him as he went down. While the world was still tilting, Maré noticed the stunned, astonished look on Harry's face.

Her added weight drove Joss into the coffee table – and through it. She forgot about Harry; her entire world came down to throwing herself at this man, meeting him with what force she could muster, stopping him with her entire being. Of the music in her head all she could hear was the building thunder of the timpanies, or perhaps it was the mad crashing of her heart throwing itself against the bars of her rib cage; she neither knew nor cared.

She screeched at the top of her lungs and thrashed at him with balled fists as more blood began to curd on his mouth amid the wreckage of the table. Joss' eyes were still wide with disbelief, but the intensity in them was dwindling away. He tried to fend off her blows, but his arms were moving as if they wouldn't work properly, weak and wooden.

—∧=∨—

Harry watched through what remained of his dazed wits as Luna appeared next to her. "Let him go, Maré! Let him go!" she said, but Maré kept hitting him until Luna took her by the shoulders. She stopped flailing at Joss and looked up at her, quizzically, and then began to squall miserably as she leaned into Luna. As fast as she had rocketed at him, her fugue broke.

Something clicked into place. "Get her off him, Luna!" Harry barked. "The glass from the table!"

Luna looked down as she held Maré, and her jaw dropped in horror. A narrow, thick spire of green glass was jutting out of Joss' abdomen. It was decorated with the brilliant red of Joss' life, and more of it was beginning to saturate his shirt.

"Grab her arm!" Harry took the other and they guided her off Joss. Luna took her crying into her arms, but when she hugged her Maré loosed a sharp hiss. Luna let her go, and a red stain began to snake its way down the side of her shirt.

Luna said "Oh, Shit!" as Maré squeezed her eyes shut and clamped her hands over her own wound. She sat down hard on the couch, Breylin forgotten.

"Harry..." said Joss in a wet whisper as he reached up. "Help me..."

He looked at Luna and said, "Go get some towels! Move! Get whatever you have for tape, too!"

He knelt down beside Joss, yanked one of the cushions off the couch and put it under his head. As he worked he said to Ridder, "Are you going to be alright? I need help, dammit!"

"Yeah, he rang my bell, but I'm getting there," he said as he stood up shaking his head.

"Fine," Harry said as he bent over and began to examine Joss.

Joss spoke, and Harry forgot about Ridder. "Harry... how bad is it?"

"Hang on Joss, I don't know yet. It sure as hell ain't good. Let me look at it..." he said as he stripped the shirt away from his wound. The glass was keen – it went right through him. Beyond the couple of large pieces under him, it doesn't seemed to have shattered much, but there was a pool of blood slowly spreading out beneath him on the plastic floor.

Luna ran back into the living room carrying a first aid kit. "This was under the sink! It's got some tape in it and a bunch of other stuff!"

"Good job," he said. "Get it open and find the bandages and tape. See if there's any surgical foam, too – we're going to need it. I need whatever towels you have in this place!"

She bolted from the room, then hurried back with several. "Here. That's all of them!" she said through her tears.

"Get one of those over her wound, Luna. Take a look at it and see what you can see."

"Maré?" said Luna. "You with me?"

"Pain, Luna," she replied distantly. "It hurts like hell."

"Let me see, hon." Luna kneeled down beside her, but Ridder joined them.

"I have some training, let me look at it."

Figuring they had it under control for the moment, Harry turned back to Breylin. "I'm going to have to roll you, man, so I can see what this thing looks like in the back. It's going to hurt like hell, but hang on."

"Yeah... go..."

Breylin screamed as he tilted him away, exposing the wound from behind. *Crap, the glass is a lot wider back there!* He eased him back down again amid more groaning. His breathing started to become shallow, and sweat was standing out on his forehead.

He looked up at Harry with a question in his eyes. He laid his hand on Joss' shoulder as he spoke. "It's bad, Joss, but I'll do what I can."

"Harry..."

"Yeah, man?" he said quietly.

"I'm sorry for everything..."

"Let it go, Joss – just focus on staying alive for now."

Looking up, he spoke to the others. "Okay, we're going to have to get him up on the couch. Luna, wad one of those and press it to the wound on his back once I have the damn thing out. How's Maré?"

"I don't think she's bad," Ridder said. "It'll need stitches, but that's probably about it."

"Here, I got the stuff," Luna said as she held out a small wad of bandages. "I found surgical foam, but the stuff seems old."

"It can't be helped. Those bandages are useless for a wound this size, though – throw them away. We'll just have to use the towels." He turned back to Breylin. "You ready?"

"Shit, the pain..."

"I know. Once I've done what I can to stop the blood loss I'll give you whatever there is in this kit." He took him by the arms and said, "Okay, hold on, Joss."

Breylin nodded and Harry hauled him into a sitting position. Breylin screamed again, though weaker this time, ending with a few more bloody coughs. "Ridder, get down here and hold him up."

"I'm not helping that damn psycho!"

Harry shot him a deadly look and seized his arm. "I don't give a rat's ass if you don't like him – you get your ass down here now!"

"Fine." He kneeled and grabbed Joss' arms, as Harry moved around his back and knelt in warm, red gore. "Hang on, Joss!" And he pulled the glass out in one quick motion. Breylin just groaned. Reaching into the case, he took out the foam applicator, pressed it to the raw, puckered hole in his back and depressed the button. The device sputtered, and he shook it, tried again. It sputtered once more, then filled the hole with a thick, expanding goo. Moving to the front, he eased the nozzle in and pumped the button again. A little came out, then quit. "Shit!" Harry shook it again, more violently this time and tried it again, but nothing happened. The indicator showed it was empty, and it wasn't enough. Harry tossed it to the side.

"Call emergency services, Ridder! Tell them what happened and see if they'll come. Wait!"

"What?"

"Don't tell them anything you don't have to – nothing. You read me?"

"I'll handle it," he said as he moved to the comm equipment, and began to work its interface.

Harry grabbed a towel from Luna and pressed it to Joss' stomach tightly, then put her hands over it. "Hold it in place and keep a little pressure on it – got it?"

When she nodded, he said to Maré, "I need to get him up there – you need to move, okay? I'm sorry..."

She shook her head with fearful, wet eyes as she moved to get out of the way. Maré was coming around – it was probably the gash in her side prodding her – but taking care of her would have to wait. Harry took Joss by the arms and hauled him up and onto the couch. He continued to moan as Harry checked his wounds. The one in front was still seeping, and he figured Joss was probably bleeding internally anyway. The blood coming out of his mouth with every cough probably meant that he'd at least nicked a lung. There was nothing for it, though. Lying back on the cushions, Breylin looked pale and sweaty, and Harry was sure it meant shock was setting in.

"Any idea how much blood he's lost?" Ridder said. "They want to know."

"Tell them I don't know. A lot, though. I applied surgical foam, but I don't know if it will help."

Ridder spoke for a few more seconds, then came back. "They'll come – they should be her within twenty or thirty minutes – but they didn't sound all that hopeful when I described his wound," he breathed.

Breylin looked up and gave a weak smile. "I've had it, haven't I?"

Looking at his friend, he nodded. "I'm sorry, Joss. I can't do anything else..." He broke eye contact and went to the first aid kid. Looking through what was there, he located a small stash of sedative. He worked the notches on the hypo-spray and pressed it to Joss' neck, injecting him with about a quarter of its contents.

"Give it a couple of seconds, and that should dull the pain, man," he said quietly.

"Thanks," he said, then looked at the girls. "Maré, Luna..."

Luna was kneeling next to him, and Maré moved behind her, standing there impassively with her hands at her sides. Harry noticed that she was crying, but it seemed like she was mostly in her head, not here in this room that was beginning to stink with the coppery odor of blood.

"We're here... Dad," said Luna, and a tremor passed through Maré. *Maybe she isn't totally here,* he thought, *but that had definitely registered.*

He smiled as he looked up at her. "I'm sorry... for everything. I'm sorry I didn't... love you like I should have."

Luna, still holding the towel to his stomach, said, "just get better, and maybe we can figure it out."

Joss reached up and brushed her face with bloody fingers. "I'm not going to pull through this one, honey." When she let out a sob he said, "it's okay, Luna. I'm going to join your mother..."

Without taking her hands off of him, she turned and buried her face in Maré's side. Harry couldn't tell if the laceration was bothering her less or if she had just gone numb to it, but either way she hugged Luna to herself, if awkwardly, and watched Breylin with stiletto-focused eyes. *She went away for a little while there,* he thought. *But she's definitely back now.*

"Could you –" he coughed a few times, wincing as each one wracked him. He settled and slowly relaxed. "Would you put on one of the holos of your mother?"

Luna looked up at her, and Maré sighed. She let her go and walked over to the entertainment center. She navigated the menus of the system for a few seconds, and it sprung to life.

It showed a tableau of Larissa and the girls sitting around a campfire somewhere outside. The fire illuminated their faces as Joss was moving away from the camera to sit back down in the circle. He picked up a long stick and stirred the coals, sending a shower of bright orange photons upwards. The sparks seemed so real that Harry almost felt like he was really there, in the shade of some unknown hill or mountain. He understood that the exothermic reaction of combustion was producing motes of red hot carbon, that they were propelled upward on the rising thermals of the fire, but that wasn't it, or even a part of it. He couldn't feel the heat, but in some unqualifiable but no less real way it was also magical, and the magic pulled at him. Stealing a quick look around, he saw that the others were raptly attentive to the unfolding scene. Joss was smiling, for a dead man, and he seemed completely lost in the moment out of time most of all.

"I have a small surprise, for you two," said Larissa, and she pulled a small book out of her pack.

"Hang on now, we haven't even eaten!" Joss said playfully. The real Joss snorted, and when Harry looked at him, he saw that he was shedding tears of his own.

"Hush you," Riss said and pointed at Joss. "The Queen has spoken," she retorted with a playful smile.

Joss laughed and Luna, with bright eyes, snuggled into Mom's armpit.

Smiling ear to ear, Maré said, "go ahead, Mom, we love it when you read to us."

"I suppose I can cook *while* you read..." he said. As Riss was paging through a book, he picked up a few more sharp sticks and produced a pack of sausages. He skewered two and handed them to Maré, who was watching Larissa too closely to notice. He bumped her with his shoulder and handed them to her when she turned. He gestured towards the fire and she held them over it to cook. He speared two more and held them over the flames himself.

"Here we go," said Larissa. "*Snow White and Rose Red.*"

"I knew it – I love this one," said Luna sweetly.

"You gonna let Mom read or keep talking?" said Maré with a giggle, and Luna stuck her tongue out at her.

Larissa cleared her throat loudly, then began to read...

"There was once a beautiful queen who ruled from a grand castle. Near a fountain in the castle's courtyard was a bright garden, and at the center stood two huge rose bushes, one of which bore white and the other red blossoms. She had two daughters who were like the two rose bushes, one named Snow White and the other Rose Red. They were as good and happy, as busy and cheerful as ever two children in the world were, only Snow-white was quieter and more gentle than Rose-red. Rose-red liked better to run about in the meadows and fields seeking flowers and catching butterflies; but Snow-white sat at home with her mother, and helped her with her house-work, or read to her when there was nothing to do.

"The two children were so fond of each another that they always held each other by the hand when they went out together, and when Snow-white said,"

Larissa motioned to Maré, who emphasized, "We will not leave each other!"

"Rose-red answered," Larissa said, then pointed to Luna, who nearly shouted her answer: "Never so long as we live!"

Larissa said, "and their mother would add,"

The three of them finished gleefully with, "What one has she must share with the other!"

All four of the people in the image erupted in laughter, while Joss watched, smiled at the happy memory and cried softly. The holo of Riss reading to their daughters and Joss cooking continued to play. Luna was tearing up too, and despite everything that had just happened, Harry was embarrassed to find his own eyes leaking.

After a few moments, Joss dragged his hand across his nose and said, "Girls, will you get your old man to the window?"

They looked at each other, and Maré nodded. Together, they took his arms and got him to his feet, causing him to suck air in sharply. They put his arms around their shoulders, and helped him over to the chair by the picture window. Slowly they lowered him, and he moaned through his clenched teeth the whole way down.

Harry put his hand on his shoulder. "Joss, you want the rest of the painkiller?" He paused – it was just too much. When he continued, his voice cracked with raw emotion. "There's a good bit here. It will... make you sleep."

"No... I can barely feel it now, Harry. Will you tell Sirvon... I said I'm sorry?"

Harry nodded, and he cried as the realization hit home that his friend was about to die – and soon, judging by the wet sounds he was making as he breathed.

"Girls, give me your hands."

Luna cried harder as she answered him, swept up in the emotion of the moment. "You are holding our hands, Dad." Maré wasn't, though – she was holding onto Luna – and she made no move to participate further.

He nodded. "I'm sorry, girls." He coughed up more blood, and Luna wiped his chin with one of the smaller towels. "I should have... been kinder to you. I should have loved you more like a father. Please forgive me..." He spoke slow, quiet as he continued. "Things were sometimes confused... but I remember what it felt like..." Another fit of coughing choked off anything else he might have said.

Maré looked at Harry and Tomas with resignation and a question on her face. "Can you do anything for him?"

Tomas snorted and turned away, but Harry shook his head, wishing he could turn away, too. He wanted to; he felt like an invader now, out of place, and way out of his league. He was angry with himself, and he was certainly angry with Joss, his now dying friend, but he wouldn't turn from this. No matter what he'd done, he was still Harry's friend, and as awful as watching him slip away felt, he wouldn't walk out that damn door to make himself feel better. *How could I face Sirvon if I did?* And that was what hardened his resolve; her image floated in his mind, and he forced that cowardly need to run to the back of his mind and breathed slowly.

"It's okay, Dad – there's nothing to forgive," Luna said, her voice cracking with barely contained emotion.

"Your mother used to sit here for hours at a time... do you remember? She loved the view... but she was very unhappy. I couldn't make it better..."

Maré kneeled down beside the chair and looked into his eyes. "Can you hear me, Dad?" she said in a near whisper.

"I hear you, Maré."

"A lot of your blood is cooling on the floor, and you haven't got long... do you have regrets?"

He breathed and said nothing, but he shook his head.

"This is what it feels like when you've lost everything, when you're finally at the end of all things, that there's nothing left. It's the way you've made everyone who trusts you feel, most especially Mom."

He nodded again. "Yeah... I know."

"Maré!" said Luna.

"No, dammit! He's sitting in that chair, looking out at the fucking sunset and dying because of what *he* did!"

"She's right, Luna," he said. "There was too much hurt and anger... I should have moved on..." He paused to gather more breath. "Joined your Mom when she died, but I wasn't strong enough... like my Dad was... I finally understand what he meant all those years ago... But it's my time now. Luna, Maré, will you understand? Will you forgive me when I'm gone?"

"All's forgiven, Dad," said Luna.

"I can't listen to this anymore," and Ridder went to the front door, opened it and walked out.

Joss' eyes cleared and he sat a little straighter. He squeezed Luna's hands tight and said, "Do you think God will forgive a wretch like me?"

Maré pressed the bloody towel to her side and stood back up. She opened her mouth to say something undeniably caustic, but Luna shot her a pleading look, and she closed it. Instead of speaking, she gestured with her chin towards him, a gesture that seemed to Harry to say *Go ahead Luna, go ahead and comfort him if it quiets your mind, and hastens his death.* As she clamped her eyes shut and tears fell, the tight line of her mouth seemed to finish the thought. *I'll remain silent for your sake, but don't ask me to ease his passing.*

"Love covers many wrongs, Dad," said Luna. "You can rest now."

Relaxing, he said, "yeah, rest... that will be good..." He slumped, laid his head on the back of the chair and stared up at the ceiling. He coughed a few times, but feebly. He shut his eyes, and after a few seconds of winding down, he spoke quietly. "Oh, Riss, there you are... the girls and I were just..." He trailed off, shuddered, and stayed silent.

A miserable Luna rose and went to Maré, who held her while she sobbed.

Harry went to Joss, and putting his fingers on his neck looked for a pulse. He thought he felt something weak at first, but as he repositioned he felt nothing.

Harry shook his head in futility. "He's gone."

Maré leveled a look at him over Luna's shoulder. "But the wind's still howling." With the tears she'd shed drying on her face and the muscles working along her jaw, he couldn't for the life of him figure out what she was thinking, and he wasn't sure he wanted to know.

Elegy

When Emergency Services and Corporate Security finally arrived, there was nothing left to do but the paperwork.

After the medics had patched the laceration in Maré's abdomen, they zipped Breylin into a large, black satchel and stowed him in their meat wagon with brutal efficiency. Since he had been dead for nearly two hours, they cared little for the details of what had happened, and left almost before the two CorpSec investigators had begun making notes.

"Mr. Westport, I'm Detective Joe Agabe, and my associate is Detective Portumna." Agabe was a tall and dark skinned man with close cropped hair. Though he wasn't thin, his unusual height made him seem lanky. His face was smooth, and his carefully fitted suit seemed to be at odds with his vaguely indifferent manner. His partner was a fiery redhead with a pinched face who kept hugging herself in her long coat, as if she were cold. She looked around the living room, remained silent and avoided Harry's eyes as she was introduced.

"I don't want to take a lot of your time; can you tell me what happened?" Agabe said as he pulled out a pad and began to tap in notes with a small stylus.

"Not much to tell, really," replied Harry. "I came out here with one of Breylin's simulant subordinates, Tomas Ridder. They'd had an altercation at work, and I was hoping we could resolve it."

"Seems odd – why didn't you just do it at work?"

"Well… Joss is – was – my friend, and I was hoping we could keep the issue quiet."

"I see, please continue."

"To make a long story short, he didn't want to talk about it. We argued and said things we'd both regret, it escalated and got out of hand. We fought and grappled. When we tipped over the couch and landed on the table, he was on the bottom. I tried to seal his wound as best I could, but I was..." Harry shook his head and sighed. "In over my head, I guess. He knew his number was up. We got him over to the window so he could look out at the sunset, and he died moments later."

"You shouldn't have pulled that shard out, but you were probably in over your head more than you realize. The paramedics tell us the glass pierced through his liver. It's possible he might not have lived had it happened in the medical facility down in Twilight. Pulling it out of his wound may have hastened his death, but not by much. Nothing you did or might have done would have made much of a difference either way."

"Thanks... I still feel pretty crappy." Harry massaged his forehead as he spoke. "He was my friend."

"I see that one of the simulants," He consulted his notes. "Maré I believe, has a laceration and quite a bit of blood on her. Can you tell me how that happened?"

"She got hurt while we were trying to help me work on Breylin. Would you like to speak to her yourself... or either of the others?"

"No, I don't think that will be necessary, Mr. Westport. This seems like it was an accident, and I have enough information for the mandatory reporting agencies. We're nearly done here – I just need to tie up the loose ends."

"Loose ends?" said Harry nervously. "Like what?"

"I need to verify that the dwelling is still useable before I secure it. Other than that, I assume as a representative of your company that you'll return Ridder to where he belongs, but I'll need to take the other two with me as abandoned simulants. They'll be institutionalized until they are either sold off or expire."

This is it, Harry thought to himself. *Really sell it.* "Of course I'll get Ridder to where he belongs, but maybe I can help with the disposition of the other two. My wife and I don't actually have any simulants; I was thinking maybe we could take them on. It's the least I could do for him, and my wife and I've been thinking about it for a while. Anyway, it'd keep you from having to walk them through the system."

Agabe wagged his head side to side as he mulled it over. "That would make my job a lot easier – it's a hassle taking care of simulants on the weekends. I'll just have the forms sent your way during the week, if that's okay."

"Thanks," Harry said with what he hoped was nonchalance.

"If you would have them retrieve any of their effects, I would appreciate it. Once they gather everything they want or need, you may go, and we can secure the place."

"Yeah, sure – you should be able to salvage most of the afternoon."

"Exactly, Mr. Westport," he replied. "Oh, one last thing – what of Mr. Breylin's belongings; did he have a next of kin recorded at work? If you don't recall I can look it up."

"No, his family's all gone, here and back on Earth. I suppose there might be a few things we want to take with us, but you may do whatever you want with the rest. May I keep his lift? I might be able to get a few credits for it."

"Normally we just leave everything for the next tenants, though it's highly unlikely this place will ever be used again." He gave

Harry a bored smile. "Not too many folks have Zarmina as a destination anymore. Do what you like with the lift."

"I see what you mean. Well, if you'll give me a couple of minutes, I'll have everyone out of your way."

Agabe nodded, and Harry breathed a sigh of relief as he went down the hall to the girl's bedroom.

After he dropped them off with Sirvon at their apartment, Harry took Ridder back to his quarters in the work complex. It was a short but silently tense ride.

When he pulled the lift into the compound, he shut down and turned to his moody passenger. "You're not going to be able to talk about this with anyone. Regardless of what would happen to me, those girls would be warehoused somewhere unpleasant, and you can probably guess what would happen to yourself."

"I know – you don't have to worry about me talking... and for what it's worth, it didn't go down the way I would have wanted it to," he responded. "I mean his death. You know that, right? I didn't give a damn about him, but I didn't want him dead."

Harry sighed loudly. "Yeah... Me either. No one killed him, Tomas – not you or me and not Maré. Breylin killed himself. He did it a long time ago, his body just didn't know it."

Ridder nodded in acceptance. "Are you really going to take care of those two girls?"

Harry turned and stared out the side window at the approaching clouds. "Yeah, I meant what I said."

He paused. "May I politely ask you why you'd bother?"

It definitely looked as if another storm would be rolling in soon. "It's like I said... my wife and I don't have simulants, and we'd like to keep them." *Now leave it go, please,* he thought.

"If you say so. Listen, I know we're going to have to go back to being what we were before this happened, but sitting here... well, between us, you've earned my respect. Very few humans go out of their way to help my kind."

Harry turned back to him. "As long as we're being honest, thanks for helping. You didn't have to get involved, but you did. You are what you are, but you're a person in my book, Tomas."

Ridder nodded once more as he spoke. "Damn straight I am." He pushed the door up and climbed out of the lift. He stuck his head back in. "One last thing."

"What?" Harry said tiredly.

"When you're lying in bed tonight and you're thinking about the two simulants in your home, and how you brought them back from hell today..."

"Yeah?"

"Before you congratulate yourself too much, remember that there are lots of others around that aren't happy where they are, either."

"I don't know what to tell you, man," he said and sighed. "Ridder... The truth is I can't save every starfish that washes up on the beach."

"Yeah, that's the spirit," he said. "Call someone else for the next psycho, okay?"

Harry nodded, and Ridder shut the door.

Back at their apartment, Harry found Sirvon and the girls with their heads together in the small sitting area. Everything the girls owned sat in a couple of boxes a few feet away on the floor, and they looked understandably tired.

"Hey," he said.

Sirvon smiled when she saw him coming in the door. "Hey yourself."

"How's everyone doing?"

"Better," said Luna. "It's been a long day though. Thanks for taking us in."

"We appreciate everything, Harry," Maré whispered.

Sirvon took their hands. "Of course, dears. It's going to be cramped around here, but it will be fine."

"I have a few ideas about that, but we can talk it over tomorrow. How about we have dinner and just chill out for tonight?"

"Good idea, Harry. Girls, how does pizza sound?"

Luna smiled. "I'm dying of hunger. Pizza sounds fantastic."

They turned to Maré, but she stayed quiet. "Honey?" said Sirvon.

"Girls," she said staring at the floor, so quiet that Harry wasn't sure he heard her correctly.

"What do you mean, Maré?" Harry asked.

"Girls," she said again. "Breylin always called us girls. I think we've been through enough to be called women now." She looked up, reached out for Luna and drew her into her arms. They made eye contact, then Luna laid her head down on Maré's chest and closed her eyes. It was becoming her default position when they embraced. As she absently smoothed Luna's hair, she looked to Harry and Sirvon and spoke. "Do you think that would be okay?"

Sirvon looked up at her husband when he answered. "You're

right, Maré, and I'm sorry. We'll call you anything you want, but you're definitely women."

The next morning, Harry got up at his usual time for work when the alarm went off, but he surprised Sirvon when he called in to say that after the weekend's events, he'd be taking a week off.

"Good thinking," she said to him when he ended the comm. "We should get this place sorted out."

"Not exactly what I had in mind. We can talk about it when our guests rise. Would you make me some coffee please? I'm going to step outside and have a cigarette."

Sirvon scrunched up her face, but she said nothing as she began to make the coffee.

He stopped. "Okay, honey, you win. Today's a new day, and I'm quitting."

She stopped and turned to him with raised eyebrows. "Are you serious?"

"Why not? I give. It seems like the right time to start making positive changes."

She gave him a smile warm with pride. "You'd better get some nicotine patches before you get moody."

"A remarkable idea, my darling."

"And make the gym a priority – I don't want you getting fat, either."

He laughed as he reached for her, and she came to him. They stared into each other's eyes for a few quiet seconds, then rubbed noses.

Movement from the sofa broke their private moment, and they

turned to see their house guests sitting up.

"Good morning," Sirvon said with a splash of joy.

"That's easy for you to say. Maré had some wicked elbows last night."

Maré looked at her silently as she rose. She regarded their new hosts but continued in her silence.

Luna gave her a big smile, but the only reply Maré gave her was to caress her cheek.

Harry cleared his throat to break the tension. "Let's eat some breakfast, and then we can discuss our collective future," he declared. "For what I have in mind, we've got a lot of work to do."

A couple of days later, Maré and Luna were settling into their new home down on the shaded floor of Amity Canyon. Luna had remarked she could hardly believe the changes they had been through in such a short time, or the kindness of Harry and his family. They had rearranged their entire lives to help them, and to be near them. Maré had become a little more talkative – and a little more possessive where Luna was concerned – but not much.

"Are you sure you don't want to look at one of the other houses?" Sirvon asked with a wrinkled nose as she ran her finger through the thick layer of dust on the kitchen counter top. "Maybe one of them had been sealed up better and is a little less musty."

"No, it's fine. We'll take our time and clean it little by little," answered Maré while running the water out of the long unused faucet. "The old house was out; even if it didn't hold bad memories and blood stained furniture, we'd still have to look at that damn horizon. Down here... I guess it's like the sun has finally set."

"And the electronics work," said Luna. "Not a whole lot of automation here, but more than we had, and we can listen to music whenever we want."

Sirvon bobbed her head in agreement. "This and the house next door *are* the only ones close to each other." She smiled at the younger women. "And we do want to be close to you."

Sitting at the table, Luna wrung her hands and looked pensive. "But are we sure no one will find out about us here? I guess I'm afraid this'll be taken from us."

Harry placed the satchel he was holding on the table, sat down next to her and took a serious tone. "Are we sure? No... but it's extremely unlikely. Maré, in the year you were out here, how many times did anyone come through?"

She snorted, came behind Luna, bent down and put her arms around her. "Before you folks came to dinner, never." She moved her lips near her ear and spoke quietly, though just loud enough for the others to hear. "We're safe here, Chroma. This place isn't as isolated as it had been," she said with a relieved nod towards the Westports, "but we'll have the seclusion we'll need."

Luna closed her eyes and pressed Maré's head to her own.

After a few seconds Harry said, "I have a small house warming gift for you." Opening the satchel, he pulled out two image frames. "After you mentioned pictures of your parents the other day, I dug through the archives and found a couple of 2D scenes of them. There are a couple more out there, if you want them. Sorry they're flat – I couldn't get the dimensional paper fast enough."

"Oh..." said Luna as she looked at one of them. "I hadn't seen this one before."

Maré leaned forward and picked up the other and held it so they could both see it. "Here's the one from the wall in our room." She turned it around so Harry and Sirvon could see it. "This is supposed to be us in front."

"Thank you, Harry," said Luna. "This means more to me than you know."

Maré nodded in agreement. "Yeah – thanks, for everything."

Harry smiled and craned his head in acceptance.

"I've kept pictures of my family, too. I don't look at them all that often, but I do like to."

"So do I," said Luna. "This is really an awesome gift, you guys."

"Doesn't it feel... artificial though?" Mare asked. "At least a little?"

"Is that how you feel when you look at them, Maré?" asked Sirvon.

She stood, went back over to the sink and shut the water off. Resting her elbows on the edge, she looked out the window at the weather-eroded rocks, not really seeing them. "I guess it's something of a *novelty* to me, but... well, to be honest, my connection to those people isn't strong. *Luna* is my family. In important ways, *you* guys are becoming my family. Them though?" She shrugged. "Not so much. But then I've struggled with what I am."

"I'm sorry, Maré," replied Sirvon. "Having our memories makes it much easier on us. I haven't tried very hard to see things from your point of view. I'm sorry."

She waved her hand. "No, that's fine, Sirvon. I mean... I do appreciate the love they had for their children; I've been able to see it through Luna's eyes, and I'm going to work on strengthening that connection. All of my connections." She looked at Luna. "I certainly don't have all the answers, but I'm finding that it's okay. Maybe I'm fortunate to be like a blank screen – I get to determine what I am, not what someone else thinks I should be. I'm beginning to feel that I'm truer, more genuine this way, somehow."

Luna nodded. "I know you've wrestled with it, Chroma. But I don't think I *did* know, not really. I've been insensitive."

"Let it go, Luna. After all we've been through, it's not worth wasting energy on. Let it go."

A strange hush cropped up, one that was half comfortable, half unsettled. She knew she was responsible for it, but it was okay. It was okay to be a little weird with her family.

Mare broke it anyway. "There *is* one connection I'd like to forget," she said with a rueful snort. "It's bizarre, but I do feel something for that unhappy bastard Breylin." She turned back to the others and sat down at the table. "I hated him – he deserved that... but I feel a..." She put her palms flat on the table and let out a long, tired sigh. "A loss, too, I guess. I don't know why. A little for his wife, too, and I *never* knew her. It might have been watching that holo of them as he was bleeding out." She rubbed her eyes. "Stars, that got to me; not all at once, but it definitely showed me what family can be like. I'm not sure any of us were thinking straight at the time, though. Am I making sense? That holo could've been of us, sitting there at that fire, and listening to her read. That really felt weird..."

"Yeah," agreed Luna. "I felt it, too."

"You've both been through a lot," Harry said charitably. "You're going to have to allow yourselves time to feel, and to process those feelings."

Sirvon took a hand from both of them, put them together, and then covered them with hers. "It's okay, dear. Like you said, maybe you don't need all of the answers. Don't expect too much too quickly."

"Pitying him..." Luna confessed. "It feels wrong. In the end, I didn't want him to die, but maybe a part of me did because he was so cruel to Maré. But at the same time, I forgive him."

"Both of you... listen to me and try to think of it this way." He paused for a moment. "Joss did awful things... but he could be funny and kind, and he was capable of tremendous love, too. We all sensed it watching the holos he took. But what you experienced with him... well, I think maybe life dealt him a bigger pile of shit than he could handle, and it broke him. When his sanity left, I think it took a lot of his humanity with it. It could have all been quite different given better circumstances. That the two of you feel conflicted shows how developed your sensitivity is."

Harry added his hands to the pile in the middle. "What I mean is that whether you have your memories or not, even whether you're humans or simulants, what matters is that you *are* genuine, good people."

Sirvon gave him a warm smile and laid her hand on his arm. "You're talking too much, husband, and you're getting maudlin."

"No, I'm serious! And I'm *not* maudlin!" he said with a small laugh. "Am I?"

Sirvon just shook her head.

Maré smiled too, but she tucked his words away. They felt right, if difficult, and she'd have to give them consideration. After all he'd done he deserved that.

"Anyway, it's not up to me," he continued more seriously. "But I think you should try to put all those confusing feelings into a bucket, and over time, pull them out one by one. Talk to each other, and you can talk to us, too."

"It may seem crazy now, but I think we should all forgive him, no matter what he did," Sirvon said.

"Hey, I said I felt something for him, but don't you think forgiving him is awfully generous?" Maré asked dubiously. "C'mon, I'm working on it, but I just don't know if I'm able to go that far."

"He's gone, dear," said Sirvon. "Forgiveness isn't about making him feel better, but you. If you can find it within yourself to let your anger go, then you'll have less to carry around. You and your Chroma can be what you are in the present and moving towards the future, and not defined by the past. What were the words you used? Start a new song?"

Maré nodded.

"And if I may say... I think Luna needs you to get what she understands. If you don't then it won't matter how close you get – you'll always have this between you."

"Maré," Luna said. "You once asked me to get past an ugliness that controlled me. Remember how I didn't want to give it up? We had to do it together, and that's how we'll do it now."

"It's a big ask," said Maré. "But yeah, you may be right. Give me a little space, and I'll think it through."

"I hate to bring up practical matters," apologized Harry with a sigh. "But maybe this is a good time to mention that the authorities are gonna release Joss' body to me tomorrow, if I want it. Those idiots can't find the records of where Larissa was buried. Otherwise if I don't take him, they'll inter him in the pauper's grave outside the city." He sighed. "I thought maybe we could bury him above the rim of the canyon. Maybe poke through the ruins of the fire and see if there's anything left. We might come across a memento, or something."

Luna broke the pregnant quiet, speaking directly to Maré. "Our love could cover many wrongs, Chroma..."

Maré blanched. "Maybe, Luna," she replied. "But there's more than mementos left after the fire..."

With her arm around Luna and the light breeze streaming their hair around their faces, Maré watched Harry place the last shovelful of rocky soil on the grave that had been dug large enough to hold four sets of remains. It had been a long tiring piece of work, and when he stood up he wiped the sweat from his face with his grimy shirtsleeve. Sirvon handed him a flask of water; and he thanked her with a nod of his head before taking a long pull from its contents.

Maré and Luna picked up the rock that they had taken turns working with a couple of Harry's screwdrivers. It had taken them more than four hours, but they'd managed to legibly carve the Breylin name upon it. They carried it over to the grave and placed it at the top and turned so that the sun shone on the name. With Zarmina's predisposition for wind and rain, the carving upon the rock would wear with time, but they would keep after it. Brushing off their hands, they moved to where Harry and Sirvon were standing.

Yesterday, they'd gone to the burned out remnants of the house. The fire hadn't left much, and exposure had worked its processes, but they'd found the bones – pitted, bleached, and caked with muddy soot.

At first, Maré wouldn't go in, but finally she'd willed her legs to move.

Luna looked at her. "You didn't have to come over." She touched her arm. "You okay? You look pale."

"Yeah. My stomach's going crazy, and I nearly left you to deal with it." She pointed to her temple. "But the memory's a lot worse than anything here."

"I didn't want to believe it, Maré." Harry held his stomach and looked like he might throw up. "I knew you weren't lying, but this is too much."

"It's okay, Harry – you're not responsible." She closed her eyes and held her face up to the breeze. "Let's just do what we came to do and finish this."

Once they'd collected Riss and two simulants, they muddied their shoes poking around the rest of the house. There had been furniture springs, warped utensils, melted electronics. The fire had left plenty behind, but all of it was destroyed.

Luna had spotted a bit of color sticking out from under a piece of collapsed wall that had fallen in towards the back of the house. Once Harry had picked it up, they found a few books and a small, simple rag doll. They were in bad shape; they'd been mostly covered, but time and weather had worked their inexorable processes regardless. With effort and care, the books might be salvaged, but the doll nearly fell apart at Luna's touch. In the same hollow, they'd also found a small resin display case that contained the two paper flowers that had figured prominently in some of the holo recordings of the Breylin women. It had been exposed too, but both it and the things it held had survived everything almost completely unscathed.

At the gravesite, Sirvon handed Luna the doll and Maré the case.

They turned and walked back slowly with gravel crunching underfoot. Maré crouched and laid the box near the headstone, with her fingers lingering upon its smooth, cool surface. Luna bent down and positioned the rag doll between the cased flowers and the stone marker. Leaning on her Chroma's shoulder, she had to twist it just right so that it would sit up, but she was able to get it settled, and now it too looked upon the sunlight streaming in from the horizon.

"So that's it," Maré said as she looked down upon the small memorial.

She stood up and took Luna's hand, and they walked back to stand next to Harry and his wife. Luna put her arms around Maré's neck and laid her head on her shoulder. Without taking her eyes from the grave, Maré circled Luna's waist and drew her closer with her arms.

Harry and Sirvon were holding each other, too, and both couples silently absorbed the somber scene.

Maré squared her shoulders and took a couple of cleansing breaths. "Joss, Larissa, and your daughters, may your family find the comfort and happiness you lacked in life."

Luna's lashes had served as breakers against the tide of her tears, but they flowed over them now and down onto Maré's shoulder. She loved the feel of the innocent delicacy that Luna had, yet she possessed an inner strength upon which they would both need to lean. She possessively tightened her embrace on her and kissed the top of her head.

Maré looked to Harry. "When the time comes, would you lay us here too, please?"

"I don't know what to say..." he said, not meeting her eyes. "Are you sure?"

"We all return to the ground, Harry," she breathed. "Ending up here with them makes as much sense as anything else."

Harry nodded his head as he spoke. "I guess it does."

Maré nodded. "Thanks."

"Have you two thought about marrying?" he asked. "You're really quite beautiful together."

"Still trying to save simulants, Harry?" said Luna. "Careful, Sirvon – he's going to bring more home."

"Yeah, he does that – it's part of why I love him."

"Marrying is what humans do, Harry," Maré said with a reserved smile, as she pulled Luna in tighter. "We do something else."

"I stand corrected," he said with a smile of his own, "but maybe you're not as different from us as you think." He and Sirvon turned and headed down the hill, hand in hand.

A few minutes passed, and Maré said, "Are you ready to head back?"

"You go ahead," she said as she turned to the sun stretched out in the distance and sat down on the headstone. "I want to sit for a little while and think."

"Then I'll wait for you," said Maré as she moved to stand behind her and began to gently comb Luna's hair back with her fingers. "You know," she said, "you've had to pull me off two people I've seriously hurt or killed."

Luna nodded, but said nothing.

"Do you forgive me?"

Luna turned, and Maré was surprised to see her eyebrows raised in question. "You were protecting me both times. I was useless, you did what you had to do, and there's no issue." She shrugged her shoulders. "How could there be?"

When she turned back, Maré smiled and resumed combing her hair.

"I love it when you do that," she said.

"Of course, that's why I do it."

"We had a rough start, Maré, and maybe you more than I." She turned and looked up at her, and Maré silently nodded. Luna turned back to the horizon and they stayed that way for a while. Normally, Maré would have preferred to be in out of the wind, but it had turned out to be one of those rare days where the breeze was light and the clouds were few, and even though they'd just buried their past, she was still feeling pretty content. This day had been a big punctuation in their lives, and it had turned out well.

"I know you think of it as a sunset, Chroma," she said as she gestured toward the unchanging horizon. "But we have a new life now, and I think of it as a sunrise."

Maré bent down low, tucked her hair behind her ear and moved close enough to smell her natural scent. "*You* are my sunrise."

As Luna leaned into her, Maré traced the palm of her hand over her opposing cheek, applying just enough pressure so that she turned her head. She moved her fingers lightly along her jawline, back under her ear and finally threaded them into her hair. Maré searched her eyes. "You know that, don't you?"

Luna closed her eyes as she craned her neck to offer herself. Their lips met, and Maré felt her cheeks flush at the safety and love that flowed through the moist physical connection. When they parted, Luna breathed her words. "And you are the only sunset I ever want."

"C'mon, Chroma – it's time to begin our song. Leave the rag doll if you like, but we bring the book and the roses home."

THE END

OF

The Way of All Flesh

TO BE CONTINUED IN...

The Dawn of All New Life

Glossary

Chroma (KRO-ma): A close, personal relationship between two simulants.

Chromanity (kro-MAN-uh-tee): A term used to describe all simulants.

Crop (KRAHP): The simulants from one bloodline produced in one cycle.

Gabacho (ha-BACH-oh): A derogatory slang term generally used for simulants. Female simulants are *gabachas*.

Mimetiosis (mi-MESH-ee-oh-sis): The process by which a human is copied to create a simulant.

Premisant (PREH-mi-sahnt): The human template from which the simulant is a copy.

Simulant (SIM-yoo-lahnt): An artificially grown person with a pre-defined lifespan and no legal rights.